ENCHANTED

Also by Elizabeth Lowell
in Thorndike Large Print ®

Forbidden
Untamed

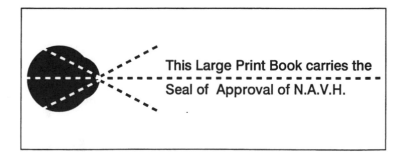

This Large Print Book carries the
Seal of Approval of N.A.V.H.

ENCHANTED

Elizabeth Lowell

Thorndike Press • Thorndike, Maine

Published in 1995 by arrangement with Avon Books.

Thorndike Large Print ® Romance Series.

The tree indicium is a trademark of Thorndike Press.

The text of this Large Print edition is unabridged.
Other aspects of the book may vary from the original edition.

Set in 16 pt. News Plantin by Juanita Macdonald.

Printed in the United States on permanent paper.

Library of Congress Cataloging in Publication Data

Lowell, Elizabeth, 1944–
    Enchanted / Elizabeth Lowell.
        p.   cm.
    ISBN 0-7862-0223-8 (lg. print : hc)
    1. Large type books.   I. Title.
[PS3562.O8847E53   1995]
813'.54—dc20   94-14259

for
DEBBY TOBIAS

first class all the way

1

Autumn in the reign of King Henry I.
Stone Ring Keep, home of Lord Duncan and
Lady Amber, in the Disputed Lands at the
northern reaches of Norman England.

"Which will it be," Ariane whispered to herself, "a wedding or a wake?"

Ariane stared at the dagger in her hands, but no answer came to her save that of candlelight running like silver blood over the blade. As she looked at the ghostly blood, the question rang again within the silence of her mind.

A wedding or a wake?

The answer that finally came was no comfort to Ariane.

It matters not. They are but different words for the same thing.

Beyond Stone Ring Keep's high walls, the wind wailed of coming winter.

Ariane didn't hear the mournful cry. She heard nothing but echoes of the past, when her mother had pressed the jeweled dagger into her daughter's small hands.

In her mind Ariane could still see the dark flash of amethysts and feel the cold weight of silver. Her mother's words had been even more chilling.

Hell has no punishment greater than a cruel marriage bed. Use this rather than lie beneath a man you do not love.

Unfortunately, Ariane's mother had not lived long enough to tell her daughter how to use the weapon, or upon whom. Whose wake should it be, the groom's or bride's?

Should I kill myself or should I kill Simon, whose only crime is to agree to marry me out of loyalty to his brother, Lord Dominic of Blackthorne Keep?

Loyalty.

A yearning tremor went through Ariane, making the rich cream and russet of her tunic quiver as though alive.

Dear God, to be so blessed as to know that kind of fidelity from my family!

Dark nightmare turned, threatening to break through the wall Ariane had built against it. Grimly she shifted her thoughts from the night she had been betrayed first by Geoffrey the Fair and then by her own father.

The blade of the dagger bit delicately into Ariane's hand, telling her that she was holding the weapon too tightly. Distantly she wondered what it would feel like when the dagger bit far more deeply into her flesh.

Certainly it could be no worse than her nightmares.

"Ariane, have you seen my — oh, what a lovely dagger," Amber said, spotting the quicksilver gleam as she walked into the room. " 'Tis as finely made as any brooch."

The voice startled Ariane out of her grim reverie. Taking a slow, hidden breath, she loosened her grip on the jeweled dagger and looked toward the young woman whose golden outer tunic highlighted the color of her eyes and hair.

"It was my mother's dagger," Ariane said to Amber.

"Such extraordinary amethysts. They are the exact color of your eyes. Were hers violet, too?"

"Yes."

Ariane said no more.

"And your thoughts," Amber continued matter-of-factly, "are the exact color of your hair. The darkest part of night."

Ariane's breath caught. Warily she eyed the Learned lady of Stone Ring Keep, who could discern truth simply by touching someone.

Yet Amber wasn't touching Ariane now.

"I don't have to touch you," Amber said,

guessing the other girl's thoughts. "The darkness is in your eyes. And in your heart."

"I feel nothing."

"Ah, but you do. Your emotions are a wound that has been concealed rather than healed."

"Are they?" Ariane asked indifferently.

"Aye," Amber said. "I felt it when I touched you the first time. Surely you must feel it too."

"Only when I sleep."

Ariane slid the dagger back into its sheath at her waist and reached for the lap harp that once had been her joy. Now it was her consolation. The dark, graceful curves of the wood were inlaid with silver, mother-of-pearl and carnelian in the form of a flowering vine.

But it wasn't the harp's elegance that lured Ariane. It was the instrument's voice. Her long fingers moved, calling from the strings a chord that was in eerie harmony with the storm wind, a wildness that was barely contained.

Concealed, not healed.

Hearing the harp speak for the silent harpist, Amber wanted to protest the combination of fear and rage and grief that burned just beneath the Norman girl's calm surface.

"You have nothing to dread from becoming Simon's wife," Amber said, her voice urgent. "He is a man of intense passion, but it is always disciplined."

10

For an instant Ariane's fingers paused. Then she nodded slowly. Gradually the sounds she drew from the harp became less wild.

"Aye," Ariane said in a low voice. "He has been gentle enough with me."

Much gentler than he will be when he discovers that his wife is no maiden.

Wars have begun over lesser insults. Men have killed. Women have died.

The last thought held a dark allure for Ariane. It whispered of an escape from the brutal trap of pain and betrayal that life had become.

"Simon is strong of body and fair of face," Amber added, "with a quickness to put the keep's cats to shame."

Ariane's fingers hesitated. After a moment she murmured, "His eyes are very . . . dark."

" 'Tis only that sun-colored hair of his that makes his eyes seem so black," Amber said instantly.

Ariane shook her head. "It is more than that."

Hesitating, sighing, Amber agreed.

" 'Tis the same with many of the men who came back from the Saracen battles," she admitted. "They returned less light of heart."

A minor chord quivered in the silence.

"Simon mistrusts me," Ariane said.

"You?" Amber laughed without humor.

11

"He trusts you enough to show you his back. I am the one he mistrusts. In the silence of his heart, Simon calls me hell-witch."

Surprise lightened the bleak violet of Ariane's eyes for a moment.

"If it helps," Amber said dryly, "your own eyes, for all their fey beauty, are as remote as a Druid moon."

"Should that comfort me?"

"Can anything comfort you?"

Ariane's fingers paused in their delicate stroking of the harp as she considered the question. Then her fingers struck like snow falcons, ripping a harsh sound from the strings.

"Why does he call you hell-witch?" Ariane asked after a moment.

Before Amber could answer, a deep male voice spoke behind her, answering Ariane's question.

"Because," Simon said, "I thought she had stolen Duncan's mind."

Both women turned and saw Simon standing at the entrance to the small corner chamber that had been turned over to Ariane for the length of her stay at Stone Ring Keep. Ariane didn't expect the visit to be long; all that held Lord Dominic of Blackthorne Keep here was his determination to see Ariane wed to one of his loyal men before anything else could go awry.

Simon was the second groom chosen for the Baron Deguerre's daughter. Though Ariane had never been drawn to her first fiancé — Duncan — in any way at all, just seeing Simon sent odd currents through Ariane. He filled the doorway with little left over. Because most people first saw him standing next to his brother Dominic, or to Amber's even larger husband Duncan, Simon's size often passed without particular comment, as did the width of his shoulders.

Yet Ariane noticed everything about Simon, and had from the first instant he had strode up to her at Blackthorne Keep and told her to prepare for a hard ride to Stone Ring Keep. She had been vividly aware of Simon's quickness and grace, and of his supple, powerful body. His eyes had burned like black fire with the force of his intelligence and will.

And sometimes, if Ariane turned to him unexpectedly, she had seen Simon's eyes burning with an intense sensual heat. He desired her.

She had waited in dread for him to force that desire upon her. Yet he had not. He had been unfailingly civil, treating her with a courtesy and disciplined restraint that she found as reassuring as it was . . . alluring.

Simon could have been standing in a forest of giants and he would have towered over them in Ariane's sight. There was something about the feline quickness and male elegance of Simon's body that in her eyes overshadowed men more brawny.

Or perhaps it was simply that he had been kind to her in his own sardonic way. The ride from Blackthorne Keep, where she had just arrived from Normandy, to Stone Ring Keep had been hard indeed. Blackthorne Keep was in the far north of England, on the edge of the Disputed Lands where Norman and Saxon still fought over estates.

Stone Ring Keep was still farther north, in the very heart of the lands where Normans claimed estates and Saxons held those same estates by force of arms. The Battle of Hastings had been won more than a generation ago by the Normans, yet the Saxons were far from subdued.

"It seems," Simon said as he walked into the room, "I was wrong about Amber. It was only Duncan's heart that she had stolen. A far more trifling matter than a mind, surely."

The Learned girl refused to rise to the deftly presented bait, though the amber pendant she wore between her breasts shimmered with secret laughter.

Simon's smile warmed.

"I no longer think of you as the devil's tool," he said to Amber. "Will you ever forgive me for making you faint with pain and fear?"

"Sooner than you will forgive all women for whatever one woman did to you," Amber said.

The room became so silent that the leap of flame in the brazier sounded loud. When Simon spoke again, there was no warmth in his voice or his smile.

"Poor Duncan," Simon said distinctly. "He will have no secrets from his witch-wife."

"He will need none," Duncan said from behind Simon.

On hearing Duncan's voice, Amber spun toward the doorway, glowing as though lit from within.

Ariane stared. In the seven-day she had been at Stone Ring Keep, she had yet to become accustomed to the sheer joy Amber took in her new husband. Duncan's joy was no less, a fact that was simply beyond Ariane's comprehension.

When Amber rushed across the room, holding out her hands to Duncan, Simon gave Ariane a wry sidelong glance. The look told her that he was as bemused as she was by Duncan and Amber.

The moment of silent, shared understanding was both warming and disconcerting to Ariane. It made her want to trust Simon.

Fool, Ariane told herself coldly. *The smile is but a charming ruse to make you more at ease, so that you won't fight the brutal coils of marital duty.*

"I thought you were going to take all morning listening to the serfs' complaints," Amber said to Duncan.

"So did I." Duncan gathered Amber's hands in his much larger ones. "But Erik took pity on me and sent the wolfhounds in to lounge by the fire."

"Stagkiller, too?" she asked, for her brother was rarely without his canine shadow.

"Mmm," Duncan agreed. He kissed Amber's fingertips and tickled her palms with his mustache. "Shortly afterward, everyone left."

Simon smothered a laugh.

The serfs revered Amber's brother Erik, the former lord of Stone Ring Keep, but they were distinctly wary of the Learned man's animals. More than one tenant and cotter had been overheard thanking God that the new lord of Stone Ring Keep was a brawny warrior not given to ancient ways, Learned teachings, and animals more clever by half than common folks.

"I shall miss your brother when he goes back to Sea Home Keep," Duncan said.

"My brother or his hounds?" Amber asked, smiling.

"Both. Perhaps Erik could leave us a few."

"Large ones?"

16

"Does he have any other kind?" Duncan retorted. "Stagkiller is nearly as tall at the shoulder as my war stallion."

Laughing, shaking her head at the exaggeration, Amber brushed her cheek against one of Duncan's battle-scarred hands.

Ariane watched the newly married couple as a hunting falcon would watch an unexpected movement on the ground far below its wings. The words the lovers spoke were unimportant; it was the way each looked at the other, the touches they shared, the heightened awareness that flowed between them like an invisible river between opposite shores.

"Baffling, isn't it?" Simon asked softly.

He had moved so close to Ariane that his breath stirred the hair at the nape of her neck.

Too close.

"What?" Ariane asked, startled.

It took all of her courage not to draw away as she looked into Simon's clear midnight eyes. But retreat would do no good. Nor would pleas to be left alone.

Geoffrey had taught her that, and much else that she had buried behind walls of pain and betrayal.

" 'Tis baffling," Simon explained, "how a formidable warrior such as the Scots Hammer becomes as river clay in a girl's hands."

"I would say rather the reverse," Ariane

muttered, "that it is the amber witch who is the clay and he the strong hands molding it."

Simon's blond eyebrows rose in silent surprise. He turned and looked at Duncan and Amber for a few moments.

"You have a point," Simon agreed. "Her eyes are as lovestruck as his. Or is it dumbstruck?"

When Simon turned back to Ariane, he bent over her once more, ensuring the privacy of their conversation. Before Ariane could stop herself, she pulled away. She covered the action by pretending to see to the tuning of her harp.

Simon wasn't fooled. His black eyes narrowed and he straightened swiftly. While he didn't consider himself as handsome as Erik — and certainly not as wealthy in land or goods — Simon was not accustomed to having a woman withdraw from him as though he were unclean.

What made the matter even more irritating was that Simon had been certain his body called to Ariane as surely as her body called to him. She had taken one look at him walking toward her across Blackthorne Keep's bailey the first time they met, and then she had kept on looking as though she had never seen a man before.

Simon had looked at Ariane in just the same

way, a recognition that defied understanding. He had seen more beautiful women in his life, but never had he seen one who compelled his senses so deeply. Even the siren Marie.

At the time, it had seemed to Simon a cruel jest from God that Ariane was betrothed to Duncan of Maxwell, the Scots Hammer, a man who was Simon's friend and Dominic's ally. When it was discovered that Duncan loved another woman, Simon immediately had offered to wed the daughter of the powerful Norman baron. The marriage would ensure the peace that Dominic desperately needed in the Disputed Lands if his own Blackthorne Keep were to prosper.

When Simon had proposed the marriage, he had been sure that Ariane preferred him above other men. Now he wasn't so certain. Perhaps it was simply that she strove to keep him off-balance. That had certainly been Marie's game, one that she had played exceedingly well.

"Have I done something to offend you, Lady Ariane?" Simon asked coolly.

"Nay."

"Such a quick answer. So false, too."

"You startled me, 'tis all. I didn't expect to find you that close to me."

Simon's only answer was a thin smile.

"Shall I have Meg blend me a special soap

to please your dainty nostrils?" he asked.

"Your scent is quite pleasant to me as it is," Ariane said politely.

As she spoke, she realized that she meant it. Unlike many men, Simon didn't smell of old sweat and clothes worn too long.

"You look surprised that I don't stink like a midden," Simon said. "Shall I test the truth of your words?"

With disconcerting quickness, he bent close to Ariane once more. She flinched in the instant before she managed to control her alarm. Very carefully she shifted her body on the wooden chair until she was no longer leaning away from Simon.

"You may breathe now," he said dryly.

Ariane's breath came in with a swift, husky sound that could have been a gasp of fear or pleasure. Considering the circumstances, Simon decided that fear was more likely.

Or disgust.

Simon's lips flattened beneath his soft, closely clipped beard. He remembered all too well Ariane's words when Duncan had asked if she would be a wife in fact as well as in name:

I will do my duty, but I am repelled by the prospect of the marriage bed.

When asked if her coldness came because her heart belonged to another man, Ariane had been quite blunt.

I have no heart.

There had been no doubt that she spoke the truth, for Amber had been touching Ariane the whole time and had found nothing but the bleakest honesty in the Norman heiress's words.

Ariane had agreed to marriage, but she had also made it clear that the thought of coupling with a man revolted her. Even the man who was soon to be her husband.

Or, perhaps, especially him?

Simon's mouth took on a grim line as he looked at the Norman heiress who had agreed to be his bride.

When we first saw one another, was she watching me with fear while I watched her with desire?

The thought chilled Simon, for he had vowed never again to want a woman more than she wanted him. That kind of wanting gave women power over a man, a cruel power that destroyed men.

Could it be that Ariane is another Marie, playing hot and cold by turns, chaining a man to her with uncertainty, driving him mad with desire half-slaked?

Or slaked not at all.

But that game of feint and lure, retreat and summon, can be played by more than one.

It was a game Simon had learned quite well

21

at Marie's hands. So well that he had ultimately beaten her at her own sport.

Without a word, Simon straightened and stepped back from Ariane, not touching her in any way.

Though relieved, Ariane sensed that her flinching from Simon had cut his pride. The thought worried her, for he had done nothing to earn such a wounding from her.

Yet even as Ariane opened her mouth to tell Simon so, no words came. There was no point in denying the truth: the thought of coupling with a man made her blood freeze.

Simon hadn't earned her coldness, but she could do nothing to change it. All warmth had been torn from her months ago, during the long night when she had lain drugged and helpless while Geoffrey the Fair grunted over her like a pig rooting in a virgin orchard.

A shudder of revulsion coursed through Ariane. Her memories of that terrible night were vague, distorted by whatever black potion Geoffrey had given to her to keep her silent and helpless.

Sometimes Ariane thought the blurring was merciful.

And sometimes she thought it only increased the horror.

"Simon," Ariane whispered, not knowing that she had called his name aloud.

For a moment Simon paused as though he had heard her. Then he turned his back to her with cool finality.

2

The teasing words of the newlyweds filled the taut silence that had grown between Simon and Ariane.

"Have you time to ride with me?" Duncan asked Amber.

"For you, I have all the time in the world."

"Just the world?" he asked, feigning hurt. "What of heaven and the hereafter?"

"Are you bargaining with me, husband?"

"Do I have something you would like to lay hand upon?" Duncan parried.

Amber's smile was as old as Eve and as young as the blush mounting her cheeks.

Duncan's answering laughter was a sound of pure masculine delight.

"Precious Amber, how you please me."

"Do I?"

"Always."

"How?" she teased.

Duncan started to tell her, then remembered they weren't alone.

"Ask me tonight," he said in a low voice, "when the fire in the brazier is little more than scarlet coals veiled in silver ash."

"You have my vow on it," Amber said, resting her fingers on Duncan's powerful forearm.

"I will hold you to it," he murmured. "Now, if you are finished here, let us be off to the horses."

"Finished here?" Amber blinked. "Oh, my comb. I had forgotten."

She turned to Ariane, who was watching her with eyes as clear and remote as gems.

"Have you seen a comb with red amber set in it?" Amber asked. "I think it must have fallen out of my hair somewhere in the keep."

"Once, you would have had but to ask, and the comb's hiding place would come to me," Ariane said in a low voice. "Once, but no more."

"I don't understand."

Ariane shrugged. "It matters not. I haven't seen your comb. I'll ask Blanche."

"Is your maid feeling better today?"

"Nay." Ariane's mouth turned down. "I fear Blanche has a more common illness than that which laid my knights low on our travels from Normandy."

"Oh?" Amber asked.

"I believe Blanche is breeding."

" 'Tis not an illness, but a blessing," Simon said.

"To a married girl, perhaps," Ariane said. "But Blanche is far from her home, her people, and, likely, from the boy who set her to breeding in the first place. Hardly a blessing, is it?"

A lithe movement of Simon's shoulders dismissed Ariane's objections.

"As your husband, I will see that your maid is well cared for," Simon said coolly. "We have need of more babes in the Disputed Lands."

"Babes," Ariane said in an odd voice.

"Aye, my future wife. Babes. Do you object?"

"Only to the means."

"Means?"

"Coupling." A shudder rippled through Ariane's body. " 'Tis a sorry way to such a sweet goal."

"It won't seem so after you have been married," Amber said kindly. "Then you will know that your maidenly fears are as groundless as the wind itself."

"Aye," Ariane said distantly. "Of course."

But no one believed her, least of all herself.

Blindly Ariane's hands sought the solace of the harp once more. The sounds that came from the graceful instrument were as dark as her thoughts. Even so, stroking the instrument brought a small measure of peace to her. It made her believe that she could endure what must be endured — grim, painful couplings and nightmares that tried to follow her into day.

Amber gave Ariane an odd look, but the Norman heiress didn't notice.

"Perhaps it would be better not to rush the marriage," Amber said in a low voice to Simon. "Ariane is . . . unsettled."

"Dominic is afraid that something else will go awry if we wait."

"Something else?" Then Amber realized what Simon meant. "Oh. Duncan's marriage to me rather than to Lady Ariane."

"Aye," Simon said sardonically.

"In any event," Simon said, "the northern boundary of Blackthorne Keep is secure once more, now that your brother Erik is pleased with your marriage."

Amber nodded.

"But that security could vanish," Simon said bluntly, "if Baron Deguerre were to think that Duncan had jilted his daughter for love of you."

Amber glanced quickly at Ariane. If she were listening, it didn't show in her face or in the measured drawing of her fingers over the lap harp.

"Do not fear for Lady Ariane's tender feelings," Simon said sardonically. "She was raised a highborn maid. She knows her duty is to wed whoever enters into the marriage bargain."

"Lady Ariane must be married to a loyal vassal of Dominic le Sabre," Duncan said flatly. "The quicker it happens, the better for all of us."

"But —" began Amber, only to be overridden by Simon.

"And her husband must be someone who has the approval of both King Henry and Deguerre himself," Simon added.

"But you don't have that approval!" Amber retorted.

"Simon is as loyal to Dominic as any man alive," Duncan said, "so the English king will approve the marriage. Simon is Norman rather than Scots or Saxon, so Baron Deguerre will have less to complain of in that regard than if the groom had been me."

"Aye. In all ways that matter," Simon said, "I am a more desirable husband for Deguerre's daughter than Duncan."

"This baron," Amber said, frowning. "Is he so powerful that kings are wary of him?"

"Yes," Ariane said distinctly.

A ripple of discordant notes accompanied the single word.

"Had he married me to Geoffrey the Fair, who is the son of another great Norman baron," Ariane continued, "my father soon

28

would have been the equal of your English Henry in wealth and military might, if not in law. So I was betrothed instead to a knight whose loyalty is to Henry rather than to a Norman duke."

"Now," Simon said dryly, "all we have to do is convince Baron Deguerre that his daughter is well pleased with me. That way there will be no excuse for war."

"Ah," Amber said. "That explains the story Sven has been spreading among the people of the keep and countryside."

"Story?" Ariane asked.

Simon laughed mirthlessly. "Aye, and quite a tale it is, too."

Ariane said nothing more, but her fingers plucked an ascending series of notes from the harp. As though she had spoken a question, Simon answered her.

"Sven is saying that we fell in love when I escorted you from Blackthorne to Stone Ring Keep."

Ariane's hands jerked as the outrageous tale yanked her out of her unhappy thoughts.

"*Love?*" she muttered. "What a pail of slops that is! Men have no love of their betrothed. They love only the dowry and the power."

Amber winced, but Simon laughed.

"Aye, my lady," he said. "Slops indeed."

"But 'tis a clever tale," Duncan said ad-

29

miringly. "Even the king himself must bow before a girl's absolute right to choose her husband. Deguerre can do no less."

"Dominic indeed deserves to be called the Glendruid Wolf," Amber said. "His clever plans bring peace, not war."

"It was Simon's idea to marry me, not his brother's," Ariane said. "Simon's mind is even quicker than his hands."

A brief expression of surprise showed on Simon's face. The last thing he expected from Ariane was a compliment, however casually it was delivered.

On the other hand, perhaps she was simply picking up the threads of the teasing game once more.

"Do you think that Deguerre will believe you?" Amber asked Simon doubtfully.

"Believe what? That I've married his daughter?"

"That it was a . . ." Amber groped for words.

" '. . . drawing together of hearts that defied English king and Norman father equally,' " Ariane quoted. " 'For *love*, of course.' "

Ariane's tone exactly captured the mockery that had been in Simon's voice when he had proposed marrying Ariane himself as a solution to the dangerous dilemma of her broken engagement.

Simon shrugged. "Deguerre can believe the tale or he can go begging in Jerusalem. Either way, before midnight mass is sung, Lady Ariane will be my wife."

A shout from the bailey below distracted Simon. He went to the slit window, listened, and gave Duncan a sideways look.

"You waited too long to escape, O mighty lord of Stone Ring Keep," Simon said, bowing as low as a Saracen would to his sultan. "The serf with the wandering pig — what is his name?"

"The pig's?" Duncan asked in disbelief.

"The serf's," Simon corrected, deadpan.

"Ethelrod."

"Ah, how could one forget?" Simon said. "Apparently the pig has acquired a taste for apples. By the bushel basket."

"That is why pigs are turned loose to root in the orchard after harvest," Duncan retorted. "Otherwise only the worms would fatten."

"At present, the pig in question is underground, rooting in one of *your* cellars."

"God's blood," Duncan said through his teeth as he strode out the door. "I told Ethelrod to build a pen stout enough to hold that clever swine."

"Excuse me," Amber said, trying not to laugh out loud. "I must see this. Ethelrod's pig is a source of much amusement to the people of the keep."

"Unless that swine is kept under control," Simon said dryly, "it will be the source of much bacon."

Amber burst out laughing and hurried after her husband.

Simon's quick eyes caught the shadow of a smile on Ariane's lips. The beauty of it reminded him of the first instant he had seen the Norman heiress. He had felt as though the breath had been driven from his body by a mailed fist.

Even now it was hard to believe that Ariane was almost within his reach, a highborn girl engaged to a bastard whose only claim to wealth or worth lay in his quick sword arm.

Without meaning to, Simon reached out to her.

"Ariane . . ." he whispered.

Ariane blinked at the sound of her name. For a few moments she had forgotten she wasn't alone.

When Simon's hand touched her hair, she flinched away.

Slowly Simon lowered his hand. The effort not to clench it into a fist was so great it left him aching. Yet he made the effort without knowing it, for he had vowed never again to let lust for a woman rule his actions.

"Soon we will be husband and wife," he said flatly.

A shudder went over Ariane.

"Do you react like this to all men," Simon asked, "or just to me?"

"I will do my duty," Ariane said in a low voice.

Yet even as she spoke, she realized that the words were a lie. She had thought she could go through with her wifely duties. Now she knew she could not. She simply couldn't force herself to submit to rape again.

Unfortunately the realization had come too late. The wedding was set. The trap was sprung.

No way out.

Except one.

Yet this time the thought of death brought no comfort to Ariane.

How can I kill Simon, whose only crime is love of his brother?

Failing that, how can I endure rape again, and then again, all the years of my life?

"My duty," she whispered.

"Duty," Simon repeated in a low voice. "Is that all you will be able to bring to the marriage? Is your beauty like the whore Marie's, a lush fabric wrapped around a soul of icy calculations?"

Ariane said nothing, for she was afraid if

her mouth opened, a scream of rage and betrayal would be all that came out.

"Your anticipation of our marriage overwhelms me," Simon said sardonically. "See that I don't have to send a man-at-arms to fetch you to the altar. For by Christ's blue eyes, I will do just that if I must."

Simon turned and left the room without another word.

None was needed. Ariane had no doubt that Simon would do exactly as he said. He was, in all things, a man who kept his vows.

No escape.

Save one . . .

Without knowing it, Ariane's fingers closed around the harp strings. A despairing, dissonant wail was ripped from the instrument.

It was the only sound Ariane made.

The wedding would begin before the sun set and end before the moon rose. Before the moon set once more, the bride must find a way to kill.

Or die.

3

Melancholy, subtly clashing chords quivered through Ariane's corner room. Although Stone Ring Keep seethed with hurried preparations for the coming wedding, no one disturbed Ariane until the maid Blanche belatedly arrived to see to her mistress's needs.

A glance was all it took for Ariane to see that nothing had changed in the handmaiden's health. The girl's face was still too pale. Beneath a kerchief of indifferent cleanliness, Blanche's light brown hair had no luster. Nor did her blue eyes. Obviously she felt no better today than she had since the middle of the voyage from Normandy to England.

"Good morning, Blanche. Or is it afternoon?"

There was no censure in Ariane's voice, rather simple curiosity.

"Did you not hear the sentries crying the time?" Blanche asked.

"No."

"Well, 'tis to be expected, what with finding yourself so soon to be married to a groom who is not the man you expected to wed," Blanche said with a maturity far beyond her fifteen years.

Ariane shrugged. "One man is much the same as another."

Blanche gave Ariane a startled look.

"Beg your pardon, mistress, but there is considerable difference."

Ariane's only answer was a series of quickly plucked notes that sounded like dissent.

"Not that I blame you for being uneasy," Blanche said hurriedly. "There are some surpassing odd folk here. 'Tis enough to make a body start at shadows."

"Odd?" Ariane asked absently, drawing a questioning trill from the harp strings.

"Tch, m'lady, you have been talking to your harp so long your mind has gone as numb as your fingers must be. The Learned are odd ones, don't you think?"

Ariane blinked. Her fingers stilled for a few moments.

"I don't think the Learned are odd," Ariane said finally. "Lady Amber is as kind as she is lovely. Sir Erik is better educated — and more handsome — than all but a few knights I've known."

"But those great hounds of his, and that devil peregrine on his arm. I say it isn't natural."

" 'Tis as natural as breathing. All knights love hounds and hawks."

"But —" Blanche protested, only to be cut off.

"Enough useless chatter," Ariane said firmly. "All keeps and their folk seem strange when you haven't lived within them very long."

Blanche said nothing as she set about readying her mistress's bath needs. The sight of a long ebony comb reminded Ariane of her earlier conversation with the mistress of the keep.

"Have you seen a comb set with red amber?" Ariane asked. "Lady Amber misplaced one."

Blanche was so startled by the question that she simply stared at Ariane and gnawed on one ragged fingernail, speechless.

"Blanche? Are you going to be sick again?"

Numbly Blanche shook her head, causing a few lank tresses to escape from the kerchief that was her only headpiece.

"If you do find the comb," Ariane said, "please tell me."

" 'Tis unlikely I will find aught before you do, lady. Sir Geoffrey said many times how like your aunt you were."

Ariane went taut and said nothing.

"Was it true?" Blanche asked.

"What?"

"That your aunt could find a silver needle in a field of haystacks?"

"Aye."

Blanche grinned, showing the gap where she had lost a tooth to the blacksmith's pincers when she was twelve.

"It would be a fine gift to have, finding lost things," Blanche said, sighing. "Lady Eleanor was always beating me for losing her silver embroidery needles."

"I know."

"Don't look so sad," Blanche said. "If Lady Amber has lost her comb, you soon will find it for her."

"Nay."

The flat denial made Blanche blink.

"But Geoffrey said you found a silver goblet and ewer that no one —" began the handmaiden.

"Is my bath ready?" Ariane interrupted, cutting across the girl's words.

"Aye, lady," Blanche said in a low voice.

The handmaiden's unhappiness tugged at Ariane's compassion, but Ariane had no desire to explain that she had lost her fey gift along with her maidenhead.

She also was weary of having her stomach clench every time she heard Geoffrey's name.

"Lay out my best chemise and my scarlet dress," Ariane said in a low voice.

Whether a wedding or a wake, the dress would do quite well.

"I dare not!" blurted the handmaiden.

"Why?" asked Ariane.

"Lady Amber instructed me that she would bring your wedding dress to you personally."

Uneasiness rippled through Ariane.

"When did this pass?" she asked.

"Another Learned witch — er, woman — came to the keep," Blanche said.

"When?"

"Just at dawn. Didn't you hear the baying of those hellhounds?"

"I thought it was but a lingering of my dream."

"Nay," Blanche said. " 'Twas a Learned woman come to the keep with a gift for you. A dress to be wed in."

Ariane frowned and set her harp aside. "Amber said nothing to me."

"Mayhap she couldn't. The Learned woman was special fierce. White hair and eyes like ice." Blanche crossed herself quickly. "It was the one they call Cassandra. 'Tis said she sees the future. There be witches here, m'lady."

Ariane shrugged. "According to some, there were witches at my home. My aunt was one of them. So was I. Remember?"

Blanche looked confused.

"If it makes you feel better, I have met the

Learned woman face-to-face," Ariane said. "Cassandra is quite human."

The handmaiden's frown eased and she sighed.

"The chaplain here told me that this was a godly place no matter what the whispers," Blanche said. " 'Tis a relief to hear. I would be fearful for my ba—"

As though cut with a knife, Blanche's words stopped.

"Do not worry, handmaid," Ariane said calmly. "I know you are breeding. The babe will come to no harm. Simon has promised it."

Blanche still looked alarmed.

"Would you like Simon to arrange a husband for you?" Ariane asked.

Wistfulness replaced alarm on Blanche's face. Then she shook her head.

"No, thank you, lady."

Black eyebrows lifted in surprise, but all Ariane said was, "Do you know who the father of your baby is?"

Blanche hesitated, then nodded.

"Is he back in Normandy?"

"Nay."

"Ah, then he must be one of my men. Is he a squire or a man-at-arms?"

Blanche shook her head.

"A knight, then," Ariane said in a low voice.

"Was he one of those who died of that savage disease?"

"It matters not," Blanche said, clearing her throat. "No knight would marry a servant girl who has no kin, no dowry, and no particular beauty."

Tears stood in the handmaiden's eyes, making their light blue irises glitter with unusual clarity.

"Be at ease," Ariane said. "At least no man pursues you because of what you can bring to him. Nor would any man take from you by strength or wile what you would keep as your own."

Blanche looked at her mistress oddly and said nothing.

"Put away your fears," Ariane said crisply. "You and your babe will be well cared for, and you won't have to endure a husband in your bed if you don't wish."

"Oh, that." Blanche smiled. " 'Tis not such a trial. In the winter, a man is warmer than a swine and stinks not half so much. At least, most men don't."

Unbidden, the memory came to Ariane of Simon leaning down until his breath brushed her nape.

Shall I have Meg blend me a special soap to please your dainty nostrils?

Your scent is quite pleasant to me as it is.

An odd sensation whispered through Ariane as she realized anew just how true her words had been. Simon was as clean to her senses as the sunlight that caught and tangled in his hair, making it appear to burn.

If all I had to do as a wife was to see to Simon's house, his accounts, and his comforts. . . .

But that is not all a man wants from a wife. Nor is it all God requires.

"M'lady? Are you well?"

"Yes," Ariane said faintly.

Leaning forward, Blanche peered more closely at her mistress.

"You look white as salt," the handmaiden said. "Are you with child, too?"

Ariane made a harsh sound.

"No," she said distinctly.

"I'm sorry, I meant no insult," Blanche said hastily, her words stumbling. "It's just that babes are on my mind and Sir Geoffrey said you were particularly eager to breed."

"Sir Geoffrey was wrong."

The lethal calm of Ariane's voice told Blanche that she had once again stepped beyond the boundaries of her half-learned duties as a lady's maid.

Blanche sighed and wished that all the highborn were as charming and easy of manner as Geoffrey the Fair had been. No wonder that Lady Ariane had become grim and removed after being told that she would be sent to England to wed a rude Saxon stranger, rather than remaining at home to marry Sir Geoffrey, son of a great Norman baron.

Ariane the Betrayed.

"Your things are ready, my lady," Blanche said sympathetically. "Do you wish me to attend your bath?"

"No."

Though the marks of Ariane's ordeal at Geoffrey's hands had long since faded from her body, she could not bear even the casual touch of her lady's maid.

Particularly not when Blanche kept bringing up the name of Geoffrey the Fair.

4

A brazier sent warmth and a small bit of fragrant smoke into the third-floor room of Stone Ring Keep. The draperies around the canopied bed were drawn. A frowning Dominic le Sabre sat next to a table set with cold meat, bread, fresh fruit and ale.

His expression gave a saturnine cast to his face that made strong men uneasy. Coupled with his size, and the Glendruid ornament on his black cloak — an ancient silver pin cast in the shape of a wolf's head with clear, uncanny crystal eyes — Dominic was a forbidding presence.

Thinking about the marriage that would take place in a few hours had done nothing to improve Dominic's peace of mind. The bonds of love between the two brothers were far deeper than blood or custom required.

"You sent for me?" Simon said.

Dominic's frown vanished as he looked up at the tall, lithe warrior who stood before him. Simon's fair hair was windswept and his indigo mantle was thrown back to reveal the scarlet tunic with purple and silver embroidery that had been a gift from Erik. Beneath the elegant clothing was a body honed to battle readiness. Despite being Dominic's right hand, Simon never shirked the endless battle practice that the Glendruid Wolf decreed for his knights — and for himself.

"You are looking particularly fit," Dominic said approvingly.

"You sent me running from the outer bailey all the way up here to determine my fitness?" retorted Simon. "Next time, run with me. It will give you a better idea of my stamina and wind."

Dominic laughed. Too quickly, his laughter faded and his mouth once again fell into rather grim lines. He knew his brother too well to be deflected for long by Simon's quick wit.

"What is it?" Simon asked, eyeing Dominic's expression. "Have you news from Blackthorne? Is something amiss?"

"Blackthorne is fine. Ariane's dowry chests still lie unopened and undisturbed in the treasure room, guarded by Thomas the Strong."

"Then why are you so gloomy? Has Sven brought news of Norsemen or Saxon raiders nearby?"

"Nay."

"Where is Meg? Has that handsome sorcerer Erik managed to charm her from your grasp?"

This time Dominic's laughter was truly amused.

"Erik is as comely a knight as I've seen," Dominic said, "but my wife would no more fly from me than I from her."

Smiling, Simon conceded what he knew quite well was true. Lady Margaret's loyalty to Dominic was as great as Simon's.

"I am glad you found it in your heart to welcome Meg as your sister," Dominic said. "Sit with me, brother. Eat from my plate and drink from my mug."

Simon looked at the dainty chair opposite Dominic and grabbed a bench from along the wall instead. As he sat, he resettled his broadsword on his left hip, hilt ready to his right hand. The unconscious grace of the gesture said much about his ease with the weapon.

"Of course I accepted Meg into my heart," Simon said, reaching for the ale jug.

"You have no love of witches, whether they do good or evil."

Simon poured ale into the nearly empty mug, saluted Dominic silently, and drank. After a few deep swallows, he put the mug aside and looked at his brother with eyes as clear as a spring and as black as midnight.

"Meg risked her life to save yours," Simon said. "She could be Satan's own sister and I would love her for saving your life."

"Simon, called the Loyal," Dominic said softly. "There is little you wouldn't do for me."

"There is nothing."

The finality in Simon's voice didn't reassure Dominic. Rather, it brought back his frown. He reached for the mug, lifted it, drained it, and refilled it.

"You were loyal to me before we fought the Saracen," Dominic said after a time, "but it was a different kind of bond."

"We are brothers."

"No," Dominic said, pushing the mug of ale toward Simon. "It is more than that. And less."

The quality of Dominic's voice caught Simon. Mug half-raised to his lips, he looked at his brother.

And found himself pinned by a glance that was as unblinking as that of the wolf's head pin.

"It is as though you feel responsible for my torture by the sultan," Dominic said.

"I am," Simon said bluntly, and drank.

"Nay!" Dominic said. "It was my error that led men into ambush."

"It was a woman's treachery that led us to ambush," Simon said flatly, setting the mug down with a thump. "The whore Marie bewitched Robert, and then she cuckolded him with any man who caught her fancy."

"She wasn't the first wife to do so, nor the last," Dominic said. "But I couldn't leave a Christian woman to the mercy of the Saracens, no matter that she lived among them since she was stolen as a child."

"Nor would your knights have allowed it," Simon said sardonically. "They were bewitched by Marie's harem tricks."

Dominic smiled slightly. "Aye. She is a skilled whore, and I have need of such to keep my Norman knights from seducing Saxon daughters and causing more strife."

Leaning back in the heavy oak chair that had been brought up from the lord's solar for the Glendruid Wolf's comfort, Dominic fixed Simon with shrewd, quicksilver eyes.

"Sometimes I worried that Marie had bewitched you," Dominic said after a few moments.

"She did. For a time."

Dominic hid his suspense. He had always wondered just how deeply Simon had succumbed to Marie's practiced lures.

"She tried to bewitch you, too," Simon pointed out.

Dominic nodded.

"You saw through her cold game sooner than I," Simon said.

"I am four years older than you. Marie

wasn't my first woman."

Simon snorted. "She wasn't my first, either."

"The others were girls with less experience than you. Marie was . . ." Dominic shrugged. "Marie was trained in a seraglio for the pleasure of a corrupt despot."

"She could have been trained by Lilith in hell and it would all be the same. Marie cannot stir me anymore."

"Aye," Dominic said. "I watched her try the whole journey from Jerusalem to Blackthorne Keep. You were polite, but you would handle a snake sooner than her. Why?"

Simon's expression changed. "Did you send for me to talk about whores, *lord?*"

After the space of a breath Dominic accepted that he would get no more from Simon on the subject of Marie.

"Nay," Dominic said. "I wanted to ask in private about your coming marriage."

"Has Ariane objected?" Simon demanded sharply.

Black eyebrows shot up, but all Dominic said was, "No."

Simon expelled a pent breath. "Excellent."

"Is it? Lady Ariane has little taste for marriage."

"Blackthorne can't survive a war over a Norman heiress who was jilted by a nameless

Scots warrior," Simon said bluntly. "Ariane will be my wife before the moon sets tonight."

"I am reluctant to give you over to such a cold union," Dominic said.

Faint amusement showed on Simon's face. With a speed and skill that had unnerved more than one enemy, he drew his belt dagger and casually speared a piece of cold meat. Strong white teeth sank into the venison and chewed.

An instant later the tip of the dagger flicked out like a snake's tongue. A brief movement of Simon's wrist flipped the slice of meat toward Dominic, who caught it deftly.

"Your marriage was little warmer, at first," Simon pointed out as his brother ate the venison.

Dominic smiled slightly.

"My small falcon was a worthy adversary," he agreed.

Simon laughed. "She fair ran you ragged, brother. She still does. I'll settle for less passion and more ease in my marriage."

The Glendruid Wolf's silver-grey eyes weighed Simon for a time. Beyond the stone walls, an early winter wind howled around the keep so fiercely that heavy draperies stirred.

The room was luxuriously furnished, having been designed for the lady of Stone Ring Keep. Now it was serving as temporary quarters for

Dominic and Meg, Lord and Lady of Blackthorne Keep. But even the stout stone walls, thick draperies, and slit windows could not wholly turn aside the ice-tipped talons of an unseasonable storm.

"You are a passionate man," Dominic said simply.

The quality of Simon's eyes changed from clear black to something deeper, more distant, night in a sky that held neither stars nor moon.

"Boys are controlled by passion," Simon said distinctly. "Men are not."

"Aye. Yet men are passionate all the same."

"There is a point to this catechism, I presume."

Dominic's mouth turned down at one corner. Though he was Simon's older brother and his lord, Simon had little patience for advice. Yet a more loyal knight had never lived. Dominic was as certain of that as he was of his wife's love.

"I have discovered," Dominic said, "that a passionate marriage is a pearl beyond price."

Simon grunted and said nothing.

"You disagree?" Dominic asked.

The impatience in Simon's shrug was repeated in the flat line of his mouth.

"Whether I agree or disagree matters not one bit," Simon said.

51

"When you rescued me from that sultan's hell —"

"*After* you gave yourself to the sultan as ransom for me and eleven other knights," cut in Simon.

"— I came out of it a lesser man," Dominic said, ignoring his brother's interruption.

"Truly?" Simon asked in a biting tone. "The few Saracens who survived your sword afterward must have been relieved."

Dominic's mouth shifted into a smile that was every bit as hard as his brother's.

"I wasn't discussing my fighting skills," Dominic said.

"Excellent. For a time I feared that your sweet witch-wife had addled your brain."

"I was discussing my lack of passion."

Again, Simon shrugged. "The whore Marie never complained of anything lacking in you before her marriage to Robert. Afterward, she complained of little else."

Dominic made an impatient sound. "Do not play the slackwitted serf with me, Simon. I know too well just how quick your mind is."

Simon waited.

"Lust is one thing," Dominic said flatly. "Love is quite another."

"To you, perhaps. To me, both mean a singular stupi— um, vulnerability in a man."

Dominic's grin was wolfish. He knew quite

well how Simon felt about men who loved women. Stupid was the least insulting word he had heard Simon use.

But it had not always been thus. Only since the Holy Crusade and the Saracen dungeon.

"Nothing I learned among the Saracens led me to believe that a vulnerable knight was a wise one," Simon concluded.

"Love isn't a war between enemies to be won or lost."

"For you, yes," conceded Simon. "For other men, no."

"What of Duncan?"

"Nothing I have seen of Duncan recommends love to me," Simon said coolly.

Dominic looked surprised.

"God's teeth," Simon snarled. "Duncan nearly died in that hellish Druid place where he found Amber!"

"But he didn't die. Love was stronger."

"Love?" Simon grunted. "Duncan was simply too thick-skulled and stubborn to let feminine witchery defeat him."

The Glendruid Wolf looked broodingly at the handsome, sun-haired brother whom he loved more than anything on earth save his wife Meg.

"You are wrong," Dominic said finally, "just as I was wrong when I came out of the sultan's hell."

Simon started to argue, thought better of it, and shrugged instead.

"Aye," Dominic said, "you do understand what I am talking about. You were the first to see the difference in me. I had no warmth."

Again, Simon didn't disagree.

"Meg brought warmth to my soul," Dominic said. "And then I noticed something that has troubled me ever since."

"Weakness?" Simon asked ironically.

A wolf's smile flashed and vanished.

"Nay. It is you, Simon."

"I?"

"Yes. Like me, you left all warmth in the Saracen land."

Simon shrugged. "Then the cold Norman heiress and I are well matched."

"That is what worries me," Dominic said. "You are too well matched. Who will bring warmth to you if you marry Ariane?"

Simon speared another piece of meat.

"Do not worry, Wolf of Glendruid. Warmth will be no problem for me."

"Oh? You sound quite certain."

"I am."

"And how will you achieve this miracle?" Dominic asked skeptically.

"I shall line my mantle with fur."

5

Between shouts of wind and bursts of icy rain, the sentry called out the hour. The call was repeated through the bailey and into the settlement beyond, telling serf and villein to set aside their tools and bring their animals into the fold even though there was still light in the stormy sky.

Motionless but for her own breaths, Ariane stared through the slit window down to the bailey, fighting her fear of the coming night by concentrating on the view below. Fragrant smoke poured from the uncertain shelter of the kitchen area. Servants bustled about the ovens and spits that had begun working well before dawn, baking and roasting all that was necessary for the hurried marriage feast.

" 'Tis fortunate that the harvest is good," Cassandra said from the doorway. "Otherwise the keep would have been sore put to create a feast worthy of the coming marriage. There has been scant time to prepare for such an important alliance."

Slowly Ariane turned around. She wasn't

surprised to see Cassandra, for she had recognized the Learned woman's voice even before she saw her distinctive scarlet robes. But Ariane was surprised by the fabric Cassandra held in her hands.

With a sound of wonder, Ariane walked closer. Her first thought was that she had never seen a dress more beautifully embroidered. Intricate silver stitches flashed at neckline and hem, and ran like curved lightning through the lining of the long, very full sleeves.

Ariane's second thought was that the color of the rich cloth itself was an exact match for the amethyst ring she wore. Her third thought was that such a magnificent dress should be worn by a happy bride, rather than by one looking for any way out of the marital trap.

Even death.

Cassandra's pale eyes watched each shade of Ariane's response, from the pleased light in the Norman heiress's otherwise dark eyes at the sight of the cloth, to the slender fingers reaching for the fabric . . . and curling into a fist short of their goal.

"You may touch the dress, Lady Ariane. It is our gift to you."

"Our?"

"The Learned. Despite Simon's dislike of

our ways, we . . . value him."

"Why?"

The blunt question didn't displease Cassandra. Rather, it made her smile.

"He is capable of Learning," Cassandra said. "Not everyone is."

The shimmering richness of the gift in Cassandra's hands captivated Ariane. The subtle play of light over the lush, dark fabric was entrancing.

Abruptly Ariane blinked and went quite still, compelled by something she could not name, only sense. Something was condensing within the fabric, a picture calling to her like chords from an ancient harp. Beneath the lightning strokes of embroidery, embedded in the color and texture of the fabric itself, there was a suggestion of two figures . . .

Unknowingly, Ariane reached out to trace the design. It shimmered throughout the cloth like an amethyst beneath a full harvest moon. The play of color and light was as subtle as a sigh breathed into a storm. Yet like a sigh, the design was unmistakable to anyone who had the sensitivity to discover it.

As soon as Ariane's fingertips touched the cloth, she knew that the figures were not those of two knights fighting or two noblemen hawking or two monks transfixed by prayer. The figures were a man and a woman, and they were intertwined in one another as surely as the threads of the cloth itself.

Silently Ariane traced the figures with her fingertips, beginning with the woman's darkly flying hair. The cloth had a whisper of warmth. It was soft yet resilient, as though it were alive.

The feel of it was marvelous, but even more fascinating was the pattern that became clearer with each moment Ariane's fingertips lingered. Though the faces of the figures were concealed by the subtle sheen of the fabric, the weaver had been so skilled that there was no difficulty in telling male from female.

A woman of intense feeling, head thrown back, hair wild, lips open upon a cry of unbelievable pleasure.

The enchanted.

A warrior both disciplined and passionate, his whole being focused in the moment.

The enchanter.

Now he was bending down to her, drinking her cries even as he drew more sounds from her. His powerful body was poised over hers, waiting, shivering with a sensual hunger that was as great as his restraint.

Simon?

With a startled sound, Ariane snatched back her fingers.

"That cannot be," she whispered.

Cassandra's eyes narrowed, but when she spoke, her voice was soft, almost supplicating.

"What is it?" the Learned woman asked. "What do you see?"

Ariane didn't answer. Rather she simply stared at the fabric.

It was changing again even as she watched. Now Simon's midnight eyes were staring back at her, promising her a world she no longer believed in, a world as warm and darkly shimmering as amethysts and wine.

Enchantment.

"Nay," Ariane whispered, "it cannot be! It is but a mummer's trick!"

"What cannot be?"

This time the Learned woman's voice was less soft, more compelling.

Ariane's answer was a wild shaking of her head that sent black locks flying from their careful confinement. Yet even as she stepped back from the fabric, she reached for it once more.

Or did it reach for her?

"No," Ariane said. "It cannot be!"

Cassandra draped the cloth over Ariane's hands.

"There is no need to be afraid," the Learned woman said casually. " 'Tis but cloth."

"It appears — the fabric appears too fragile to wear."

Ariane spoke the half-truth quickly, forcing herself to look at Cassandra's pale eyes rather than at the dress that even now was curling caressingly over her hands.

"Fragile?" Cassandra laughed. "Far from it, lady. The fabric is as strong as hope itself. Do you not see the unspoken dreams woven into the very warp and weft?"

"Hope is for fools."

"Is it?"

Ariane's mouth turned down in a curve too bitter to call a smile. "Yes."

"Then Serena's cloth will drape calmly around you," Cassandra said. "It responds only to dreams, and without hope there are no dreams."

"You make no sense."

" 'Tis a charge often leveled against the Learned. Is your handmaid feeling well?"

"Er, yes," Ariane said, caught off guard by the abrupt change in subject.

"Good. Please remind her not to take more of the potion than I advised. Too much will muddle her wits."

"How would I know the difference?" Ariane said beneath her breath. "The girl has little more wit than a goose as it is."

Cassandra smiled. It changed her face from austere to quite striking.

"Blanche is more like a raven than a goose,"

Cassandra said dryly. "Though she is quite shrewd in her own way, she will always be distracted by whatever trinket shines the brightest at any moment."

Ariane couldn't help smiling at the Learned woman's astute assessment of her handmaiden.

With a nod, Cassandra withdrew, leaving Ariane alone but for the fey dress that precisely matched her eyes. Rather warily she looked at it.

Nothing looked back at her but the ripple of light over rich cloth.

Ariane didn't know whether she was relieved or disappointed. With a muttered word, she reached out to drape the dress across the bed.

The same bed she and Simon would share tonight.

I cannot bear it. Not again.

Never again!

Instead of releasing the dress, Ariane's hands clenched more tightly in it. The cloth became a soothing richness, whispering of a sensuous amethyst world where a woman's cries were of pleasure rather than pain.

Without meaning to, Ariane looked at the cloth, admiring it. Then she looked *into* it. . . .

A warrior both disciplined and passionate, his

whole being focused in the moment.

His powerful body was poised over hers.

The thought sent a surge of emotion through Ariane, shaking her, making her feel more trapped than ever.

Hope is for fools! There is no way out but one and I can only pray that I am strong enough to take it.

"Lady Ariane?"

The voice made Ariane start as though she had been slapped. Hastily she dropped the dress on the bed and turned toward the doorway.

Lady Margaret, the wife of the Glendruid Wolf, was standing quietly there, waiting for Ariane's attention. There was both curiosity and compassion in Meg's green eyes.

"I'm sorry to disturb you," Meg said.

" 'Tis nothing."

Ariane's voice was hoarse, as though it hadn't been used in some time. Distantly she wondered how long she had been staring into the fabric, fighting its enchantment even as a stubborn part of her soul reached out for the dream that shimmered just beyond her reach.

Fool.

"I made some soap for you and left it near the bath," Meg said. "I hope the scent of it pleases you."

Shall I have Meg blend me a special soap to please your dainty nostrils?

Your scent is quite pleasant to me as it is.

Ariane made a small sound as the memory of Simon looming over her bloomed in her mind, mingling with amethyst images from the dress.

Could I be the woman with the darkly flying hair? Is it possible?

Fool! It is but a sorcerer's trick to bewitch you into accepting marriage to a man the Learned value. All pleasure in the marriage bed is for men.

"Lady?" Meg asked, stepping into the room. "Are you well? Should I send for Simon?"

"Whatever for?" Ariane asked hoarsely.

"He has a gentle hand with illness."

"Simon?"

Meg smiled at the blunt skepticism in Ariane's voice.

"Aye," Meg said. "For all his black eyes and bladelike smile, Simon has great kindness in him."

Ariane suspected that her outright disbelief showed on her face, for Meg kept singing Simon's praises.

"When Dominic lay too ill to know friend from foe, Simon slept across the doorway so that the least whisper of need would alert him."

"Ah, Dominic," Ariane said, as though the single name explained everything.

And it did. Simon was called the Loyal for his unswerving fealty to his brother.

"Not only Dominic knows Simon's kindness," Meg said. "The keep's cats vie for his petting."

"Do they?"

Meg nodded, sending light like tongues of fire through her hair. The golden bells on the ends of her long red braids chimed sweetly with every motion of her head.

"The cats? How curious," Ariane said, frowning.

"Simon has an uncanny way with them."

"Perhaps they see themselves in him. Cruelty, not kindness."

"Do you truly believe that?"

Ariane didn't answer.

"Was Simon so harsh with you when he brought you from Blackthorne to Stone Ring Keep?" Meg asked sharply.

Ariane hesitated, wishing she had a harp to conceal the trembling of her hands. And her soul. But the harp was across the room and she was reluctant to show weakness in front of the Glendruid girl with the uncanny green eyes.

"Lady?" Meg asked.

"No," Ariane said reluctantly. "The road

was harsh, and the weather foul, but Simon was no worse than necessity required."

"Then why do you think him cruel?"

"He is a man," Ariane said simply.

"Aye," Meg said smiling. " 'Tis usual for a bridegroom to be a man."

Ariane kept speaking as though she hadn't heard Meg's words. "Beneath that flashing smile and sun-bright hair, he is waiting only for the most telling moment to reveal his cruelty."

Meg's breath came in with an odd sound.

" 'Tis no special disparagement of Simon," Ariane added. "All men are cruel. To expect otherwise is to be a fool."

Abruptly Meg looked at Ariane in the Glendruid way, *seeing* the truth in her.

Ariane, the Betrayed.

"Simon would never betray you," Meg said. "You must believe me."

A single bleak look was Ariane's only answer.

"He would never take a leman," Meg continued earnestly. "He and Dominic are alike in that. They expect no less honor from themselves than they do from a wife."

"Simon may have lemans and concubines with my blessings. Better he loose his cruelty and rutting on them than on me."

Meg tried to hide her shock, but couldn't.

"Lady Ariane, you have been misled as to the nature of what passes between man and woman in the marriage bed," Meg said urgently.

"You are mistaken. I have been well prepared for what is coming."

Each word Ariane spoke was clipped, precise, and cold.

Even as Meg opened her mouth to argue the point, her Glendruid eyes saw the futility of further words. However Ariane had been betrayed, the act had wounded her too deeply for mere words to heal. Only deeds could touch her now. Only deeds could heal her soul.

"In a fortnight or two," Meg said quietly, "we will speak again of cruelty and betrayal. By then, you will have had more experience of Simon's gentleness."

Ariane barely repressed a shudder.

"If you will excuse me, Lady Margaret," Ariane said tightly, "my bath grows cool waiting for me."

"Of course. I'll send Blanche with more hot —"

"No," Ariane interrupted.

Hearing the curtness of her own voice, she took a deep breath and forced a smile.

"Thank you, Lady of Blackthorne," Ariane said, "but I much prefer to see to my own needs in the bath."

Ariane left the room without looking back, for she was very much afraid she would see speculation in the Saxon girl's shrewd green eyes. Ariane didn't want that. She didn't want to know what Meg would do if she discovered that the bride intended to take a deadly silver dagger to her wedding bed.

How can I possibly kill Simon?

How can I possibly not kill him?

And failing all, can I kill myself?

The conflicting questions raged through Ariane as she bathed. There was no answer to her wild thoughts save one.

She could not lie beneath a man again.

Any man.

Even one who called to her from deep within an uncanny amethyst dream.

6

The marriage toasts from the assembled knights grew more and more unrestrained with each mug of ale and goblet of wine that was consumed. While the wedding ceremony itself had been elegant, brief, and reverent, the feast was making up for the previous restraint.

Lord Erik, son of Robert of the North, watched the newly married couple from his seat at Duncan's table at the head of the great hall. Nothing Erik saw stilled the uneasiness that was growing within him. Simon was courteous to his bride and no more. If he were anticipating the bedding of his Norman heiress, it didn't show.

But it was Ariane who truly disturbed Erik's peace of mind. Though the bride wore Serena's complex, fabulously beautiful weaving, there was no joy in Ariane's face or gestures. Rather there were hints of terror and rage barely contained. Her magnificent amethyst eyes were shrouded by shadows that owed nothing to the night that had wrapped coldly around the keep.

Through the ceremony and the celebration that followed, the bride's fingers had kept moving subtly, as though seeking the harp to speak for all that was unspeakable within her.

"Ariane. The Betrayed. But by whom, and in what way, and why?"

No person turned away from the feasting to answer Erik's words. They had been spoken too softly to be overheard by any of the revelers at the lord's table at the head of the great hall.

But Cassandra heard Erik clearly. As soon as the feast had ended and the rounds of increasingly rowdy toasts had commenced, she had come to stand just behind her former pupil. Silently she had watched while he lifted his goblet and responded to toasts with a gracious smile that revealed nothing of his thoughts.

"Tell me, Learned," Erik said without interrupting his study of Ariane, "what did the dress think of our Norman heiress?"

"Serena's weaving is like Serena herself," Cassandra said.

"And what might that be like?" Erik retorted. "I've never seen the old crone."

"She isn't old."

Erik made an impatient sound. This was his first opportunity to have a private conversation with Cassandra since the nuptial dress had arrived at the keep. Curiosity — and the far more urgent needs of a lord who must defend a keep within the Disputed Lands' turbulent borders — made him unusually abrupt.

With a rather fierce smile, Erik lifted his goblet in response to a toast asking that the union be as fertile as there were stars in the sky.

"I don't care if Serena is freshly hatched or so old she rattles like sticks when she walks," Erik muttered as he set down the goblet with a thump.

Cassandra's mouth formed into a line that was suspiciously close to a smile.

"God's teeth," Erik said without looking up. "Tell me what I must know and spare me the embroidery!"

The Learned woman's lips were frankly smiling now. The quicksilver grey of her eyes gleamed with amusement. It was rare to have Erik rise so easily to the bait.

"Be at rest," she murmured. " 'Tis not your wedding night."

"Be grateful," he said through his teeth. "I'm in no humor to seduce an ice queen tonight, no matter how much wealth she brought across the sea to lay at my feet."

"Ah, but Ariane isn't a goddess of ice."

A subtle change went over Erik. Though he made no move, he was somehow more alive, more alert, a predator on a fresh scent.

At Erik's other side, Stagkiller rose to his feet in a surge of power. He watched his master's golden eyes with eyes that were no less gold.

"The dress accepted Ariane!" Erik said in a low voice.

"After a fashion."

"A Learned speak clearly? What would become of tradition?"

Belatedly, Erik understood that he was being deftly teased by the woman whom he loved like a mother.

"Speak how you would, but do so quickly," Erik said. "Stagkiller is eager to course the night. And so am I."

" 'Course the night.' " Cassandra smiled. "It suits you to have the unLearned think of you as a sorcerer who changes shape between wolf and man, doesn't it?"

Erik's teeth showed in a swift, feral grin. "It has saved many a tedious negotiation with greedy cousins, outlaws, and rogue knights."

Cassandra laughed and gave in.

"Ariane saw something within the cloth," said the Learned woman.

"What was it?"

"She didn't say."

The humor vanished from Erik's face.

"Then how do you know the dress accepted her?" he asked.

"She held and stroked the cloth as though it were a puppy nuzzling for comfort. She took pleasure in it."

Erik grunted. "Then Ariane isn't dead all the way to her soul, despite what Amber felt when she touched her."

"It seems not."

"There is no 'seems' about it," he retorted. "Ariane saw something in the dress. It felt pleasant to her touch. It is hers and she is its. Passion exists in her, thank God."

"Aye. But will that passion be for Simon, or will Serena's gift be a kind of armor against him?"

For a time Erik looked broodingly out on the great hall of Stone Ring Keep.

"I don't know," he said finally. "What of you?"

"The rune stones are silent on the subject."

"Even the silver stones?"

"Yes."

Erik muttered an oath under his breath. Cassandra's ability to foresee future crossroads was useful, but not reliable. Prophecy came to her as it willed, rather than as *she* willed. Often what she saw was enigmatic, without easy interpretation, even by Learned and priests combined.

Silently Erik resumed watching the assembled lords, ladies, knights, squires, and a scattering of gently born maidens who filled the great hall with shouts and laughter. When it was appropriate to respond to a toast, he did so, but his expression held the people of the keep at bay.

From his position at the raised table, seated to the right of Duncan, lord of Stone Ring Keep, Erik could see and name each knight who drank and called out toasts. He could name each of the hounds that surged and seethed beneath the long tables, questing for scraps. He could whistle each falcon's special call and have each answer him from her perch behind a knight's chair.

It was the same for the serfs and servants, freemen and villeins of the keep and fields and countryside. Erik knew them all, knew their individual abilities, knew their kith and kin, and could predict with fair accuracy how each would respond to a given command.

But the heiress Ariane, daughter of the powerful Baron Deguerre, was from a foreign place. She had come to the Disputed Lands unlearned, ungiving, a remote beauty wrapped in a cold as deep as that of winter itself.

"Simon will find a way to her heart," Erik said.

"Is that hope or Learning speaking?" Cassandra asked.

"What girl could resist the combination of wit, warrior and lover that is Simon?"

Cassandra's hands moved slightly. A ring set with three stones sent sparks of red and blue and green into the candlelight.

"Hope or Learning?" she repeated.

"God's blood," snarled Erik, "why ask me?"

"Your gift is to see patterns and connections that elude Learned and unLearned alike."

"My so-called gift is useless when it comes to divining what lies in a woman's mind."

"Nonsense. You simply never have had a sufficient reason to try."

"Ariane makes me uneasy," Erik said flatly. "And that is Learning, not hope."

"Yes," Cassandra agreed.

"Look at her. Have you ever known a person to be accepted by one of Serena's weavings and not be calmed?"

"No."

"Is Ariane calmed?"

Erik's question was rhetorical. Cassandra answered anyway.

"Placid? No," Cassandra said. "Calmed? Quite probably. We can only guess the state

74

of Ariane's distress if she were wearing different cloth."

The low sound Erik made sent a ripple of answering emotion through Stagkiller's lean, powerful frame.

"You are a source of endless comfort," Erik said ironically.

"Learning is rarely comfortable."

"What is it within Ariane that so harshly restrains normal passion?"

"I was hoping you would tell me," Cassandra said. "Better yet, tell Simon."

"God's blood," Erik said in a low voice. "If this marriage isn't a fruitful one in all ways, the Glendruid Wolf will be brought to bay by men of blood and greed."

"Aye. And if Dominic falls, the Disputed Lands will know a harrowing such as hasn't come since Druid times."

"Then light candles for Simon the Loyal and Ariane the Betrayed," Erik said. "Their survival is ours."

As though Simon had heard, he turned and looked at Erik and Cassandra. As Simon turned, his long fingers closed around one of Ariane's restless hands. The reflexive jerking away of her fingers was so quickly controlled that only Simon noticed.

The line of his mouth flattened even more. The closer it came to the time when the bride would withdraw to her bedchamber to prepare for her groom, the colder Ariane's flesh became.

He began to fear it was no game that she played, nor even maidenly anxiety that made her draw away. Rather it was a simple truth: Ariane was cold to the marrow of her bones.

"Come, my passionate bride," Simon said sardonically.

Eyes the violet of a wild summer storm gave Simon a swift glance.

"It is time to take your leave of the feasting you so obviously have enjoyed," he said.

Ariane looked out over the raucous knights and wished herself far away, alone, listening to her harp instead of Simon's rich voice vibrating with irony and bitterness.

"So set aside your unused goblet and leave your untouched plate for the hounds," Simon continued. "We will pay our respects to the lord of Stone Ring Keep together, as befits a married couple."

Though Ariane said nothing, she didn't fight the easy power of Simon's hand pulling her to her feet. She had known this moment would come.

Without realizing it, Ariane's free hand sought the soothing folds of the dress whose rich color matched her eyes. The longer she wore the luxurious fabric, the more she appreciated its calming texture.

As much as Ariane enjoyed stroking the cloth, she was careful not to look *into* the uncanny fabric. She needed no more frightening, tempting visions of herself arching like a drawn bow at Simon's touch, pleasure a rush of silver lightning stitching through her soul. . . .

Simon felt the subtle tremor that went through Ariane's body as he led her toward Amber and Duncan.

God's teeth, am I that disgusting to my bride?

The icy anger of Simon's thought didn't show on his face or in the gentleness with which he drew Ariane to his side.

"Ah, there you are," Duncan said, spotting Simon. "Impatient for the rest of the festivities, are you?"

The laughter that went through the knights gathered nearby left no doubt as to what the remaining "festivities" were.

"Not as impatient as my lovely bride," Simon said, smiling down at Ariane. "Isn't that so?"

The smile she gave him in return was little more than a baring of teeth. No one but Simon seemed to notice. He squeezed her fingers between his in silent warning that she bridle her dislike of him while in public.

Ariane looked at the black clarity of Simon's

eyes and knew he sensed with great precision her distaste for being touched.

"I am . . . overwhelmed by all that has happened," Ariane said.

Her voice was hoarse from the fierce restraint she applied not to scream.

"Lord and lady, you have been both generous and kind in your gifts," Ariane said.

"The pleasure is ours," Duncan said.

"The dress becomes you," Amber said. "I am glad."

Ariane's slender fingers stroked the length of her sleeve. Silver embroidery flashed and gleamed with each motion of her body.

"I would like to have thanked the weaver," Ariane said. "Will you carry my gratitude to her?"

"You can tell her yourself," Amber said.

"You told me Serena was a recluse," Duncan objected.

"She is, but she will see Ariane."

"Why?" Duncan asked.

"Because Ariane completes the weaving," Amber said simply.

Simon looked at his bride with hooded eyes. There was no doubt that Ariane's beauty was enhanced to an extraordinary degree by the vivid, lush fabric.

"Do you not agree, Simon?" Amber asked.

"Her skin is like a pearl lit from within,"

Simon said without looking away from his bride. "And her eyes shame even the magnificent amethysts woven into her hair."

Startled, pleased, yet deeply wary of male admiration, Ariane found it impossible to breathe. The look in Simon's eyes belied the restraint with which he had touched her up to now.

He wanted her.

A warrior both disciplined and passionate, his whole being focused in the moment.

The enchanter.

And a frightening part of Ariane longed to be the enchanted. Frissons of yearning swept over her like shadows of the lightning that had been embroidered on the wedding dress.

A stray draft from the great hall sent a fold of the dress curling around Simon's free hand. His fingers caressed the fey cloth. Unwillingly he smiled with pure pleasure. It was as though warmth and laughter, passion and peace had been woven into the very fabric.

Amber looked at the cloth clinging to Simon's fingers and smiled with relief. She sensed her brother standing just behind her and turned. Erik, too, was watching the fabric being stroked by a warrior's hard hand.

"You approve of the dress?" Erik asked Simon casually.

"Aye."

"That bodes well for the marriage," Erik said, satisfaction in every syllable.

"Does it?"

"Indeed. It foretells a lasting, passionate union."

"If my bride's bed is half so beguiling as her dress," Simon said, smiling ironically, "I shall deem myself the most fortunate of men."

Ariane's breath came in with a stifled sound as fear returned in a rush. She moved to step away from Simon. His fingers tightened around her wrist. Though the pressure wasn't painful, it was a clear warning of his superior strength.

Nightmare bloomed like a black flower in Ariane's soul. It took every bit of her self-control not to fight Simon's firm grasp.

Abruptly he released the folds of her dress as though it no longer pleased him.

"Patience, my dark nightingale," Simon said, his voice very soft and his eyes as black as hell. "We cannot leave until you have been toasted by the lord of the keep."

Ariane closed her eyes briefly. "Of course. Forgive me. I am . . . anxious."

"All maids are," Amber said in a gentle voice. "There is naught to worry you. Simon is as gentle as he is quick of hand."

The smile Ariane managed was more than a trifle desperate.

"Duncan," Amber said, "toast the union. We have tormented them quite long enough."

"We have?" Duncan asked blankly.

"Have you forgotten so quickly how eager you were to consummate your own union?" Erik asked.

Duncan flashed a smile at his own recent bride. "Viewed that way, a wedding feast is indeed a form of torment."

Erik thrust a golden goblet into Duncan's hand, distracting him from Amber's blushing smile. Duncan took the hint and turned his attention to the newly wed couple. His expression changed as he studied first Ariane and then Simon. Slowly Duncan lifted his goblet.

The room became still.

"May you see the sacred rowan bloom," Duncan said clearly.

A murmuring of agreement and wonder went through the gathered knights as the story of Duncan and Amber's love was retold in scattered phrases.

"There is no danger of that, thank God," Simon retorted in a voice that went no farther than the two couples. "Ariane is no witch to enchant love from an unwilling warrior."

Ariane gave Simon a sideways look and a thin smile. "Ah, but I was, once."

"What?" he asked.

"A witch," she said succinctly.

Simon's black eyes narrowed, but before he could say anything, Ariane turned to the lord and lady of Stone Ring Keep.

"Again, I thank you for your generosity," she said clearly.

"Again, I say it was our pleasure," Duncan said.

Ariane kept speaking as though she hadn't heard, raising her voice so that it carried through the great hall. At the same time, she grabbed Amber's hand with a speed that rivaled the quickness of her husband, Simon.

A low sound came from Amber as the bleakness at the center of Ariane's soul rushed through the touch like a cold river.

"If, at any time in the future," Ariane said quickly, "either man or woman hints that I received ill treatment in the Disputed Lands, let it be known that such is a lie. Am I speaking the truth, Learned?"

"Yes," Amber said.

"Let it also be known that whatever happens in this marriage, *Simon the Loyal bears no blame.*"

Pale, swaying, Amber said, "Truth!"

Ariane released her instantly and looked to Cassandra.

"Will you be my witness, Learned?" Ariane asked.

82

"All Learned will be your witness."

"Whatever comes?"

"Whatever comes."

Without another word, Ariane turned and walked from the great hall. Each step, each breath, each motion of her body set the sweeping folds of her dress rippling and swaying. Silver shimmered and ran like springwater through the woven cloth, teasing the eye with a sense of pattern just beneath the surface, just beyond understanding, as tantalizing as the memory of summer heat in deepest winter.

Duncan turned to Cassandra.

"What is the meaning of this?" he asked bluntly.

"I know only what you do."

"I doubt that," Duncan retorted.

Amber's hand settled with a butterfly's delicacy on Duncan's thick forearm. She looked into the dangerous hazel glitter of his eyes without a bit of fear.

"Ariane spoke the truth," Amber said. "Cassandra — and through her, all Learned — witnessed Ariane's truth. That is all."

"I don't like it."

"Neither did Ariane."

Erik gave his sister a shrewd look.

"What else did you sense of Ariane's truth?" Erik asked.

"Nothing I could put words to. And even

if I could I would not. What lies within Ariane's soul is hers to share or conceal."

"Even from her husband?" Duncan asked.

"Yes."

Duncan made a frustrated sound and raked powerful fingers through his thatch of dark brown hair.

"I like it not," Duncan growled again.

"Don't fret, my friend," Simon said. "Ariane was protecting me."

Duncan gave the lithe knight a surprised look and then laughed aloud.

"Protecting *you?*" Duncan asked in disbelief.

"Aye," Simon said with an odd smile. "A beguiling thought, is it not, to be protected by a fierce little nightingale?"

"But what danger could come to you within the walls of Stone Ring Keep?" Duncan asked.

"I'll remember to ask Ariane . . . eventually."

With that, Simon turned to follow his wife.

"Wait!" called Amber. "It is customary for a bride's relatives to prepare her for the groom."

"As Ariane has neither sister nor mother, niece nor aunt, she will just have to make do with the groom," Simon said without looking back.

"But —"

"Do not worry, Amber witch. I won't tear Ariane's magnificent dress in my haste."

7

If I cut my throat, how can I be certain of doing a thorough job of it?

Ariane thought of all the horrible tales she had heard of knights and battles. While there was plenty of gore in all the stories, the blood had been drawn by warriors wielding battle-axe and hammer, broadsword and lance.

Next to such weapons, the dainty dagger gleaming in her hand seemed a joke.

God's teeth! Is the cursed blade even long enough to reach my heart?

While Ariane stared at the dagger's elegant silver blade, the dress shimmered and curled caressingly around her legs like a cat begging to be noticed.

Ariane's thoughts scattered.

Distracted, she began pacing the small room, not even noticing that Blanche had forgotten to kindle the fire in the hearth. As a result, the room had a winter chill, as though all heat had been sucked from the thick stone walls.

Why was I born a woman, with none of a

warrior's strength or skill in piercing flesh?

The wind gusted. The draperies around the bed stirred vaguely. Ariane's dress moved restively no matter what the wind did.

Even without that evil potion Geoffrey put in my wine, I would have had no chance against him.

Simon would have.

Ariane's quick steps paused.

"Aye," she said softly. "Simon. So strong. So quick. Even Geoffrey's murderous skill with the sword would be hard put to equal Simon's swiftness."

Again came the thought that had haunted Ariane throughout the wedding ceremony.

Simon.

I cannot kill him. Nor would I, even if I could. I must be the one to die.

But how? What can I do to make Simon strike me down?

Ariane couldn't think of a time he had ever lifted a hand to an unruly hound, much less to the highborn heiress who had been first Duncan's betrothed, then Simon's.

With a muttered word, Ariane resumed pacing, ignoring the soft folds of dress that seemed determined to slow her. Nothing she could think of seemed sufficient to disturb Simon's self-control. He would fight only on the order of his lord and brother.

Or to defend himself.

Ariane came to a complete stop. Motionless, she stood in the center of the room, turning the insight over and over in her mind even as she turned the dagger over in her hands.

Would he see me as enough of a threat to kill me?

The idea almost made her laugh. Simon's power and skill were so great that he would probably hurt himself laughing if she attacked him with the dagger.

Somehow, she would have to take him unawares, a move so swift that he wouldn't have time to think.

And laugh.

A man gone on drink has no control over himself. Many toasts have been drunk already. Simon will be forced to drink many more before he is free of the great hall.

Silently Ariane stood in the center of the room, the dagger turning restlessly in her hands. The violet dress seethed softly, redoubling the least flicker of lantern light.

"Yes," Ariane whispered finally. "That is the answer. Simon is a warrior. When attacked, he will attack in return with the heedless speed of a cat."

She looked at the dagger.

"I will slash at him, he will kill me before his better judgment interferes, and that will be the end of it."

A draft stirred the fabric of Ariane's dress, making it swirl around her feet with tiny, almost secret motions.

I am mad even to think of this. He will take the dagger from me and beat me most soundly.

No. I will beguile him first. I will bide my time until he is lost to the coils of lust and ale. Then I will strike.

He will strike back fiercely. It will end.

It will not. You are mad even to think of this.

Ariane ignored the inner argument just as she ignored the soothing caress of the Learned fabric. She had become used to fragments of herself arguing since the night when she lay helpless, bound by nightmare and Geoffrey's sweating, hammering body.

Far better to die than to endure such masculine savagery again.

At least death will be quick.

The thought brought a measure of comfort to Ariane. No matter how many well-wishers slowed Simon's progress through the great hall toward her bedchamber, no matter how many toasts must be drunk to avoid insult to other knights, Simon would make a swift job of her death.

She had never seen such quickness as his. Not even Geoffrey the Fair, who was renowned for fighting two and three men at once.

And winning.

No one will blame Simon for what happens. After all, he will only be defending himself against a murderous bride.

Oddly, making certain that Simon didn't suffer because of her death was important to Ariane. He had been kind to her in his own way. Not the kindness of lackeys or men seeking favors, but a simple awareness that she had neither his strength nor his stamina on the trail. He had been careful of her in a way that had nothing to do with the politeness of a knight toward a highborn maiden.

The sound of footsteps in the hall broke into Ariane's thoughts.

"Who goes?" she asked.

Her voice was so tight it was almost hoarse.

"Your husband. May I enter?"

"It is too soon," Ariane said without thinking.

"Too soon?"

"I'm not — not ready."

Simon's laughter was rather teasing and quite male. It ruffled nerves Ariane had never known existed in her body.

"It will be my pleasure to ready you most thoroughly," Simon said in a deep voice. "Open the door for me, nightingale."

Ariane moved to put the dagger in its sheath at her waist, only to remember that the dress was laced from neck to knees. There was no belt from which to hang a sheath.

Frantically she looked around for a place to put the dagger. It must be within her reach while she lay in bed. That would be when she most needed it.

The sash holding one of the bed draperies aside was the best hiding place Ariane could find for the blade. Hurriedly she slid the dagger between the folds of cloth and went to the door.

"Ariane."

Simon's voice was no longer teasing. He meant to have access to the bedchamber.

And to his wife.

With shaking hands, Ariane opened the door.

"There was no barrier to your entry," she said in a low voice.

Her glance didn't lift from the floor.

"Your lack of welcome is a bigger barrier than any contrived by a locksmith," Simon said.

Ariane said nothing. Nor did she look up to his face.

"If I am so ugly in your eyes, why did you want the Learned to witness that whatever comes of this marriage is your doing, not mine?" Simon challenged gently.

"You are not ugly in my eyes," Ariane said.

"Then look at me, nightingale."

Drawing a deep breath, Ariane forced herself to confront her husband's black glance. What she saw drew a startled sound from her.

One of the keep's cats was draped around Simon's neck. When his long, tapering fingers moved caressingly under the cat's chin, it purred with the sound of thick rain on water. Claws slid in and out of their sheaths, telling of feline ecstasy. Though the claws pierced Simon's shirt to test the flesh beneath, he showed no impatience. He simply kept stroking the cat and watching Ariane's violet eyes.

Belatedly Ariane realized that Simon held a jug of wine and two goblets in the hand that wasn't busy petting the cat.

"You drank little wine," Simon said, following her glance.

Ariane shuddered, remembering the night another man had pressed wine upon her.

"I have little liking for wine," she said tightly.

"English wine can bite the tongue. But this is Norman wine. Drink with me."

It wasn't a request. Nor was it an order. Not quite.

Ariane decided that she would pretend to drink, for it was clear that Simon hadn't yet drunk enough to lose the edge of his wit, much less his judgment.

"As you wish," Ariane murmured.

Simon stepped into the room. Instantly Ariane stepped back, then covered the action by making a fuss of closing the door. She doubted that Simon was fooled.

A glance at his face told her she was right.

"Why is there no fire?" Simon asked.

For the space of an aching breath, Ariane thought he was asking about her lack of passion. Then her lungs eased as she realized that he was looking at the barren hearth.

"Blanche has been ill."

Casually Simon set the wine and goblets on a chest that held extra coverings for the bed. He lifted the cat from his neck and settled the animal in the crook of his arm. With easy grace, he knelt and stirred the ashes, seeking any embers. There were only a few, and they were quite small.

Ariane started for the door. "I'll call for fresh coals."

"No."

Though the word was quietly spoken, Ariane stopped so quickly that her dress swirled forward.

"What is already in the hearth will be enough," Simon said.

"They are barely alive."

"Aye. But they *are* alive. Be ready to hand me kindling. Very small at first. No more than slivers."

As Simon spoke, he gathered the scarce coals and began breathing gently on them. After a few moments, the larger coal began to flush with inner heat.

"Kindling, please," Simon murmured.

Ariane started and looked around. A basket of kindling lay just beyond her reach. Between her and the basket was Simon's muscular body.

"It's to your right," Ariane said.

"I know," he said. "My right arm is full of His Laziness."

"His Laziness?"

Then Ariane understood. She laughed unexpectedly.

To Simon, the sounds were as musical as any Ariane had drawn from her harp.

"The cat," she said. "Is he truly called His Laziness?"

The sound of agreement Simon made was rather like the cat's purr.

Disarmed, Ariane reached around Simon until her fingers could close around the basket handle. It was a long reach. Simon's back was broad. Even beneath the luxurious indigo folds of his shirt, she could sense the power and heat of the long muscles on either side of his spine.

The cat's ecstatic purring vibrated in Ariane's ear as she bent far forward to retrieve the basket. When Simon drew a breath, his back brushed against Ariane's arm. She looked at him with sudden wariness.

If he noticed the contact, it didn't distract him. He was still leaning forward, his expression intent, his lips shaped to send air in a steady stream over the coals.

The sight of Simon's pursed mouth intrigued Ariane.

Odd. I thought his lips were hard, ungiving. But now they look almost . . . tender.

Simon's breath flowed out. Coals shimmered with new heat.

"Kindling," he breathed.

It was a moment before the request sank through Ariane's curious thoughts. She snatched the basket from the hearth, reached in, and grabbed the first thing that came to hand. Quickly she held the piece of wood out to Simon.

"Here," she said.

The wood was half again as long as her hand and thicker than three fingers held together.

"Too large," Simon said. "The fire is still too shy to take that burden. Something much smaller is required."

Ariane hesitated, struck by the teasing quality buried within Simon's rich voice.

"Quickly," he said without looking at her. "If the coals burn too long alone, they will spend themselves without ever creating true fire."

Blindly Ariane felt through the kindling basket until she found dry slivers of wood at the bottom. She held them out on her palm.

As Simon took the offering, his fingers drew over Ariane's hand in a gesture that was strangely caressing. She shivered and found it difficult to breathe.

When Simon felt the telltale quiver, he smiled within the concealment of his very short, fine beard.

"Just right," Simon murmured. "You will quickly learn to build a fine fire."

Ariane thought of protesting that she had Blanche to perform such tasks. In the end, Ariane held her tongue, not wanting to disturb the fragile sense of playfulness she sensed in her warrior husband.

Ariane told herself that her caution came from wanting Simon to be off guard when she finally was driven to use the dagger.

She wasn't certain she believed it.

What does it matter? Ariane mocked herself silently. *Death will come soon enough. Is it so terrible to take pleasure in the bit of softness that lies so surprisingly within this warrior?*

Intently, memorizing each deft moment with a thoroughness she neither questioned nor understood, Ariane watched as Simon added the slivers of kindling to the tiny mound of coals. Heat grew in response to his breath fanning warmly over the ashes.

"More," he said. "A bit bigger this time. The fire grows less shy."

Ariane rummaged heedlessly in the basket, winced when a sliver went into her flesh, then kept on searching without looking away from the pale gold of Simon's head.

His hair looked as soft as a kitten's ears. She wondered if it would feel half so smooth between her fingers.

"Ariane?"

"Here," she said, startled, holding out her hand.

Simon looked at the pale, slender fingers where wisps of shredded kindling were heaped like stiff straw. With careful, totally unnecessary care, he stirred a fingertip through the woody offering.

As often as not, it was Ariane's palm his finger nuzzled, not splinters of wood. At the first touch, her hand jerked subtly. The next touch startled her less. After a few moments his fingertip was tracing the lines of her palm with a gentleness that was very close to a caress.

"Mmmm," Simon said, pretending to choose among the slivers of fuel.

"You rumble like His Laziness," Ariane said.

Her voice sounded strange to her own ears.

To Simon, Ariane's breathlessness was a small victory, a sliver of wood turning smoky as it succumbed to heat.

Reluctantly he took several bits of kindling and returned his attention to the coals. He said something under his breath when he saw that the fire had all but fled the embers while he caressed Ariane's palm.

Gently he blew across the dying coals. After a time they flared again. First he placed splinters, then larger pieces of kindling over the embers. Renewed heat flushed their silvery faces.

The thought of sending a similar flush through Ariane made Simon's breath ache within his lungs.

"More," Simon said.

The huskiness of his voice intrigued Ariane for a reason she could not fathom. Forgetting the dagger waiting in the bedside drapery, she sorted eagerly through the kindling basket, relieved to think about something besides nightmare and death. Soon she had several sizes of kindling ready for Simon.

"Perfect," Simon said, leaning forward.

The rush of his breath across Ariane's cheek was warm and pleasantly spiced with wine.

Simon saw the tiny flare of her nostrils as she breathed in his own breath. When she smiled slightly, as though savoring a small part of him, heat lanced through Simon. He wanted very much to grab Ariane, push her witchy violet skirts above her hips, and bury himself in her.

Much too soon, advised the cooler part of Simon's brain. *The game — if indeed it is a game she plays — has hardly begun.*

With great precision, Simon placed gradually larger pieces of kindling on the coals, then larger still. All the while he blew carefully on the fragile fire.

Suddenly tongues of flame licked upward, consuming the kindling in a soft burst of golden heat.

One-handed, Simon laid the rest of the fire. Then he watched it in silence, stroking the steel-colored cat that hadn't budged from its privileged nest.

As Ariane watched Simon's palm smooth the length of the cat, she wondered what it would feel like to be touched with such care by a warrior's hard hand.

"Pour the wine for us, nightingale."

Ariane blinked as tension returned in a cold rush. She had been so intent upon watching Simon's hand that she had forgotten the inevitable end of the night.

Unhappily she looked at the elegant silver designs on the wine jug and wondered what savage potion lay concealed within.

"I — I don't want any," Ariane said baldly.

Simon gave her a swift black glance. When he saw that calculation had returned to her eyes, he barely suppressed a curse.

A heartbeat ago she was watching my hand with longing. I am certain of it.

And now she looks at me as though she were a terrified Saracen maid and I a Christian warrior bent on rape.

She is like a wealthy sultan's fountain, hot and cold by turns.

Is it truly fear that makes her draw back again? Or is it merely a game to tease me and addle my wits with lust?

"Bring me a goblet," Simon said evenly. "It would be a pity to waste such fine wine."

When Ariane realized that Simon meant to drink from the jug himself, she felt a rush of relief.

"If — if you are having some, I will be pleased to drink with you," she said.

Her voice was so low that it took a moment for Simon to understand. When he did, he gave her a glance that was divided between irritation and amusement.

"Were you afraid of poison?" he asked sardonically.

Ariane flinched. She shook her head. At each movement of her head, the chains of tiny amethysts woven into her hair burned with violet fire, reflecting the renewed leap of flame.

Her hair is like a midnight studded with amethyst stars. God's blood, she is beautiful beyond any man's dreams.

Longing went through Simon so violently that he had to clench his jaw against it. Slowly he set His Laziness near the fire-warmed hearth and stood to face his wife.

"What, then?" Simon persisted. "Why were you afraid to drink the wine?"

"I . . ."

Ariane's voice died. A glance at Simon's face convinced her that he meant to have an answer. For a wild instant she considered telling him the truth. Then she remembered her father's reaction and her jaws locked against words of any kind.

Whore. Daughter of a whore. Wanton spawn of Satan, you have ruined me. If I dared kill you, I would!

The truth had done Ariane no good with her father. Nor had the priest been any more sympathetic. He had accused her of lying in the sacred act of confession. Priest and father alike had believed Geoffrey.

There was little hope that the near-stranger who was her husband would believe her, when the men who had been closest to her had not.

Speaking the truth would be foolish. It would serve only to make it more difficult to catch Simon off guard.

"I've heard," Ariane said in a thin voice, "that men can put something in wine that . . ."

Again, Ariane's voice failed.

"That makes maidens into wantons?" Simon asked neutrally.

"Or makes them . . . helpless."

"I've heard of such things too," Simon said.

"Have you?" Ariane asked.

"Aye, but I've never had to resort to them to seduce a girl."

The amusement buried just beneath the surface of Simon's words made his dark eyes gleam like water touched by moonlight.

Ariane let out a breath she hadn't been aware of holding.

"And I never will."

Simon restrained his anger with difficulty. It was one thing for Ariane to play a sensual game. It was quite another to slander a man's honor.

"A man who would do that to a maid is beneath a dog's contempt," Simon said in a clipped voice.

There was no amusement in Simon's eyes now. He was icy, savage.

"Do you believe me?" he asked.

Hastily Ariane nodded again.

"Excellent," Simon said softly.

The quality of his voice made her flinch.

"I suspect you dislike me," Simon said.

"That's not —"

"I suspect I repel you physically," he said, talking over Ariane's interruption.

"Nay, 'tis not you, 'tis —"

"But I have done nothing to earn your contempt," Simon finished, his voice deadly cold.

Knowing that she had hurt Simon caused surprising pain to Ariane, further tightening her already overstrung nerves. She hadn't meant to demean him. Of all the men she had ever known, it was Simon to whom she was most drawn.

It frightened her even as it lured her.

"Simon," she whispered.

He waited.

"I never meant to insult you," Ariane managed.

Raised blond eyebrows silently contradicted her statement.

"Truly," she said.

Simon held out his hand.

She flinched.

"You insult me every time you draw back from me," Simon said flatly.

Desperately Ariane tried to convince her husband that her reticence had nothing to do with him.

"I cannot help it," she said in a rush.

"No doubt. Tell me, wife. What do you find so disgusting about me?"

Ariane's fragile hold on her self-control snapped.

"It's not you!" she raged. "You are clean of limb and sweet of breath and quick and strong and honorable and so comely it's a wonder the fairies haven't slain you out of pure jealousy!"

Simon's eyes widened.

"You are also thickheaded beyond belief!" Ariane finished in a rising voice.

There was an instant of silence in which neither could say who was more surprised by Ariane's words. Then Simon threw back his head and laughed.

"The last, at least, is true," Simon said.

"What?" asked Ariane warily.

"The part about my thick head."

With a sound of exasperation, Ariane turned her back on her maddening husband.

"You will believe the worst I say, but not the best," she muttered.

Simon's only answer was the sound of wine being poured into silver goblets. When the goblets were full, he set them near the hearth to take off their chill. He would like to have warmed himself by the fire as well, but there was no chair big enough to take his weight.

He looked around quickly. The bed was close enough to the fire to bask in warmth from the flames, but not close enough to put the draperies in danger of burning. The bed was also where Simon had every intention of spending the night.

But not alone.

"Come, my nervous nightingale. Sit with me by the fire."

The gentle rasp of Simon's voice was like a cat's tongue. Intrigued despite her anger, Ariane risked a quick look over her shoulder.

Simon was smiling and holding out his hand to her. This time she sensed she must not refuse him, or he would simply stalk from the room, leaving her to face her fate the next night, or the night after.

Ice condensed in Ariane's stomach at the thought. She doubted if she could string herself up to this pitch again. It must end here, now.

Tonight.

Be quick, Simon. Be strong.

End my nightmare.

8

Simon watched while his wary bride approached him. The hand she gave to him was trembling and cold. Her eyes were dark and almost wild.

Laughter, curiosity, flirtation, fear. She changes direction as quickly as a falcon on a storm wind.

I wonder if Dominic had this much difficulty with his bride.

God's teeth. None of the other women I've bedded has given me a tenth so much trouble.

Belatedly, Simon remembered that the other women hadn't been nervous, virginal, highborn girls. They had been widows, concubines of fallen sultans, or infertile harem girls.

Once, and only once, his lover had been married.

"Such a cold hand," Simon said.

Ariane was in too much of a turmoil to answer. Simon's hand was so warm she thought it might burn her.

"Is your other hand as cold?" he asked.

She nodded.

"I don't think that's possible," Simon said judiciously. "Show me."

The hand he held out to her was large, elegant despite that, and scarred with the inevitable marks of battle.

"Ariane."

She jumped.

"If I were going to throw you on the floor and ravish you like a slave girl, I would have done so many times over by now."

Ariane turned even more pale. Geoffrey had done his worst, but it had taken him the better part of a night, for he was much gone on drink.

When Simon realized she had taken him seriously, he didn't know whether to swear or laugh.

"Nightingale," he said, sighing, "do you have any idea what passes between a man and a woman on their wedding night?"

"Yes."

The intense stillness of Ariane's body told Simon that someone had explained full well to her what was expected of a wife in the marriage bed.

And she loathed the thought of it.

" 'Tis natural that it seem strange to you," he said. "It seems strange to a man the first time or two."

"It does?"

"Of course. 'Tis difficult to know where to put one's hands and arms and, er, other parts."

Before Ariane could respond to that surprising bit of information — or to the pronounced red on Simon's cheekbones — he took her other hand and tugged her gently down onto the bed.

"You were right," he said. "This hand is as cold as the other."

Simon blew gently across Ariane's right hand. The contrast between the chill of her flesh and the heat of Simon's breath was so great that Ariane shivered.

"Try the wine," Simon suggested.

Ariane bent and dipped her fingertip in one of the goblets. Delicately she licked up a drop of wine.

"Nay," she said. "Your hands are warmer than the wine."

Simon had meant that Ariane try to warm herself by drinking the wine, but the sight of her pink tongue licking up wine sent everything resembling thought from his head.

"Are you certain?" he asked.

The rasp was back in Simon's deep voice. The sound of it pleased Ariane. Smiling, she bent and dipped her finger in the wine once more.

Breath held, Simon watched as she circled

her wine-wet fingertip with the very tip of her tongue.

" 'Tis quite certain," Ariane said. "Your hand is far warmer than the wine."

"May I have some?"

She held out the cup.

"Nay, wife. From your fingers."

"Do you mean . . . ?" asked Ariane.

She looked at him uncertainly.

"I don't bite," Simon assured her, smiling.

"Said the wolf to the lambkin," Ariane muttered.

Simon laughed, delighted by his bride's change from fear to amusement.

Ariane bent over and dipped her finger into the wine again. As she lifted her hand toward Simon, wine ran down her fingernail, beaded into a brilliant garnet drop, and threatened to fall to the pale white lace of the bed cover. He ducked his head and caught Ariane's fingertip between his lips.

The heat of Simon's mouth made the fire seem cold. Ariane made a low sound as he gently released her finger.

"Is something wrong?" Simon asked.

"You are so very warm. It surprised me."

"You felt no displeasure?"

She shook her head.

"What of pleasure?" Simon asked.

"Now I know why the keep's cats stalk you.

The warmth of your body draws them."

Amusement gleamed in Simon's dark eyes.

"Then you liked my heat," he murmured, smiling.

Ariane wanted to scream with sudden frustration at the trap life had built around her. In her eyes, Simon was as handsome as a god. Firelight burned in the gold of his hair and gleamed within the midnight depths of his eyes.

When he smiled, it was like watching the sun rise over a bank of clouds, touching everything with warmth. Yet Ariane had to sit close to Simon while thinking coldly about the dagger that was now within her reach.

If he smiled again, she didn't know what she would do.

How can a man who is so fair to look at be such a beast when taken by lust?

There was no answer to Ariane's silent, desperate question. There never had been an answer. Geoffrey the Fair was considered the most comely knight in the Norman lands, and he had raped her without apology.

Maybe Simon would be different. More kind.

The thought was as beguiling to Ariane as Simon's smile. But on the heels of that thought came the bitterness of past experience to warn her.

A man's smile is like a rainbow. If I foolishly

chase it, I will be drawn from my true path. Then I will relive my nightmare again and again and again.

But I will be awake this time. Every time.

Ariane shuddered with fear and revulsion. Only the thought of the dagger, bright and clean and hard, made it possible for her to keep her self-control as nightmare threatened to overwhelm her.

"Bring me some more wine, nightingale."

Without a word Ariane pick up a wine goblet and held it out to Simon. He didn't take it.

"I find that wine tastes better when sipped from your fingertip," he said.

Ariane looked at Simon intently. His eyes were like his mind, clear and unclouded by drink.

Yet he must be weakened by wine if her plan had any chance of succeeding.

"It will take until dawn to drink a goblet from my hand," Ariane protested.

"A night well spent."

Ariane dipped her fingers in wine and held them out to Simon. This time the warmth of his mouth didn't startle her. The pleasure, however, remained.

It pleased him, as well. He purred.

The feline sound coming from a fierce warrior made Ariane smile.

"Do I amuse you, nightingale?" Simon asked.

" 'Tis odd to hear a warrior purr," she admitted.

Before Simon could answer, Ariane put two fingers into the wine goblet. In her haste to get more wine into him, she dipped up too much. Wine ran down her fingers to her palm, and from there to her wrist.

So did Simon's tongue.

If he had been holding her, Ariane would have fought. But Simon hadn't moved and it had been she who had offered her wine-wet fingers.

"Such an odd sound," Simon said.

"What?"

His tongue swept out and the hardened tip traced the fragile blue veins of her wrist where life beat frantically just beneath creamy skin.

"Oh!" Ariane said.

"Aye. That sound," Simon said. "Unease and surprise and pleasure combined."

"You are so unexpected," Ariane said.

The frustration in her tone nearly made Simon smile. He felt the same way about her.

"I?" Simon asked. "I am but a simple warrior who —"

Ariane made a sound of exasperated disagreement.

Simon never paused.

"— finds himself wed to an extraordinary beauty who quails at the thought of a kiss, much less the proper joining of man and wife."

"I'm not."

"Quailing at the thought of our union?" he asked smoothly.

"I'm not beautiful. Both Meg and Amber shine more brightly than I."

Simon laughed outright. "Ariane, your beauty beggars my ability to describe it."

"And your silver tongue beggars my ability to believe your words," she retorted.

"Then you like my tongue."

"More wine?" she asked, looking away from Simon's gleaming eyes. "But not from my fingertips. It will take too long that way."

"What will?"

Killing the bride.

For a terrible instant Ariane thought she had spoken aloud. When Simon only continued to look at her attentively, she realized she hadn't put her frantic thought into words. With a ragged sigh, she gathered the shreds of her self-control.

"Reaching the bottom of the goblet," she said quickly. "It will take too long drop by drop."

"Does something await us at the bottom of the goblet?"

"Whatever we wish."

Simon blinked. "Really."

"Aye," Ariane said, improvising swiftly. " 'Tis an old belief in Norman lands that a wish made on a nuptial cup is granted, but the cup must be quickly drunk."

"Odd. I'm an old Norman and I've never heard of it."

"You're teasing me."

"The thought appeals."

"Simon," Ariane said a trifle desperately.

"A whole goblet?" he asked.

"Aye."

"One wish per cup?"

"Aye," she said.

"What if I have two wishes?"

"Then you must drink two goblets. Quickly."

"And you?" he asked.

"I have only one wish."

Simon saw the sudden return of darkness to Ariane's eyes and wondered what her thoughts were.

"What wish is that, nightingale?"

"I cannot tell you."

"Ever?"

For a moment Ariane didn't answer. Then she lowered long black lashes over her eyes, concealing the darkness within.

"Not yet," she whispered.

"But someday?"

"Someday you will know."

The fire crackled in the silence, sending up sparks that died almost before they lived. Broodingly, Simon looked from the fire to his enigmatic wife.

You are like those sparks, nightingale. Flashes of brilliant heat against a consuming darkness.

What was it Amber said about you? You had endured a betrayal so deep it all but killed your soul.

Yet I can call fiery sparks from your darkness.

"Make your wish," Simon said huskily.

Ariane looked at the goblet that he was holding out to her and shook her head.

"You go first," she said.

"Another 'old' tradition?"

Ignoring the teasing in Simon's voice, she nodded urgently.

Without looking away from Ariane, Simon lifted the goblet.

"May I burn like the phoenix within your amethyst fire," he said. "And like the phoenix, may I arise to burn again."

Simon drank to the last drop, turned the goblet upside down to show that it was empty, and poured more wine from the ewer.

"Your turn," he said.

Ariane eyed the goblet with faint alarm. Though Simon had filled it barely half-full, it still was a daunting amount of wine to her.

"I cannot drink so quickly as you," she said.

He smiled. " 'Tis just as well, nightingale. You would be too addled to crawl, much less to fly."

Taking a deep breath, Ariane raised the goblet to her lips.

"Your wish," Simon said.

" 'Tis for you."

Surprised, Simon couldn't think of anything to say.

"May nothing of what passes here tonight cause you difficulty," Ariane said in a rush.

Before Simon could ask what Ariane meant by that toast, she lifted the goblet to her lips and drank as quickly as she could without choking. Wine spread over her tongue and through her body in a dizzying wave of warmth.

"Here," she said breathlessly, pressing the goblet into his hands. "Your second wish."

"There's no hurry."

Ariane looked so disappointed that Simon shrugged, filled the goblet, and toasted her again.

"May I some day understand the darkness in which my nightingale flies," he said distinctly.

With an anxiousness Ariane couldn't conceal, she watched Simon drink. When he finished the last drop, she let out a sigh.

Surely that will be enough to slow him. He drank toasts downstairs while I but pretended to drink mine. He has had two full goblets while I have had but half of one.

Surely . . .

"Don't look so nervous," Simon said dryly, lowering the goblet. "I won't fall senseless after this small bit of drink."

He poured more wine in the goblet and turned to Ariane.

"Oh, no," she said quickly. "I had only the one wish."

"For me, not for you."

" 'Tis enough. If that wish comes true, none other matters."

The intensity of Ariane's voice and eyes told Simon that she meant exactly what she said. Whatever her game, it was deadly serious.

Frowning, he looked into the burgundy depths of the wine. The liquid swirled slightly, capturing streamers of light from the hearth.

"Then we will have to do it a few drops at a time," Simon said. "Slower that way," his smile flashed, "but never tedious."

"I don't understand."

Saying nothing, Simon drank a small bit of wine. Deliberately, he left a gleaming trail of liquid on his lips.

"Sip from me," he said simply.

Surprise showed on Ariane's face, but she

lifted her fingertips to Simon's mouth, preparing to blot up the wine.

He turned his head aside.

"Nay, nightingale. With your lips."

Ariane's eyes widened, revealing magnificent amethyst depths framed in thick black lashes. She had kissed Geoffrey only a few times, and never on the mouth. Even in nightmare, she had avoided that.

Hesitantly Ariane leaned forward. The first brush of her lips over Simon's startled her. He was warm, smooth, resilient. His beard was soft, tempting her to stroke it with her cheek. And he tasted quite wonderful.

Slowly, savoring each drop, she licked up every bit of the wine on Simon's lips. When she realized what she had done, she froze, expecting to be grabbed and flung down onto the bed as lust overcame him.

Ariane looked at Simon with eyes that revealed her sudden fear.

"Was it so terrible?" Simon asked.

She shook her head.

"But you were expecting it to be?"

"I — I've never kissed a man's mouth."

Her words sank into Simon like light through darkness, illuminating everything.

I begin to believe that Ariane is indeed what she most often seems to be — a skittish virgin rather than an accomplished flirt.

"Did you expect me to bite you?" he asked, only half-joking.

"Nay. I expected you to throw me on the bed and —"

Abruptly Ariane stopped speaking.

"Ravish you?" Simon suggested.

She nodded.

"Sorry to disappoint you," he said, smiling crookedly. "I find you most alluring, but not so much so that lust will overcome me after a single chaste kiss."

"Chaste? I don't understand."

"You will."

With that, Simon wet his lips once more with wine and turned to Ariane. His lips were smooth and shining. They tasted firm and warm to her, sweet and oddly salt. But nothing was as heady as the hot darkness behind his lips, where her tongue received a caress for each one it gave.

The half-goblet of wine Ariane had drained bloomed in a rush of heat through her blood. Before this moment, the heady feeling would have unnerved her. Now it simply made her want to crowd closer to Simon, for he was her anchor in a warmly seething sea.

Simon felt Ariane leaning toward him. Triumph and something much hotter flared through him. Only the discipline learned at such cost during the Holy Crusade allowed

Simon to keep himself from reaching out and wrapping Ariane up in his arms. He knew it was too soon for the fiery, headlong joining he wanted. She was only beginning to lose her fear of what was to come.

Silently cursing the vicious old maid who must have filled Ariane's ears with horror stories of the marriage bed, Simon lured his bride into a deeper kiss, then deeper still, until their mouths were fully mated and each knew no taste but the other.

It was unlike anything Ariane had ever experienced. A caressing warmth that was sunlight and velvet combined. A complex flavor to be savored again and yet again, always changing, always new. A hushed intimacy rising like a silent silver tide, lapping at the nightmare, forcing it to retreat.

Thinking nothing, feeling everything with shivering intensity, Ariane gave herself to the kiss.

Slowly, carefully, Simon's arms circled his bride. Though he would have liked very much to lie down with Ariane on the bed, her blunt expectation of being thrown down and ravished made him decide to stay upright for a while longer.

Gently Simon pulled back from the kiss. Ariane's murmured complaint and blind seeking for his lips made him smile with both triumph and tenderness.

"Simon?"

"The wine is gone."

"Nay," Ariane protested. "I can taste it still."

"Can you?"

"Aye. Can't you?"

"Shall we see, nightingale? Part your lips for me once more."

Without thinking, Ariane obeyed. Simon bent and captured her mouth with a single smooth movement, claiming it completely with deep rhythms of penetration and retreat.

At the back of Ariane's mind, black warnings stirred. Before she could act on them, the kiss changed. Simon's tongue caressed her mouth, touching every soft bit of it from the satin behind her lips to the different textures of her tongue. The tender teasing so pleased Ariane that she forgot to be wary. She joined in the sweet duel of tongue with tongue.

This time when the rhythmic penetration and retreat began again, Ariane moaned softly and gave even more of her mouth to Simon.

The tiny sound sent desire ripping through him, swiftly undermining his self-control. Ariane was succumbing to him so delicately, so hotly, that he wanted to protect and ravish her in the same wild instant. Everything about her called to his senses, from the subtle perfume in her hair to the taste of their joined mouths, from the soft warmth of her neck beneath his fingertips to the fey fabric that caressed him even as he caressed the female flesh beneath.

The silver laces at the neckline seemed as eager to be undone as Simon was to undo them. He had but to touch, to think of tugging, and warm silver strings curled around his fingers and slid away, leaving the sweet territory beneath undefended. It was the same for the violet cloth, a caressing welcome even as the fabric folded aside to admit him to the secrets of his bride's body.

Ariane never felt the bodice of her dress give way to Simon's quick hands. She was lost to a kiss that was like Simon himself, intense and controlled, fierce and tender, honest and complex to the very core.

The pleasure of giving herself to Simon's kiss and taking from his mouth in return was as dizzying to Ariane as the wine sliding through her blood, bringing heat in its wake.

Simon's fingertips glided from Ariane's cheek to her ears and down to the hollow of her throat, adding to her pleasure. Instinctively she threaded her hands through his golden hair in return, stroking him like a cat. And like a cat he responded, crowding closer, silently demanding more.

Not understanding what her response was

doing to Simon, Ariane drew her fingernails from his crown to his nape even as she sucked lightly on his tongue.

Within a heartbeat Simon's kiss changed from pleasuring to something far more urgent. The rhythms became more elemental, more hungry, a frank sexual claiming.

Abruptly Ariane became aware of the heat radiating from Simon and of the hardness in every muscle of his body. The kisses had been new and sweet to her, far removed from her nightmare.

But this was not.

Male hands were closing on her bare breasts even as powerful shoulders pushed her over onto her back with frightening ease. Soon her legs would be wrenched apart and the pain and degradation would begin, never to end short of death.

Nightmare and desperation exploded through Ariane. Her hand swept out, seeking the dagger she had concealed among the bed-side draperies. The weapon's cool silver haft came to her as though summoned. Recklessly she slashed outward.

Ariane was very quick. The blade scored Simon's arm in the instant before he grabbed her wrist. For a taut moment he looked from the jewel-studded dagger to his bride's wild eyes.

Swiftly Simon shifted his grip, disarming Ariane before she knew what was happening. He flipped the dagger end over end with quick, expert motions of his hand. With equal speed, he caught the haft, stilling the weapon.

Ariane watched the silver cartwheels of the dagger and knew that Simon was as thoroughly acquainted with the lethal uses of a dagger as he was with those of the sword.

"Do not play with me like a cat with a baby bird," she said harshly. "Finish it."

For a moment Simon looked at Ariane.

"Kill you?" he asked neutrally.

"Yes!"

An odd smile played over Simon's lips. Belatedly Ariane realized that he was amused rather than angered by her attack.

"I'm not that harsh a lover, nightingale. We'll both survive the night very nicely."

Simon's arm moved with deceptively casual ease. The dagger flew straight to the far wall where a streak of pale wood no wider than a finger provided a target. An inch of the blade sank into the wood.

Before the haft stopped quivering, Simon reached for his bride.

When Ariane realized that she had lost her only chance to escape her nightmare, she went mad. She fought Simon's grasp with mindless, silent desperation, knowing only that she could not submit to rape again.

Simon accepted the blows only long enough to subdue Ariane without striking her in return. Very quickly she lay full length under him, pinned beneath his much greater strength, barely able to breathe, much less to fight him.

"God's teeth," said Simon in exasperation. "What's wrong with you?"

"Never!" Ariane said wildly. "Never, do you hear me? I will never lie beneath a man while he hammers into my body. *Never!*"

"Really," Simon said in a silky voice. "And just how do you propose to stop me?"

He watched the understanding of helplessness sink into Ariane. With it came the same kind of pure animal terror he had seen in the eyes of Saracen girls after a fortress had fallen and the invading soldiers vented their lust on whomever they could catch.

The chill of Ariane's skin and the clammy sweat that gleamed between her breasts spoke eloquently of her fear, as did the violent tremors that raked her from head to toe.

With grim clarity Simon remembered when Duncan had questioned Ariane less than a fortnight ago, and Amber had been there to underline the brutal truth of Ariane's response.

I will do my duty, but I am repelled by the prospect of the marriage bed.

An icy fury descended on Simon.

Up until this instant he hadn't truly believed Ariane's words. He had sensed the currents of sensual awareness running between himself and the Norman heiress. Whether her fear was real or simply an enhancement of the sensual game, he had assumed that he could seduce her.

He had been wrong.

"So," Simon said through his teeth. "I am tied by sacred bonds and earthly necessity to a woman who loathes her marital duties."

"I was honest from the first," Ariane said tonelessly. "I told everyone who would listen that I had no heart."

"I can do quite well without your heart," Simon retorted in a savage voice. "It is your body I want, both for pleasure and for children."

Ariane said nothing.

In a single swift movement, Simon released Ariane and stood up. For aching moments he said nothing. He simply looked at the ravishing, unattainable beauty whom he had married.

Another, different kind of shudder went through Ariane as she realized that she would not be raped tonight.

Nor would she be set free.

"Are you so dead in what passes for your

soul that you don't want children?" Simon asked with appalling softness.

Even as Ariane opened her mouth to agree, she knew it was a lie. Defeated, she turned her head away from Simon.

From the corner of her eye, she saw his arm coming toward her. With a hoarse sound she threw herself to the far edge of the bed.

Saying nothing, Simon yanked the bed covers from beneath Ariane, leaving only a single layer over the rustling, rose-scented mattress. Too spent to flinch, she watched numbly as he held out his arm once more.

Blood dripped slowly but steadily onto the mattress.

"That should do," he said.

Blankly, Ariane looked up at Simon.

"A substitute for the blood of your maidenhead," he said distinctly. "Were the linen not stained, there would be much gossip in the keep about the man who was so great a fool as to marry a soiled woman."

Ariane made a small sound and looked away, seeing nothing at all.

" 'Tis a good thing that your dowry is great," Simon said, shrugging his mantle about his shoulders. "It is the only joy I will have of this union for a time."

"Forever," Ariane said dully.

"Nay, *wife*. There is a fire in you that is

126

great enough to burn stone. I have felt it. One day you will plead that I take the very thing you refuse me now. You may look forward to it. I certainly will!"

Slowly Ariane shook her head, as much in despair as in response to Simon's words.

"Have a care how you mock me," Simon said with deadly gentleness, "else I will take what God and king have given to me, and to hell with your virginal fears."

With that, Simon turned and stalked from the bed chamber.

9

Dominic swept aside the last scraps of the previous night's wedding feast, dragged a senseless man-at-arms from the only upright bench, and continued hauling the hapless man out of the great hall to the forebuilding. When he returned to the great hall, Meg had revived the fire and was pouring fragrant tea into clean mugs.

No smell of baking bread wafted in from the outside kitchen. No meat roasted on spits. Fresh water had been drawn and little more. Few of the servants were even up and about. All were much the worse for drink.

One was snoring fit to stir the draperies.

"Ale or tea?" Meg asked as Dominic walked up.

"Tea."

Dominic looked at the limp men stacked like logs against the wall of the great hall and shook his head. Simon's wedding had been well and truly toasted, until not one of the knights could raise a goblet or untangle his tongue to speak.

" 'Tis just as well I brought headache bane with me," Meg said. "When these stout men finally awaken, they could be felled instantly by a child with a shrill voice."

"They may not have to wait that long," Dominic said in disgust. "Were they my knights, I would take them by the ears and throw them into the swine pen."

Dominic took the tea Meg offered, sat on the bench he had cleared, and drank deeply of the transparent, hot brew. As always, anything from Meg's herbal refreshed and restored him. He lowered the cup with a sound of pleasure.

Six feet away, a knight snored hard enough to choke.

"God's teeth," Dominic muttered. "Have Erik's knights no sense? Don't they know that dawn follows a riotous night as quickly as a quiet one? Nay, more quickly!"

"Don't be harsh with them," Meg said, refilling his cup. "They but shared Erik's joy in a marriage that will bring an island of peace to a troubled land."

Dominic snorted. "Aye. And in their celebrations, they kept you awake most of the night."

"Nay."

"Then what did? For you were awake, small falcon. I know it."

"I dreamed," she said simply.

Dominic went still. "Glendruid dreams?"

Meg nodded and said nothing.

"Is there anything you can tell me?" Dominic asked, for he knew that his wife's dreams could not always be put into words.

"There is danger."

"God forbid," Dominic muttered, looking pointedly at the useless warriors sleeping in the hall. "Is the danger already inside the keep?"

Meg tilted her head thoughtfully. "Not . . . quite."

"Beyond the keep?"

There was no hesitation this time.

"Aye," she said. "It comes this way."

Dominic shrugged. "Small falcon, there is always danger in the Disputed Lands."

Fleetingly Meg smiled, for she and her husband had had this same conversation many times before when talking about her dreams. It wasn't that Dominic didn't believe her. It was simply that until her dreams became more specific — if they did — there was little he could do, for he already insisted that the men under his command maintain a constant state of vigilance.

"There is far less peril than before you came to the Disputed Lands," Meg pointed out.

She bent down and kissed her husband's

hard mouth, softening it into a lover's warm smile. As she moved, the tiny golden bells at her wrists and hips chimed. A fiery braid slid forward. Golden bells trailed from it like costly jesses, chiming with piercing sweetness.

"Glendruid Wolf," she murmured. "Have I told you how much I love you?"

"Not since morning chapel," Dominic said quickly. " 'Tis a terrible long time to go without your love."

Meg's laughter was as rich and beautiful as her Glendruid hair.

Several yards away, Ariane paused at the side entrance to the great hall, gripping her harp in both hands. She was struck by the music of Meg's laughter, the autumn glory of her loosely plaited hair, and the unexpected sight of Glendruid witch and Glendruid Wolf at play.

"You are spoiled, my wolf," Meg said.

"Aye. Spoil me some more," Dominic said, pulling her down onto his lap. "I grow faint for want of kissing you."

"Faint?"

Meg laughed again. Her hands slid beneath Dominic's mantle, pushing it over his shoulders. Openly enjoying her husband's unusual strength, Meg kneaded the muscles of his chest and shoulders, approving his masculine power.

"Oh, yes," she said gravely, hiding her smile. "I can feel how faint you have become for lack of my kiss."

"Then take pity on me. Revive me."

Meg tilted her face up to Dominic. At the same time she threaded her fingers into his black hair and pulled his mouth down to hers. The kiss that followed was slow and sensual.

Unwillingly Ariane was reminded of the magic time last evening when Simon's kiss had held her enchanted, forgetful of the danger that would surely follow a man's rising lust.

Ariane had a mad impulse to cry out to the Glendruid witch, to warn her that a man's kiss was like his smile, a lure for the unwary. Common sense made Ariane bite her tongue before a single word was spoken.

"Are you revived?" Meg asked after a time.

"Aye," Dominic said huskily.

Teasingly she traced the clean line of his lip beneath his mustache with the tip of her tongue.

"Are you quite certain?" she asked.

Dominic's smile was dark, sensual, and fully male. With one hand he drew his mantle back over his shoulders so that it covered Meg and himself. With the other hand, he urged her fingers down the center of his body.

"Tell me, small falcon. Am I revived?"

Dominic's breath caught as Meg's hand moved.

"You appear to be," she said, "but it could be just the bench whose hardness lies at hand."

"Test more . . . closely."

"Someone might happen by."

"I promise not to scream."

"You are a devil."

"Nay. I am but a man whose duties have kept him too long from his wife's warm body. Can you not feel it?"

"Here?" she asked innocently, caressing his thigh.

Dominic shifted smoothly, making Meg's hand slide between his legs.

"Can you feel it now, witch?"

Her husky laugh was that of a woman who fully approved of what lay beneath her husband's fine clothes. The laughter was as sensual as fire, and like fire, it was hot.

But that wasn't what shocked Ariane. What shocked her was that there was no fear in Meg's laughter. Not even a hint. It was as though Meg anticipated the inevitable end of such teasing as much as Dominic did.

In growing disbelief Ariane stared at the couple with a rudeness that would have astonished her under other circumstances. Even though Dominic and his wife were shielded by his mantle, Ariane had no doubt that the two were involved in love play.

A play that was as much relished by wife as by husband.

"Your hands," Dominic said. "They are the sweetest kind of fire. Burn me, small falcon."

Footsteps sounded down the spiral stone stairway leading from the third floor to the great hall.

Dominic hissed something in a foreign tongue and quickly set Meg back upon her feet. By the time the footsteps resolved into Erik and Simon coming into the great hall by way of the main entrance, Meg and Dominic were quietly eating a breakfast of fruit, cheese, and yesterday's herb bread.

Simon and Erik strode into the hall with similar lithe strides. Tall, quick, broad-shouldered, strong with the lean power of a wolf rather than the muscular heft of a bear, blond of hair and beard, the two knights looked more like brothers than like men born in separate lands. All that divided them was the massive wolfhound that paced at Erik's side.

No one noticed Ariane standing in the side entrance, concealed by shadows, dark clothing and her own stillness. She wanted to walk forward, to show herself and take a place by the fire, but the sight of Simon froze her in place.

Have a care how you mock me, else I will take what God and king have given to me, and to hell with your virginal fears.

A chill condensed beneath Ariane's skin. She stood motionless, praying not to be noticed until she could withdraw as quietly as she had come.

When Simon came up to the fire, Dominic gave his brother a swift, comprehensive glance. As always since the Holy Crusade, Simon's face gave away nothing of his thoughts. Dominic was one of the few people who knew that his brother's quick wit and smile were as much an armor as any chain mail ever worn.

Usually Dominic could see beneath Simon's sun-bright surface to the reality beneath.

Usually, but not this morning.

Disappointment bloomed silently within Dominic. He needed no Learning to sense that whatever had passed between Simon and Ariane last night had increased rather than eased the cold darkness in his brother.

"God's teeth," Erik said in disgust as he stepped over a snoring man-at-arms, "Duncan and I will need a whip and a goad to get these men up and about."

"Where is Duncan? And Sven?" Simon asked. "Usually they are the first to awaken."

"I sent Sven out to gauge the temper of the countryside," Dominic said. "With all these great louts sleeping like rocks, it would be a child's work to take Stone Ring Keep."

"The sentry is at his post," Erik pointed out.

Dominic grunted, unimpressed. "As for Duncan . . ."

"Duncan is enjoying the rowan's gift," Meg said.

"Uninterrupted sleep?" Simon asked.

Cool, sardonic, Simon's voice was a good match for the crystal blackness of his eyes.

Glendruid dreams echoed in Meg's mind, speaking darkly of the violence that was gathering like a storm in the Disputed Lands.

A storm whose center would be Stone Ring Keep.

A low cry came from Meg's lips, a sound too soft for anyone but her husband to hear. Instantly Dominic was on his feet beside his wife. His arm went around her and his dark head bent down to her cheek. Though Meg needed no support, she leaned gratefully against her husband's strong arm.

"What is it?" Dominic asked urgently.

She simply shook her head.

"It isn't the babe, is it?" Dominic asked.

"Nay."

"Are you certain? For a moment it seemed as though you were in pain."

Meg let out a long breath and looked up into her husband's clear grey eyes.

"The babe is hardy as a war-horse," she said.

She took Dominic's scarred hand and held it against the taut mound of her pregnancy. Dominic felt first the heat of his wife's body, then the subtle yet unmistakable kick of the babe.

The expression that came to Dominic's face made Ariane stare. Never would she have believed that such a formidable man could have such a tender smile.

Simon stared, too. Though he had had months to become accustomed to Meg's effect on Dominic, there were still times when Simon was surprised by the depths of his brother's feeling for the girl fate had sent to him.

"The Glendruid Wolf looks not so fierce right now," Erik said in a low voice. "In their own way, he and his witch share the rowan's gift, don't they?"

"I wouldn't know," Simon said coolly.

"Ah, yes. What was it Dominic said — that your gift is to see only that which can be touched and held and weighed and measured?"

"Aye," Simon said with grim satisfaction. "It still sounds more like a curse to me."

"I don't notice you galloping to Stone Ring and its invisible rowan tree and demanding to be leg-shackled by love."

Erik glanced sideways at Simon. Though Simon was always tart of speech, his tongue seemed to have an unusual edge this morning.

"Long night?" Erik asked blandly.

"It was a night like any other."

"Brrrr."

Simon smiled thinly.

"Does this mean that you will accept my offer of a mantle lined with white weasels?" Erik asked.

Simon laughed ruefully. "Aye, Learned. I'll take your gift."

"I'm sorry. When Lady Ariane was accepted by Serena's weaving, I hoped . . ." Erik shrugged. "Ah, well, cold wives are why God gave us furred animals and lemans. I'll send for the mantle lining immediately."

"I am in your debt."

"Nay," Erik said instantly. "It is I who will be forever in your debt. You gave me a gift beyond compare when you agreed to marry the cold Norman heiress."

Simon said nothing.

Nor did Ariane, though she heard each word all too clearly. There was nothing for her to say in any case. The men but spoke the truth: A fur-lined mantle would warm Simon's body sooner than would Ariane the Betrayed.

"If you hadn't stepped forward," Erik continued, "Duncan would have wed Ariane, Amber would have died in Ghost Glen, and my father's lands would have fallen to renegades."

Simon moved restively. What had happened between Duncan and Amber in that place beyond the baffling mists was something that couldn't be weighed or measured.

It confounded him.

"It matters not to me," Simon said. "I'll never know the terrible coils of love, nor see the sacred rowan bloom."

"You are young yet."

Simon gave Erik a sidelong glance.

"I am older than you," Simon said. "And I am married to a maiden carved of ice taken from the bleak heart of the longest night of winter."

"I'm told that there is a sweet solace for such coldness. Her name is Marie and her eyes are as black as yours."

Anger and disgust snaked through Simon at the thought of the skilled, faithless Marie, but nothing of what he felt showed.

"You must have been talking to Sven," Simon said. "He sings Marie's praises in the hope that some strapping foreign knight will fall into her trap and spill all his secrets along with his seed."

Laughing, Erik bent to touch Stagkiller,

who had been prodding his master with increasing urgency.

"What is it, beast?" Erik asked. "What makes you uneasy?"

The affection in Erik's voice was as apparent as the wolfhound's great, gleaming fangs.

"Perhaps he wants to change bodies with you," Simon said blandly.

"Do you believe everything Sven hears when he listens under the eaves in the countryside?"

Simon laughed and said nothing.

Stagkiller bumped insistently against Erik.

"Are you trying to knock me off my feet?" Erik grumbled.

As he bent to look into the wolfhound's eyes, Erik caught the subdued flash of gemstones in Ariane's hair from the corner of his eye.

"Lady Ariane," Erik said, straightening. "Good morning to you."

A stillness came over Simon. Then he moved swiftly, bringing Ariane into view. Instantly he knew that she had overheard every word.

That didn't bother Simon particularly, for he had said nothing to Erik that he hadn't first said to his unwilling wife.

But the pain Simon sensed in Ariane did bother him. It both chastened and angered him.

"Have you taken breakfast?" Simon asked, his tone neutral.

Ariane gripped her harp tighter, holding it across her body as though it were a shield.

"No," she said in a low voice.

"Then do so. You are as thin as one of your beloved harp strings."

Ariane's fingers moved. A flurry of notes rose in a minor key, then fell off sharply.

"I'm not hungry," she said.

"I'm well aware of your lack of appetite."

Simon's voice was cool, unaccented, impersonal. The silence that followed his words was broken by a slight movement of Ariane's fingers.

"You were present when Amber questioned me," Ariane said tightly. "You knew how I felt."

"Thank you, gracious wife, for reminding me that night is indeed caused by the absence of the sun, and cold by the absence of heat."

This time the silence that followed Simon's words was broken by nothing at all. When it became apparent that neither of them intended to speak again, Erik cursed beneath his breath and spoke gallantly to the Norman heiress.

"The dawn that follows the longest night," Erik said, "is always the most warm."

Ariane looked at Erik for a long moment

before she spoke. "You are very kind, lord."

"Kind?"

"To suggest that all nights end with dawn, when you know full well that some nights never end."

"I know nothing of the sort."

Ariane's eyes widened slightly as she sensed the savage impatience that lay just beneath Erik's polished surface.

"As you say, lord."

Erik sighed and wished Ariane were less comely. It would have been easier to be angry at an unwilling woman who was also ugly.

"Your eyes," Erik said.

"I beg your pardon?" she asked.

"Your eyes are magnificent. 'Tis a miracle the fairies haven't stolen you away out of jealousy."

Erik's words brought back all too clearly the moment when Ariane had told Simon just how attractive he was to her.

When Ariane risked a sideways glance at her husband, Ariane saw a faint smile and knew that he, too, remembered.

"Thank you, lord," Ariane said.

Her smile was a reflex born of her childhood. She had been trained to accept just such courtly exchanges among highborn men and women.

"But if fairies were to steal from mortals,"

Ariane continued, "it would be your eyes at risk, not mine. They are a most unusual shade of gold, like an autumn sun reflected by water."

"Or like a wolf's eyes reflecting fire," Simon said blandly.

Erik shot him a sideways look. "You are too kind."

"Undoubtedly," Simon said.

With a stifled laugh, Erik turned back to Ariane.

"As your husband is likely too ill-mannered to have mentioned your beauty," Erik said, "it falls to me to point out that even the stars in the sky lack your amethyst fire."

Again Ariane smiled politely, but a bit more warmly. "You are the one who is too kind."

Simon watched with growing irritation as Erik and Ariane traded compliments. Such polite rituals shouldn't have annoyed Simon, but they did. Seeing his wife respond to Erik's handsome face and courtly manners was distinctly irksome.

"I'm not kind," Erik protested. "I merely speak the truth."

Then he looked at Ariane for the space of a breath, as though seeing her for the first time as a woman rather than as a cold obstacle to his plans for the Disputed Lands.

"Your hair is like silk cut from the night

143

sky," Erik said slowly. "Dark, yet full of light. Your skin would shame a pearl into hiding its perfect face. Your eyebrows have the elegant lines of a bird in flight. And your mouth is a bud waiting to —"

"Enough," Simon interrupted curtly. "I haven't heard such a pile of overripe compliments since I was in the court of a Saracen prince."

Though Simon hadn't raised his voice, its tone was a clear warning. Erik gave him a measuring look. Simon raised his left eyebrow in silent challenge.

Abruptly Erik smiled like the wolf he was reputed to be. Simon's message was clear: Cold or not, Ariane was Simon's wife, and he meant to make sure that everyone understood it.

That was welcome news to Erik, who had been afraid Simon would simply ignore his icy wife but for the duty of providing sons to fight for his lord and brother, the Glendruid Wolf. That kind of cold, practical liaison would result in deadly danger. Erik didn't know why, but he knew it was truth. It was his gift to see such patterns where others saw only unconnected events.

"I will leave you to compliment your lady in peace," Erik said.

"Wise of you."

Ariane glanced at Simon. He was smiling.

And he was deadly serious.

Erik withdrew, hiding his own smile of satisfaction.

"That was unnecessary," she said in a low voice.

"It was very necessary," Simon said.

"Why? What harm is there in an exchange of courtly compliments?"

Simon stepped toward Ariane. She caught herself just before she stepped back. Even so, Simon saw her reflexive flinching away.

"The harm," he said softly, savagely, "is in the fact that you flinch at my least movement, yet fawn over Erik as though bent on seducing him."

"I never —"

"The harm," interrupted Simon, "is in your beauty. Men come to you like dogs after a bitch in heat, helpless to control their own lust."

Ariane's mouth opened in shock. "That's not —"

He overrode her words without a pause.

"The harm, dear wife, is that a compliment that begins with your eyes soon ends with comparing your lips to a bud on the brink of flowering."

A small shiver of memory went through Ariane.

"The harm —" Simon continued coolly.

"You made me feel like that," she said without thinking. "A bud that was full of sweetness."

Though soft, Ariane's words cut off the rising anger in Simon. He looked at her mouth, tender as a petal, sweet as nectar, the unblemished pink of a wild rose just before it blooms.

Dominic hailed Simon from the head of the room. If Simon heard, he failed to turn away from his study of Ariane's lips.

"Simon," she whispered. "Lord Dominic calls you."

Simon ignored Ariane's words as he had ignored his brother's greeting.

"Last night," Simon said huskily, "your mouth was just like a tightly furled bud. The feel of you slowly opening to my kiss made my head spin as wine never has."

The narrowed, glittering darkness of Simon's eyes was both warning and lure to Ariane.

"When you finally did open," Simon said, "I knew how a bee feels when it slides between fragrant petals and sips nectar from the heart of the flower."

Breath wedged in Ariane's chest as Simon's words vividly recalled the sweet glide of tongue over tongue, the taste of him spreading through her mouth, making her weak with a longing she couldn't name.

Without knowing it, she whispered her husband's name.

"Aye," Simon said. "You remember it, too. Soon you will open for me in a different way, and the honey of your desire will be the nectar that drenches me."

A shimmer of heat went through Ariane. It was startling and pleasurable.

"But until that day," Simon continued smoothly, "you will trade compliments only with me, for I am the only bee whose sweet sting your petals will ever know."

Ariane opened her mouth to answer. Nothing came out but a sound that could have been Simon's name. She licked lips that were suddenly dry.

"You tempt me without mercy," Simon said fiercely beneath his breath. "Would that I could do the same to you."

He turned with startling speed and strode toward Dominic, leaving Ariane to the solace of the harp she held so tightly against her breasts.

10

" 'Tis a beautiful day, lady," Blanche said. "Almost worth the six days of storm that came before."

A sound like a cascading sigh came from the harp Ariane held. The notes were as haunted as her eyes. Ariane's fingers continued their slow drawing over the harp while Blanche set aside the comb and began braiding her lady's hair.

Ariane hardly noticed Blanche's fingers. She was caught between nightmare and unnervingly sweet memories of Simon's kiss.

Six days a wife.

Tonight will be the seventh night.

" 'Tis a blessing the weather has changed," Blanche muttered as she braided Ariane's long hair. "The knights are wild to be hunting. Or wenching. The cotters' daughters are hiding in with the swine."

Will this be the night Simon finally comes to my bedchamber again?

Or will he let my nerves string ever tighter as I wait for him to stalk to my bed, drag my nightdress up my legs and hammer within me until I bleed?

Ariane forced herself to breathe.

What a pity one cannot conceive babes with a kiss.

Her hands changed on the harp as she remembered the sweet restraint and gliding caress of Simon's mouth.

If he remembered her kiss with equal favor, it didn't show in his manner. Since the morning after their marriage, Simon had been polite to Ariane and no more.

I don't want any more from him.

It was a lie, and Ariane knew it.

Yet it was also the truth, and she knew that too.

She wanted Simon's kisses, his gentle touches, his smiles. She didn't want the passion that ran through his blood like lightning through a storm, making his eyes both dark and glittery at once. She was frightened of the male strength that so easily could overwhelm her, holding her helpless while he forced her body to admit his seed.

Have a care how you mock me, else I will take what God and king have given to me, and to hell with your virginal fears.

"Lady?" Blanche asked.

Ariane blinked. The tone of her handmaiden's voice told Ariane that she had been called more than once.

"Yes?" Ariane asked.

"Does your hair suit you?"

"Yes."

With a grimace Blanche set aside the comb. Ariane hadn't so much as glanced at her reflection in the brass mirror.

"If I had your face and form," Blanche said, "I'd not hide away up in my room like a nun in her cloister."

"Then would that we could trade forms," Ariane muttered, "as Lord Erik and his wolfhound are reputed to do upon a full moon."

Blanche shuddered and crossed herself hurriedly.

"Don't be such a goose," Ariane said. "Lord Erik has been very kind to us."

"They say Satan is charming, too."

"Satan doesn't wear the cross of a true believer."

"Lord Erik does?"

"Yes."

Blanche's expression showed her disbelief.

"Ask the chaplain of Stone Ring Keep if you don't believe me," Ariane said.

Her voice was as curt as the staccato notes she plucked from the harp.

"Will you breakfast in your bedchamber again?" Blanche asked carefully.

Ariane was on the point of agreeing when

150

restlessness overcame her. She realized that she was tired of her self-imposed exile from the keep's life. Abruptly she stood up, harp in hand.

"Nay," Ariane said. "I will breakfast in the great hall."

Blanche's pale eyes widened, but she said only, "As you wish."

Ariane started for the door, then stopped. She set aside her harp and began impatiently unlacing the dress she had chosen to wear this morning. The cloth's mauve folds and pink trimming at cuff and hem no longer pleased her.

"Bring me the dress I was married in," Ariane said.

"That one? Why?"

"It pleases me more than my other clothes."

With a sideways glance at her unpredictable lady, Blanche went to the wardrobe that held the few dresses Ariane had brought with her from Blackthorne Keep.

"A vexed odd fabric," Blanche muttered.

She held the strange cloth no more closely than she had to in order to bring the dress to her mistress.

"Odd? How so?" Ariane asked.

"The weaving looks soft as a cloud and feels rough as thistle leaves. I don't see how you can bear to have it against your skin, even

151

to please the Learned."

Startled, Ariane gave her handmaiden a long look.

"Rough?" Ariane said in disbelief. "Why, the dress is softer than the finest goose-down."

"Vexed odd goosedown," Blanche muttered beneath her breath.

Gingerly she held out the violet cloth with its lush silver threads woven through in disconcerting patterns, like leashed lightning playing through an amethyst storm. With scant patience, she waited for Ariane to take the dress.

For once, Blanche didn't insist on helping her mistress with the laces. Nor was any help needed. The dress all but laced itself, needing little help from Ariane's quick fingers.

That was one of the things that appealed to Ariane about the Learned gift; she didn't have to endure unwanted hands on her body in order to get dressed. The fabric also turned aside stains with the ease of a duck shedding water.

"I wonder how the weaving was accomplished," Ariane said, running the backs of her fingers over the cloth. "The threads are so fine I can barely distinguish them."

" 'Tis said the most expensive silk is like that."

"Nay. My father bought many bolts of silk from knights who had fought the Saracen. None of the cloth was this soft. None was as cleverly woven."

Yet even as Ariane stroked the fabric, she was careful not to look into its depths where light and shadow intertwined. The memory of Simon's kiss was unsettling enough. She didn't need the vision of a woman arched in passion beneath a warrior's caresses to further disturb her peace of mind.

Harp in hand, silver-trimmed dress seething gently around her ankles, Ariane set off for the great hall. The keep was alive with the sounds of servants. As she made her way toward the hall, Ariane heard them calling back and forth, talking of the fine day after the wild storm and of the canny swine that had once again escaped Ethelrod's pen.

The fire in the great hall's hearth leaped high and golden. Simon and Dominic were lounging nearby. The cat known as His Laziness was draped around Simon's neck like a leftover storm cloud. Leather hawking gauntlets lay on the table. From the swooping motions of the men's hands, it appeared that they were discussing the merits of hunting waterfowl with falcons of various sizes.

Other than a polite nod when Ariane entered the room, Simon made no move to join her.

Ariane was both relieved and . . . vexed. Only then did she admit to herself that she had been hoping for a chance to talk with Simon.

'Tis just as well he isn't interested in me, Ariane told herself. *How do I ask my husband if he plans to force me tonight or some other night entirely?*

With an impatient word under her breath, Ariane shoved aside the fears that had neither outlet nor encouragement. Since their disastrous wedding night, Simon had ignored his wife except to be polite when their paths crossed in the keep.

Meg was sitting along one side of the big table where the lords and ladies of the Disputed Lands normally took their meals. Instead of food, Meg had an array of lotions, balms, potions, tinctures and creams spread in front of her. Next to her sat Amber. The combination of flame-colored hair next to gold was arresting against the grey stone walls.

"Cassandra says this works very well against diseases caused by chill," Amber said. "Though, for mild cases, some Learned healers prefer nettle harvested at the height of summer to berries taken from Lucifer's ear."

Meg picked up a pot, dipped her finger briefly into it, and rubbed a bit of the cream between her thumb and forefinger. When the cream was as warm as her body, she held her fingers up to her nose, sniffed carefully, tasted lightly, and nodded.

Quietly Ariane sat down nearby. Simon's squire — a boy barely old enough to grow a wretched shadow of a beard — stepped forward instantly with a plate of cold meats, fruits, cheeses, breads and a mug of fragrant tea.

"Thank you, Edward," Ariane said, surprised.

"It is my pleasure to serve my lord's lady," the boy said carefully.

Edward glanced aside at Simon, received a fractional nod, and retreated hastily.

It was clear that Simon was overseeing Ariane's breakfast. As she looked at the plate again, she understood something else — Simon must have been monitoring her food for the past six days.

There wasn't one item on the plate that she didn't like. The tea itself was a subtle blend of rose hips and chamomile that Ariane had declared more than once was very much to her taste.

Under Simon's watchful black eyes, Ariane set aside her harp and began to eat.

"Thank our Lord," Dominic muttered as he saw the harp leave Ariane's hands. "The lady won't be making our falcons weep with her sad tunes."

Simon merely glanced from Ariane to his own gyrfalcon waiting on a perch along the wall of the great hall. Hooded, patient, Skylance waited with other birds of prey arrayed on perches in the hall. Occasionally a falcon shifted and flared its wings. The movements made bells jangle on the ends of leather jesses wrapped around the falcons' slender, cool legs.

Turning away, Simon resumed stroking the cat whose head was tucked along the right side of his neck. The motion of Simon's arm caused the sleeve of his shirt to fall away from his arm, revealing the scarlet line of healing flesh across his biceps.

"Meg's balm has healed you quickly from your, ah, accident," Dominic said.

Though the Glendruid Wolf's voice was low, Simon knew his brother well enough to understand that Dominic didn't believe the story of how Simon had gotten the cut across his left arm.

"Aye," Simon said. "Meg is very skilled."

"Odd that you were so clumsy. Tell me again how it happened."

A black look was Simon's only answer.

"Ah, it comes back to me now," Dominic said. "You had too much wine, you were showing your bride how to flip the dagger end over end, and the blade sliced you. Is that how it went?"

Simon shrugged and began demolishing an apple with neat, flashing bites.

"A pretty story," Dominic said judiciously, "but it is time to speak the truth to your lord."

"What passes between a man and his bride on their wedding night belongs to them, and only to them."

"Not when the death of one or the other would bring calamity to Blackthorne Keep," Dominic retorted.

"We live," Simon said dryly.

"And the bridal sheets were duly stained. By *your* blood, I presume?"

Silence.

"Simon."

The Glendruid Wolf's voice was low, urgent. So was his posture as he leaned toward his brother.

"My questions aren't idle," Dominic said flatly. "Each night Meg dreams Glendruid dreams. Each night her dreams are more frightening."

Simon's mouth became a line as thin as the scarlet wound across his arm. For long moments he made no motion but to stroke His Laziness, increasing the cat's ecstatic purring.

"Is Ariane your wife in deed as well as in

ceremony?" Dominic asked bluntly.

Simon's fingers paused, then resumed their caresses.

"No," he said succinctly.

Dominic cursed in the language of the Saracens.

"What happened?" Dominic asked.

"My wife is as cold as a northern sea."

"She refused you?"

A narrow, bleak smile changed the line of Simon's mouth, but the gentleness of his hand on the grey cat never varied.

"She refused me," Simon agreed.

"Why?"

"She said she would rather die than lie beneath a man."

"Then place her on top," Dominic said impatiently.

"I have it in mind."

Dominic waited.

Simon said no more.

"How were you wounded?" Dominic demanded.

Though the Glendruid Wolf's tone was insistent, it carried no farther than the two men.

"With a dagger," Simon said.

"Who was holding it?" retorted Dominic.

"My wife."

It was what Dominic had suspected, but

hearing the truth spoken was somehow shocking.

"She truly tried to kill you?" Dominic asked.

Simon shrugged.

"God's teeth," Dominic muttered. "No wonder you haven't sought her bed again. It would be enough to take the steel from even the stoutest sword."

"Would that it had that effect," Simon said beneath his breath.

"What?"

"Would that my wife's dagger could take the steel from my sword. But it can't. I fear my temper if she refuses me again."

Dominic's black eyebrows rose. Whether on the battlefield or in the bedchamber, Simon's self-control was the envy of many a knight.

"That is why you sleep alone?" Dominic asked.

"Aye. And now she is wearing that witchy dress once more," Simon said. "God's teeth, but I would love to get my hands beneath it."

Dominic looked at his brother's taut features and picked his words very carefully before he spoke.

"Do you think she prefers another man?" Dominic asked.

"Not if she wishes to live."

159

The deadly coolness of Simon's voice warned Dominic that even a brother and a lord combined had better tread warily around the subject of Ariane's desires. Dominic had not seen Simon so intense since he had pursued Marie's artfully swaying hips between battlefield campfires that burned no less hotly than Simon himself.

Abruptly Simon cursed and some of the savagery left his eyes. A flick of the cat's tail under Simon's nose reminded him of his true mission in life — making His Laziness purr.

"No," Simon said quietly. "Ariane loves no man. In some ways it might be easier if she did. I could kill him."

Dominic smiled sardonically. "Then Lady Ariane is like some of the sultan's harem. She prefers the touch of her own sex."

"Nay. Ariane prefers no touch at all. Even in the bath, no one attends her."

"The bath . . ."

Dominic smiled to himself as he remembered the pleasures of bathing with his Glendruid wife, whose love of water was even greater than that of the Saracen sultans whose palaces sang with fountains.

"Such a cream-licking smile," Simon said, half-disgusted, half-curious.

Curiosity won.

"Is that how you tamed your small falcon?"

Simon asked. "Did you catch her when her wings were too wet to fly?"

Dominic laughed softly.

Stroking the cat, Simon waited with leashed impatience.

"I trained my small falcon quite carefully," Dominic said, "whether in the bath or the forest or the bedchamber."

Simon looked at Meg. Her hair burned brightly, but nothing was as vivid as the Glendruid green of her eyes as she talked with Amber.

"Was it the golden jesses you made for her that tamed her wild heart?" Simon asked.

"Nay."

"A sound beating?"

Dominic shook his head.

" 'Tis just as well," Simon muttered. "I have no taste for thumping on things smaller than I."

"Excellent. I have it on good authority that the small things don't care for it either."

Simon laughed aloud. The sound was so unexpected, and so infectious, that Ariane looked up from her nearly empty plate. Amethyst eyes flashed in the instant before she looked down once more.

"She looks only at you," Dominic said.

"What?"

"Your wife. No matter who is in the room,

she sees only you."

"Wait until the sun god arrives," Simon retorted.

"Erik?"

"Aye," Simon said curtly.

Dominic shook his head. "You are the sun that shines in her eyes, not Erik."

"Of course. That's why she tried to put a dagger through my heart."

Dominic winced. "Win her trust, and she will fight just as fiercely *for* you."

"The thought appeals."

A rill of notes lifted from the far end of the table where Ariane sat. The music was not quite a melody, but it was melodic. It wasn't a song, yet it sang of emotions swirling beneath the cool surface of a woodland spring, making shadows turn in the clear depths.

Moments later the melody turned back upon itself, reprising itself as surely as day and night turning and returning in their ordained cycles. A clear whistle lifted to the notes, twining around them, defining them.

The piercing beauty of the joined notes stitched through Ariane's soul like silver needles. She turned to see the source of the whistle.

Simon.

Ariane's hands fumbled, then dropped to her lap.

162

"Play, nightingale," Simon said. "Or does my whistling displease you so much?"

"Displease?" Ariane took a deep breath. "Nay. It was the unexpected beauty that surprised me."

Simon's eyes widened, then narrowed at the familiar surge of fire that came whenever he was near Ariane.

Or even when he thought of her.

Abruptly Simon stood up. He plucked off His Laziness and set the grumbling cat on the warm hearth.

"I'm going to test Skylance's wings," Simon muttered.

He yanked on his hawking gauntlet, strode to one of the wall perches, and urged his hooded gyrfalcon from its perch.

"Aren't you going to wait for others?" Dominic asked.

"I'm not a lord to require attendance," Simon said impatiently.

"Your squire would probably appreciate a chance to breathe the air of the fens and fells."

Simon glanced toward Edward, but it was Ariane who caught and held his eye. She was watching the gyrfalcon with a longing that she couldn't conceal.

Swiftly Simon went to his wife. The gyrfalcon rode his arm with a quick grace that rivaled that of Simon himself.

"Would you care to go hawking with me?" Simon asked. "The falconer brought word of fat partridges on the western side of Stone Ring."

"Hawking? Aye!" Ariane said, leaping to her feet. "I grow weary of cold stone."

"Edward," Simon said without looking away from his wife. "Send to the stables for two horses. My wife and I are going hawking."

"Alone, sir?" Edward asked.

"Yes. Alone."

11

When Cassandra came into the great hall a short time after Simon and Ariane left to go hawking, only Dominic remained. On the table in front of him was an ancient Latin text. He was reading it intently, obviously engrossed.

A ripple of surprise and interest went through Cassandra. People who could read the old manuscripts were quite rare. She had trained Amber and Erik most carefully in such reading, for the Learned had inherited a wealth of old writings that required translation.

Idly Cassandra wondered if she could induce Dominic to learn the ancient rune language. Amber had little time for translation now that she was the lady of Stone Ring Keep.

Dominic nodded his head once, sharply, as though he had reached some inner conclusion. Without looking up, he went on to a new page of the manuscript, handling the parchment with a care that approached reverence.

"Good morning to you, Lord Dominic," Cassandra said politely. "Have you seen Erik?"

Dominic looked up. "Good morning, Learned. I thought Erik was with you. He didn't breakfast in the great hall."

"Do you know if he plans to return to Sea Home soon?"

"Yesterday during the hunt he mentioned something about overseeing the building of Sea Home's inner keep before the first true cold came. He's worried that the snows will be early and stay for weeks upon the ground this year. He said something about the geese coming early to the Whispering Fen."

"Aye."

Cassandra stood for a moment as though listening to something within her mind. Then she sighed.

"Your man Sven," she said.

"Yes?"

"Is he nearby?"

"No. I sent him into the countryside," Dominic said. "Meg's dreams grow more dire each night."

A shadow went over Cassandra's face.

"Yes," the Learned woman said. "I talked to her in the garden."

"What of you, Learned? What do your rune stones say when you cast them?"

"I thought you didn't believe in such things."

"I believe in anything that will help bring peace to this troubled land," Dominic said bluntly.

"You are wiser than your brother."

"I've had an excellent teacher."

"Your wife?" Cassandra asked.

Dominic nodded.

"The rune stones say much the same as your wife's dreams," Cassandra said. "Death stalks the Disputed Lands."

"Death stalks all life."

The Learned woman smiled, but there was little comfort in the cool curve of her lips.

"Does that mean," she asked, "that you want no information about where death might first strike?"

"No. It means that we are having an early, cold autumn that will likely be followed by a harsh winter in which the weakest will die. It means that men have fought and died in the Disputed Lands since long before the first Roman scribe scratched words on parchment. It means —"

"— that death is common," summarized Cassandra.

"Let's just say that prophesying death in the near future takes no more skill than a rooster prophesying dawn," Dominic said neutrally.

Cassandra laughed with genuine amusement, surprising Dominic.

"You and Simon share much in common," Cassandra said.

"We are brothers."

"You are very stubborn clay."

"Then stop trying to mold us."

"I?" Cassandra asked. "I am but clay myself. 'Tis God's hand that shapes us, not mine."

Dominic made a sound that could have meant anything from agreement to displeasure.

"When Sven returns with information about the countryside, will you make certain that Erik is present?" Cassandra asked. "Erik has a gift for taking odd incidents and finding the pattern lying just beneath."

"Of course. Erik is Blackthorne's ally, just as Duncan is. Both have my confidence."

The sound of voices calling from the bailey seeped into the great hall. Much more clearly came the clatter of shod hooves over cobblestones as men rode across the bailey toward the keep itself.

A peregrine called from outside the building. The falcon's voice was high, sweet, and wild to the last pure note.

"Erik comes," Cassandra said.

Dominic didn't doubt it. The call of Erik's peregrine was a sound not easily forgotten. No other falcon sounded quite like it.

A horse neighed and stamped impatiently. A steel shod hoof rang on the cobblestone.

"Sven comes," Dominic said.

Cassandra gave him an enigmatic look.

"His was the only shod horse to go out this morning," Dominic said coolly. "A shod horse has just crossed the bailey from the outer moat. Logic, not witchery."

Cassandra's smile was as enigmatic as her silver eyes. "Each man believes that which comforts him."

One of Dominic's black eyebrows rose questioningly.

"For your comfort," Cassandra said, "let me assure you that Erik's *logic* is far superior to most men's in all things save one."

"And that is?"

"Understanding women."

Smiling, Dominic said, " 'Tis reassuring to know that Erik is more man than sorcerer."

"It would be more reassuring if he used his head at all times," Cassandra muttered.

Before Dominic could reply, Sven and Erik came into the great hall.

"Where is Duncan?" Erik asked.

"Checking the armory," Dominic said. "He wasn't satisfied with the steward's inventory."

"We may need every blade and then some," Erik said. "There are outlaws nearby."

"Enough to threaten the keep?" Dominic asked instantly.

Erik shook his head.

"Not yet," Sven said. "But three of the outlaws ride shod horses. From the size and depth of the tracks, I would swear they are battle stallions carrying knights in chain mail."

"What else did you discover?" Dominic demanded.

"They are renegades. They attacked the household train of a northern lord who was traveling to his winter manor."

Dominic grimaced and said sardonically, "A brave knight indeed, to attack servants, children and kitchen goods."

"Fortunately, the lord's own knights came back to check on the progress of the train," Sven said. "At least, that's what it seemed from the tracks."

"It fit the pattern," Erik said.

"Pattern?" Cassandra asked sharply.

"Rumors have come from Sea Home in the past few days," Erik said. "Rumors of a knight who fights for Satan rather than Christ."

"What does this knight look like? For which lord does he ride?"

Sven shook his head. "None. 'Tis said that the design on his shield was burned off in the very fires of hell."

"More likely he destroyed the design himself," Dominic said. "If word got back to his true lord, he would be hunted down and hanged for the traitorous outlaw and craven that he is."

"That may be true of the other knights," Erik said, "but their leader is rumored to fight with the strength and skill of three men."

"Aye," Sven said. "Three of the northern lord's knights tried to kill him. He killed two of them before he fled. The third nearly died of his wounds."

"Have you talked to the one who survived?" Dominic asked.

"Aye," Erik said. "A wise woman is nursing him back to health in a hamlet just beyond the western boundary of Stone Ring Keep's land."

"What did the wounded knight say?"

"He could barely talk," Sven said. "He was half out of his mind with wound fever."

"He said that the renegade is the greatest warrior the Disputed Lands has ever known," Erik said.

"What of Duncan, the Scots Hammer?" Dominic asked mildly. "Or Erik, called the Undefeated?"

"The Scots Hammer brought me down," Erik said.

"And there sits Dominic, who defeated the Scots Hammer," Sven pointed out. "Surely

Dominic is greater than this devil knight."

"Any man may be defeated," Cassandra said. "Any man may be victorious. It depends on the man, the weapon, and the reason for fighting."

"This one fights for bloodlust, plunder, and rape," Erik said.

His tone said that the pattern he had found surrounding the renegade knight was loathsome.

"Unfortunately, the spawn of Satan fights like an archangel," Sven said.

"Did the wounded knight get close enough to see his attacker?" Dominic asked.

Sven gave a lithe shrug. "Aye, but he saw only his own defeat rushing down. To hear him, the renegade is a giant among men, with the burning eyes of a demon."

"Red, I presume," Dominic said dryly.

"What?" asked Sven.

"His eyes."

"No. Blue."

Dominic sighed. "Well, we know it isn't Simon or Erik. That leaves perhaps four score blue-eyed warriors for us to consider."

"We won't be long in wondering," Erik said. "My peregrine spotted strange knights beyond the west side of Stone Ring."

"The west side?" Dominic shot to his feet. "Are you certain?"

"Aye," Erik said. "That's why we came back here so quickly. We needed armor and war-horses."

"God's teeth," snarled Dominic as he ran toward the armory. "Simon and Ariane are hawking for partridge west of Stone Ring!"

"Who went with them?" called Erik.

"No one. Not even a squire!"

Sven and Erik didn't ask any more questions. They simply followed the Glendruid Wolf to the armory at a dead run.

12

Brightly colored fleets of leaves sailed toward the distant sea on creeks the color of battle swords. Tawny weeds and grasses bent low to the ground beneath the wind, their heads heavy with the weight of next year's life. Oak, beech, and rowan trees bowed leaf-stripped branches as an invisible river of air rushed by. Wind sent ragged white cloud banners flying from the distant peaks. The sky between the clouds was a blue as deep as the treasured lapis lazuli brought back from the Saracen lands.

But it was the sun that ruled the day. The sun was an incandescent golden disk that burned with angelic purity.

Covertly, Simon studied his wife in the rich autumn light. She sat her mare with the elegance and ease that had beguiled him on the hard ride from Blackthorne to Stone Ring Keep. To his surprise, her Learned dress had proved to be quite suited for riding. It didn't flap or fly or climb or hinder.

If it hadn't been made of cloth, Simon would

have called the dress well behaved.

The fabric fascinated him. The longer he looked at it, the more he thought he saw . . . *something* . . . woven into the very warp and weft.

A woman.

Her hair is darkest midnight, her head is thrown back in abandon, her body is drawn on passion's sweet rack.

With a soft sound, Simon looked more closely.

Her mouth calls a man's name, pleading that he lie within her and share the wild ecstasy.

Then the woman's head turned and amethyst eyes looked out at Simon.

Ariane.

Suddenly the cloth shifted, revealing another facet of the weaving.

A shape that could be a man. He is bending down to Ariane, drinking her passion, flowing over her. . . .

Yes. A man.

But who?

The shape changed, becoming more dense, more real, almost tangible. The man's head began to turn toward Simon.

"What is that?" Ariane asked, pointing to her left. "There, where the hill rises most steeply and clouds come and go."

Reluctantly Simon looked away from the fey

cloth that changed before his very eyes, weaving light and shadow until they intertwined like lovers.

When he saw where Ariane was pointing, he frowned.

"That is Stone Ring," he said.

Ariane gave him a questioning look.

Simon ignored it. He disliked talking about Stone Ring, for it was a place with at least two faces — and only one of them could be weighed and measured.

But what truly rankled Simon was the suspicion that it was the less important face of Stone Ring that he could see.

"*The* Stone Ring?" Ariane asked. "Where the sacred rowan blooms no matter the season?"

Without answering, Simon straightened one of his gyrfalcon's jesses, which had become tangled on the saddle perch. Hooded, eager, beak slightly parted, Skylance clung and shifted restlessly on the T-shaped wooden perch, waiting for the instant of release into the untamed autumn sky.

"I have been to the ring of stones," Simon said finally. "I didn't see a rowan tree, much less blossoms."

"Do you want to try now?"

"No."

"Why? Is there not time?"

"I don't care to see the rowan bloom," Simon said. "The price is too high."

"The price?"

"Love," he said succinctly.

"Ah, that. Does Duncan know how you feel?"

" 'Tis hardly a secret. Any man of common sense feels as I do."

"Any woman, too."

Ariane's cool agreement shouldn't have irritated Simon, but it did. It would be very nice to be looked at with wonder and warmth, as Meg and Amber looked at their husbands.

Eyes narrowed, Ariane stared through the ragged cloud streamers to the hill where stone monoliths lifted ancient faces to the sky.

"Then why did Duncan toast us as he did on our wedding?" Ariane asked.

May you see the sacred rowan bloom.

"Ask Duncan," Simon said. "I claim no understanding of what passes for thought in the mind of a man in love."

Simon's tone of voice didn't encourage further pursuit of the topic of Stone Ring, but Ariane found it impossible not to do just that.

"What happened when you followed Amber's trail to the Stone Ring?" Ariane asked.

"Not one thing."

"I beg your pardon?"

Simon slanted Ariane a black glance.

"You were at Stone Ring Keep," he said curtly. "Surely you heard the gossip."

"Only pieces," she said. "I barely listened in any case."

"Too busy playing sad songs on your harp?"

"Yes," she retorted. "I prefer its music to the clatter of idle tongues. Besides, the ride from Blackthorne to Stone Ring Keep, coming on the heels of a trip from leaving my home in Normandy — a trip during which my knights sickened and I lost all but my handmaiden —"

"And your dowry," Simon put in dryly.

"— left me too exhausted to care what went on in either keep," Ariane finished. "Now, however, I am quite recovered."

"And curious to sample the gossip you missed?"

"These are my people now. Have I not the right to know about them?" Ariane asked evenly.

"We will be living at Blackthorne Keep, not at Stone Ring Keep."

"Lords Erik and Duncan are joined to your lord, the Glendruid Wolf. You, as your lord's right hand, will often be among Erik's and Duncan's people."

Ariane said no more.

Nor did she have to. As Simon's wife she had not only the right, but the duty, to understand the temper of the allies who were important to her husband's lord. In short, Simon was being unreasonable, and both of them knew it.

Silently Simon tightened the rein on his temper. Talking about Stone Ring's maddening mysteries irritated him.

The place was not reasonable.

"Stagkiller coursed Amber's trail to the edge of Stone Ring," Simon said neutrally, "then stopped as though he had run into a keep wall."

"Did he find her trail out of the ring?"

"No."

"But Amber wasn't anywhere inside the ring, was she?" Ariane asked.

"No."

"Then why wasn't there a trail out?"

"Cassandra said that Amber took the Druid way," Simon said.

"What does that mean?"

"Ask Cassandra. She is the Learned one, not I."

This time Ariane heeded the curt tone of Simon's voice. For a while there was silence. Yet despite her husband's displeasure, Ariane couldn't help watching the ancient ring of stones with increasing intensity as they rode around the base of the hill.

There was something odd about the lichen-etched stones, as though they cast shadows even when there was no sun. Or perhaps it was something else she was seeing, a second ring wavering like a reflection in disturbed water. . . .

For his part, Simon looked everywhere except at the timeworn stone monoliths.

"Simon?"

He grunted.

"Is there more than one ring of stones?"

He gave Ariane a long, cool look.

"What makes you ask?" Simon said finally. "Do you see another ring?"

Amethyst eyes narrowed. Ariane stood in the stirrups and leaned forward as though a handspan closer to the stones would make a difference in the clarity of her view.

"I don't think I see another ring," she said slowly. "There is something odd about it all, though."

"Such as?"

"Such as shadows standing upright instead of on the ground. Or a second ring inside the first, a ring made of shadow stones that ripple as though seen through mist or troubled water," Ariane said slowly. "Is that possible?"

"What does gossip say?"

"Ask the maids in the buttery," retorted Ariane.

Simon smiled faintly.

"The Learned," he said, "believe that there is a second, inner ring. It is there the sacred rowan is said to bloom."

"Then you have to be Learned to see the sacred rowan?"

Slowly Simon shook his head. "Duncan isn't Learned, yet he has seen the blossoms. At least, that is what he says."

"Don't you believe him?"

Simon's jaw flexed beneath the short pelt of golden beard. This was the crux of the matter. As it had no reasonable solution, Simon would have preferred to ignore it entirely.

Ariane, however, had the look of a cat that had just spotted movement in the hay. She wasn't going to turn aside of her quarry short of an argument. An *unreasonable* argument. And Simon was nothing if not reasonable. He had learned the terrible price of letting emotion rule his actions.

Worse still, it had been his brother who had paid the price, not Simon himself. It had made Simon's lesson all the more savagely complete.

"I don't doubt Duncan's honor for even the space of a breath," Simon said flatly.

"But you don't believe there's a second ring?"

"I see none."

"Then how did Duncan see it?" Ariane asked.

"You have more curiosity than a cat."

"But less fur," she retorted.

Simon cursed softly, yet could not entirely conceal his amusement. The longer he was with Ariane the more he enjoyed her quick tongue.

Unfortunately, thinking about that self-same tongue had an annoying habit of making him harden like a boy in the first rush of understanding why God made men one way and women another.

"How can Duncan see what we cannot?" Ariane persisted.

Simon bit back a scorching curse.

"Legend has it," he said tightly, "that only those who truly love one another can see the sacred rowan's bloom."

The leashed sarcasm in Simon's voice was as clear as the first ring of stones silhouetted against the windswept autumn sky.

"And the second ring of stones?" Ariane asked. "Is love required to see them too?"

Simon blew out an impatient breath. "No. Erik and Cassandra say they see the second ring, and neither of them has been foolish enough to become enchanted by love."

"So they don't see the sacred rowan?"

"God's teeth," muttered Simon, "is there no end?"

Ariane waited, watching him with eyes that

were more beautiful than the silver and amethyst circlet she wore about her head.

"They see the rowan," Simon said grimly, "but its branches are always barren for them."

"So . . ." Ariane's fingers drummed thoughtfully on her saddle. "One must be Learned to see the second ring and truly in love to see the rowan bloom?"

A tight shrug was Simon's only answer.

"Then Duncan must be Learned," Ariane concluded.

"I suspect the bolt of lighting that felled him simply muddled his wits," muttered Simon. "God knows it took his memories for a time."

Ariane tilted her head thoughtfully. Simon was certain that if she had been holding her harp, a questioning rill of notes would have come forth.

"What happened in Ghost Glen?" she asked.

Simon all but smacked his forehead in frustration. After Stone Ring itself, Ghost Glen was his least favorite topic. It was another of the incidents that reason could not fully explain.

It was also the primary reason that Duncan's quest for Amber was rapidly becoming a legend in the Disputed Lands.

"Ask Amber or Duncan," Simon said. "I

wasn't there. They were."

"Yet Duncan left the keep with you, Erik and Cassandra, didn't he?"

Simon's mouth tightened.

"Our horses refused the trail to Ghost Glen," Simon said neutrally. "Duncan switched to the mare we had brought for Amber to ride back. The mare took the trail without difficulty."

Ariane watched her husband's face, sensing that there was a great deal of emotion beneath his dispassionate words.

"Duncan went into Ghost Glen," Simon said. "We did not. In time he rode out of the mist with Amber in his arms."

"Odd that your horses refused."

Shrugging, Simon said, "The mare had been over the trail before. The mist didn't confuse her."

"Hadn't Cassandra and Erik been to the glen before? It's part of Sea Home's lands, isn't it?"

"No, they hadn't. Yes, it is."

"Why hadn't they gone? It sounds as though it's a rich and wonderful place, able to support at least one keep, probably more."

"God's *blood*," muttered Simon.

Watching her husband rather warily, Ariane waited for the answer with an urgency that she herself didn't understand. She only knew that somehow, in some unknowable way, Stone Ring and its attendant mysteries were important to her.

It was the same kind of uncanny certainty she had once had when she envisioned the location of items that had been lost.

"Simon?" Ariane coaxed, wanting the rest of the story.

Needing it.

"Cassandra said that the sacred places accept or reject people as they will," Simon said tightly. "She said that Ghost Glen rejected her, and Erik as well."

"Did you try?"

He nodded curtly.

"And it rejected you?" she whispered.

Simon made a disgusted sound. "Nay, nothing *rejected* me. The cursed mist was impenetrable."

Simon's tone said more. Much more. It revealed how maddening it had been for Simon to know there was a trail ahead that could be coursed by neither hound nor hunter . . . unless some incomprehensible, impossible, illogical force permitted his presence.

"But Duncan was accepted," Ariane said. "And Amber."

"Accepted?" Simon shrugged. "The mist was lesser then, 'tis all."

"Is the mist there all the time?"

"I don't know."

"Are you certain Duncan isn't Learned?"

"Why does it matter to you?" Simon retorted with barely leashed irritation. "You're not married to him."

"Are you and Cassandra allies?"

The change of subject made Simon blink. He looked at his wife's eyes. Their violet clarity was breathtaking. It reminded him of how she had looked by lantern light, eyes half-closed, shimmering, fully in thrall to his kiss.

"Dominic respects Cassandra's gift of prophecy," Simon said finally.

"And you?" Ariane asked.

"I respect Dominic."

Ariane frowned and looked again toward the shifting, enigmatic shadows inside the first of Stone Ring's circle of monoliths.

"You reject Learning," Ariane said slowly, "yet the Learned value you."

Simon gave her a dark, sideways glance.

"What makes you think that?" he asked sardonically.

"Cassandra told me. It was because of you that they gave me this dress."

Surprise showed clearly on Simon's face.

"Perhaps they value me because they value Dominic," Simon said after a few moments.

"No."

"You sound quite certain."

"I am."

"Second sight?" he asked sarcastically.

"Firsthand knowledge," she retorted. "Cassandra told me that they value you because you have the potential of being Learned. Few men do."

"By the Cross," muttered Simon, "what flatulence."

Abruptly he removed the gyrfalcon's hood, put Skylance on his gauntlet and urged his horse into a faster pace. The bird responded with an open beak and mantling wings. Only the jesses firmly held in Simon's fist prevented the falcon from leaping onto the back of the wild wind.

"Come," Simon said curtly. "Skylance grows impatient and so do I. The Lake of the Mists lies just over the next rise."

With that, Simon galloped off beyond the reach of more questions whose answers were as uncomfortable as they were unknowable.

Simon's mount was fleet, long-legged and eager to run. The mare Ariane rode was a heavy-boned, broad-beamed, muscular animal whose colts were destined to carry fully armed knights into battle rather than to race after stags in a hunt.

Ariane's mount had a singular lack of interest in galloping anywhere unless a pack of wolves was in close pursuit. Despite smart kicks from her rider's heels, the mare was just cresting the rise when Simon's blood-freezing shout of warning rang back to Ariane.

"Renegades! Flee to the keep, Ariane!"

13

As soon as Ariane heard Simon's warning shout, she hauled back on the reins. The unexpected pressure on the bit made the mare rear back onto her thick haunches. Ariane swayed effortlessly in the saddle, balancing herself even as she stared intently down the rise and into the misty trail ahead.

One sweeping look told it all. Scattered oaks and grass, a lake gleaming like quicksilver between gaps in the mist, and two groups of outlaws spurring their horses toward Simon. The closest men were perhaps six furlongs away from her and only one from Simon. The two quickest outlaws wore old battle helms and rode horses like Simon's, long-legged beasts bred for the hunt rather than for the battlefield.

But there were three more outlaws a furlong farther back, and those men were fully protected by chain mail from lips to heels. Even their horses had chests and rumps covered by mantles of mail. Though the men were knights, their shields and lances were barren of any lord's colors or symbol.

Simon made no attempt to flee the renegade knights. Grimly he held his mount at a standstill, guarding the approach to the rise.

Guarding Ariane.

Before Ariane's horrified eyes, the first two outlaws thundered up to Simon, broadswords raised for a killing blow. Ariane screamed her husband's name, but the sound was lost in the clash of steel on steel as Simon's broadsword met and slashed right through an outlaw's inferior weapon — and through far more vulnerable flesh and bone as well.

The outlaw fell in bloody ruin onto the grass. Panicked, his mount raced off among the trees.

The second outlaw shouted a curse. Enraged, he swung mightily at Simon. Fighting one-handed with a broadsword meant for two hands, Simon wheeled his horse to meet the outlaw's blow. Then, with a quickness so great the eye could barely follow, Simon dropped the rein and swung his broadsword two-handed.

The second outlaw died even more swiftly than the first.

Three renegade knights spurred their war stallions from a heavy trot into a canter, eating up the distance between Simon and themselves.

"Flee, Simon!" Ariane shouted. "Your horse is faster than theirs!"

The brief battle had taken Simon farther from Ariane. He could not hear her cries. He heard only the renegades thundering closer to him with each heartbeat. One hand wrapped firmly around the rein, the other grasping his heavy broadsword, Simon waited.

As he waited, he wished for Dominic's oaklike strength, or that of Duncan of Maxwell. But Simon had only his quickness of hand and his wits and a driving need to protect the violet-eyed girl whom fate had given into his keeping.

Ariane's whip whistled through the air and cut across her mare's haunches. Before the startled animal could collect itself, Ariane's arm rose and fell once more. The mare broke into a lumbering canter, then a gallop, dodging between trees and around boulders.

But it was down the slope toward Simon that Ariane galloped, not toward the safety of Stone Ring Keep.

Intent on the attacking knights, Simon kept his back toward the slope. There was no question that the renegades meant to fight three against one, though Simon had neither armor nor war stallion with which to defend himself.

Simon was hopelessly overmatched, and he knew it.

Even worse, he wasn't certain he could stay alive long enough to give Ariane's heavy-footed mare sufficient time for her to outrun the powerful war stallions and reach the haven of Stone Ring Keep.

Tautly Simon waited, eyes searching for any weakness in the trio charging toward him. One of the knights was already dropping back a bit. His horse ran as though stiff in the hindquarters. Another of the men, the biggest of the three, was pressing ahead of the pace, obviously eager for the kill. The smallest man sat his mount awkwardly, protecting his ribs as though he had recently taken a blow across his left side.

Whoever fought you last gave a good account of himself, Simon thought bleakly. *He must have worn armor.*

Lance leveled, the most eager renegade shouted in foretaste of victory as he spurred his stallion at Simon. With a harsh grip on the rein and unrelenting pressure from his powerful legs, Simon held his frightened mount in place.

At the last instant Simon yanked the bridle, spun his horse on its hocks, and spurred it to the side.

The war stallion swept past like a landslide, but Simon was already beyond reach. Immediately the renegade yanked on the rein, turning his stallion. But at a full gallop, the turn would be wide. For a minute or two the eager renegade would be out of the battle.

Simon had no chance to appreciate his small strategic victory. The smallest of the renegades was upon him. Again Simon forced his horse to wait, then spurred it into flight so swiftly that great clots of earth leaped from beneath the horse's hooves.

The renegade was expecting such a maneuver and had slowed to counter it. Still, Simon's quickness and the agility of his horse kept them beyond range of the renegade's deadly lance.

Instead of retreating as he had done before, Simon spurred his horse forward. As he had planned, he was now on the knight's left side, the side the renegade had been taking such care to protect.

A short, backhanded blow was all Simon could manage from the saddle of his untrained mount, but it was enough. Simon's broadsword thudded into the renegade's ribs. Though the edge of the blade was stopped by chain mail, the force of the blow itself was not. The renegade screamed in pain and rage, dropped his lance, and doubled over in the saddle.

Before Simon could follow up the advantage, the last of the three knights galloped up.

A glance told Simon that the first knight had managed to complete his wide turn, the second knight was out of the battle, and the third knight was planning to pin Simon against the second knight's horse.

Simon spurred his own mount forward, trying to evade the third knight and still not come any closer to the first, bloodthirsty knight who was charging toward him again.

Evading the third stallion wasn't difficult, for the horse was somewhat lame in the left hindquarter. But Simon's horse couldn't spin aside quickly enough to escape entirely the first knight's charge.

In a last, desperate attempt at avoiding the deadly lance, Simon yanked harshly back and up on the bit and at the same time raked his mount with spurs. Simon's horse reared wildly, hooves flailing. It was a maneuver familiar to war-horses, but totally unexpected from an untrained animal.

A hoof hit the first knight's lance with numbing force. The big knight grunted as the shaft was wrenched from his suddenly weak grip.

Yet even before the lance hit the earth, Simon knew his luck and skill had reached an end. By the time his horse had four feet on the ground again, the third knight would be on him. There would be no room to maneuver. No escape.

Simon's only solace was that he had bought enough time for Ariane's mare to outrun the war stallions.

Grimly Simon hauled at the bit, forcing his horse around to confront the death that he knew was coming with the next breath, or the one after, as the third knight's sword descended on Simon's unprotected back.

What Simon saw as he turned wasn't death, but a chestnut juggernaut hurtling over the grass at a right angle to the third knight. On the back of the thundering mare was a girl dressed in amethyst, her black hair whipping behind like hell's own pennant, and her mouth open with a scream that was his name.

Just before the renegade's sword would have split Simon's skull, the heavy mare slammed broadside into the renegade's stallion. The horse's weak hind leg gave way, tumbling the two mounts with their riders into a pile of threshing, steel-shod hooves and flailing limbs.

Even as the felled knight went down, he drew his battle dagger and turned on the one who had caused his downfall, either not knowing or not caring that it was an unarmed girl he sought to kill.

Simon's own horse staggered and went to its knees, but Simon had already kicked free of the stirrups. He landed as he had trained all his life to land, upright, running, wielding the heavy broadsword as though it were made of smoke.

The wide blade descended on the third knight at the same instant that his dagger slashed out at Ariane. The renegade's helm saved his life, turning Simon's blow aside.

Ariane had no such armor. She screamed as she felt the burning edge of steel cut into her.

Simon went mad. His broadsword whistled through the air as he brought it down over his head to cut the renegade in two, regardless of the armor the man wore.

Before the sword bit into flesh, a mailed fist descended on Simon from behind, knocking him aside. If it hadn't been a left-handed, looping blow, it would have knocked Simon senseless. As it was, he was merely dazed.

Instinctively he turned to face his enemy as he fell. He was rewarded by a glimpse of a stallion's strong legs, a sword, and ice-blue eyes glaring out from beneath the first knight's hammered steel helm.

Though slowed by the blow, Simon managed to roll aside as he hit the ground. At that, he barely got beyond the reach of the first knight's sword.

The big renegade cursed savagely and struck

again at Simon. The blow was awkwardly aimed, for the man's hand was still half-numbed from the strike that had broken his lance. Despite that, Simon barely raised his own sword quickly enough to deflect the blow.

Before Simon could draw a breath, the war-horse's mailed shoulder slammed into him, knocking him off his feet and sending his heavy sword spinning beyond his reach. Winded, all but senseless, Simon sank to the ground. With a triumphant shout, the renegade lifted his sword for the killing blow.

A peregrine's uncanny cry split the air. The bird plummeted down with blinding speed, talons held forward as though to rake prey from the air.

But a war-horse rather than a fat partridge was the bird's target.

Talons slashed at the stallion's unprotected ears. The horse reared wildly, ruining the renegade's aim. No sooner did the stallion recover than the peregrine attacked again, this time going for the war-horse's eyes. Retreating, the stallion screamed in fear and fury, but there was no way for the earthbound animal to attack the peregrine that hovered just beyond reach, waiting for another opening.

In the distance came the shouts of men. Much closer came the full-throated howl of a wolfhound on a fresh trail.

Cursing, the renegade made one last, futile slash with his sword before he spurred his horse away from the voices. The stallion leaped forward, eager to leave the savage, unexpected peregrine behind.

No sooner had the war-horse turned to run away than Simon lurched to his feet. His sword was but two strides distant. As his hand closed around the cold, familiar haft, the world spun dizzily around him.

Simon sank to his hands and knees and crawled toward Ariane, dragging his sword alongside, knowing only that he had to protect her.

Dimly he realized that Ariane's mare and the war-horse had both scrambled onto their feet once more. The remaining renegade knight had managed to remount, but neither he nor his stallion had any heart for fighting on alone. Awkwardly, favoring his left haunch, the stallion cantered off and was soon lost among the trees.

Simon didn't spare the fleeing renegade so much as a look, for Ariane was lying on the battle-churned ground. Blood trailed like a ragged scarlet ribbon down the left side of her body.

"Ariane," Simon said harshly.

The word was almost a groan.

"I am — here," she said.

Ariane's voice was thin, her face pale, her eyes huge in her ashen face.

A peregrine's uncanny, sweet greeting trilled through the silence. It was answered by a wolfhound's deep-throated bay.

Stagkiller raced down the slope, scanned eagerly for enemies, and found none. The hound's presence told Simon what he had already guessed from the peregrine's attack.

Erik was nearby.

As three war-horses thundered down the rise toward Simon, he braced himself upright on his sword next to Ariane.

"Nightingale," he said hoarsely.

It was all he could say.

Magnificent amethyst eyes focused on Simon. Ariane opened her mouth. Nothing came out but a choked cry of surprise as pain and darkness closed around her, taking the very breath from her lungs.

When Erik, Dominic, and Sven galloped up, they saw the bodies of two outlaws. Just beyond, Simon lay on the ground, his wife in his arms.

"There were five," Erik said flatly.

Dominic didn't ask how Erik knew.

"Track them," Dominic said curtly.

At an unseen signal from Erik, Stagkiller raced off, coursing the trail of the bandits.

Sven followed without an instant's hesitation.

The two remaining war-horses came to a sliding, ground-gouging stop a few yards from Ariane and Simon. Both knights dismounted as Simon had earlier, a muscular leap that set them upright on the ground, running. As Erik ran, he stripped off his chain mail gauntlets and stuffed them into his belt.

"Simon?" Dominic called urgently.

Simon simply tightened his arms around Ariane, pulling her even closer.

"There is blood," Dominic said, bending down to his brother.

"Not mine," Simon said hoarsely. "Ariane's."

"Let me see to her," Erik said, kneeling.

His voice, like his expression, was surprisingly gentle. Even so, Simon made no move to release Ariane.

"I have some small training in wounds," Erik said. "Permit me to help your wife."

Painfully Simon shifted, but not enough to allow Erik to see Ariane's wounded side. The violet fabric of the dress moved with Simon, covering both him and Ariane from the waist down.

"Release her," Erik said in a low voice.

"Nay. She will die if I don't hold her next to me."

Simon's eyes were black, savage.

Erik's eyebrows rose in surprise, but he said nothing. He simply looked to Dominic for help.

After a single glance at his brother's eyes, the Glendruid Wolf shook his head, cautioning Erik. Erik didn't argue. He had seen enough battles to know that reason was too often the first casualty.

Slowly Dominic knelt by Simon's side. A hand wrapped in chain mail settled as delicately as a butterfly onto Simon's leg. Beneath the mail gauntlet, the fey dress rippled and shivered with every breath of wind as though alive.

"Simon," Dominic said urgently. "Let us help you."

A shudder coursed through Simon. Gradually the wildness left his eyes. He moved aside just enough for Erik to reach Ariane's wounded side. The amethyst fabric moved with Simon, clinging to his thigh. Absently he stroked the cloth as he would have one of the keep's cats.

With great care, Erik's fingers probed down the side of Ariane's dress.

"I couldn't find a wound," Simon said roughly.

"The dress is binding it," Erik said.

"Then make it bind more tightly. She bleeds too much."

"The dress is only cloth," Erik said. "Very clever cloth, but still . . . cloth."

Delicately Erik began to run his fingertips down Ariane's side once more.

"What happened?" Dominic asked Simon quietly.

"I was ahead of Ariane. Two outlaws and three renegade knights struck. The knights were in armor and riding war stallions."

"God's wounds," hissed Dominic.

"I killed the two who weren't in armor."

"You should have fled," Dominic said curtly. "Your horse was more than a match for war stallions carrying fully armored knights."

"Ariane's mare was not."

Dominic blew breath through clenched teeth, making a hissing noise.

"You are as fine a knight as I've ever known," Dominic said after a moment, "but even you couldn't defeat three knights in chain mail riding war stallions. How did you survive?"

"I had help."

"Who?" Dominic asked, looking around.

"A brave, foolish nightingale."

Dominic's head snapped back around to his brother.

"Ariane?" Dominic asked, shocked.

"Aye," Simon said. "I sent one knight running, but another was set to slice me in two. I was a dead man. Then Ariane came out of the mist at a hard gallop and slammed that blocky little mare right into the knight's stallion."

Dominic and Erik were too surprised to speak.

"Before that tangle was sorted out," Simon said, "a peregrine came out of the sky like feathered lightning and sent another stallion fleeing. I guess the remaining knight decided that he had fought enough for one day and quit the field."

"Was Ariane struck on the head?" Erik asked.

"I don't know. All I saw was the dagger blow. I would have killed the cursed knight, had not the blue-eyed devil intervened."

No one interrupted the silence that came after Simon's bleak statement.

"What of your wounds?" Dominic asked finally.

"I've taken worse during your endless drills."

"You can thank those drills that you lived long enough for help to arrive," Dominic muttered.

"That and the big renegade's bloodlust," Simon agreed. "It made him too eager."

Erik and Dominic exchanged a look.

"Would you recognize this renegade if you saw him again?" Erik asked Simon.

"I think not. Thick-chested, blue-eyed bastards are as common as rocks in the Disputed Lands."

"What insignia was on his shield?" Dominic asked.

"None," Simon said succinctly.

"Do —"

"Enough," Simon interrupted impatiently. " 'Tis Ariane who matters now, not the misbegotten bastards who attacked us."

While he spoke, Simon's hand caressed Ariane's cheek as delicately as a shadow. The tenderness of the gesture was at odds with the gaunt planes of Simon's face and the marks of recent battle on his body.

"Try to tear a strip of cloth from the hem of her dress," Erik suggested.

Dominic reached for the dress, only to be stopped by Erik's hand.

"Nay, let Simon do it," Erik said. Then, turning to Simon, "When you hold the fabric, think of Ariane's need to have the flow of blood staunched."

Simon stripped off his hawking gauntlet, took the fabric between his strong hands, and pulled. The cloth parted as though along a hidden seam. Nor were any raveling edges left behind.

"You did that as well as any Learned healer," Erik said with satisfaction.

"Did what?" retorted Simon. "The stuff came apart in my hands. 'Tis a wonder the dress hasn't fallen to pieces and left Ariane wearing only her chemise."

Erik smiled slightly and said, "Now, bind the strip around Ariane's wound. Do it so tightly that a dagger would have difficulty getting between cloth and skin."

When Simon shifted Ariane in order to bind the wound, she moaned. The sound hurt Simon more than any of the blows he had received fighting renegade knights.

"Why didn't you run to safety, nightingale?" Simon asked, his voice both soft and rough.

There was no answer but that of the Learned fabric clinging like lint to Simon's thigh while he worked to bind Ariane's wound.

"You would have been safe," Simon said to Ariane under his breath.

"And you would have been dead," Erik pointed out.

Simon opened his mouth but no words came for a time. He hissed a Saracen phrase.

"I am a knight," Simon said finally. "Death in battle is my lot. But Ariane . . . Ariane shouldn't have to fight for her own life, much less for the life of her husband!"

"Cassandra would disagree with you," Erik said. "The Learned believe that we all fight — man, woman, and child — each according to need and skill."

Simon grunted. Yet despite the grimness of his expression, his hands were gentle on Ariane's body. Even so, she moaned from time to time as he worked.

"Nightingale," he said softly. "I'm sorry, but I must hurt you in order to help you."

"She knows," Erik said.

"How can she?" Simon asked coldly. "She is senseless."

Erik looked at the amethyst fabric lying placidly within Simon's grasp and said nothing.

Overhead, a peregrine arrowed down out of the sky, trilling a sweet, uncanny greeting. A second falcon followed, its pale feathers bright against the sky.

Dominic pulled on Simon's hawking gauntlet and whistled Skylance's special call. The gyrfalcon hovered, then settled onto Dominic's arm, accepting captivity once more.

When Erik stood and held out his arm, his peregrine swooped down with heart-stopping speed. At the last possible instant, the falcon's wings flared. With dainty care, the peregrine landed on Erik's hawking gauntlet.

"Well, Winter, what have you to show

me?" he asked softly.

Then he whistled an ascending trill. The peregrine cocked her head, watching him with clear, knowing eyes. Her hooked beak opened and astonishingly sweet trills poured out. For a few moments bird of prey and Learned man whistled to one another.

Then Erik's arm moved with swift, muscular ease, launching the peregrine back into the sky. Winter climbed rapidly, vanishing into the distance.

"The outlaws are still running," Erik said, turning back to his human friends. "Stagkiller and Sven still follow. They hold to an ancient trail."

"Do you know where it leads?" Dominic asked.

"To Silverfells. Stagkiller will bring Sven back to the keep."

"Why?" Dominic asked. "Shouldn't we know where the renegades are camped?"

Erik said nothing.

Simon glanced from the gyrfalcon on Dominic's arm to the equally fierce profile of Erik, son of a great Northern lord.

"Lord Erik?" Dominic asked.

The Glendruid Wolf's voice was polite, but he meant to have an answer. The well-being of too many keeps rested on peace in the Disputed Lands.

"The land of the Silverfells clan is forbidden to the Learned," Erik said curtly.

"Why?" asked Dominic.

Again, Erik said nothing.

Simon stood, lifting Ariane with him.

"Come," Simon said impatiently to his brother. "We must get Ariane to safety."

For a few instants Dominic's eyes glittered with the same hard light as the fey crystal in the wolf's head pin that fastened his mantle.

Then the Glendruid Wolf turned away from Erik to his brother. The amethyst of Ariane's dress flowed like twilight against the indigo of Simon's mantle.

"To the keep, then," Dominic said curtly.

"Quickly," Simon urged, striding to his horse, "before the renegades realize they were defeated by a Learned peregrine and a reckless little nightingale."

14

" 'Tis like an oiled eel," Meg muttered, turning to Cassandra. "Have you a dagger? I can't get a grip on the bandage to make it come free."

Cassandra looked from Ariane's white face to the violet fabric covering her wound. Only a small amount of blood had seeped through the Learned weaving.

"Simon," Cassandra said.

"I'm here." Simon stepped forward from the doorway, where he had stayed to avoid getting in the healers' way. "What do you need?"

Simon's glance took in the room he had not come to since his wedding night. Nothing had changed, except that the bride lay more dead than alive on her bed.

"Take off your wife's bindings," Cassandra said.

Without a word, Simon went to Ariane. A few deft motions of his hands unwrapped the bandage he had put on after the battle with the renegades.

Baffled by Simon's ease with the slippery cloth, Meg looked from the bandage to the Learned woman. Cassandra didn't notice, for she was intent upon Simon's handling of the odd fabric.

"Now," Cassandra said. "The dress."

Ariane neither stirred nor even moaned as Simon swiftly unlaced the front of the dress. She lay as limp as sea wrack stranded on a rocky shore.

Silver laces slid free of their moorings with gratifying speed. The dress opened, revealing fine linen underclothing. The pale gold perfection of the linen was ruined by a scarlet blotch running all the way down one side.

"God have mercy," Simon said starkly.

"Amen," said Meg and Cassandra as one.

Then, briskly, Cassandra said, "Stand aside, Simon. This is work for healers."

Reluctantly he moved away from the bed.

"Stay close," Cassandra cautioned as Simon once more headed for the doorway. "We may need Serena's fabric to stem the flow of blood."

"What does that have to do with Simon?" Meg asked.

"More than I have time to explain."

With that, Cassandra bent over Ariane, prodding lightly along the senseless girl's body with hands that smelled of astringent herbs.

Meg, dressed as Glendruid ritual required in the clean linen shift of a healer, dipped her hands once more in a pan of herbal water. A pungent, complex aroma rose from the hot liquid.

"Her bones seem intact," Cassandra said. "Her ribs turned aside some of the blade."

Cool sweat bloomed beneath Simon's tunic at the thought of steel meeting Ariane's delicate bones. He made an inarticulate sound and flexed his hands as though hungry to feel a renegade's neck between them.

"Let me cleanse the wound," Meg said.

Cassandra straightened and stepped away. As she did, she gave Simon a sideways glance. His face looked carved from stone, with a grimness his closely clipped beard couldn't soften.

"Are you well, sir?" the Learned woman asked.

"Well?" Simon choked off a curse. "Aye. Quite well, thanks to my wife lying near death on the bed."

Cassandra gestured toward a trunk whose open top revealed tray after tray of small pots, bundles of cloth, herbs, sharp blades and even sharper needles.

"If you feel faint, have a care not to fall into the medicines," she said.

"Faint?" Simon said. "I've seen blood before."

"And I've seen many a fine warrior fall senseless at the sight of another's wound," Cassandra retorted.

"Simon won't," Meg said without looking up from her task. "He nursed Dominic back to life after a sultan amused himself for many days torturing his captive Christian knight."

Cassandra looked at Simon with new interest.

" 'Tis rare to find a man with a gift for healing," Cassandra said. "Rarer still to find a warrior so gifted."

The assessing look in Cassandra' s grey eyes made Simon uncomfortable.

"It was no more than common sense," Simon said curtly. "I simply cared for my brother until he was able to care for himself again."

Simon might as well have saved his breath. Cassandra was bent over Ariane once more. Learned woman and Glendruid witch conferred in low voices, discussing plants by their ancient names, the names incised in rune stones by women who died long before Roman legions marched into the Disputed Lands.

To Simon, it seemed a lifetime before the two healers stepped back from Ariane's motionless body.

With a murmured word to Cassandra, Meg went behind a screen, took off the soiled linen shift, and put on her ordinary tunic once more. The linen shift would be ritually cleansed before it was worn again.

"She is sleeping as peacefully as could be expected," Meg said to Simon.

"Dominic's squire asked that you go to your husband when you are finished," Simon said.

Meg touched Simon's hand in silent reassurance and went out the door to seek Dominic. She found him with Duncan in the lord's solar.

"How is Lady Ariane?" Dominic asked the instant Meg appeared in the doorway.

Duncan looked up from his steward's inventory of the food. The remains of a cold meal lay nearby on a table that was covered by a colorfully woven cloth. Duncan's hazel eyes were intent, bright with the leap of flames in the hearth. He knew that much depended upon Ariane's alliance with Simon — and through her, Normandy's alliance with Henry, the English king.

"Well enough," Meg said. "With care, good fortune, and God's blessing, Ariane will mend. Unless wound fever comes . . ."

Meg sighed wearily and rubbed the small of her back. Pregnancy hadn't been difficult for her until recently, when the weight of the babe seemed to increase overnight, every night.

"Come here, small falcon," Dominic said, holding out his hand to his wife.

When Meg was seated, Dominic stood and began rubbing the aches from her back.

"Ariane is doing better than I feared when I saw her linen underclothes," Meg said after a moment. "Whatever fiber the dress is woven of apparently stems the flow of blood as well as any powder or salve known to Glendruid healers. Or Learned ones, for that matter."

"What of Simon?" Duncan asked. "Erik said he was rather bloodied by the fight."

"Scrapes, cuts, bruises, lumps," she summarized. "None of which he would let us tend."

Meg sighed and leaned gratefully against her husband's knowing hands.

"He blames himself for Ariane's wound," Dominic said.

"Why? How did it happen?" Meg asked.

"Simon faced down five renegades in order to give Ariane time to run away," Dominic said.

Meg caught her breath sharply. She looked over her shoulder at her husband with wide green eyes.

"But instead of running," Dominic said, "Ariane galloped right into the middle of the battle. Because of her reckless courage, Simon lives."

"It was that close?" Meg asked in a low voice.

"Aye," Dominic said, his expression bleak. "I owe the cold Norman heiress a great debt."

"Cold?" Duncan asked. "A cold woman would have watched Simon die without blinking. Rather I would say that Ariane is a woman of deep passion."

"But not for men," Dominic said bluntly.

The certainty in his voice made Duncan wince and shake his head in silent sympathy for Simon the Loyal.

There was a sudden rush and moan of wind around the keep. A shutter banged on the third floor. Simon's gyrfalcon, alone among all the unoccupied perches in the great hall, cried out to her own kind. There was no answer.

The sentry called the time from the battlements.

Dominic stood and paced uneasily. After a moment he headed for the battlements with a determined stride.

"There has been no sign of renegades," Duncan called after him.

" 'Tis not renegades I fear, but winter," Dominic said without pausing.

A few moments later the sound of his boots on the keep's spiral stone stairway echoed back down to the lord's solar.

Duncan glanced at Meg.

215

"What eats him, Meggie?" Duncan asked.

She smiled at hearing the childhood name, but her smile quickly faded.

"Blackthorne Keep is much on my husband's mind," Meg said simply.

"Have you heard rumors of trouble?"

"Nay. Since Dominic dealt so harshly with the Reevers, outlaws either avoid our lands or ride on through, leaving our people untroubled."

"Then what makes Dominic as restive as a chained wolf?"

Meg closed her eyes for a moment. Beneath her clothes the babe kicked strongly. She put her hands over her womb, reassured by the life within her. However uncomfortable pregnancy was, the babe's obvious health heartened her.

" 'Tis simple," Meg said, sighing. "I have dreamed."

Duncan snorted. "Where your Glendruid heritage is concerned, Meggie, nothing is simple."

Meg shook her head. Golden bells sang and her long, loosely plaited braids gleamed redly in the light.

"I dreamed of two wolves, one black, one tawny," Meg said. "I dreamed of an oak with hazel eyes. I dreamed of a harp that sang with a nightingale's pure, poignant notes while held

216

within the arms of a golden knight. I dreamed of a storm around all of them. An evil storm."

" 'Tis no wonder Dominic is restless," Duncan said wryly.

"Aye. Thomas the Strong guards Blackthorne while we are away. Thomas is a loyal knight and a brave warrior, but he is no leader of men. If winter bars our return and trouble comes in our absence . . ."

Cursing under his breath, Duncan raked blunt fingers through his hair. In the firelight, scars from long-forgotten battles gleamed palely across the back of his hand.

"You must return to Blackthorne Keep," Duncan said abruptly. " 'Tis long enough you have spent at Stone Ring Keep dealing with problems I've caused."

"That isn't what I meant," Meg protested.

"I know. But 'tis true all the same."

Duncan surged to his feet with a grace surprising in a man so large. He looked into the fire for a moment.

"I'll send men-at-arms with you as far as Carlysle Manor," he said. "After that, you will be safe. I'd go myself, but . . ."

"Stone Ring Keep needs you," Meg finished for Duncan.

"Aye. Especially with this thrice-damned renegade knight preying upon the weak."

Duncan's hands worked for a moment as

though feeling the chill weight of a battle hammer sliding over his palms, coming into his grasp as though created solely for him; and then the eerie hum of the hammer slicing deadly circles from the air.

"I'll send word that your horses and goods be ready at dawn," Duncan said. "Dinna worry, Meggie. We'll care for Simon's wife in his absence as though she were one of our own. When Ariane is well, we will bring her to Blackthorne and her husband."

Duncan didn't doubt for an instant that Simon would leave Stone Ring Keep with his lord and brother, Dominic. The Glendruid Wolf had made no secret of how much he valued his brother's advice, companionship, and fighting skills.

Simon, called the Loyal.

Meg sighed and started to push herself to her feet.

"Stay by the fire," Duncan said quickly, going to her.

"I have a patient to watch."

Duncan lifted Meg to her feet and smiled down at her with real affection.

"In better times," Duncan said softly, "you must take your Glendruid Wolf to the Stone Ring. The rowan will bloom for the two of you, Meggie. I am as certain of it as I am of my own heartbeat."

Meg's smile was like sunshine, all warmth and light. Standing on tiptoe, she touched Duncan's cheek with her lips.

"We would like that," she said.

Still smiling, Meg climbed the stairs to Ariane's room. As expected, Cassandra was there, sitting by the bed, embroidering a tiny garment.

The bed curtains had been pulled, cutting off stray drafts from the slit windows.

"How is she?" Meg asked.

"Asleep."

"Fever?"

"None so far," Cassandra said. "Thank God for it."

"Is Simon on the battlements with Dominic?"

"Nay," said a deep voice from behind the bed curtains.

Simon pulled one of the curtains aside in time to catch the surprised look on Meg's face.

"Don't worry," he said. "I'm careful not to harm her. But she is restless unless I'm here."

Meg looked beyond Simon to where Ariane lay. She was curled beneath the bed covers, her face toward Simon. The violet dress lay like a bridge between man and wife.

Frowning, Meg turned to Cassandra.

"I don't know your Learned healing rituals," Meg said, "but Glendruids are quite firm about giving nothing to the patient that hasn't first been purified."

"Examine the dress," Cassandra said. "You will find it as pure as herbs, water and fire can make anything."

" 'Tis true," Simon said. "I went over the dress myself, for I know how particular you are about such things."

Meg went to the bed. She picked up an edge of the fabric, ran it lightly between her fingertips and sniffed. Slowly she released the cloth. It fluttered down to rest once more against Simon's shoulder and Ariane's cheek.

" 'Tis as though newly woven," Meg said, baffled.

"Aye," Cassandra said. "Serena's weavings are much prized among the Learned."

Meg watched Simon's fingers stroking the fabric as though it were a cat.

And like a cat, the fabric seemed to cling more closely in response.

"Does Dominic need me?" Simon asked.

"Now? Nay. But we leave tomorrow for Blackthorne Keep."

As though in silent protest, Simon's hand clenched on the fabric.

"Ariane isn't well enough to travel," Simon said carefully.

"Aye. Duncan promised that he would care

for Ariane as though she were his own," Meg said.

"I will stay with her," Cassandra said.

Simon made no response.

"Don't worry," Meg said. "Cassandra is as skilled in healing as I am."

Simon nodded and said nothing.

There was no question that his duty lay with his lord and brother, the Glendruid Wolf. For the first time, such duty was more burden than pleasure for Simon.

Broodingly he looked at Ariane, who had saved his life at the risk of her own, yet had refused to share her body in the marriage bed as God, custom, and necessity required.

Reckless little nightingale. Will you be pleased to have me gone from your side?

Will your songs be happier without me?

Cassandra put aside her embroidery, stood, and went to the bed. Thoughtfully she looked down at Ariane's relaxed body and Simon's taut one.

But most of all, the Learned woman looked at the fabric stretched between the two.

"Come, Simon," Cassandra said softly. "Stand by me."

His black eyes narrowed at the gentle command, but Simon said nothing. Instead, he set aside the violet fabric and eased from the bed so as not to disturb Ariane.

When he stood, the dress fell forward over its own soft folds until it brushed against Simon's thigh.

"Farther," Cassandra said, stepping backward.

Puzzled, Simon followed.

The fabric slid away.

Simon had to bite back an instinctive protest. Only now did he realize how rewarding it was for him to touch the weaving.

"Watch," said the Learned woman to Meg.

After a few moments the posture of Ariane's body changed subtly. No longer was she relaxed in a healing sleep. Rather she lay slackly. Her skin seemed more pale, more chalky, less supple.

"What is it?" Meg asked Cassandra. "What's wrong?"

"A few times within Learned memory, the Silverfells clan has woven cloth that covers more than the body," Cassandra whispered. "Serena is from that clan."

Simon made a hoarse sound and spun to face the Learned woman.

"Are you saying there is witchery woven into that dress?" he demanded harshly.

Cassandra gave Simon a measuring glance.

"Nay," she said flatly. "I am saying the Learned know that there is more to the world than that which can be weighed, measured, touched, and seen."

Simon's expression became hard, closed. "Explain."

"Of course."

Simon waited, his body taut.

"But first," Cassandra said coolly, "you must explain a moonrise to Edgar the Blind, and relate the call of a nightingale to the miller's deaf child."

The blackness of Simon's eyes narrowed into two glittering strips of midnight. He turned to Meg.

"Is that cursed dress harming Ariane?" he demanded.

Thoughtfully, Meg bent and rested her hand on the dress, *seeing* the dress as she would have *seen* a person, with Glendruid eyes.

" 'Tis of a surpassing odd texture," Meg said, straightening, "but there is no whiff of evil."

"Are you certain?" Simon asked.

"I am certain of this," Meg said. "No other cloth could have kept the life's blood inside Ariane's body. Is that evil?"

Simon closed his eyes. His jaw clenched visibly as he struggled to contain his temper.

Will I never be free of witchery?

Will I ever be clean of what Marie's witchery did to me, and I to Dominic?

Simon let out a pent breath. His eyes opened

clear and savage with all that had not been said, the past a poison within his soul.

"I have no fondness for witchery," he said finally.

The stillness of his voice was more dangerous than a shout would have been.

"Except yours, Meg," Simon said, his expression and voice gentling. "Yours I abide because it saved Dominic's life. And because you would die before you would betray him."

"What of Amber?" Meg asked.

"She is Duncan's to contend with."

Ariane groaned softly. Her head turned from side to side as though she were searching for something.

"It is you she seeks," Cassandra said.

Simon looked at the Learned woman.

"I?" he asked.

"Yes."

"You, are wrong, madam. My wife has no fondness for me."

"Indeed?" Cassandra murmured. "Well, that explains it."

"Explains what?" Simon asked impatiently.

"Why she nearly died so that you could live."

Simon's mouth shut with a distinct clicking of teeth. His jaw muscle worked.

"I don't know why she galloped into the middle of the battle," he said, biting off each word. "It will be the first thing I ask her when she awakens."

"If you leave tomorrow, I doubt that Ariane will ever awaken," Cassandra said matter-of-factly.

Simon's face paled. He spun to look at his wife again. Her skin appeared to have been rubbed with chalk. Each time she breathed, she groaned as though a knife were sticking between her ribs.

"Explain it how you will, Simon," Cassandra said, "or ignore it entirely, but Ariane heals more quickly when you lie close to her."

"Can she travel?" he asked.

"Tomorrow? Nay," Cassandra said. "In a fortnight? Probably."

Simon looked to Meg, but she was already on her way out of the room.

"Meg?" he asked.

"I will bring Dominic here," Meg said.

Simon headed for Ariane's bed, only to be stopped by Cassandra's hand. He looked at the cool white fingers wrapped around his wrist. A ring set with a red, a green, and a blue stone gleamed like a captive rainbow on the Learned woman's hand.

"First, let the Glendruid Wolf see Ariane as she is, without your vitality infusing the cloth," Cassandra said.

Simon started to ask a question, saw the gleam of amused anticipation in Cassandra's eyes, and decided to say nothing at all.

"What is this?" Dominic asked, striding into the room. "Meg says that Ariane is suddenly worse."

"Watch her closely, Wolf of Glendruid," Cassandra said.

The tone of the Learned woman's voice told Dominic far more than her words. He watched Ariane as carefully as a hunter would watch for the first sight of a stag leaping from cover.

"How does she appear to you?" Cassandra asked.

Dominic glanced at Simon.

"Speak freely," Cassandra said. "Simon assures us that there is no affection between him and his wife."

"She looks like a woman with childbed fever," Dominic said bluntly.

"Or a knight with wound fever?" Cassandra offered.

"Aye."

"Glendruid healer," Cassandra said, turning to Meg. "Go to Ariane. Lay your hand upon the cloth Serena wove."

With a questioning glance, Meg did so.

Nothing happened.

"Now your husband," Cassandra said.

As Meg withdrew, Dominic went to the bed

and touched the fabric.

"Strange stuff," he muttered. "I can't say I like the feel of it at all."

"Step back," Cassandra said.

She placed her own hand on the fabric. After the space of four breaths, she moved away.

Throughout it all, Ariane continued to whimper and thrash restlessly. Scarlet burned along her cheekbones, telling of fever's fires rising within.

"Simon," Cassandra said.

Reluctantly, Simon stepped forward and touched the fabric.

As always, the texture pleased him. It was like Ariane's kiss, never the same twice, changing even while he savored it. The look of the fabric itself was also endlessly intriguing, as though brilliant shadows of amethyst and violet and ebony had been threaded through, creating pictures that shifted with each breath, each moment.

A woman of intense feeling, head thrown back, hair wild, lips open upon a cry of unbelievable pleasure.

The enchanted.

A warrior both disciplined and passionate, his whole being focused in the moment.

The enchanter.

Now he was bending down to her, drinking her cries . . .

"Do you see now?" Cassandra asked Dominic.

The sound of Cassandra's voice sent a shudder ripping through Simon. Raw yearning twisted within him.

He felt as though he had almost touched something that could be neither weighed nor measured nor seen.

Nor touched.

"Aye," Dominic said. "Ariane rests now. Is it a Learned thing?"

"Not really," Cassandra said. "It is an aspect of some Silverfells clan weavings. Each is different. Each becomes more different as it is worn. It simply . . . *is*."

Dominic rubbed his nose thoughtfully, then turned to his brother.

"You will stay with Ariane," Dominic said.

Simon opened his mouth to protest, but the Glendruid Wolf was still talking.

"As soon as it is safe to travel, bring your wife to Blackthorne Keep."

"What if winter keeps us here?" Simon asked.

"So be it. Baron Deguerre's daughter is more important than having one more knight at Blackthorne, even a knight such as you. Unless . . ."

Dominic's voice died as he turned to look at his wife.

"Unless you dream of greater danger, small falcon. Then I will reconsider Simon's value to Blackthorne Keep."

15

Cool water soothed Ariane's dry lips and poured gently over her parched tongue. She swallowed eagerly. When no more liquid came to her mouth, she tried to lift herself toward the source of the water.

Liquid overflowed Ariane's lips and down her chin to her neck. Something warm and velvety ran over her skin, following the trail of the water.

"Gently, nightingale."

With the words came a warm exhalation in the hollow of Ariane's throat. Where drops of water had collected, the soft velvet brushed again, taking away the liquid.

Thirst combined with a need to be closer to the gentle voice made her whimper and strain toward the words.

"There is no need to fear. Neither the water nor I will leave you."

A hand stroked Ariane from crown to nape with slow, tender motions, reassuring her. Sighing raggedly, she turned toward the source of comfort. Her lips skimmed across something both hard and warm, slightly rough and wonderfully reassuring at the same time. At a distance she realized it was a hand.

A man's hand.

Ariane tried to stiffen and pull away, but her body simply refused to obey the alarms of her awakening mind.

"Softly, nightingale. Your wound is still healing. Lie still. You are safe."

Ariane sighed and turned her face once more into the large male hand that was being used not to hurt her, but rather to soothe her fears.

"Open your lips," Simon whispered. " 'Tis water you need, and then gruel, and then tiny bits of minced meat and honey, and —"

With an effort, Simon stopped the rushing words. He wanted Ariane to be well with an urgency that grew greater with each hour. The nine days he had spent caring for her had been the longest of his life.

'Tis savage enough that Dominic suffered torment because of my lust for Marie. But at least Dominic was a knight fully trained for pain and blood.

'Tis unbearable that my melancholy nightingale lies wounded and in pain because of me.

"Why didn't you flee when I gave you the chance?" Simon whispered.

No answer came from Ariane's pale lips

except a kiss breathed into the center of his palm.

Awake, she fears me.

Asleep, she kisses me.

Simon closed his eyes as the simple caress sank to the marrow of his bones and then deeper still, spreading through his soul like quicksilver ripples through black water.

After a time Simon sipped from a cup, bent down to Ariane, and once again allowed a few drops to pass from his lips to hers. It was a method of giving liquid medicine that he had first seen used by Meg on Dominic. Meg's patient, persistent attempts to get water within Dominic had saved his life.

It was working on Ariane, too. Though she wasn't truly awake, her body knew what it needed. Her mouth opened. Her tongue came out to lick up the wonderful moisture that had appeared on her lips. A few more drops flowed over her tongue in reward. She swallowed and lifted herself greedily, wanting more.

This time Simon was prepared. Nothing spilled from Ariane's lips to her throat. He caught his wife's mouth beneath his own and trickled water over her tongue. She drank from him thirstily again and again, until the cup of medicine was empty. Then she sighed and relaxed once more.

But like the amethyst cloth swirling around Ariane's body, she clung to the warmth and vitality that was Simon.

He looked at the pale fingers woven through his own much stronger fingers and felt an odd tightness in his throat. Tenderly he lifted their entwined hands, kissed Ariane's cool skin, and resumed stroking her hair with his free hand.

Gradually Simon became aware that someone had come into the room and was standing patiently behind him. The fragrance of incense cedar told him that it was Cassandra who had come so quietly into Ariane's room.

It wasn't the first time that the Learned healer had come to stand vigil near her patient. While Cassandra had been adamant that it must be Simon who nursed Ariane, an hour rarely passed during the day when Cassandra didn't look in.

"The balm I brought three days ago," the Learned woman said, "have you used it?"

"Aye."

"And?"

"She seems . . ." Simon hesitated.

"What?" asked Cassandra sharply.

"She seems almost to enjoy it."

Cassandra's grey eyes gleamed. "Excellent. And you?"

"I?"

"Does the balm please you as well?"

Simon gave the healer a sideways glance.

Cassandra simply waited, saying nothing.

"Aye, it pleases me," Simon said, "if that matters."

The Learned woman tilted her head and smiled. "It matters, Simon."

"Why?"

"The balm was exactly blended to enhance all that is Ariane."

"Midnight, moonrise, roses, a storm," Simon said, looking back at his wife. "Ariane."

"Has she awakened?" Cassandra asked.

"Almost."

Cassandra went to the bed, watched Ariane for a moment, then shook her head slowly.

"She won't fully awaken this day, nor even on the morrow," the Learned woman said.

"In the past two days, she follows my touch as though more awake than asleep. Sometimes I almost believe she understands my words."

"She may."

Simon gave the Learned woman a quick glance.

" 'Tis the balm," Cassandra said simply. "It reaches past what we know of the world to another place, a place where waking and sleeping are combined. It is a special kind of dreaming."

"I don't understand."

Cassandra almost smiled. "Ariane will awaken feeling as though she has dreamed deeply. And within the dream, she will also feel deeply. As will you."

"Will she feel pain?" Simon asked sharply.

"Nay, unless you intend it."

"Never. She has suffered enough on my behalf." Simon hesitated. "Will she remember aught else?"

"Such as?"

"Disgust at my touch," he said bluntly.

"Are you disgusted to be touching her?" Cassandra asked.

"No."

"Does she seem to draw away when you touch her?"

"She draws closer."

"Excellent," Cassandra said succinctly. "She progresses."

Simon stroked Ariane's long, loose hair in silence for a time. As had happened before, she turned her face toward him, taking ease from his touch.

"Will Ariane remember what she dreamed when she awakens?" Simon asked.

"Very few do. Healing dreams are . . ." Cassandra shrugged. "Such dreams are very different from ordinary sleep."

When Cassandra turned away to stoke the

fire, Simon picked up the herbs she had brought with her. He sniffed each packet carefully. When he was satisfied that the correct medicine lay within, he rubbed a bit of each herb delicately between thumb and forefinger, sniffed, tasted, waited for five breaths, and then either accepted or rejected the mix.

"The yarrow is a bit musty," Simon said at one point.

"You have a very keen nose. I have sent for more yarrow. Until it comes, 'tis better to have some a bit musty than none at all."

Simon's mouth drew down at one corner, but he said nothing. He mixed some of the herbs into water that had been heated on the brazier. Under Cassandra's watchful eyes, he picked up a mortar and pestle, added various herbs, and ground them to dust with efficient, powerful strokes. The resulting powder was worked into a pungent salve.

Throughout the room, the smell of the fires in the brazier and hearth gave way to the complex interplay of medicinal herbs and fragrant balm. Simon's nostrils flared subtly, testing the salve for any false or overly potent scent. He rubbed some of the balm on the tender skin inside his wrist and waited.

No burning arose. No itching. Nothing to suggest that the salve would do anything except what it was supposed to do. Heal.

"You are very careful of your unwanted wife," Cassandra said after a time.

Simon threw her a black, slanting glance and said nothing.

"Many men in your position would have been happy enough to make a token effort and then flee," the Learned woman added.

"I am not a coward, madam."

Though soft, the words cut like an ice-tipped wind.

"Your bravery is well-known," Cassandra said calmly. "No man would have raised a question if you had failed to save your wife from the rogue knight who had slain better-armed and more numerous enemies than you."

"Is there a point to this?" Simon asked in a low, impatient voice.

"Simple curiosity."

"There is nothing simple about Learned curiosity."

The tone of Simon's voice penetrated Ariane's hazy awareness. She turned restlessly. Her fingers tightened on his hand as though afraid he would withdraw.

"Exercise your curiosity elsewhere," Simon said softly. "You are disturbing my wife."

"As you wish, healer. But remember, all of Ariane's skin must know the healing kiss of the balm. Every bit."

Cassandra was out of the door before Simon realized what she had called him.

Healer.

Broodingly he looked down at Ariane's wan face.

If only it were that easy.

If only I could heal her body with a handful of herbs and a soothing touch.

Then perhaps I could heal my dark nightingale's soul as well.

Or my own soul. Equally dark.

Unbidden, unwanted, Dominic's words echoed in Simon's mind.

Like me, you left all warmth in the Saracen land. . . . Who will bring warmth to you if you marry Ariane?

Ariane made a low noise, as though protesting something only she could understand.

The sound brought Simon out of his bleak thoughts. What was past was irretrievable. What remained had to be lived with, whether sweet or bitter, savory or sour, fire or ice.

Abruptly Simon turned away from his sleeping wife. Despite her muted, unknowing protests, he slid his hand from hers and began the cleansing ritual that Meg had insisted he learn before she left with Dominic for Blackthorne Keep.

With deft, gentle hands that smelled of medicinal soap, Simon partially undid the silver laces on Ariane's dress and eased amethyst fabric from her shoulders. As he handled the dress, he no longer questioned Cassandra's edict that Serena's weaving remain against Ariane's skin. He had seen for himself that she rested more easily when wrapped in the cloth.

And when Simon was touching her, she rested most deeply of all.

When she is truly well, will she trust me enough to let me touch her as a husband rather than a healer?

The unexpected thought made Simon's hands stop in mid-movement. Violet cloth and cool silver laces slid from his motionless fingers.

The bodice of Ariane's dress fell away. Flickering fire from the brazier cast shadows of light and darkness over her smooth breasts. The ripples of shadow and firelight made her breasts look as though they were being stroked by immaterial fingers.

And as though stroked, her nipples became taut.

"Nightingale," Simon whispered.

Ariane's head moved restlessly. Her breasts shifted with subtle, enticing movements, as though asking to be admired by Simon's eyes, his hands, his mouth.

With a silent curse, Simon closed his eyes. He had undressed Ariane thrice daily for nine days, and despite the beautiful temptation of her body, never once had he touched her in any way other than as a healer. But now . . .

Now he wanted to be the light on her breasts, caressing her in shades of dusk and fire.

Now he wanted to take the weight of her breasts in his palms while his thumbs flicked her nipples into full pink buds.

Now he wanted to curl his tongue around those buds and draw her into his mouth.

And then he wanted more. Much more.

He wanted things he could neither name nor describe. He wanted to burn as the phoenix burned, and know what the phoenix knew as it rose from the flames only to return again and then again, feeling the ecstatic fire burn all the way through to his soul.

A low sound was dragged from deep within Simon. It shocked him, but not as much as the violence of his need for Ariane's unwilling body. He was full to bursting, hard as a battle sword, and burning as though fresh from the forge.

"God's teeth," he hissed beneath his breath. "Does Cassandra think I'm a eunuch not to lust for the very flesh I am supposed to heal? Seeing Ariane's breasts in the firelight . . . 'tis like having hot coals spilled between my legs!"

Shaken by his own sudden lack of control,

Simon clenched his hands into fists, squeezing the amethyst cloth between his fingers until his arms ached.

After too long a time for his own comfort, Simon could breathe without feeling as though it were flames rather than air he was taking into his lungs. Slowly he released Ariane's dress and began unwinding from around her ribs the strip of violet cloth that was acting as both binding and bandage.

The wound was a thin scarlet line centered between two ribs. Already the skin had knitted back together as though never sliced by a renegade's dagger. The flesh around the wound was warm but not hot, flushed with the pink of healing rather than with the livid red of a wound gone to deadly fever.

" 'Tis worth putting up with Learned and Glendruid witchery combined to see you healing so cleanly," Simon murmured to Ariane. "When I saw that dagger go into you . . ."

His voice faded to a raspy sound. He had relived that moment many times; seeing the savage gleam of steel, knowing that her tender flesh was no match for the blade, feeling the sickening certainty that he could not reach her in time to save her.

And he hadn't. She had fallen even as he screamed her name. She hadn't answered his cry then.

She still hadn't answered him.

Ariane.

But now Simon's cry went no farther than the turmoil of his soul, where Ariane's wounding had become another raw scar lying next to the still-livid scar that had come when Dominic paid for the sins of his brother.

Slowly Simon reached for the pan of medicinal water that had been warming near the brazier. He squeezed out a small cloth and began to wash Ariane with great gentleness. As he worked from her face to her breasts, he did his best to ignore the warm rush of Ariane's breath and the even warmer brush of her breasts against his hand with each motion of the cloth.

He was more successful with the bathing than with the ignoring.

It had been easier not to see Ariane's sensual appeal when her body was flushed with illness or chill with the aftermath of fever. Then he could think of her not as a girl whose aloof, dark beauty had set his body on fire from the first time he had seen her, but as flesh that needed to be washed and dried and salved, and then wrapped up once more against the autumn cold.

But the very feel of Ariane was different tonight. After she had taken the last of the medicine from his lips, she had changed.

There was no subtle slackness in her body, as though all her strength were being spent in surviving an outlaw's dagger. Though still unnaturally calm, her mind and body were throwing off the drugs and medicines that had held her in a healing thrall.

The elegant line of Ariane's waist and hips had changed subtly, vibrantly. It was as though she were giving herself to his touch while he bathed her, transforming the bath from a cleansing ritual into something far more sensual.

Now her torso sang with a siren's call to Simon, as did the long curves of her legs while he washed her. The lush thicket of her femininity made his breath wedge deep in his chest. He forced himself to look away from the midnight triangle, else his touch change from healing to loving.

'Tis foolish! I am not a green squire to stare as though I have never seen a woman's soft cleft.

Simon took a deep breath and finished his work quickly, forcing himself to think of her as a patient.

Even so, Simon decided to forego rubbing scented salve into Ariane's skin from her delicate toes to her graceful nape. The ointment smelled too sensuous to be a medicine in any case, though Cassandra had insisted it was necessary for Ariane's cure.

Abruptly Simon began drawing the amethyst dress back up Ariane's legs. Yet no matter how quickly he moved, how little he touched her, she felt different to his hands. Her limbs were more alive. More vital.

Inviting.

She was flushed with the kind of womanly fever that knew only one cure.

"God's teeth," Simon hissed. "What is wrong with me to lust after a girl who is in no condition to say aye or nay?"

Ariane is my wife.

"She isn't well," he muttered, pulling the dress up Ariane's hips with unusual urgency.

Her body follows my touch like a flower follows the sun.

"She isn't awake!"

Her body is awakened. I can sense it. I can feel it. Were I to bathe her softness with my tongue, I could taste it.

The thought sent a bolt of raw sensation through Simon, followed by a temptation so strong that it shook his body the way thunder shakes the ground.

Simon quit arguing with himself and concentrated on covering as much as possible of Ariane before he rubbed salve into her tender wound. But the dress's long, flowing sleeves seemed to have a mind of their own. They tangled. They twisted. They were as elusive as smoke. They frustrated every approach.

And each time Simon lifted Ariane a different way in order to work on the sleeves, her breasts swayed and brushed over his arms, his hands. Once, his cheek knew her warmth and softness.

She smiled dreamily at the caress.

Blistering Saracen phrases whispered through the still room. Simon released Ariane, picked up a sleeve and eyed it as he would an ill-trained hound.

The fabric curled softly around his fingers and breathed a subtle perfume into his nostrils, moonrise and wild roses and a hint of storm.

Ariane's scent.

The scent of the very balm Simon didn't trust himself to rub into her changed flesh.

The balm that Cassandra insisted was vital for Ariane's full recovery.

Closing his eyes, Simon groaned too softly for anyone to hear, even himself. Slowly his clenched fingers opened. The amethyst fabric slid from his grasp with a sound like a sigh.

He picked up one of the small pots that were arrayed on a chest near Ariane's bed. The odor of the balm was astringent, bracing, brisk.

Medicinal not passionate.

Rather grimly Simon dabbed his index finger in the balm and began applying it with care to the scarlet scar between Ariane's ribs. She lay very still, breathing softly, not quite asleep. A slight smile made her so beautiful that he felt a hand squeeze his heart.

Your body wants me, nightingale.

It has wanted me from the first, when you were Duncan's betrothed.

And you fought that wanting as hard as I did.

Fight no more. You are no longer betrothed to another. I am your husband. You are my wife.

Your smile ravishes my soul.

Just as Simon lifted his hand from Ariane's wound, she turned on her side toward him. His fingers were caught in a sensuous vise between her breasts.

Heat flushed Simon from his forehead to his heels, but most of all he burned where erect flesh strained against his breeches. He counted his heartbeat in aching pulses that surged against restraining cloth.

With a long, hissing breath, Simon forced himself to withdraw from the sweet vise. As he retreated, his fingertips brushed one of Ariane's nipples. It drew taut.

"God's blood, 'tis too much," Simon groaned through his teeth.

He told himself that he must stand up and leave Ariane. He meant to do just that. But the wretched sleeves had fallen across his lap, chaining him.

Simon reached for the pot of scented ointment that Cassandra had blended just for Ariane. The pot felt warm, smooth, the size and weight of a breast nestled against his palm.

The scent of roses and storm drifted into the room as Simon opened the pot. He inhaled deeply, taking into himself the perfume that, like the dress, enhanced rather than concealed the essence of Ariane.

Slowly Simon dipped his fingertips into the balm. It was warm, creamy, sleek, infused with all that was feminine.

And it burned like desire.

16

For nine days Simon had been tending Ariane as though she were a babe. For nine days he had told himself that he didn't see the feminine allure of her breasts and hips. That he didn't take a purely sensual pleasure in smoothing ointment into every bit of her skin. That he didn't want to be like the balm, sinking into her very flesh, becoming part of it.

For nine days he had lied.

God's aching teeth!

What was Cassandra thinking of when she ordered me to rub scented cream over every inch of Ariane? Am I made of stone not to burn with passion?

Ariane turned her head from side to side, sending gleaming coils of black hair sliding over her breasts. Her hands moved languidly, yet almost impatiently, questing for . . . something.

"Ariane," Simon said in a low voice.

Her head turned as though in response, yet her eyes were closed. Deliberately Simon brushed the back of his fingers over her cheek.

Her hand lifted, holding his fingers against her face.

She turned even more toward him, plainly accepting his touch.

Nay. Wanting it.

Demanding it.

"I wish I dared awaken you," Simon whispered.

But that had been specifically forbidden by Cassandra. She had said that when Ariane was healed she would throw off the effects of the medicines. Until then, she would sleep. Rushing her awakening would only delay the healing.

When Simon began applying balm, the warmth of Ariane's breath flowed over him. He told himself he was doing nothing different, nothing new, certainly nothing sensual . . .

Yet he couldn't help noticing as though for the first time the winged grace of Ariane's eyebrows. The black fringe of her lashes was so long that it rested against her skin. Her nose was a clean, straight line with delicately arched nostrils. Her cheekbones tempted his fingertips, as did the hollows beneath where shadows of firelight played.

The scent of the balm curled upward, increased by the warmth of Ariane's body. The perfume caressed Simon invisibly with every touch of his skin against hers. He drew the scent deep into his lungs while sensual heat burned from his navel to his knees.

He let out his breath and lightly stroked the violet cloth that concealed Ariane's hips and legs. The fabric slid aside with the ease of water flowing, leaving Ariane naked.

Careful not to jar her, Simon lifted Ariane and turned her onto her unwounded side. He told himself that his hands hadn't lingered on the swell of her hip. Nor had he molded his palm to her leg and curled his fingertips around to skim the lush darkness that lay concealed between her thighs.

A stifled sound came from Simon as the sword between his legs grew more adamant to be sheathed. It was as if he had never touched a woman before, never known the heady scent of a woman's desire, never parted soft, perfumed lips and delved between to the very heart of desire.

Abruptly Simon jerked back his hands as though he had been holding them too close to flame.

This is madness.

Neither Simon's reasoning side nor his unruly, passionate one disagreed with his conclusion.

He closed his eyes and dipped his fingertips into the small pot of balm. Slowly he began stroking balm down Ariane's back. When he reached the flare of her buttocks, he hesitated.

Ariane's long legs moved restlessly. The motion brought her hip up against the palm of Simon's hand.

His fingers flexed in sensual answer, testing the resilience of her flesh. When he realized what he had done, he froze, afraid that he had disturbed Ariane's healing sleep. After several breaths, he slowly relaxed. Ariane hadn't awakened.

Nor had she moved away from the long fingers cupping her hip.

Slowly Simon lifted his hand. He dipped up more balm and followed the line of Ariane's spine to its base. Without truly intending to, he skimmed over the shadow cleft beyond.

Fire licked up his fingertips and shot through his arm, sending a surge of heat through his loins. Reluctantly he removed his hand while he could still trust himself to do so.

Simon wanted to give more to Ariane than a caress that ended almost before it began. He wanted to follow the curve of her bottom all the way around, until his palm was pressed between her thighs, snug against her softness while his fingers penetrated her sleek, scented heat.

Then he would retreat slowly, drawing her moisture with him, letting it wash against his palm until he slid into her again, penetrating

251

her deeply, withdrawing, spreading the scent of her desire until it clung to both of them like heat to fire.

I cannot. She isn't awake.

But I am.

Sweet Jesus, I am on fire.

Simon would have cursed, but hadn't the breath. He felt both potent and immensely alive, blood pouring through him in powerful waves, making him even harder than before.

A deep, almost soundless groan threaded between Simon's clenched teeth. Carefully thinking of nothing at all, he rubbed the scented ointment down the curving length of Ariane's legs and into the finely wrought arch of her feet.

Sighing, Ariane turned onto her back as though her body had memorized the routine of balm and stroking. As she turned, long black hair fanned across her breasts and belly. The faintly curling ends of her hair caught and held on the triangle of thicker, more curly hair that protected her most feminine flesh.

As though entranced, Simon reached out and slowly, very slowly, separated the two shades of midnight that were Ariane's hair. The temptation also to part the black triangle with just one fingertip and seek the heat beneath was so great that Simon's hand shook.

I must not.

Yet as quickly as he told himself it was wrong, another part of himself rebelled.

Why? Look at her shifting, sighing, wanting. Look at her breasts swelling in hope of my touch, her nipples drawing taut, needing to be stroked.

Rather grimly, Simon silenced his inner argument by dipping his fingertips into the creamy ointment. He massaged it into Ariane's shoulders, her arms, her hands, until nothing above her collarbones remained untouched.

Wishing that he were finished with the maddening duty — and simultaneously glad that he wasn't — Simon probed deeply in the pot, scooping up more balm. He rubbed the ointment over his palms and began speedily to complete his task.

Ariane's breasts were fuller than Simon remembered, vibrant, taut. Even when he closed his eyes, he could see the image of her burned against his eyelids. Her skin was as fine-grained and pale as a sultan's most prized pearl. The tips of her breasts were tight pink buds waiting only for the dewy moisture of his tongue to complete their perfection.

Without knowing, without thinking, Simon lowered his head to Ariane. Her breasts knew the caress of his forehead, his cheek, his lips. Then his mouth parted and his tongue touched one delicate bud.

She tasted of roses.

With a soundless groan Simon traced the tip of Ariane's breast, savoring her heat and changing textures with his tongue.

"Silk," he whispered, drawing his tongue over the pale swell of her breast.

Ariane murmured and shifted. The motion brought an erect nipple against his lips.

"Velvet," he breathed, tasting lightly.

She arched as though caught within a sensual dream. Her taut, pink nipple rubbed along his lips.

"I cannot bear it," Simon said in a low voice.

He took Ariane into his mouth and loved her as he had wanted to do since the first moment he had seen her standing proud and frightened, waiting for a man she had never met to claim her body for his bed and her womb for his heirs.

The sultry pleasure of Simon's mouth quickened Ariane's heartbeat. With a dreamy murmur, she drew up one knee.

Or had his hand slid beneath her knee, raising and opening her as a lover would?

No. I am a healer, not a lover.

Then I should heal her. All of her.

But —

The passionate part of Simon overrode the caution he had learned at such great cost.

Isn't that what Cassandra said? Every bit of

Ariane's skin must know the healing kiss of the balm.

That was true enough. Cassandra had repeated the warning more than once, as though the balm were the most important part of the healing ritual.

Can I trust myself to touch her so intimately?
And not take her.
Merciful God. Is it possible?

Simon closed his eyes and forced himself not to move, for he couldn't say whether his next motion would have been toward or away from Ariane.

And if it were toward, he wasn't certain where healing would stop and loving would begin.

"Nightingale," Simon said in a ragged voice. "If only you were awake."

Ariane made a low, anxious sound. The line of her body became less relaxed. Her legs moved restlessly, as though she were trying to run after something but found herself hopelessly mired. One arm thrashed out, bumping into Simon's thigh.

As soon as she felt his muscular presence, she let out a long breath and became calmer. Very shortly her hand relaxed and slid from his thigh to the bed cover, but the back of her fingers remained pressed against him.

Nor was the contact accidental, for when

Simon eased away, Ariane's hand soon sought out the timeless reassurance of flesh against flesh.

His flesh.

Her desire.

"Was I right about that, nightingale?" Simon whispered. "Did you look at me with more favor and less disgust than you looked at other men?"

No answer came save that of Ariane's hand pressed against Simon's thigh.

"And desire," he said, bending down to Ariane once more. "Did I see it in you? Did I taste it in your kisses?"

Simon ran his strong hands down Ariane's body from breasts to the dark triangle he wanted more than he wanted to breathe. The perfume of balm spread in the wake of his palms.

"When you first saw me, your eyes widened," Simon said. "Was that less than a month ago? By the saints, it seems a lifetime. You belonged to another, then. I could scarcely allow myself to look at you."

Simon's palm shaped the back of Ariane's flexed leg, massaging in balm and revealing more of her beauty with every slow pressure of his hand.

"The setting sun struck amethyst fire from your eyes," he whispered. "And your mouth

. . . Dear God, the sight of your tongue sliding along your lower lip nearly made me spill my seed."

A shudder ripped through Simon as he remembered. And remembering, he pressed small kisses beneath Ariane's breasts, over her belly, lingering to test the sweet dimple of her navel with his tongue.

"I didn't want to desire any woman," Simon whispered. "Not like this. Not like a brand burning below my belly."

Simon's warm breath washed over Ariane's skin while his hands and mouth continued caressing her, healer and lover combined.

"I saw the quickening of your pulse whenever I approached. It could have been fear, but whenever you thought I wouldn't know, you *watched* me."

His hand slid down Ariane's body until at last he felt the dense, sensuous triangle of hair pressing against his palm. He rubbed as delicately as a sigh, teasing the seductive mound whose heat rose to meet him. A low sound came from Ariane, half moan, half whimper.

And she moved toward Simon's touch, not away.

His own breath became a groan. He wanted to wake her, to take her, to watch her eyes shimmer with passion as he sheathed himself deep within her body. He felt as though he had wanted that all of his life.

Simon dipped his fingers into the balm one last time. With great care he rubbed the creamy mixture from Ariane's navel to her thighs. Her leg flexed more deeply. The motion caused her hips to lift just a little.

It was enough. Simon's fingertips skimmed the secret flesh that was flushed by desire. Ariane made a murmurous sound of pleasure and stretched dreamily, stroking herself against his fingers.

Delicately he drew his fingertips between her thighs, discovering and tracing her sultry softness in the same hushed moments. He sensed the ripple of pleasure radiating through her, heard it in her ragged sigh, saw it in the languid movement of her hips.

"What are your dreams, nightingale?" Simon asked in a soft, rough voice. "Do you want me now the way I wanted you the first time I saw you?"

Very gently, Simon caressed the edges of Ariane's tightly furled petals. The hot, sensuous dew of her response gilded his fingers and made his heartbeat quicken. With exquisite care, he eased a fingertip just between the sultry folds. His touch eased slowly forward, caressing and parting her at the same time.

At the peak of the caress, Simon discovered the hidden pearl. It was sleek, firm, full. When his moist fingertip circled, Ariane sighed brokenly. Her hips moved subtly, luxuriously, as though seeking more.

Simon's hand withdrew until nothing of his body was touching Ariane. She made a protesting sound and turned her head from side to side with a languid restlessness that spoke eloquently of both her desire and the healing thrall of the dream.

It was as Cassandra had said. *Ariane will awaken feeling as though she has dreamed deeply. And within the dream, she will also feel deeply. As will you.*

"What are you feeling, nightingale?" Simon asked huskily. "Is it disgust?"

He ran his fingertips down the inside of Ariane's thigh. She arched up to him as though swimming through heavy liquid. Each movement was slowed to a shadow of her usual quickness. Each small motion was a sensuous reflection of her dreams.

"Nay, it isn't disgust that moves you," Simon whispered. "Is it the heat swelling deep within that drives you? Do you lift to me, knowing it is I who stroke you?"

His fingertips caressed petals that were no longer so tightly furled. They were swollen, hot, and they wept with Ariane's desire.

Simon's breath hissed out as though he were in pain.

"I could test the depth of your heat," he whispered, "but I do not trust myself to be content with the feel of your virginity snug around my finger. It would be too easy to open you more and then still more, until I could press my hungry sword deeply into your sheath."

Closing his eyes, Simon fought the desire that clenched his whole being.

"Do you wonder what it would feel like to look at me and I at you while our hearts hammer and our bodies strain to be locked ever more closely in loving combat?"

Ariane didn't awaken to answer Simon's question, though the flesh beneath his grazing, skimming caresses was an answer in itself.

She was hot, fevered.

Nor was it the dry heat of illness whose presence burned Simon's fingertips. This was the liquid heat of a woman whose hunger had been summoned by a lover's touch.

Simon opened his eyes and measured Ariane's arousal in the slow, voluptuous movements of her hips. The heightened color brought by passion had flushed her lips and nipples deep rose.

Motionless, Simon sat on the bed, fighting himself with every ragged breath he drew, knowing he should get up and leave the enthralled girl who could say neither yes nor no.

But I can choose for her.

The thought was agony.

"Do you want me so deeply inside you that you feel my seed leaping as surely as I do?" Simon asked in a raw whisper.

Ariane's answer was as silent as it was unmistakable. Her body was no longer utterly languid. She was taut, vibrant, open, lush with expectation. The scent of her desire sank into him, setting his mind on fire.

Simon made an anguished sound.

By Christ's blue eyes, what is wrong with me? Why can't I stand up and walk away?

Yet even as the words battered within Simon's mind, the pounding of his own heartbeat overwhelmed them. Not trusting himself to touch Ariane with his hands again, unable to turn away from her sensuous, expectant beauty, he bent down to his wife once more.

Ariane murmured dreamily at the caress of Simon's cheek against her thigh. He breathed deeply, infusing himself with her perfume, immersing himself in the fragrance of passion as though it were a healing thrall.

He kissed the creamy flesh with a languid care that equaled her dreamlike movements. When he sucked lightly, creating a rush of heat beneath her fair skin, she sighed raggedly

and shifted, making a deeper nest for him between her legs.

Heal me.

He whispered her name against her softness
as he tasted the essence of moonlight and roses
and the wild, leashed storm that seethed
dreamily between them, enthralling both.

A slow heat went through Ariane, a burning
that was all the more thorough for its lan-
guorous pace.

I am on fire.

I can taste it.

Yes. Taste me.

Swirling slowly, succumbing wholly to the
sultry thrall, Simon knew only the feel and
taste of Ariane, her heat flushing his skin until
he breathed only pure fragrance and fire.

I burn.

Yes.

Burn with me.

Always.

We are.

Burning.

17

Warily Simon eyed the pot of fresh balm Cassandra was handing to him. He uncapped it and sniffed.

A luxuriant shudder went through him, memory and desire combined.

"Ariane," Simon said huskily.

"Of course," said the Learned woman.

Saying nothing more, Simon put the cap back on the pot with quick, final gestures and turned to Ariane's bed.

"Does the balm displease you?" Cassandra asked.

A ripple of memory and dream entwined cascaded through Simon. He had tried not to think about the past night, when he had awakened half-dressed with his wholly naked wife lying asleep in his arms . . . and the healing fragrance of the balm had risen from his body as much as from hers.

Simon had tried not to think of what had happened between himself and his wife, because it made no sense. It had neither reason nor logic. It could not be weighed or measured, held or examined.

It could not have happened.

I can't have shared her healing.

I can't have felt her burning.

But he could have burned.

He had.

And so had she.

"Thrice," Cassandra said.

Simon started, wondering how she had known.

"What?" he demanded.

"Until Ariane awakens, you must apply the balm three times each day," the Learned woman said patiently.

Despite Cassandra's neutral expression, Simon thought he detected an amused gleam in her quicksilver eyes.

"Aye, you explained that to me several times already," Simon said shortly.

This time he was certain the Learned woman smiled.

"Have you checked her wound this morning?" Cassandra asked.

"Not yet."

Simon's tone was curt. He had no desire to explain that he didn't trust himself to undress his wife again, much less to smooth fragrant, artful balm all over her skin until there was nothing between them but roses and moonlight, a distant storm, and a slow, consuming fire.

He breathed deeply, trying to control the savage response of his body.

Just a dream. 'Tis all.

I fell asleep. And I dreamed.

Sweet God, I pray that I could dream such dreams while still awake!

And Ariane dream with me . . .

With a silent, searing curse, Simon went to the bed and began undressing Ariane. When the last of the dress and bandage fell away, he drew in a swift breath.

The crimson line of the wound had faded to a pale pink. There was not even the faintest shadow of bruising beneath her creamy skin.

"She will awaken soon," Cassandra said with satisfaction. "The healing is almost complete."

"Almost?" Simon asked. "What remains?"

"We will know when she awakens."

With that cryptic comment, Cassandra turned and left the room.

In the silence that followed, the cry of yet another storm came to Simon, muted by thick stone walls. He picked up a pot of medicinal ointment and sat on the bed next to Ariane as he had so many times since she had been wounded.

" 'Tis just as well Meg and Dominic left for Blackthorne days ago," Simon said as he rubbed the pungent salve into what remained of the knife wound. "Despite Meg's determination and spirit, she would have suffered during a cold, stormy ride back home."

Simon spoke aloud as had become his habit during the long days when he sat by Ariane's bedside, waiting for color to come back into her face. He had discovered that the sound of his voice had a calming effect on Ariane.

"Dominic would have been an utter churl by the time we reached Blackthorne Keep," Simon added. "He is very fierce in defense of his small falcon."

Simon smiled slightly, remembering Meg's golden jesses.

"Do you know, I miss the sound of those tiny gold bells. And Meg's laughter. I miss that, too."

From the floor below came the sound of a man's laughter, followed a moment later by a woman's.

"But there is the sound of Duncan's and Amber's laughter to replace Meg's," Simon said. "They drink not a drop, yet they romp like a squire after his first jug of wine."

While Simon spoke, he turned away to rinse the bandage in a pan of water laced with astringent herbs. He wrung out the amethyst cloth, shook it hard, and felt its dry length with an amazement that hadn't lessened in all the days he had cared for Ariane.

"A canny piece of work, as Duncan would say."

Simon looked at the bandage and then at the pale pink scar that lay between Ariane's ribs.

"I think not," he said, setting the bandage aside. "Fresh scars are too tender for even this clever cloth."

No matter the topic, Simon's voice was low and soothing. He had learned while nursing Dominic back to life that a calm voice acted like a tonic to whatever part of a person's mind it was that didn't sleep.

And it soothed Simon, too.

The first thing Ariane understood as she slowly awakened was that she was propped half-upright by strong hands and arms. The touch was as warm and gentle as the fabric that was being smoothed up over her arms.

In a rush of sensation Ariane knew that the cloth was her wedding dress. She also knew that it was Simon's breath and his soft beard brushing against her breasts.

Pleasure cascaded through Ariane. For an instant she wondered if it had been Simon who had brought her the healing, shimmering fire of her dreams.

Nay, that cannot be. 'Tis madness even to think such a thing! I was defenseless. Held in thrall.

I know full well how a man treats a helpless girl.

My nightmares tell me.

The bleak thought quenched the silvery sensations that had made Ariane feel awake in a way she had never known before. Except once, in Simon's arms, when he had kissed her with sensual deliberateness.

I tasted him.

Or did he taste me?

Have we tasted one another?

Fire streaked from Ariane's breasts to her thighs, startling her with its intensity. Disoriented, she closed her eyes, wondering what was wrong with her.

Simon carefully was trying not to look at Ariane's elegant body while he dressed her. Certainly he wasn't looking at the creamy breasts whose tips had drawn up into taut, velvety pink buds at the accidental caress of his cheek.

And he most certainly wasn't remembering the feel and scent and taste of those very breasts.

With grim efficiency, Simon pulled the long, full sleeves into place and began to lace up the front of Ariane's witchy amethyst dress. The instant Simon touched them, the laces seemed to go from pure silver to quicksilver. They became impossible to hold on to, much less to thread through the many tiny embroidered eyelets that reached from Ariane's thighs to the soft hollow of her throat.

"God's teeth," Simon seethed at the laces. "Don't go all stubborn on me now. No matter how delectable her breasts are, they must be covered."

A lace slipped from Simon's hand to the creamy skin of Ariane's abdomen. For a moment the lace nestled against the triangle of midnight hair that peeked through the front opening in the dress. Before Simon could retrieve the lace, it shifted and slid away like bright water, vanishing between Ariane's legs.

The feel of Simon's fingers probing between her thighs brought Ariane bolt upright. Nightmare exploded.

"Nay!" she said hoarsely, clawing at Simon's wrist. "Only a beast would use a helpless woman so!"

Simon's head snapped up. Ariane's wild amethyst eyes stared right through him, but it wasn't her eyes he saw; it was the fear and revulsion on her face.

And what else did I expect — a miracle? Simon asked himself sardonically. *She is what she was before she was wounded.*

Cold.

"Good morning, wife," Simon said. "I trust that nine days of sleep has refreshed you?"

The chill in Simon's voice poured over Ariane like a basin of water fresh from the well. She drew another ragged breath and focused on her husband instead of her dream.

"If you will take your fingernails out of my wrist," Simon said, "I will resume dressing you. Or is it that you like having me snugged up close to your warm nest?"

As he spoke, Simon deliberately flexed his hand, pressing his fingers against Ariane, caressing the soft petals whose every contour he had learned with lips and teeth and tongue.

Did I dream that?

Could I have?

Ariane's breath came in with a gasp as conflicting feelings shuddered through her. The first was frank fear. The second was an equally frank pleasure.

And the second was even more frightening than the first.

"Please," she whispered brokenly. "Don't. I can't — I can't bear it."

Disgust with himself rose like bile in Simon's throat. He jerked his hand free of its soft confinement.

"Then kindly retrieve your own lace, madam," he said through his teeth.

Ariane gave him a bewildered look.

"Your silver lace," he said curtly. "I was fastening your dress when the cursed thing slipped free."

Ariane looked down. The front of her dress was undone all the way to her thighs. Except for folds of amethyst cloth that revealed more than they concealed, she was quite naked.

"My undergarments . . ." Ariane's voice dried up.

Simon waited for her to finish.

Licking her dry lips, Ariane tried again.

"I have nothing on but my dress," she said huskily.

"I am well aware of that."

And of much more besides. God's wounds, how can a girl whose body is so plainly made for passion draw back in disgust from it?

Or perhaps, despite her protests, it is I who disgust her, not passion.

Aye. That must be the truth. No girl who was repelled by passion itself could have responded as she did last night.

A dream.

Just a dream.

Ariane flushed from her breasts to her forehead as she looked down at her own near nudity.

"I usually wear . . ."

Her voice frayed. She licked her dry lips again.

The sight of Ariane's elegant pink tongue could not have been more arousing to Simon if it had been his own aching flesh that was being licked.

"God blind me!" Simon said savagely.

He surged to his feet, poured a cup of water from the ewer on the chest, and stalked back to the bed.

"Drink this," Simon said. "If you lick your lips any more you'll make them raw."

Ariane lifted trembling fingers to the mug. Simon took one look and waved her hands aside.

"You have less strength than a kitten," he muttered. "Here."

Simon held the mug against Ariane's lips and tilted it. Very quickly she choked and water spilled in cool silver streams down her chin.

"By the Cross," cursed Simon, lowering the cup. "It was easier when you were senseless."

"What —" Ariane coughed and cleared her throat. "What do you mean?"

"When you were senseless, I fed you from my own lips."

Ariane's mouth dropped open. "I beg your pardon?"

Simon drank from the cup, bent to Ariane, and fed her the water as he had so many times when she lay in thrall to Learned healing.

The giving of water was so swiftly done that Ariane had no time to object. And even if she wanted to object, she had to swallow before she spoke.

"More?" Simon asked, holding the mug to his lips.

Again Ariane's mouth opened in amazement as she understood just how Simon had cared for her.

Again he sipped and again leaned down to her mouth.

She watched him with dazed amethyst eyes. The sight of him bending down to her sent odd sensations cascading through her body.

She swallowed convulsively.

"You do that so . . . casually," Ariane said.

"I have had near ten days to become adept at nursing you," Simon said.

Ariane's mouth opened again. She closed it hastily when Simon raised the mug once more.

"You?" she whispered. "You tended me?"

He nodded.

"Why?" she asked.

"Cassandra required it."

Ariane blinked.

"Cassandra," Ariane repeated slowly, as though she had never heard the name. "Why in the name of all that is holy did she require that?"

"Why does a Learned one do anything?" Simon retorted. "And while we're asking questions, why in the name of God didn't you gallop for the keep when you had a chance?"

"The keep?"

"When the renegade knights attacked."

Suddenly it all came back to Ariane — the shout from Simon, the attacking knights, and the realization that he was going to stand and defend her when he could have outrun them quite easily.

"You stayed," she said simply.

"What?"

"You defended me when you would have been better served if you let the renegades have me."

"What kind of a beast do you think I am?" Simon asked in an icy tone.

Then, remembering his response to the enthralling sensuality of the balm, Simon went pale.

"I may be a beast when it comes to matters of the bedchamber," he said tonelessly, "but I am not a craven to leave a girl to be torn apart by marauding bastards dressed as knights."

"Simon," Ariane whispered, knowing she had wounded him without meaning to.

He looked at the elegant fingers placed in silent plea on his forearm.

"Simon, the Loyal," Ariane said in a shaking voice. "You stayed, though you knew it would cost your life. You stayed, when many another man would have betrayed me."

Simon's breath locked in his throat as he

looked deep into Ariane's shadowed amethyst eyes.

"Very few men would have turned their back on you," Simon said. "And no knight would have done such a craven thing."

Ariane's smile was as bleak as her experience of men.

"You are wrong, Simon. In the ways of betrayal, I am wiser than you. I have never known a man — knight or common serf — who would put my well-being above his own pleasure."

"Ariane, the Betrayed," Simon whispered. "Who was it, nightingale? Who betrayed you, and how?"

Ariane didn't acknowledge Simon's words. Instead, she tried to explain something to him that she herself was just now understanding.

"When I saw you standing across the trail, I thought instantly that your horse was speedy enough to carry you to safety."

"Your mare wasn't fleet."

"Aye. Thus you stood across the trail, prepared to spend your life so that I might live."

"I stood prepared to kill renegades."

"Who were armored and riding war-horses and outnumbered you five to —"

"You should have run when I told you to," Simon said, cutting across Ariane's words.

"Nay!" she cried, leaning toward him. "I

would rather have died than have lived a single day knowing that I had betrayed the very man who had been loyal to me!"

Simon looked at Ariane's flushed face and blazing eyes and wanted nothing so much as to taste the emotion that was visibly running through her blood.

"Yet you flinch from my touch," he said.

Ariane closed her eyes.

"It isn't *you,* Simon. It is something that once happened."

"Was it my doing?"

She shook her head. Strands of loose black hair slid forward, concealing all but a bit of the pale skin that showed through her unlaced dress.

"I . . ." Her voice cracked.

Simon put his hand gently over Ariane's. Instead of pulling away, she twined her fingers in his and held on with a power that was surprising in a girl who looked so slender.

"Once," Ariane whispered, "the daughter of a baron was fostered in a noble house. She was closer to me than a sister, young, naive . . ."

Ariane swallowed convulsively and closed her eyes.

Simon kissed the pale fingers that were clenched around his own.

"She was to wed a certain knight," Ariane

said hoarsely. "But her father found a better match for her, and the knight . . ."

Ariane dragged breath into her aching lungs. Tremors shook her body as though she were a leaf in the wind.

"Nightingale," Simon said. "You can tell me when you're stronger."

"Nay," she said fiercely. "If I don't tell you now, I'll lack the courage later."

"No girl who gallops bare-handed into combat with armed knights lacks courage of any kind. Good sense, perhaps, but not courage."

"That was easier to do than this."

The clenched tightness of Ariane's body radiated through to Simon.

"The spurned knight," Ariane said in a rush, "decided that if he deflowered the girl, the other knight wouldn't have her. So he forced himself on her. Then he went to her father, said that *she* had seduced him but he would be noble and marry her."

Simon said something savage under his breath.

"The father went to the girl's room and found her naked in bed, the blood of her lost virginity and more besides still drying on her legs, and he didn't believe her cries of innocence. He called her a whore and a wanton and turned his back on her."

"She told you this?" Simon asked softly. "She?"

"The girl."

Ariane took a wrenching, shuddering breath.

"Aye," Ariane said. "She told me all of it, each cruel and disgusting thing the knight did to her."

"And you've been afraid of the marriage bed ever since."

Ariane shuddered convulsively. "I bathed her afterward, when no one else would soil their hands touching her."

Simon took a swift, audible breath. He had seen enough of war and rapine to know what must have greeted Ariane's innocent eyes when she washed her friend.

"I bathed her, and I knew what it was like to plead for mercy and yet have your legs yanked apart and a man hammering into you, tearing at you, hammering and hammering while he slobbered and —"

Simon's hand came over Ariane's mouth, stopping the words that were like knives sinking into both of them.

"Hush, nightingale," he whispered. "It would not be like that between us. Never. I would sooner die than take you while you fought me and begged for mercy."

Ariane looked into Simon's dark eyes and

found herself hoping that he spoke the truth.

Though she knew it was foolish to hope. And yet . . .

"You fought for me," she whispered.

"You fought for me," he countered.

"You were loyal to me." Ariane drew a shaking breath. "As soon as I am well once more, I will . . ."

Simon waited.

"I will endure the marriage embrace," she whispered. "For you, my loyal knight. Only for you."

"I want more than clenched teeth and duty."

"I will give you all that I have."

Simon closed his eyes. He could ask for no more and he knew it.

But he needed far more.

And he knew that, too.

18

The cobblestones in the bailey of Stone Ring Keep were crisp with frost. White plumes of breath rushed out from the horses standing patiently in the bailey. Erik's lean, tall wolf-hounds lounged near the gate, watching for the signal to leave. Men-at-arms talked loudly among themselves, eating cold meat as each bragged of what would happen were he the one to cross weapons with the renegade knight.

Smells of peat, woodsmoke and baking bread mingled with the earthy scents of field and stable. Small children chased one another through the pack animals, daring the stable boys to catch them. Their shrill voices rose and mingled with the silver breath of the horses whose packs were heavy with gifts from the lord of Stone Ring Keep to Simon and his wife.

Shod hooves rang like hammers against cobblestone when Simon's riderless war-horse pranced into place at the front of the line. Muscular, fierce, glittering with swaths of chain mail, the steel-colored battle stallion was a fearsome sight. A squire walked next to the war-horse, firmly holding the bit.

Suddenly a reckless child took a dare and darted forward. Before he could get close enough to touch the war stallion, a man-at-arms collared the child, shook him by the scruff like a naughty puppy, and sent him chastened back to his friends.

The squire spoke in a low voice and held Shield's bit tightly. The stallion's nostrils flared widely as though testing the air for the smell of danger. Finding none, the war-horse snorted and shook his head, nearly sending the squire flying.

A groom came from the stables leading a sleek, long-legged mount whose color was that of ripe chestnuts. Normally used by Simon for hunting, the horse today was equipped with a small saddle that had been draped in a rich gold fabric. The horse's hooves rang as clearly on the cobbles as any battle stallion's, for Simon had personally overseen the shoeing of Ariane's mount.

Never again would Simon's lady be in danger because her horse lacked speed.

A stir went through the bailey as three people descended the steps of the forebuilding down to the grey cobblestones. A strong, gusting wind tugged at colorful mantles and sent

Ariane's headcloth swirling out from her hair.

The corner of Erik's crimson mantle lifted, revealing the richly embroidered cloth of the lining. A chain mail hauberk gleamed beneath the mantle. His shoulder-length hair burned the color of the autumn sun as he threw back his head to call his falcon from her flight. A clear, uncanny whistle soared from his lips upward into the sky.

The wind gusted again. Ariane's dress rippled and shone like amethyst water, and like water it lapped against Simon's metal chausses and curled up beneath his chain mail hauberk. The leather garments he wore under his armor were midnight blue, a color so dark it appeared black in all but the brightest light.

Even through steel links, Simon sensed the fey cloth clinging to him. He slid off one gauntlet and gathered up the errant fabric as gently as though it were a kitten, taking care not to snag the cloth on his armor. Before he released the dress, he stroked it with his fingertips. The alluring texture of the weaving caressed him in return.

His fingers opened, allowing the cloth to fall. For a time it clung to his hand. Then it slid reluctantly from his fingertips and settled back around Ariane's legs.

When Simon looked up, Ariane was watching him with a curious intensity. Her lips were parted, her eyes half-shut, her breath uneven. She looked like a woman who had just received a secret caress.

Or would like to.

Hunger lanced through Simon. In the seven days since Ariane had awakened, he had been careful not to touch her in any but the most casual ways. He had overseen her meals, but he had not fed her medicine from his own lips. Nor had he spent the day bathing her in her bedchamber.

He had not spent the nights with her, either. Even when she gathered her courage and invited him to do just that the previous night.

Save your clenched teeth and endurance for the journey, wife. You will need it. I don't.

Simon knew that the rage he felt at Ariane's lack of passion wasn't reasonable. He also knew that rage existed just the same. Until he was more certain of his temper in that regard, he planned to touch Ariane no more than custom and politeness required.

While Ariane had stayed in her bedchamber regaining her full strength, Simon and Erik — often accompanied by Amber and Duncan — had fattened Stone Ring Keep's larder with the fruits of hunting and hawking. When not pursuing stag or waterfowl, Simon, Erik, and Duncan had hunted much more dangerous game.

They had found none. All sign of the renegade knights had dissolved in the icy autumn rains.

Nor would Erik permit the hunt to go into the area known as Silverfells. Because the mysterious fells lay within Erik's Sea Home lands rather than those of Stone Ring Keep, Simon had little choice but to bow to Erik's edict.

As though Erik understood Simon's frustration, he had offered himself as a partner in the daily battle practice that Dominic — and now Duncan — required of his men. When the two sinewy, fair-haired, astonishingly agile warriors went at one another with sword and shield, the other men stood and watched with something close to fear, whispering among themselves about the duel of Archangel and Sorcerer, each sun-bright and lightning-swift.

Yet the vigorous hunts and even more strenuous workouts with Erik had not given Simon the peace of mind he sought at night. He still dreamed of scented balm and sultry, yielding flesh; and he awoke knotted with hunger.

All that had kept Simon from Ariane's bed was pride . . . and his fear that his hunger would be too strong for him to control, that he would take whatever mummery of passion Ariane offered.

And then he would hate himself for being so weak.

Again.

It doesn't matter. Ariane isn't well enough to put to the test of passion.

Is she?

Despite Ariane's protestations, Simon didn't see how she could be well. He had never known even the strongest knight to recover from such a deep wound so swiftly.

Surely she isn't healed. Not completely. There might be something still wounded deep inside her, something that she is too proud and reckless — and dutiful — *to acknowledge.*

The thought of causing Ariane any more hurt made Simon cold.

And so did the thought that she might turn from him despite her promise.

Are you fully healed now, nightingale? If I go to your bed, will you come to me without disgust?

Do you remember the balm's sultry enchantment, when you lifted yourself toward my touch?

Night after night the questions had echoed in Simon's mind with the same frequency as his heartbeat. He didn't know what he would do if Ariane's lush body were offered to him only to be withheld at the ultimate moment, when her disgust overcame her promise to him.

I will endure the marriage embrace.
For you.

Simon didn't want dry endurance from Ariane. He wanted the sleek heat of her passion sheathing him. He wanted to bend down and taste desire consuming her. He wanted the dream that awakened him each night, sweating and shaking, aching with the need to bathe once more in the sultry fountains of her desire.

I will give you all that I have.

In the thrall of healing, Ariane had been passion incarnate. But the thrall was broken. Now Simon was afraid that all he would be able to call from Ariane was cold duty and even colder disgust.

He wasn't certain what he would do if that happened.

He was certain that he didn't want to find out.

A falcon's keening cry arrowed down from overhead, pulling Simon from his bleak thoughts. Moments later, Winter plummeted from the sapphire sky toward Erik's outstretched arm. Talons sank into leather gauntlet. Wide, steel-grey wings flared and then settled crisply along the bird's sides. Peregrine and tawny-eyed sorcerer whistled to one another.

"She found no sign of armed men between here and Stone Ring," Erik said.

Ariane let out a breath that she hadn't been aware of holding.

Simon grunted and held his tongue.

Erik was hardly the first knight who claimed to understand his falcon's mind, but he was the first knight Simon had encountered who actually appeared to do so. Although Simon didn't understand how man and falcon communicated, he was practical enough to accept that it happened — and that it had saved the day when the renegades attacked.

"Thank God," Ariane said.

Simon said nothing.

"You seem unconvinced," Erik said blandly to Simon. "Would you like to query Winter yourself?"

"I'm not Learned."

"So you say."

"So I *know*," Simon corrected curtly.

"You are a most curious unLearned man," Erik murmured.

"How so?"

Erik looked pointedly at Simon's legs.

Simon glanced down and saw that Ariane's dress had become entangled in his chausses again.

"God's teeth," Simon muttered. "The stuff clings worse than cat fur."

"Only to you," Erik said.

Simon looked up sharply at Erik. So did

Ariane, who was discreetly — and futilely — tugging at her dress, trying to free it without snagging the lovely fabric.

"What do you mean?" Simon asked.

Erik shifted the peregrine to his shoulder, removed one gauntlet, and reached for the dress.

A subtle bit of wind shifted the fabric just out of reach. The corner of Erik's mouth curled up.

"See?" he said. "It eludes me."

"The wind eludes you," retorted Simon as he plucked at the dress.

As quickly as Simon released one bit of material, another part of the cloth got caught anew on his armor. Erik watched and hid his smile behind his hand.

Ariane bent over to help her husband. When her bare fingers brushed Simon's, a surge of pleasure went through her at the contact of skin with skin. The pleasure was so sharp and so startling that her breath broke. She snatched back her fingers as though it had been fire rather than flesh she touched.

Simon's mouth flattened at the fresh evidence that his wife disliked even the most casual physical contact with him. But other than the line of his mouth, nothing of his reaction showed. His fingers remained patient as they dealt with the stubborn, beautiful fabric.

"I am sorry," Ariane said. "It must be the autumn wind that makes the fabric cling. I will change to another dress."

"No need," Simon muttered without looking up. "We should have left immediately after morning chapel. If we delay while you change your clothes, it will be eventide before we set out."

Before Ariane could open her mouth to protest that it would require only a brief time for her to change, Erik took a long stride forward. When he stopped, he was standing very close to Ariane.

Simon noted and said nothing, though he very much disliked having his wife so close to the handsome blond sorcerer.

"Lady, if you will be so kind as to help me demonstrate the special nature of Serena's weaving?" Erik asked.

Simon gave him a sidelong glance. Though nothing showed in Erik's expression or tone of voice, the amusement in him fairly radiated from his tawny eyes.

"Of course, sir," Ariane said. "How may I help you?"

"Take a fold of cloth and try to snag it on my hauberk or chausses."

"I'll do it," Simon said curtly.

His voice said a lot more. It said that he had no desire to have Ariane touch the muscular young sorcerer with anything, even a fold of her dress.

Simon's hand shot out and gathered up a fistful of cloth. He pulled it across Erik's chain mail hauberk. Nothing caught or snagged. Nor did the cloth show any inclination to cling to the hauberk.

"You have an extraordinary armorer," Simon said.

"No armorer could take out the dents, nicks, and cuts your sword has left on my hauberk in the past week," Erik said dryly.

Simon's eyes narrowed. With startling speed he bent and dragged the amethyst fabric across Erik's chausses. Cloth slid like sunlight over metal. There was no hesitation, no catching, no holding.

"By the Cross," Simon said, straightening.

He looked at the cloth in his fist, then at Erik. Without a word Simon released the cloth. It slid as far down as his own thigh.

And stuck.

Simon stepped back as though burned. The amethyst cloth followed until Ariane grabbed it and shook it down into place around her ankles.

"You see?" Erik asked Simon.

Ariane and Simon exchanged a dismayed glance.

"That's why you could rip a bandage from

the dress," Erik explained. "Anyone else would have had to fight the cloth, and his own distaste for handling it, to make a bandage. And even then, it would have required a knife to sever the threads."

"I don't understand," Ariane said.

Simon wasn't sure he wanted to.

"The weavings of the Silverfell clan can be a kind of armor," Erik said. "Whoever the fabric's wearer trusts may do anything to the cloth, including tear it. Ariane trusts you."

A black glance was Simon's only answer.

"The cloth pleases you," Erik said.

It wasn't quite a question, but Simon nodded, compelled by the intensity that burned just beneath Erik's calm surface.

"Yes. The cloth pleases me. Very much." The words came from Simon as though dragged. "Witchery."

But there was no heat in his voice, for the cloth had saved Ariane's life.

"Learning, not witchery," Erik corrected. "You have a gift for it, no matter how you fight and deny. *And so does Ariane.* Were she not Norman, I would swear she had the blood of ancient Druids in her veins."

"I do," Ariane said.

Her voice was so soft that it took a moment for both men to realize that she had spoken.

"What did you say?" Erik asked, pinning

her with eyes that could have belonged to a falcon.

"My mother's people were whispered to be witches," Ariane said simply. "It wasn't true. If you cut them, they bled the same as anyone. If you put a knife in their heart, they died. They cast no spells. Nor did they consort with the Dark Prince. They wore the holy cross and spoke God's prayers without difficulty or fault."

"But some of your ancestors were different nonetheless," Erik said.

Again, it wasn't quite a question.

"Different, not evil," Ariane said instantly.

"Aye," Erik agreed. " 'Tis a hard thing for some men to accept, that difference isn't evil."

Simon said nothing at all. The quality of his silence was chilling.

"You need not fear," Ariane said, turning to Simon. "My gift of finding things didn't survive my . . . illness."

"Your knife wound?" Simon asked.

"Nay. An illness that came to me in Normandy."

Erik looked at Ariane coolly as his mind sorted through the various possibilities and patterns that would fit what he knew of Ariane. No pattern emerged save one.

And that one made him fear for the peace of the Disputed Lands.

"Illness?" Erik asked softly. "When?"

In an instant Simon's body came to battle readiness. The softness of Erik's voice was more dangerous than the sound of a sword being drawn.

Ariane, too, heard the change in Erik's voice. He was every inch the heir of Lord Robert of the North, a man whose wealth rivaled that of the king of the Scots.

"I fell ill shortly before I left Normandy," Ariane said to Erik.

"What kind of illness."

Not a question. A demand.

Ariane flushed to the roots of her hair, then went quite pale, wishing she had never brought up the subject. She had no intention of telling Erik the circumstances that had resulted in the loss of her gift.

"My wife," Simon said distinctly, "answers only to her husband, to her king, and to God."

For an instant it seemed that Erik would disregard the challenge in Simon's words. Then the Learned man changed, intensity fading until he was once more an entertaining companion for the hunt and the hearth.

"Forgive me," Erik murmured to Ariane. "I meant no rudeness."

She nodded, relieved.

"But if ever you would like to regain your gift," he said softly to her, "come to Cassandra. Or to me."

Before Simon could speak, Ariane did. "My gift can never be regained."

The flatness of her voice closed the subject with the finality of a door slamming shut.

"Just as well," Simon said into the uncomfortable silence. "I have no love of witchery."

"And Learning?" Erik challenged softly. "What of it?"

"The Disputed Lands are welcome to their Learning. I will put my faith in this."

Simon drew his sword with startling speed. The somber length of the blade gleamed in the daylight.

"Ah, your black sword," Erik murmured.

He looked at the weapon with open curiosity. It was the first time he had seen it closely, for Simon used a different, blunter weapon for mock battles.

There was something about the black sword that intrigued Erik. It was as though a pattern had once existed, then been erased.

Holding out his hand, Erik said, "May I?"

However much the Learned sorcerer might irritate Simon on occasion, he had no doubt of Erik's trustworthiness. With a deft movement of his hands, Simon reversed the sword and held it out pommel first.

The pommel was as black as the blade, and as austere. It lacked decoration of any kind.

Erik grasped the heavy blade carefully and held the pommel up to the light. As he turned the blade, sunshine poured over the dark metal of the pommel, revealing that it had been reworked.

"As I thought," Erik said. "It held jewels once. Gold inlay, too, I would guess."

"Aye," Simon said.

Something in Simon's voice made Erik look up from his study of the sword.

"Spoils of war?" Erik asked blandly.

"Aye."

"A pity the pommel has been ruined."

"Ruined?" Simon laughed curtly. "It affects the blade's balance and edge not one whit. In any case, Dominic's life was worth far more than the handful of gems I pried out of the pommel."

"Ransom?" asked Erik.

"Yes."

"An ancient Saracen custom."

"So is treachery," Simon retorted.

Erik's smile was as cruel as the curve of a falcon's beak. "Treachery knows no single people. Like Original Sin, it is a common heritage of Man."

Simon's answering smile was a replica of Erik's.

"In the end, we freed Dominic by force," Simon said. "Then we tore down the sultan's palace stone by stone and scattered it across the desert."

With a smooth, swift motion, Simon sheathed the sword.

"They are coming," Erik said.

Together Simon and Erik turned as Amber and Duncan hurried across the bailey's cobblestones to bid their guests Godspeed.

Duncan's appearance had been a signal for one of his grooms. The young man came from the stable area at a trot, leading two horses. The first was the stout mare that had been Ariane's mount while at Stone Ring Keep. The second was a filly with the same muscular build and clear, steady eye.

"The dark mare is no racer," Duncan said to Simon, "but she has the unflinching heart of a war-horse. So does her daughter. Take them, breed them to your stallion, and let their sons carry your sons into battle and safely home again."

"Lord Duncan . . ." Simon began formally. His voice died. "You are too generous. Already you have given me enough to furnish a keep, yet I have no keep to my name."

"I could give you all I have and still be in your debt," Duncan said simply. "If you had not taken my place next to Ariane, there would have been bloody chaos and death where there now is peace and life."

Duncan gave Simon a quick, hard hug while their wives exchanged farewells.

"I will miss you, Simon the Loyal," Duncan said quietly.

"And I you," Simon said, returning the hug.

As Simon stepped back, he smiled wryly at Duncan.

"To think," Simon said, "that I first met you at my brother's wedding, when I held my knife between your thighs to assure your good behavior."

Duncan gave a crack of laughter.

"Glad I am that you have a steady hand," Duncan said.

"So am I," Amber said dryly.

Smiling, Simon turned to Ariane and held out his hand.

"Allow me to assist you," he said. "We must be on our way before more clouds gather."

Before Ariane could agree or disagree, Simon swept her up in his arms and deposited her on the back of his long-legged hunting horse. The animal snorted and sidestepped, sending shod hooves ringing against stone.

Ariane curbed the spirited beast with an ease that made Simon smile. He turned to his own war stallion and vaulted into the saddle.

Amid cries of Godspeed, the clatter of hooves, and the eager barking of Erik's wolf-

hounds, Simon, Ariane, Erik, and their retainers set off for Stone Ring Keep. Very
quickly the cultivated fields fell away behind
them. Forest rose around the horses, an ex-
panse of trees broken only by rare hamlets
and even more rare circles where ancient, uneven stones lifted their faces to the sun.

Unseasonable storms had largely stolen the
blazing reds and golds from the trees, leaving
naked branches black against the cloud-
streaked vault of the sky. Drifts of leaves
swirled on every gust of wind and piled against
boulders and sacred stones alike.

The closer the riders came to Stone Ring,
the more uneasy Simon became. Perhaps it
was simply the loss of leaves from the trees,
but it seemed to him that there were more
of the ragged stone ruins now than there had
been the last time he had taken the trail.

Ariane watched intently also, as though
sharing Simon's feeling that something about
the nature of the land itself had changed.

But it wasn't until they reached Stone Ring
that Simon's unease became urgent to the
point of discomfort. He didn't want to look
at the ragged curve of stone that made up the
single rocky ring.

Yet he couldn't look away.

"What do you think of the land?" he asked
Erik.

"There is nothing amiss that I can see. Perhaps Winter and Stagkiller will have different news."

Erik pulled up where the trail divided. To the south lay Blackthorne Keep. To the west lay Sea Home.

Stagkiller emerged from the forest and bounded up the slope back to Erik. Moments later Winter appeared from behind a cloud and shot down to her saddle perch in front of Erik.

The arrival of Erik's beasts was noted only absently by Simon. The longer he waited at the fork in the trail, the more certain he became that the party was being watched.

"The trail out of the Disputed Lands is empty," Erik said to Simon. "You should have no trouble with renegades of any stripe."

Simon grunted.

"Is something wrong?" Erik asked.

Almost impatiently, Simon looked around the forest again. No matter how carefully he watched, he saw nothing except moss and lichen, ageless stone and living branches barren of all but green tangles of mistletoe.

There was only one ring of stones. He was quite certain of it. The only shadows were those cast by the sun in its normal fashion. There was no mist to obscure the inside of the circle that was bounded by stones.

Yet when Simon turned his back on the ring in order to talk to Erik, he was uneasy.

"Nay," Simon said. "All is well. Or seems to be."

"You sense something, don't you?" Erik asked.

"A cold wind."

Erik gave Simon a sidelong glance and turned to Ariane.

"What of you, lady? Are you at ease?"

"It seems," Ariane said hesitantly, "that there are more stones than before."

Erik looked at her sharply. "How so?"

She shrugged. "Just that. I see more stones than I did the last time I came this way."

"The last time you came this way," Simon said curtly, "you were senseless from your wound."

While Simon spoke, he glanced around again. His eyes narrowed against the sunlight lancing between gathering clouds. Yet no matter how hard he looked, he saw nothing to justify the odd prickling sensation over his skin.

"What do you feel?" Erik asked in a low voice.

"A cold —"

"Wind," Erik interrupted impatiently. "I feel it too. What else?"

Simon looked at Erik. The tawny eyes look-

ing back at Simon were clear, intent, as fath-
omless as the sky.

"I feel a prickling beneath my skin," Simon
admitted.

"Danger?"

"Not quite. But not quite safety, either."

"Ariane?" Erik asked, turning to her.

"Yes. A prickling. 'Tis . . . odd."

"Excellent," Erik said with satisfaction.

"Not to me," Simon said bluntly. " 'Tis like
we're being watched."

"We are, but most people wouldn't know."

Steel whispered against its sheath as Simon
drew his sword with unnerving speed.

"I knew those renegades wouldn't stay in
Silverfell," Simon said.

"Be at ease," Erik said. " 'Tis only the
rowan."

"What?"

Erik gestured with his head toward the stone
ring.

"The sacred rowan waits," Erik said simply.

"For what?" Ariane asked.

"Even the Druids didn't know," Erik said.
"They knew only that she waited."

"God's teeth," hissed Simon. "What
drivel."

He sheathed his sword with a single sweeping motion.

Erik laughed like a sorcerer and turned his

mount toward Sea Home. The stallion reared and fought the bit, not wanting to leave the other horses. Erik rode out the stallion's temper with the ease of sunlight riding water.

"Godspeed," Erik said to Ariane and Simon. "If you have need of anything, send to Sea Home. If it is within Learned power, your need will be answered. You have our vow on it."

For a moment Simon was too surprised to say anything.

"The Learned? Why?" Simon asked bluntly.

"Cassandra has cast the silver rune stones."

Simon waited in taut silence. He sensed that he wouldn't like what was said next.

He was right.

"Your fate is also that of the Learned," Erik said. "Whether you wish it or not, we are being woven into a tapestry of unknown design."

"Perhaps," Simon said.

His tone said he did not believe it at all.

Erik's eyes blazed.

"Don't hold on to your blindness too long," Erik said softly. "The cost of seeing the truth too late will be more than any of us want to pay. *Especially you.*"

19

Thunder leaped down from the peaks and through the glen in a deafening drumroll of sound. Behind the thunder came a seething quicksilver curtain of rain. The air was cold and fresh, infused with the myriad scents of woodland and meadow.

Just below the brow of the hill, in a place that commanded a sweeping view of fells, woodland, and glen, Simon had made camp in the ruins of a Roman fort. The fort itself had been built on the ruins of an even more ancient fortification. Though the ceiling of the long room was only half in place, that half provided shelter from the driving rain for Ariane. Warmth came from a bonfire burning wildly beneath an opening in the ceiling timbers.

Another fire winked and leaped on the opposite side of one of the fort's inner walls, where Simon's squire and the three men-at-arms had set up their own shelter. The highest flames of their fire were visible, for the interior wall had crumbled until it was barely waist-high. Rich scents of meat and vegetables simmering in a pot rose with the smoke into the watery twilight.

Men talked among themselves, sharing coarse jokes and rough laughter. Blanche's voice wove through the darker tones of the men like high, trilled birdsong. Her laughter was breathless, sensual, as teasing as a lover's hand sliding up a thigh to stop just short of the goal . . . and then seizing the trophy with thorough care.

Simon had no doubt that Blanche was giving the men quite a chase. For all of Blanche's whining about lack of luxury on the trail, and the long hours of riding at the pace of a walking man, she had been very generous with her favors at the end of the day.

For that, Simon was grateful. If Blanche had simply teased the men, or lain with one and taunted the others, there would have been the kind of ugliness that Marie once had created among Dominic's warriors during the Holy Crusade. But apparently those kinds of vicious female games didn't please Blanche. Having a warm man between her legs did.

Her girlish laughter pealed through the twilight, followed by masculine shouts as she flipped an ancient brass coin and they called out their choice.

"Heads!"
"Heads!"
"Heads!"

The coin gleamed and turned almost lazily above the wall, reflecting the nearby flames. Blanche's pale, dirty fingers flashed as she snagged the coin out of the air. Invisible behind the wall, she smacked the coin against her bare thigh.

"Heads it is, lads," Blanche said.

A round of groans went up. Now the men would have to wait to discover who would have the first turn with Blanche.

"Oh, blind me," she said, laughing. "Come on. Come on. 'Tis room for all. Oh! Mind you warm your hands first, you cold bastard!"

Hiding his smile, Simon turned back to the fire. Blanche might be as loose as a hound's lips, but she wasn't a girl to cause trouble among the men.

He only hoped that Ariane didn't understand the meaning of the grunts, giggles, and skirmishes that were going on barely four yards away. The ruined inner wall provided the illusion of privacy, but no more.

"Are you certain that you're warm enough?" Simon asked.

Ariane looked up at the question. In the firelight, Simon's eyes were both dark and golden with reflected fire. His hauberk gleamed with every muscular shift of his body.

Ariane nodded, silently telling Simon that she was warm enough.

The motion of her head sent firelight sliding like a lover's hands through her unbound hair. Midnight strands coiled damply against her face and steamed slightly from the heat of the fire.

"Are you certain?" Simon asked. "You were wet to the skin."

He had reason to know. He had stripped a shivering Ariane of all garments save a long chemise. The rest of her clothes were drying on lances wedged into cracks in the stone floor.

Again Ariane nodded, for she knew her teeth would chatter were she to risk unlocking her jaw to speak.

Simon bent down and pulled his fur-lined mantle more tightly around his wife. As he drew back his hands, his thumbs traced the line of her jaw.

A shiver coursed through Ariane that had nothing to do with the temperature.

"You're chilled," Simon said instantly.

"N-no. 'Tis you who wears nothing but cold metal. Take b-back your mantle and warm yourself."

"God's *teeth*."

Impatiently Simon undid the fastenings on his chain mail hauberk and set it aside with an ease that belied the weight of the armor. The task would have been more quickly accomplished with his squire's aid, but Edward

306

was otherwise involved.

Even if the lad had been standing about on one foot and then the other, waiting to be of service, Simon wouldn't have called. He wanted no male to see Ariane in such an arresting state of disarray.

"Tomorrow you will wear that witchy dress," Simon said as he stripped off his soft leather shirt. "It turns water like a duck's back."

Ariane gave him a mutinous look. She hadn't worn the amethyst dress since she had realized that it was more than it appeared to be.

Or at least, the dress seemed to be more. It was difficult to be certain when dealing with Learned things.

In any case, the thought of the supple, warm fabric stropping itself on Simon like a cat was unsettling. It made Ariane wonder what it would feel like if it were her own hand stroking him rather than the fabric.

"I will wear what I p-please," Ariane said.

Simon said something rude beneath his breath, threw more wood on the bonfire, and sat next to his wife.

The boughs the men-at-arms had gathered formed a surprisingly comfortable mattress. The bedding that had been thrown over the boughs was dry. So was Simon's mantle, for the Learned had done something to the fur lining they had given to Simon that made it shed water. When it rained, he simply reversed the mantle so that the fur side faced out.

Ariane's mantle, however, was of the more usual variety. It was wet clear through, as were the clothes she had worn. They steamed gently by the fire, hanging from lances like bedraggled pennants.

"By your leave, madam," Simon said sardonically.

Simon took the fur mantle from Ariane's hands and whipped it around his own shoulders, which were now bare. She made a startled sound as she felt herself lifted up. Very quickly she was resettled in Simon's lap.

"Is something wrong?" he asked blandly, drawing the warm mantle closely around both of them.

"I — you are so q-quick. It makes me f-forget that you are very strong as well."

"And you look like a drowned cat. It makes me forget that you still have claws and a haughty disposition."

"At l-least I don't shed," she muttered.

Simon laughed.

For a time there was silence but for the crackle of flames, the liquid murmur of rain, and random noises from beyond the wall.

Slowly the chills that had been racking Ariane subsided. As the warmth of fire and man seeped into her cold flesh, she sighed and relaxed a bit against Simon's seductive heat.

When her cheek rested against the muscular pad of his shoulder, Ariane was reminded that Simon wore no shirt. Except for his supple leather breeches he was naked.

The thought sent an odd sensation glittering through her. It wasn't quite unease.

And it certainly wasn't relaxation.

From beyond the crumbling interior wall came a breathless, definitely female cry.

"Do you think Blanche is comfortable and warm?" Ariane asked after a moment.

Beneath her cheek, Simon's chest moved as though with silent laughter.

"Warmer than you are," he assured her.

"How so?"

"She is lying between at least two strapping young men."

Ariane made a startled sound.

"Two?" she asked after a moment.

A rumbling sound came from Simon that could have been agreement. Or it could have been the contented purr of a very, very large cat.

"At once?" Ariane pressed.

"Aye."

"Is that . . . comfortable?"

"In what way?" Simon countered.

Ariane couldn't see the laughter in Simon's narrowed eyes, but she could sense it very clearly.

"It must be quite, ah, intimate," Ariane said carefully.

"Like eggs in a nest."

"Do you sleep thus?"

"Of course not."

Sighing, Ariane leaned back once more.

"I prefer having wenches rather than men-at-arms to warm me," Simon said blandly.

Ariane's mouth opened. A flush swept up her cheeks when she realized that her husband was teasing her.

At least, she thought he was.

Simon laughed at the expressions crossing Ariane's face. It occurred to him that she was truly an innocent in the ways of men and women.

Except in her dreams.

Heat lanced through Simon as echoes of an inexplicable, impossible dream coursed through his mind.

The memories both haunted and restrained him. During the Holy Crusade, he had learned to his cost that his own intense sensuality could be a weapon turned against him.

In his dreams, Ariane had matched that sensuality perfectly.

If it had been a dream. . . .

Not knowing truth from enchantment was an acid eating at Simon, for he believed only in those things that could be weighed and measured and counted. He had to know whether Ariane was as cold as she seemed or as warm as the dream.

We tasted one another.

"Don't worry about your handmaiden," Simon said against the scented dampness of Ariane's hair. "She is the warmest person in this miserable camp."

"But —"

"Have you heard Blanche complain?" Simon interrupted.

Ariane blinked. "All I've heard is laughter."

"Then she must be well pleased. Unlike you, Blanche has never failed to complain when things weren't to her liking. She should have been born a queen."

"Aye."

Ariane sighed again and unwittingly snuggled closer to Simon's warmth. Blanche's ceaseless complaints had made the past three days on the road rather trying for everyone, but most of all for Ariane, whom Blanche was supposed to be tending. As often as not, it had been the other way around.

" 'Tis kind of the men to see to Blanche's warmth," Ariane said after a time. "It must be quite uncomfortable for them."

Simon made a sound that could have been stifled amusement or a wordless question.

"How so?" Simon asked carefully.

"Blanche's clothes were even wetter than mine," Ariane explained. "She must feel quite clammy to the men warming her."

"I think not."

"No?"

"No. When I saw her, the girl was naked as an egg."

Ariane sat up abruptly, barely avoiding banging into Simon's chin.

"What were you doing watching my naked handmaiden?" Ariane demanded.

The crackle in Ariane's eyes was more than matched by the tartness of her voice.

The lady was not pleased.

Simon smiled lazily, warmed by the fire in his wife's eyes.

"Have you had carnal knowledge of Blanche?" Ariane demanded.

He raised his eyebrows. "When would I have done that?"

"While I was ill."

"Not so, nightingale. Between bathing you, rubbing balm into you, bandaging you, and dosing you, I barely had time to eat, much less to dally with unappealing wenches."

Ariane opened her mouth, then closed it.

"Unappealing?" she asked softly after a moment.

"Aye."

"She has hair the color of honey and eyes the blue of a robin's egg," Ariane pointed out.

"I prefer hair the color of midnight and eyes that make amethysts pale by comparison."

Ariane looked into Simon's dark, intense eyes and wondered how she could ever have thought them bleak or austere.

They were extraordinarily beautiful.

"Are you certain Blanche doesn't appeal to you?" Ariane asked. "She has a . . . a warm nature toward men."

"So does a muddy hound."

Ariane smiled, then snickered, then put her head against Simon's shoulder and laughed until she was breathless.

A ripple of pleasure went through Simon when he felt the complete relaxation of Ariane's body against his. She had not been so at ease with him since she had awakened from her healing dreams.

It gave him hope even as it ignited his blood.

Simon shifted his weight slightly, drawing Ariane even closer. As always, his body responded to her presence by becoming more sensitive, more alert. His blood was quickened by the mere scent of her. Already he was drawn as taut as a harp string.

He wondered what Ariane would do when she discovered his arousal. Perhaps enough of the healing thrall remained deep within her that she wouldn't draw back in cold distaste.

The thought that Ariane might find his body appealing sent a shudder of raw desire through Simon.

"Are you warm enough?" Ariane asked instantly.

"Wherever you touch me, I am warm enough."

Ariane thought that over for a time.

"I cannot cover your back," she said seriously, "and I barely cover half of your chest."

"The mantle serves for my back."

"And your front?"

"You could rub me with your hands."

Ariane lifted her hands to chafe warmth into Simon's skin, but found that her position crosswise on his lap made giving him a thorough rubdown difficult. She squirmed about, trying to lever herself into a better position.

Simon's breath came in swiftly when Ariane's soft bottom moved over his own hardened flesh.

"Sorry," Ariane said in a low voice. "Sitting thus, I can reach you with only one hand."

Common sense told Simon that he shouldn't do what he was about to do, but the temptation was too great.

"Allow me," he murmured.

Ariane made a startled sound as Simon's arms closed around her body, lifting and turning her in the same swift motion. When she settled once more, she found herself astride his lap.

"Comfortable?" he asked blandly.

"Er . . ."

"Think of me as your mount."

Ariane bit her lip against a nervous smile. The part of her that was still chained to nightmare was screaming that she wasn't safe. The part of her that had known the healing enchantment of balm and Simon's caressing hands was more than ready to rise to the sensual lure.

"Er . . . you lack a saddle," Ariane pointed out.

"I wear leather," Simon countered. "Think of that as your saddle."

"But where are the stirrups to keep me upright?"

There was more amusement than reluctance in Ariane's tone. The realization increased Simon's heartbeat, which further quickened the flesh straining against his supple breeches.

"I will not let you fall," Simon said. Then he added softly, "And I promise to heed your hand on the reins."

When Ariane realized what Simon meant, her eyes widened.

"Simon?"

"I had a chance to learn your body while I cared for you," he whispered. "Will you care for me just a little now that you are well?"

"I . . ." Ariane's voice died.

The hands that Ariane put against Simon's chest were cold. They trembled between fear and yearning.

"Am I so disgusting to you?" he asked evenly.

"Nay! 'Tis only that . . ."

Simon waited, his jaw clenched against the hunger to have just one caress freely given by his wife.

"I am nervous," Ariane confessed in a whisper.

Her hands moved from Simon's breastbone across the width of his chest to his arms.

"And there is so much of you," she added under her breath.

Smiling a bit fiercely, Simon fought against the need to bury himself in the softness that now lay open to him between Ariane's widespread thighs.

"Duncan and Dominic are larger than I am," Simon pointed out in a low, reasonable tone.

"You would make two of me."

"I would rather make a meal of you. And you of me."

We tasted each other.

Ariane's breath caught as a curious shudder unfolded deep within her body.

Simon felt his wife's trembling and swore silently.

"You misunderstand my meaning," he whispered. "There would be no pain in such a 'meal.' You would feel only pleasure."

"Said the wolf to the lambkin."

Surprised, Simon gave a crack of laughter.

Tentatively Ariane smiled.

"Where is the balm?" she asked.

He blinked. "Balm?"

"For healing. That is, if I am to learn you as you learned me?"

When Simon remembered the way he had learned Ariane that last night before she awakened, he thought he might burst.

She doesn't know what she is saying. She couldn't have been awake.

Could she?

20

The possibility that Ariane might actually have shared his dream made Simon's blood run so hotly that he was afraid to speak. With one hand he felt along the bedding for the embroidered bag of medicines that Cassandra had sent with him. His fingers quickly found the familiar shape of the pot of balm.

"Here," Simon said huskily, holding out his hand to Ariane. "Use this."

Ariane opened the pot and dipped two fingertips into the creamy balm.

"What a lovely fragrance," she murmured.

"It smells of you. Moonrise and roses and a distant storm."

Ariane smiled slightly and shook her head. "I don't smell like that."

"You smell more beautiful than I can say. I could bathe in your fragrance."

The look in Simon's eyes sent a ripple of awareness chasing over Ariane. Nervousness came in its wake.

"I feel you tugging at the reins," she whispered.

"Do you trust me not to run away with you?"

Ariane's breath caught. Then she sighed, nodded her head, and began applying balm.

"Thank you," Simon said.

"For the balm?"

"For trusting me." He smiled slightly. "Although I appreciate the balm as well. No matter how cleverly made, chain mail always chafes."

Tentatively, then with more assurance, Ariane rubbed her hands and the balm over Simon's bare chest. Once she got past the unfamiliarity of such intimacy, she discovered that touching him felt quite nice. Intriguing, even.

Pleasurable.

As Ariane rubbed in more balm, she realized that touching Simon was much more than merely pleasant. It made her shiver with enjoyment.

And a bit of apprehension, her nightmare seething with warnings.

"You are so warm," Ariane whispered.

"When you touch me, I burn."

A single look at Simon's heavy-lidded eyes told Ariane that he was speaking the truth. Another odd shiver worked through her body. Heedlessly her hands flexed, pressing her nails against the muscular pads of flesh that made

Simon's breasts so unlike her own.

His breath hissed in.

She jerked back her hands.

"I'm sorry," Ariane said quickly. "I didn't mean to hurt you."

"Then do it again, nightingale."

"What?"

"Test me with those sweet claws."

"It doesn't hurt?"

"Only when you stop."

Hesitantly Ariane's hands settled on Simon's skin once more.

"Go ahead," he whispered against her forehead. "Test me. And yourself."

Fingers flexed. Nails lightly scored skin.

Simon's breath quickened as a sensual shudder raced through him, tightening his loins.

"Are you certain you like it?" Ariane asked doubtfully.

"Aye. Someday, I will show you how much you like it, too."

The huskiness of Simon's voice intrigued Ariane.

"Someday?" she whispered.

"When you no longer draw back in disgust when I touch you."

"You don't disgust me," Ariane said.

"Only in my dreams," he said beneath his breath.

"What?"

"If I don't disgust you," Simon challenged softly, "would you kiss me while you touch me?"

"How? Like this?"

The warmth of Ariane's mouth — and then her tongue — against Simon's shoulder drew a low oath from him.

Ariane straightened quickly.

"Isn't that what you wanted?" she asked.

" 'Tis exactly what I wanted and more than I expected," he said huskily.

"Oh. Would you like another?"

"And another and another and —" Simon reined in his hungry words. "Yes. Please. Another kiss from your warm mouth."

With a sigh that sent her breath rushing over Simon's chest, Ariane bent her head and caressed him with her mouth once more. While her hands stroked healing balm into his skin and tangled sweetly in the thatch of hair that covered his chest, her mouth explored him with a growing urgency she didn't question.

The sleek texture of Simon's skin stretching over supple muscle intrigued Ariane's tongue, as did the taut line of tendon up Simon's neck. She decided that his beard was made for nuzzling and nibbling upon, as was the soft lobe of his ear.

Without understanding why, Ariane closed

her teeth on the rim of Simon's ear and bit delicately.

The sensual laughter that met her caress — and the fact that Simon wasn't forcing her in any way — made Ariane more confident in her explorations. Soon she found herself tracing Simon's ear with the damp tip of her tongue, following the curves down and in until she could go no farther.

Ariane's tongue probed repeatedly, her teeth biting gently all the while. She enjoyed the shivers of sensation that coursed through her own flesh while she explored Simon. As her mouth caressed, her fingers returned to the tiny male nipples that she had felt harden when she had first stroked the curly hair on his chest. Sucking lightly on his neck, Ariane plucked and teased his nipples.

"Who taught you?" Simon groaned when he could take no more

Reluctantly Ariane lifted her head from its warm nuzzling of his neck.

"Taught me what?" she murmured.

"This."

Simon lifted Ariane's hair aside. His teeth and tongue caressed her ear until she shivered and sank her nails heedlessly into his skin. Delicately his fingertips circled the tips of her breasts. Her nipples budded in a velvet rush that made Simon's whole body clench.

Ariane cried out softly and covered his hands with her own. Simon froze, expecting her to pull away. Instead she swayed subtly, pressing against his hands, caught in the sensual thrall of his touch.

"Who taught you?" Simon repeated against her ear.

Then his tongue thrust down again. The burst of sensation that went through Ariane made it impossible to think, much less to speak.

"I dreamed — it was — done to me," she whispered.

A ripple of hunger went through Simon at the thought that Ariane might have shared his sensual dream.

"Did it disgust you in your dream?" he whispered.

"Dear God, no."

"And now?"

Simon caught the tight velvet peaks of Ariane's breasts and rolled them lovingly between his fingertips.

"Does this disgust you?" he whispered.

"Nay."

Ariane made a ragged sound as Simon's tongue and teeth caressed her ear. Dimly she realized that her hands were covering his as they roamed over her breasts, flicking and squeezing and arousing until her nipples pouted, flushed with heat.

Then he bent his head and curled his tongue around a taut pink bud. The amethyst cloth served to magnify rather than diminish the sensuality of the caress. Her head rolled back on her neck and she shivered as his mouth suckled her.

"Are you afraid?" Simon whispered.

"Aye. Nay. I . . . do not know. I feel like a bud must at the first touch of the sun. Flushed and quivering on the edge of . . . something."

Simon took a deep, steadying breath and straightened until he could see Ariane's face. Her eyes were both shadowed and sultry, caught like her between nightmare and dream.

"What else did you dream?" Simon whispered. "Tell me, nightingale."

"I cannot!" Ariane whispered.

The heat of her blush radiated out to Simon through the thin cloth that was all she wore.

"Then show me," Simon said, smiling against Ariane's ear.

She shook her head. "It will shock you."

"If I faint, bring me wine."

The thought of being able to fell with mere words the man whose body flexed powerfully beneath her hands disarmed Ariane. She dipped up some more balm and resumed rubbing it into Simon's body.

When her fingers swept over his nipples, he groaned softly. She repeated the caress, thrilling to the sense of power it gave her to so affect him.

"Tell me your dream," Simon said huskily.

"You tempt me, my lord."

"How can I? 'Tis your hand on the reins, not mine."

The reminder quivered through Ariane, a brightness that pushed her dark fears back a bit more.

"Tempt me, nightingale. Share the dream that makes you blush like the dawn."

Delicately Simon plucked at Ariane's nipples, which still thrust hungrily between his fingers. He felt again the heat of the blood rushing from Ariane's breasts to her forehead. Slowly he released her nipples from sensuous captivity.

She gave a ragged sigh and leaned her forehead against Simon's shoulder. The tips of her breasts brushed against his chest. It both soothed her and made her restless.

"In my dream . . ." Ariane whispered.

"Yes?" he encouraged.

"I can't say it."

"Then show me."

"On your body?" she asked.

"Would it be easier that way?"

"I don't know. Simon . . ."

"Yes?"

"Would it disgust you to be touched?"

"By you? Never."

"I mean . . ." Ariane took a swift breath, gathered her courage, and ran her hands down Simon's torso. "Here."

"Mother of God," he said through clenched teeth.

Ariane snatched back her hands.

"I'm sorry," she said unhappily. "I warned you that you would be disgusted but you didn't listen."

Breath hissed back in through Simon's teeth.

"You misunderstand," he said raggedly.

"Nay, 'tis you who don't understand!"

Simon put his forehead against Ariane's.

"Again, nightingale."

"What?"

"Touch me again."

"There?"

"Aye."

"Are you certain?"

"By all the saints, *yes.*"

Hesitantly Ariane's hands slid down to Simon's waist, then skimmed over his abdomen to a point between his legs. Her thumbs went back up, tracing the blunt flesh that poked out above the waist of his breeches.

"You are very hard," she whispered.

"How can you tell?" he asked huskily. "Your touch is light as a butterfly's."

When Ariane ran her hands over Simon again, he groaned and moved urgently against her palms.

Fear rushed through her, a harsh warning of a lesson that had been learned at great cost. A man in the throes of lust was a beast.

"Simon?" she whispered.

"Again, nightingale. Or do I . . . disgust you?"

Ariane drew a broken breath and then another, nightmare and dream warring within her. Simon didn't sound mindless or brutal. But neither had Geoffrey the Fair, until that final night when he had raped and ruined her in the eyes of Church and family.

Dear God, what am I to do? Despite all common sense, despite all past pain, I yearn to become Simon's true wife.

And the moment I do, he will hate me as my father did. Whore. Wanton. Witch.

"Ariane?"

"You don't disgust me. But I am . . . frightened."

"Of what?"

The seething thoughts within Ariane's mind were too complex to sort out. So she chose the most simple, potent truth.

"I am afraid of this," she said, running her fingers over Simon's aroused flesh. " 'Tis made to tear a woman apart."

"Not so. It is made to pleasure a woman."

"I've heard no woman describe it thus," Ariane said bleakly.

Simon would have argued if her touch hadn't drawn his whole body upon a rack of passion so intense it was painful.

"Smooth balm into me," he said in a low, hoarse voice. "It will help me and it will be a way for you to learn that not all men are vicious beasts."

He took Ariane's lower lip between his teeth, bit gently, and flicked his tongue over her lip. She made a small sound and trembled.

But she leaned toward rather than away from him.

"Touch me," Simon whispered. "Learn me. It is your hands upon the rein, not mine. This time."

Even Ariane couldn't say if it was fear or excitement that made her hands tremble as she lowered them to his body once more. After a few hesitant strokes, she pressed more firmly.

Then she lingered, curious about the contours of Simon's surprising masculinity. She stroked the length of him several times before returning to explore the inch of hot flesh that had pushed above the waist of his breeches.

"So smooth," Ariane murmured, circling Simon with curious fingertips. "I hadn't expected that of something so hard. Are you sensitive here?"

"Dear Christ," Simon hissed. "I ache."

Ariane froze. "I didn't mean to wound you. Truly. I —"

"You can heal me," he said across her quick apology.

"How?"

"My breeches are too tight. Pick apart the laces."

For the space of several ragged breaths, Ariane looked into Simon's smoldering eyes.

Touch me. Learn me. It is your hands upon the rein, not mine. This time.

With trembling fingers, Ariane did as Simon asked, loosening the laces until the length of him lay hot and hard between her palms. She stroked with gentle care.

"Is this better?" she asked anxiously.

Simon groaned and bit back a searing curse. Sweat broke over his whole body.

In the firelight, his face seemed drawn by pain.

"Do you truly hurt so much?" Ariane whispered, shaken.

"God's teeth," he said hoarsely.

"Would balm help?"

329

A shudder went through Simon.

"Yes. Oh God, yes," he said through his teeth. "Heal me, nightingale."

The fragrance of balm rose from Simon's heated flesh as Ariane caressed him within the concealing warmth of his fur-lined mantle.

"Some day I will caress you like this," Simon said huskily.

"I am not shaped as you."

"Aye. You are softer than any petal ever made by God."

Ariane's fingertips found the single, unseeing eye and explored it delicately while Simon's passionate words sent streamers of heat through her.

"The flower of your womanhood is a softness beyond imagining," he whispered. "I yearn to caress that softness, taste it, bathe in the sultry fountains of your desire and bathe you in turn with my own passion."

Simon's words flicked Ariane like a whip of fire, flushing her skin, making her breath shorten. Her hands slipped lower as unfamiliar sensations made her whole body tremble. Her fingertips found the taut, aching spheres that held generations yet unborn. Curiously, caressingly, Ariane explored his very different flesh.

Simon watched her face through slitted eyes. Her expression was shuttered by a veil of midnight hair. Flames from the brazier sent more shadows than illumination over Ariane's expression. He could not decide whether her response to the intimacy was hot or cold or merely . . . dutiful.

Simon closed his eyes and stopped asking questions that had no answers. All that mattered to him was here, now, and it was on fire.

"Your fingers are like tongues of flame," Simon whispered, shuddering. "Licking all over me, making me burn. Sweet God, you are killing me."

"No," Ariane whispered, caught by the strain in his voice. "I wanted to heal your pain, not make it worse."

"Then heal me."

"Can it be done without . . ." Her voice died.

Oh God, bad enough that Geoffrey taught me to fear what other women seem to enjoy. But it is worse, far worse, that he took from me the virginity that should have been my gift to Simon.

I cannot bear to look at Simon and see disgust for me in his eyes.

Like my father.

Like my priest.

Loathing me, believing that I was wanton rather than innocent.

How could Simon believe differently? Look at me with him, touching him, stroking him, wanting nothing more than to be closer to him and then closer still.

He lures me rather than pins me down with his greater strength. He doesn't hold me in a vise of male power that leaves me helpless to escape.

"Can it be done without coupling?" Simon asked when Ariane did not speak. "Is that what you're asking?"

"Yes," she whispered.

"Aye. It can be done. 'Tis less than a grain against a bushel, but 'tis one grain better than naught."

Simon's words made little sense to Ariane. She understood only that there was something she could do to ease the tension raking through Simon's hard, hot body.

"Tell me," Ariane urged. "Let me heal you."

Simon's only answer was that of his hands fitting over hers, teaching her how to stroke and how to hold, when to tease and when to end the teasing.

Suddenly Ariane felt the shudder that convulsed Simon, heard his ragged groan, and sensed something spilling between her fingers like silky blood. She looked down, but saw only his mantle and a wedge of darkness that was his body.

"Simon?" Ariane asked anxiously. "Are you all right? I felt . . . blood."

Simon almost smiled despite the shocks of pleasure that went through him at each delicate probe of her fingertips over his still aroused flesh.

"Nay, nightingale."

"But I did," she insisted. "It was too thick to be anything but blood."

"What you felt was the children you will never know unless I taste ecstasy while our bodies are joined."

Ariane's eyes widened into mysterious pools of darkness. Her breath caught as fire licked through her. She became aware of herself in an unfamiliar way — breasts both taut and heavy with sensation, a throbbing promise that was repeated in the sultry flesh between her legs.

Slowly, gently, Ariane stroked Simon's still swollen flesh, thinking to soothe him, for shudders came to him with almost every breath. Warmth and the scent of balm laced with something even more elemental rose from the opening of the mantle. She breathed deeply, infusing herself with the heady mixture.

And then something that was more than a dream and less than a memory blossomed within Ariane.

Firelight and the scent of roses. Balm smoothed

over my skin, sinking into me.

Everywhere.

"Did you care for me in this way while I lay healing?" Ariane asked starkly.

The accusation in her voice caught Simon on the raw. She had just given him sweet release, her hands were even now making him swollen with new need, and she was looking at him as though he were a dangerous stranger.

Simon's jaw clenched as he fought to still the wild race of his blood. He wasn't successful. Ariane was too close, her hands too soft, the smell of ecstasy too fresh.

"Only once," Simon said in a low, rough voice.

"When?"

"When you were almost well. Do you remember?"

"I . . ."

Ariane's breath caught as a streamer of memory coursed through her.

She had been held in thrall, but not in the darkness and rage of her nightmare. The hands and mouth caressing her body had been gentle rather than harsh, the voice husky rather than drunken, the breath sweet rather than rancid with ale.

"You touched me," she whispered.

"Yes."

"Even . . ."

Her voice died, but Simon understood.

"Yes," he said. "Even here."

Simon's hand moved between Ariane's thighs. His palm cupped her tenderly.

Ariane gasped and jerked back as though Simon had taken a whip to her. Even as Ariane's mind reassured her that Simon would never brutalize her as Geoffrey had, echoes of pain and humiliation made her stiffen.

Cursing his own lack of control and her lack of desire, Simon snatched back his hand.

"You were less cold while you were healing," he said curtly.

"*I wasn't awake.*"

"Nor were you asleep."

"I don't remember," Ariane said frantically.

"I do. When I touched you like that, you lifted toward me!"

Eyes wide, Ariane looked at Simon. The fire transformed his hair and clipped beard into a halo of golden light. His black eyes were like night itself; clear, deep, flecked with glittering light.

"Now do you understand?" he asked in a harsh whisper.

Ariane shook her head so hard that her hair seethed like black flames.

Simon whipped off the mantle, revealing to the chill air and dancing firelight everything that had been concealed.

"Look at yourself," he whispered fiercely. "You are all but naked, sitting astride me."

Ariane shivered.

"Think how close is the sword," Simon said in a low, relentless voice. "Think how open and vulnerable is the sheath."

Ariane looked down. A ragged sound was torn from her.

If he moves at all, he will learn that he has been deceived. Then there will be no more kindness, no more gentleness, nothing but pain.

"No!" Ariane whispered.

When she would have retreated, Simon's hands clamped onto her thighs, holding her as she was.

Open.

"Do you fear rape?" Simon asked sardonically. "For nine long days and nights you lay vulnerable to me. Did you awaken torn asunder and crying your violation to God?"

Ariane barely heard. All she knew was that she couldn't move, couldn't escape, yet she must do both.

"Let me go!" Ariane cried, clawing futilely at Simon's hands.

The raw emotion in Ariane's voice chilled Simon's blood as nothing else could have. An icy rage at his own weakness and the coldness of his bride broke over him.

He set Ariane aside so swiftly that she fell

back onto the bedding. As he came to his feet, he whipped the mantle around his shoulders. For the space of three heartbeats he stood looking down at her with eyes darker than any nightmare she had ever known.

"Sleep well, wife. You need not fear my unwanted touch again. Ever."

21

The lord's solar in Blackthorne Keep was spacious and luxurious. The walls were hung with draperies in shades of wine and jade green and lapis lazuli, and threads of precious metal ran through the cloth like captive sunlight.

The draperies had been brought back from the Holy Land, as had the rugs that warmed the floor. The clean scent of herbs and spices was everywhere, for it pleased Meg's spirit.

It pleased Ariane as well. Even after nearly ten days spent at the keep, the rushes covering the floor continually surprised her with their scent. She took a deep breath and then another, savoring the complex interplay of fragrances.

Her fingers danced over the strings of her lap harp as she tried to match music with a room that was masculine in its size and decoration, yet had the fragrance of a woman's garden.

The individual sounds that Ariane drew from her harp turned slowly into chords. The quivering harmonies rose and swirled until it seemed that the very notes shimmered in the air, describing a time and a place where male was partnered with female . . . and both were enhanced by the union rather than diminished.

When Ariane paused to consider the beauty of the solar once more, she heard a delicate chiming music coming from the great hall beyond. The sound was approaching the lord's solar.

Ariane turned and rose to her feet, knowing that it would be Meg coming into the room. Only the lady of Blackthorne Keep wore sweetly singing golden bells.

"Good morning to you, Lady Margaret," Ariane said.

"Good morning to you," Meg said. "Did you sleep well?"

Slowly Ariane's mouth took on a curve that was too sad to be a smile.

"Aye," she said quietly.

What Ariane didn't say was that sleep was becoming more and more difficult each night. On the trail she had shared Simon's bed as much from necessity as from any particular desire on his part. Once at Blackthorne Keep, Ariane had assumed she would be given quarters of her own, for it had been quite clear that Simon had no intention of pursuing the consummation of his marriage.

Sleep well, wife. You need not fear my unwanted touch again. Ever.

But Blackthorne Keep hadn't enough rooms to spare two for a married couple. Ariane and Simon had been given a room close to the bathing room. The room had been Meg's before her marriage to Dominic le Sabre. The other rooms on that floor of the keep were unavailable, for they were being renovated with an eye toward children.

Simon could have slept in the barracks with the rest of the keep's fighting men, but that area was filled to overflowing. Dominic had been recruiting knights returning from the Holy War, as well as men-at-arms, squires, grooms, and the servants necessary to support the growing number of people living at the keep.

Though Ariane understood the necessity of combined quarters, she found it difficult to sleep next to a man whose very breath made curious threads of heat gather throughout her body. A man whose shimmering sensuality came to her in dreams, setting her afire. A man whose restraint she trusted. A man much beloved by the keep's cats. A man whose own feline grace made her heartbeat speed.

But not with fear.

How can I fear a man whose chain mail hauberk serves as a ladder for kittens?

The answer was as swift as it was unavoidable.

I fear what will happen when Simon discovers that I am no maiden, but a girl hard-used by a dishonorable knight.

Will I finally find the death I once sought?

Once, but no more. Now the rainbow possibilities of life called to Ariane.

Somehow, while she had lain in thrall to Learned medicine and fragrant balm, much of the poison of her past rape had drained away, allowing another kind of healing to begin. Nightmare rarely came to Ariane now unless she was in some way restrained.

As she had been by Simon when she sat astride his lap and discovered that some things burn far more deeply than fire.

The downward curve of Ariane's mouth became deeper as she remembered how she had cried out and clawed at Simon's hands. The pride and anger in him at her rejection — and the hurt — had been almost tangible.

He had no way of knowing it had been past nightmare that she rejected, not Simon himself.

I must tell him.

Soon.

Tonight?

A shudder coursed through Ariane at the thought of how Simon would react. He deserved better than a bride whose emotions and body had been savaged by a cruel knight.

Just as Ariane herself had deserved better than rape and betrayal by the very men who should have honored and protected her.

I can't tell him. Not yet.

Not tonight.

If Simon has a chance to know me better, perhaps he will believe that it was rape rather than seduction that forced my maidenhead.

But my own father did not believe.

"Lady Ariane?" Meg said gently. "Do sit down. You look quite pale."

Ariane straightened her shoulders and released a breath she hadn't been aware of holding. Her fingers moved restlessly on the strings of her harp.

It was jagged sorrow rather than completion that she drew from the instrument.

"I am well," Ariane said neutrally. "The medicines you and Cassandra used healed me."

"Not quite."

"What do you mean?"

"Listen to your own music," Meg said. "It is darker than even Simon's eyes."

"Betrayed by my own harp."

Ariane had meant the words lightly, but they came out as a bleak statement of fact.

"Are the men still out hawking?" Ariane asked quickly.

"No. We just came back."

Slowly Ariane absorbed the fact that she hadn't been awakened to go hawking in the glorious dawn, but Meg had.

It shouldn't have hurt Ariane, but it did.

"Simon said you had slept badly and shouldn't be disturbed," Meg said.

A ripple of discordant notes was Ariane's only response.

"Was the hawking successful?" Ariane asked politely while the strings were still quivering.

"Aye. Dominic's peregrine brought down enough fat waterfowl to assure a feast. Simon's gyrfalcon did just as well. They earned so many morsels of freshly killed fowl that the falcons could barely fly toward the end of the morning."

Ariane forced a smile. "Skylance is a fine falcon, worthy of Simon in every way."

The tone of Ariane's voice said much more, implying that other things — such as his wife — were not quite so worthy of Simon.

Meg's green eyes widened. She *saw* Ariane with Glendruid eyes, and what Meg saw was unsettling: Ariane did indeed feel that Simon had been cheated in the marriage bargain.

As for Simon . . . Meg didn't need Glendruid eyes to know that Simon was like a wildcat that had been caged and tormented until it savaged everything within reach.

"Lady Ariane," Meg said. "Is there some way in which I could serve you?"

Ariane gave the Glendruid girl a curious glance.

" 'Tis I who should be serving you," Ariane said. "You are the lady of the keep, and heavy with child. I am but a guest."

"Nay." Meg's response was instant and earnest. "You and your marriage to Simon are very important to Blackthorne and to the Disputed Lands."

Silently Ariane nodded while her fingers strummed without purpose on the harp.

"Without your marriage," Meg said urgently, "war would once again claw at the very life of my people."

Again Ariane nodded.

"Yet I fear it isn't enough for you and Simon to be joined in the sight of God and man," Meg said in a strained voice. "I have dreamed in the Glendruid way."

Ariane went still. "Of what?"

"Of two halves that refuse to be made whole. Of rage. Of betrayal. *Of ravens pecking out the eyes of my unborn babe.*"

A shocked sound was all Ariane could manage. Her throat closed around protests and questions that were futile. There was nothing to be said that could undo Meg's grim Glendruid dream.

344

"What must I do?" asked Ariane.

Her voice was dry, aching, barely more than a whisper.

"Heal that which lies festering between you and Simon," Meg said bluntly. "You are the two stubborn halves that threaten the whole of Blackthorne and the Disputed Lands."

"What of Simon?" Ariane retorted. "Has he no part in this healing?"

Meg's normally full lips flattened into a harsh line. "Simon says he has done all that he can. I believe him."

Ariane looked down at her harp and said nothing.

"I know my husband's brother," Meg said evenly. "Simon is proud, stubborn, and as quick with his temper as he is with his sword. Simon is also as loyal a man as ever drew breath. It is Dominic who commands Simon's loyalty."

"Yes," whispered Ariane. "To be blessed with another's loyalty like that . . ."

She couldn't finish. Eyes closed, fearing even to breathe, Ariane waited for the trap to close around her.

Again.

"If there were aught to be done for his brother's benefit, Simon would do it," Meg said simply.

Ariane nodded, fighting back the unexpected tightness of her throat as she thought of Simon's loyalty. With each heartbeat, the tension in her throat increased until she was afraid she would cry out. It was as though sorrow somehow burned inside her, waiting to be quenched by tears.

But that was impossible.

She hadn't wept since nightmare had closed cruelly around her. She wouldn't weep now. A woman's tears accomplished nothing, save to call down the contempt of priests, fathers, and dishonorable knights.

"Thus," Meg continued relentlessly, "the cause for your marriage being less than it seems comes from you, rather than from Simon."

"Yes," Ariane whispered.

Meg waited.

Silence expanded until it filled the room to suffocation.

"I ask again, Lady Ariane: How may I serve you?"

It was more a demand than a request.

"Can you change the nature of man and woman and betrayal?" Ariane asked.

"Nay."

"Then there is nothing to be done to make Simon's marriage better."

" 'Tis your marriage as well," Meg pointed out crisply.

"Yes."

"You lie with Simon at night, yet there is a distance between you two that is greater than that lying between the Disputed Lands and the Holy Land."

Ariane gave Meg a sideways glance.

"It takes no special Glendruid sight to see the estrangement between you and your husband. The people of the keep talk of little else," Meg said bluntly. "God's teeth, what is wrong?"

"Nothing that can be set aright."

Meg blinked and then went quite still. "What do you mean? Speak plainly."

"You seek to cure an ailing marriage by sexual congress," Ariane said, each word precise. "I tell you that such a 'cure' will result in the very disaster you seek to avoid."

There was silence while Meg absorbed Ariane's unexpected words.

"I don't believe I understand," Meg said carefully.

"Be grateful. I understand all of betrayal's cruel aspects. Such knowledge is a curse I wouldn't wish upon Satan himself, much less upon Simon the Loyal."

"Don't juggle words with me," snarled Meg. "It is my unborn babe at risk!"

Startled, Ariane looked at the smaller woman's searing green eyes. For the first time Ariane understood that Glendruid healers had the same elemental ferocity as spring itself; only something that untamed could burn through the lifeless coils of winter to ignite the life beneath.

"I meant no disrespect," Ariane said in a low voice.

"Then tell me what I must know!"

Ariane closed her eyes and clenched her hands on the harp's cold, smooth frame. Into the silence came the crackle of fire in the hearth and the odd, strained humming of harp strings that were far too tightly drawn.

"Tell me, witch of Glendruid, can you take a broken egg and make it whole again?"

"No."

"Given that, do the details of how and when and where and why the egg was broken matter so much to you?"

"You are not an egg," Meg said impatiently.

"No. I am a chattel that was transferred first to one man and then to another. I am a pawn in a masculine game of pride and power. I am a 'stubborn half' that *cannot* be made whole."

Abruptly Ariane released the strings. They cried out as though being torn apart.

"Does Simon know the cause of your stubbornness?" Meg asked.

"No."

"Tell him."

"If you knew what —" Ariane began.

"But I don't," Meg interrupted fiercely. "Tell Simon. He would move Heaven and Earth to help Dominic."

"You ask too much of Simon. There is no justice in that."

"Ravens don't care about justice or the tender nature of their prey. Neither do Glendruid healers."

Before Ariane could argue further, she heard Dominic and Simon striding through the great hall, laughing and comparing the skill of their falcons.

"Tell him," Meg said in a voice that went no farther than Ariane's ears. "Or else I will."

"Now? Nay! 'Tis a private thing!"

"So is death," Meg retorted. Then she released a pent breath. "You have until tomorrow. Not one breath longer. My dreams grow dire."

"I cannot. It needs more time."

"You must. There is no more time."

" 'Tis too soon," Ariane whispered.

"Nay," Meg said flatly. "I fear it is already too late!"

Ariane saw the determination in Meg and knew there would be no evading the demands of the Glendruid witch.

With a sinking heart, Ariane watched Simon and Dominic stride into the lord's solar. Both men smelled of sunlight, dried grass and cold, fresh air. Their mantles swirled and flared with each muscular motion of the men's bodies. Proud, hooded falcons rode on gauntleted wrists.

As Dominic urged his peregrine onto a perch behind his big chair, he looked from Meg to Ariane. In that instant Ariane realized that Dominic knew his wife had planned a private conversation with Simon's reluctant wife.

No doubt Dominic knew what had been discussed as well.

It takes no special Glendruid sight to see the distance between you and your husband. The people of the keep talk of little else.

The idea that the estrangement between herself and her husband provided gossip for lords and villeins alike made Ariane both angry and embarrassed.

How tongues will flap when it becomes known that I brought a fine dowry and no maidenhead to my wedding.

The bitter thought brought no comfort to Ariane. She would suffer for her lack of virginity, though she hadn't surrendered it willingly.

Numbly her hands tightened on the cool, smooth wood of the harp. She drew a few soft, sweet notes from the strings, trying to soothe herself.

"Good morning, Lady Ariane," Dominic said, smiling. "What gentle sounds you're calling from that harp. I trust the morning finds you well?"

"Aye, lord. Your hospitality leaves nothing to be desired."

"Good. Have you eaten?"

"Aye."

"Did Blanche bring you the latest gossip?" Dominic asked.

"Er, no."

"There are rumors that your father is in England."

Ariane's fingers jerked, scattering notes like leaves in the silence.

"Lord?" she asked. "Are you certain?"

Dominic assessed Ariane's shock, gave Simon a sideways glance, and spoke again.

" 'Tis as certain as any gossip," Dominic said, shrugging. "Simon thought you might have forgotten to tell us that your father planned to visit you."

"My father — if it is indeed my father — keeps his own counsel," Ariane said.

The careful lack of emotion in her voice said as much as the curt plucking of harp strings by her fingers.

"The noble in question has a large entourage with him. Does your father travel thus?" Dominic asked.

351

"My father go nowhere without his hawking, hunting, and whoring partners."

"Are they also knights?"

Ariane's mouth turned down. The notes she pulled from the harp were mocking.

"They name themselves such," she said.

"You have no liking for them," Dominic said.

Ariane shrugged. "I have no liking for any man who spends much of the day and all of the night half-blind with wine."

Dominic turned to Meg. "It seems we will have to prepare for an unexpected visit from Baron Deguerre and his knights."

"How many guests?"

"Gossip ranges from twenty to thirty-five, according to Sven," Simon said. "He is riding out to make certain, both of the number and of the lord's identity."

Meg frowned and began making mental lists of what must be done.

Simon urged Skylance onto a perch near the other falcon. With a careless nod in Ariane's direction, Simon went to the fire, stripping off his hawking gauntlet and supple gloves as he went. The white of his mantle's fur lining gleamed when he removed the garment with a casual twist of his shoulders.

Unbidden, the memory came to Ariane of the instant when Simon had swept her from his lap, leaped to his feet, and whipped his mantle around his nearly naked body. He had towered over her, fierce and hotly aroused despite his recent release, but his eyes had been the black of coldest ice.

Simon had kept the bitter vow he had made to Ariane that night. He hadn't touched her again. Not even in the most casual way.

Not once.

Does every serf and serving maid know that my husband beds down on the floor like a peasant in a stable, so that he won't touch me even while he sleeps?

"I have been considering the matter of Simon's future," Dominic said to no one in particular.

Simon glanced up sharply from the fire. "You said nothing about this while we were hawking."

Smiling, Dominic ignored his brother.

"With Baron Deguerre's generous dowry," Dominic said, "and Duncan's gifts, it is obvious that you will have the means to support a keep of your own."

"I am happy serving you," Simon said distinctly.

"I am honored. But I was your brother before I was your lord, and I know that your dream of the future was the same as mine — land of your own, a noble wife, and children."

Beneath the short beard, Simon's jaw flexed as though he had clenched his teeth.

"You have the noble wife," Dominic said, "the children are in God's hands, and the land is in mine."

"Dominic —" Simon began.

"Nay. Let me speak."

Though Dominic's smile was warm, the silver wolf's head that fastened his black mantle flashed in blunt reminder of Dominic's power.

"Carlysle Manor lies partly in my land and partly in land claimed by Robert of the North, father of Erik," Dominic said. "With Erik's goodwill, and Duncan of Maxwell's, the manor and its wide domain are secure enough. For now."

A stillness came over Simon as he listened to his brother.

"But if Erik and his father were to argue . . ." Dominic shrugged. "What say you, Simon?"

"Erik and Robert of the North are as unlike one another as any father and son I have ever known."

"Meg?" Dominic asked.

"Simon is correct," Meg agreed. "Erik is Learned. Robert despises Learning."

"Erik believes in husbanding the land and its people," Simon said. "Robert believes in taxing them until another babe to feed is a curse rather than a blessing for the serfs."

Dominic looked at Ariane in silent query. "Lady Ariane? Have you an opinion?"

"Erik is a warrior," Ariane said succinctly. "His father is a conspirator. In Normandy we call him Robert the Whisperer."

Dominic's eyes narrowed in sudden, intense interest at Ariane's words.

"Robert has even tried to make secret alliances with my father," Ariane said, "against the wishes of the king of the Scots, the king of the English, and the greatest of all Norman barons."

"Did your father agree to any alliance?" Dominic asked sharply.

Ariane paused, considering her words. Her fingers drifted across the harp strings, drawing random chords. The sounds were oddly pensive, as though the instrument were partner to Ariane's hidden thoughts.

Meg suspected that such was precisely the case. She also suspected that Ariane was unaware of how much her music gave away of the very emotions she denied having.

"The Whisperer and my father court one another like spiders," Ariane said finally. "Each is cautious to evade the other's sticky web."

Simon's smile was sardonic.

"I understand now why the Learned 'value'

me," Simon said. "Erik knows that a well-married Ariane will thwart Deguerre's ambitions in the Disputed Lands."

"What do you believe will happen between Robert and your father?" Meg asked.

"It depends on which man gets careless first," Ariane said matter-of-factly. "Behind both men, kings also spin intricate webs."

Almost absently, Dominic nodded. He was caught by Simon's statement about being of "value" to the Learned. It explained Erik's willingness to become an ally of the very Glendruid Wolf whom the king of the Scots would just as soon sweep from the Disputed Lands; and Erik's father was very much vassal to the Scots king.

A cascade of notes poured from the harp, drawing Dominic's attention back to Ariane.

"Were I a man with land and a keep that lay in the Disputed Lands between Scotland and England," Ariane said, "I would drill my warriors as faithfully as priests toll the hours of the day."

Dominic laughed. "I am glad Simon volunteered to become your husband, Lady Ariane. You are a good match for his quickness."

Ariane's smile slipped. "You are too kind, lord."

"Aye," Simon said sardonically. "Too kind indeed."

Dominic simply smiled like a Glendruid Wolf.

"Ariane's words reinforce my decision," Dominic said.

Simon lifted his tawny eyebrows and waited.

"In order to hold Carlysle Manor," Dominic said, "I learned I would have to take Meg from her beloved Blackthorne and establish a true keep where the Carlysle house is. Then Carlysle would have become our primary residence."

Meg made a small sound that was quickly smothered, but Dominic heard it just the same. He stepped forward and put his hand on her cheek.

"Be at ease, small falcon," Dominic said with the gentleness he showed to no one else. "I know your special bond with Blackthorne's people and theirs with you."

"If necessary, I can —" Meg began.

"Nay. 'Tis not necessary," Dominic said softly. "Simon will hold Carlysle for me. Ariane's dowry will pay to fortify Carlysle against raiders, renegade knights, and greedy kings."

Dominic turned from his wife to Simon.

"Come, brother," Dominic said. "Let us all go to the armory. It is time to tally the wealth Baron Deguerre sent to you with his daughter."

Simon didn't move.

"What is it?" Dominic asked. "Have you no interest in your own goods?"

"I give them all to you," Simon said. "For Blackthorne. For Meg. For the security of your unborn children. Because it is certain I will have none to concern me."

22

Dominic flashed a silvery glance at Meg, who shook her head.

"The number of your children is for God to decide," Dominic said. "It is for me to decide which of my knights shall hold land in fief for me . . . and which shall hold land in fee simple, owning nothing to me save the loyalty of a valued ally."

The smile Dominic gave Simon made Ariane feel like weeping. In that instant the love Dominic had for his brother was almost tangible. She well understood why Simon was utterly loyal to such a man, lord and brother and friend in one.

"Carlysle Manor," Dominic said, "shall become Carlysle Keep. And you, Simon, shall be lord and sole owner of all of Carlysle's land."

Simon's breath came in with an audible sound.

"I would have done it sooner," Dominic said, "but I hadn't the wealth to divide between two keeps. As Ariane's husband, you are nearly as wealthy as I."

" 'Tis too much," Simon said, his voice low. "I am not worthy."

Dominic laughed and gave Simon a hard hug.

"There is no man on earth more worthy than you, Simon the Loyal," Dominic said.

"But —"

"Were it not for your rallying the knights," Dominic said, talking over Simon's objections, "I would have died in a sultan's prison. Is that not true?"

"What I did was nothing! You ransomed me with your own body!"

"Were it not for you," Dominic said, ignoring Simon's words, "I would be preparing for war over the jilted daughter of Baron Deguerre."

"Aye, but —"

"Come," Dominic said, talking over Simon's words and taking his arm. "Let us count Deguerre's bounty and spend the remainder of the day listing what you will need to make Carlysle a secure and profitable keep."

Looking a bit dazed, Simon allowed an amused Dominic to lead him in the direction of the keep's armory. Smiling, Meg waited for Ariane to accompany them.

Carefully Ariane set her harp on a side table. As she turned back to Meg, light from a nearby lamp danced and glittered over the haft of the jeweled dagger she wore on the girdle that rode low on her hips. An answering flash of amethysts gleamed at her wrist and neck.

The two women hurried from the solar, their long skirts whispering over the keep's stone floors. Golden bells chimed sweetly with each step Meg took.

As Meg and Ariane descended the stairway, lamplight gave way to torches set in holders along the walls. Air disturbed by their bodies made the torch flames dip and sway, sending shadows sliding crazily over the stones.

The armory was near the barracks, for men-at-arms guarded both the costly weapons and the wellhead that was the keep's source of water. At Blackthorne Keep, the armory with its iron door and impregnable stone walls also served as a treasure room. There Thomas the Strong stood guard over weapons and wealth alike.

As often was the case, Marie, widow of Robert the Cuckold, was nearby. Thomas was her favorite among the knights garrisoned within the keep.

Except, of course, for Dominic and Simon.

"Lord," Marie said, bowing low to Dominic in the Saracen fashion. "We see too little of you."

The sensual light in Marie's dark eyes and

the huskiness of her voice carried another message — should Dominic ever tire of his Glendruid wife, Marie would be ready to serve him in any fashion he desired.

Meg smiled with genuine amusement. She and Marie had reached an agreement, one that had been privately struck. Marie would cease lying in wait for Dominic and confine her seraglio-learned wiles to unmarried men, or Meg would see that Marie found a position as a whore in a London brothel.

"And you, Simon," Marie murmured, smiling up at him from under long black lashes. " 'Tis sad that such a generously endowed man is so stingy with his . . . presence."

Lips more red than a ripe cherry pouted for an instant, only to widen into a sensual smile that was for Simon and Simon alone. Marie stepped very close to him, stood on tiptoe, and kissed him on the lips.

For an instant Simon stiffened as though he had been slapped. Then his hands unclenched and he accepted Marie's kiss with an ease that spoke of long familiarity.

Ariane watched and thought how lovely her jeweled dagger would look between Marie's shoulder blades.

"Congratulations on your fine marriage, sir," Marie said when Simon ended the kiss.

The huskiness in Marie's voice had doubled.

Her eyes were heavy-lidded, watching only Simon. Her clever hands smoothed down the bodice of her dress and over her full, flaring hips. The red silk — a parting gift from Dominic — glowed in the torchlight as though alive.

"Thank you," Simon said.

Casually he widened the space between them, but not far enough to suit Ariane. Each time Marie took a deep breath, and it seemed the wench took no other kind, the tips of her full breasts nearly brushed against Simon.

" 'Tis my hope that you won't forget old friends who shared . . . everything . . . with you through the Holy War," Marie said.

"I forget nothing," Simon promised softly.

For a moment Marie's long lashes swept down, shielding her eyes. Then she looked up at Simon once more. Her lips gleamed from a recent licking and her eyes were half-closed. The hardened tips of her breasts showed clearly through the red silk.

"Nor do I forget," Marie murmured. "You least of all, for you were best of all. Do you remember that, too?"

"Marie," Meg said clearly. "Remember our bargain?"

"Aye, Lady Margaret."

"Simon, too, is married."

Marie smiled and flashed a sideways look

at Ariane before speaking.

"Aye, lady," Marie said. "But 'tis said freely about the keep that Lady Ariane has no interest whose bed her husband warms, so long as it isn't her own."

"That is not true," Ariane said distinctly.

Marie's smile said she didn't believe it.

"I am glad," Marie murmured, but it was to Simon she spoke. "A sword too long without a sheath grows rusty."

Marie's fingers went directly from the laces at the neck of Simon's shirt to the lacing of his breeches. His hand shot out with startling quickness, keeping Marie's prowling fingers from their goal.

"Ah, Simon," Marie said huskily, leaning toward him, "I am happy that yours is a true marriage. Your sword is far too fine an instrument to suffer neglect. It deserves to be as I well remember it, hard and gleaming from careful rubbing."

Before Ariane could speak, Simon did.

"Thomas," Simon said neutrally.

"Aye?" Thomas asked, grinning.

Simon looked at the accomplished whore whose fingers were even now sliding against his wrist, stroking sensitive skin as though his hold on her were that of a lover rather than a man whose impatience was barely leashed. Slowly he smiled down at her.

364

Only Marie was close enough to see that Simon's eyes were black stones that held neither warmth nor humor.

"Take your leman elsewhere," Simon said gently, "before Ariane decides upon a place to stick that dagger she is holding."

Ariane looked down at her right hand. The amethyst-studded hilt flashed between her fingers. The blade itself was bright, gleaming, and obviously sharp.

She had no memory of drawing the dagger from its sheath.

"Perhaps," Meg said, amused, "Marie would do well to strike the same bargain with Lady Ariane that was struck with me."

Marie looked at the dagger and then at Ariane. Surprisingly, Marie laughed.

"Aye," Marie agreed. "Perhaps I should."

"What bargain is this?" Dominic and Simon asked at the same time.

Marie winked at Dominic, gave Simon a sideways, remembering kind of look, and turned toward Ariane.

"I will stop teasing your husband," Marie said.

Stiffly Ariane nodded.

"But," Marie said, "I live at the sufferance of Lord Dominic and his brother. If either of them desires me, *at any time,* I am theirs for as long as I hold their interest."

Dominic and Simon exchanged a swift look.

"It is the nature of men to grow bored with bedding just one woman," Marie explained matter-of-factly. "When Dominic and Simon call for me, neither Glendruid curses nor jeweled daggers will keep me from their beds. They are master here, not I. And not you, ladies Margaret and Ariane."

"Marie," Dominic said softly. "At your husband's death in the Holy Land, I vowed to keep you safe until you died. I did not give you leave to bait the ladies of the keep."

Marie curtsied deeply to the two women. "If I have offended you, I am sorry. I am harem raised and see the world differently."

"Thomas," Dominic said distinctly.

"Aye, lord!"

Thomas stepped forward from his guard position at the armory door. He was thick as an oak, unimaginative, and possessed of a genial temperament.

He also was renowned for his stamina between a woman's thighs.

"Exercise your strength on Marie's behalf," Dominic said to Thomas.

"Now, lord?"

"Now."

"My pleasure, lord."

One of Thomas the Strong's massive hands

descended on Marie's rump with a hearty smack. Then he stood close behind her and squeezed her buttocks with great care.

Marie's breath came in with a rush. She turned slowly toward Thomas, rubbing her soft bottom over him as she turned. The smile he gave her was that of a man anticipating what was to come.

Saying not one word, Thomas lifted Marie with one thick arm. Smiling, she circled his muscular hips with her legs, locking herself in place. The position was obviously a familiar one for both of them, because Thomas started walking away from the armory without hesitation.

Marie leaned close, nipped his neck, and put her clever hands to work on every fastening within her reach.

Very quickly the two people vanished from sight, leaving nothing behind but for Marie's high, oddly sweet laughter trailing back through the stone passageway. Then, even that stopped, as though cut off by a man's kiss.

"Thank God for Thomas the Strong," Dominic said.

"Amen," Simon said.

Simon turned and gave his wife a hooded, enigmatic glance. He looked her over from head to toe as though examining something utterly unexpected.

And he was.

The fact that Ariane was jealous of Simon was as startling as anything that had ever happened to him, including the moment when Ariane had crashed her strong little mare right into a war stallion on his behalf.

Ariane had nearly died to save Simon's life.

She had been ready to use her dagger on a leman who wanted him.

She melted and ran like rich, sun-warmed honey when he came to her in her dreams.

Yet awake, Ariane scorned the ultimate sensual feast.

Distantly Simon wondered if any man ever had understood women.

Even a Learned man.

"You may put away the dagger, nightingale."

Ariane's eyes widened as she looked at her husband. A curl of warmth went through her at the nickname, and at the speculative gleam in Simon's eyes.

"Or are you planning to stick the blade into me?" Simon asked politely.

Ariane's cheeks burned. She sheathed the weapon with a swift motion.

"Excellent," Simon said. "We progress. I think."

With a muffled sound of laughter, Dominic

turned away to deal with the huge iron lock that secured the armory. Moments later the lock gave way with a rattle and clang of iron. As the door swung open, a faint odor of spices pervaded the air.

"Torches," Dominic said.

Simon took two from the wall holders and held one out to Dominic as he stepped into the dark armory. Simon gestured the women to go before him. Meg went first. Then Ariane walked forward.

As she went by, Simon swiftly moved so that Ariane had to brush against his body to get past. His movement was unexpected, startling.

Ariane jerked away before she knew what she had done.

The smile Simon gave her was that of a man who has called another's bluff — and found it hollow. The look in his eyes said that there was no joy in winning that particular game.

Ariane reached out to touch Simon's arm. Deliberately he stepped beyond reach.

"I prefer the honesty of your first response," he said in a voice too soft for the others to hear.

"You are so cursed quick! You startled me, 'tis all."

"I think not."

"Simon?" Dominic asked impatiently without looking over his shoulder. "Where are you?"

"Here."

"You don't seem overeager to see your wealth."

"I don't need to see. I can smell it," Simon said dryly.

Dominic laughed. "Indeed, the pepper in particular."

Meg sniffed, drew in a deep breath, and then frowned.

"What is it?" Dominic asked immediately.

She hesitated, took another deep breath, and shook her head as though confused.

"The smell is mild for the amount of spices those chests should hold," Meg said finally. "Perhaps they are simply well sealed."

"Or old," Dominic said bluntly. "The smell fades with time."

"They are quite fresh," Ariane said. "Father's steward complained endlessly about the cost of sending the finest grade of spices to be wasted on the barbarian Scots palate of my future husband."

"Odd," Dominic said.

"Hardly," Ariane said in a dry tone. "Baron Deguerre is generous only with his knights, and even then he complains of their cost. I am but a daughter required to wed a foreign knight not of my father's choosing."

"Then he should be pleased to find you safely wed to a fine Norman knight," Dominic said.

"Pleased? By his daughter?" Ariane laughed humorlessly. "That would be unprecedented, lord."

Dominic swept the armory with torchlight. The flame was reflected back countless times over from weapons hanging on the walls, from chain mail hauberks hung on wooden rests, and from helms and gauntlets stacked neatly on shelves.

In one corner, seventeen chests were neatly laid out according to size. The brass bindings of the chests were dulled by salt air and neglect, but the locks were oiled and gleaming.

Dominic set his torch in a holder, reached beneath his mantle, and pulled out a large purse. Inside were various keys and a rolled parchment. The parchment's neat printing detailed the exact contents of the dowry chests, as well as other aspects of the nuptial contract. The heavy wax seal at the bottom of the document was repeated on the lids of all the chests in such a way as to make it impossible to open the chest without breaking the seal.

"The silks first," Dominic muttered. "Have you seen them, Ariane?"

"Aye, sir. They are very fine, with colors

to shame a rainbow. Some are sheer enough to permit sunlight to pass through. Others are embroidered so cleverly that it is as if silk had been woven upon silk until the fabric can all but stand on its own."

"Fine silks indeed," Dominic said.

"If Simon agrees," Ariane continued, "I would like to give Lady Amber some cloth for her kindness to me. And there is a green that would exactly match Lady Margaret's eyes."

"Done," Simon said instantly.

"There is no need," said Meg.

"Thank you," Dominic said over his wife's words. "I enjoy seeing Meg in green."

"I fear the cloth is too sheer for ordinary use," Ariane cautioned. "From what I overheard father telling one of his knights, 'tis more suited to a harem than a cold English keep."

A sensual smile changed the lines of Dominic's face.

"I will look forward to that cloth most particularly," he said. "The sultan's concubines wore very, um, intriguing clothing."

As Dominic spoke, he shook out the bag of keys. Clattering and clanging, they fell onto a stone ledge next to battle gauntlets. He selected a key and went to the biggest chest. Grudgingly the lock gave way. The seal broke a moment later. With a creak of brass hinges, Dominic heaved up the lid and looked within.

"God's teeth, what is this?" he muttered. "Simon."

At the sound of his name, Simon went to Dominic's side and glanced into the chest. Torchlight showed sacks made of coarse fabric. With a speed that made Ariane blink, Simon drew his dagger and opened one bag.

Coarsely ground flour spilled out. Simon grabbed a handful, worked it through his fingers, and sniffed it. With a sound of disgust he opened his fist and let the contents spill out over the armory's stone floor.

"Spoiled," he said curtly.

"The silk?" Ariane asked, for Simon's broad back stood between her and a view of the chest.

"Flour," Simon said.

Dominic began poking around in the chest.

"What of the silk?" Ariane asked, perplexed.

"There's none in this chest," Dominic said, straightening. "The rest of the bags are dirt rather than flour."

With a startled sound Ariane pushed between the two men. She looked at the scarred chest, then at the broken seal, and then at the chest again.

"The seal," she said. "Was it intact?"

"Aye," Dominic said.

"I don't understand. I saw my father's steward fill the chests."

"One chest often looks like another," Dominic said. "Perhaps there was an error."

Simon said nothing. He simply took a key from the pile and sought the correct lock. This key fit a smaller chest. He inserted the key, broke the seal, and lifted the lid. The smell of cinnamon and cloves wafted upward.

Simon didn't speak.

"Well?" Ariane said.

"Sand," said Dominic curtly.

"I beg your pardon?" she asked.

"Sand," Dominic repeated.

"But there was cinnamon once," Simon said. "And cloves. The wood reeks of it."

"I don't understand," Ariane said.

Yet her tone said she was very much afraid that she did.

In a silence that grew deeper with each chest opened, Dominic and Simon went through Ariane's dowry. The creak of a lid was followed by a single terse word that described worthless goods in place of gems, gold, silver, silks, furs, and spices.

"Stones."

"Sand."

A Saracen curse was followed by more understandable descriptions of what the chests held.

"Rotten flour."

"Rocks."

"Dirt."

Ariane swayed and felt like stopping up her ears so that she wouldn't have to hear the ugly truth.

Betrayed.

When the final chest stood open, Dominic surveyed the lot with his hands on his hips. Ballast rocks still smelling of the sea were all the chest contained.

The wolf's head pin on Dominic's mantle seemed to snarl as he turned to face Ariane. His eyes were like hammered silver.

"It would seem," Dominic said smoothly, "that there is a discrepancy between the dowry promised by Baron Deguerre and that which was delivered."

"Aye," Ariane said in a raw voice.

Though Dominic waited, she said nothing more.

"Lady Ariane," he said sharply, "what say you?"

"I have been betrayed. Again."

The bleakness in Ariane's voice touched Dominic in spite of his anger, as did the sight of her fingers reaching for the strings of the harp she had left behind.

"It would seem that the baron is trying to provoke a war," Dominic said.

If Ariane heard, she didn't answer.

"Aye," Meg said tightly. Her small hands became fists. "But what does he gain from such dishonesty?"

"Freedom from an alliance he never sought," Dominic said.

"But he went back on his given vow," Meg protested. "Surely such dishonor in the eyes of his peers costs him more than a few chests of spices and gold?"

"My father's steward saw those chests filled, sealed, and put under the guard of his finest knights," Ariane said tonelessly. "So did I. Those same knights guarded the dowry until Blackthorne Keep."

"In other words, if I claim there was no dowry, I will be declaring war," Simon summarized.

"A war that Deguerre will certainly be in a position to win, for he believes Duncan of Maxwell to be too poor to hire knights without the dowry," Meg said.

"Nor will King Henry look kindly upon being asked to go to war over holdings that some believe belong to Robert the Whisperer in any case," Dominic concluded.

He turned to Ariane. "Your father is gambling that he will have won the battle before

King Henry has time to take the field."

"It would be like my father," Ariane said, her voice flat, emotionless. "He is extremely good at finding weakness where others see only strength. 'Tis why he is called Charles the Shrewd."

"Then we say nothing," Simon said.

"What?" Dominic demanded. "We can't —"

"I have no quarrel with my wife's dowry," Simon said succinctly.

Silence spread through the armory.

Ariane's bitter smile gleamed for an instant in the torchlight. The tears she had not shed when she had awakened shamed and dishonored at Geoffrey's hands now threatened to choke her.

"Simon," she whispered. "It would have been kinder to kill me when I offered the chance."

His eyes narrowed, but he said nothing.

"The spider spins," Ariane said tightly, "and it is I who am caught like an insect. And through me, you. No matter how we struggle, Baron Deguerre will win."

"Explain," Dominic said curtly. "And explain most carefully."

"My father foresaw weakness and division. He didn't foresee loyalty and restraint."

Dominic gave a sideways look to his brother, who was watching Ariane with dark, emotionless eyes.

"My father expected me to die on my wedding night," Ariane said starkly.

"God's blood. What nonsense is this?" Dominic demanded.

Ariane turned to Meg.

"This is the truth you sought so harshly, Lady Margaret. I hope it pleases you."

"No," Meg said, reaching out as though to stop Ariane.

But Ariane was already speaking, letting pain wash through her, surprised only that she could still feel.

"My father is coming to Blackthorne Keep expecting to start a war on the pretext of avenging my death at the hands of my husband."

"He will be disappointed," Simon said neutrally. "You are alive."

"Aye. But will I still live when you discover that I came to this marriage not a maiden?"

Simon became very still.

"You knew this?" Dominic demanded of Simon.

Simon said nothing.

"Our marriage is unconsummated," Ariane said. "I will swear that before a priest. An annulment will —"

"Nay," Simon said, cutting across her words. "I have no complaint with my marriage. No reason to seek an annulment. *No reason for war.*"

"By Christ's holy blood," Dominic snarled, "what of your honor?"

"I gave up my honor the moment I lay with another man's wife in the Holy Land."

"Marie?" Dominic asked, startled.

"Yes. I am the man Marie's husband saw sneaking into her tent. I am the reason the cuckold struck his devil's bargain with the sultan. I am the reason we were betrayed and you were so cruelly tortured."

"Simon, it wasn't your doing," Dominic said bluntly. "It was Robert the Cuckold's!"

"I hold myself responsible. As does God."

"You can't know that."

"Ah, but I do. Don't you see the perfection of the punishment God designed for me?"

"I see nothing but —"

Simon kept talking over Dominic, wanting his brother to understand once and for all time that what had happened in the Holy Land was finally being paid for in the Disputed Lands.

And Simon had no quarrel with the payment.

"I married for wealth, beauty and heirs," Simon said calmly. "The wealth is a chimera, the heirs will never be conceived, and Ariane lies alone in her bed every night as she prefers, her cold beauty a mortification of my body. Aye, my bride is a fitting chastisement indeed for my sin of lust and adultery."

"But —"

"If it had been you in Marie's bed and I the one who had been tortured by the sultan," Simon said, "would you feel differently than I do now?"

Dominic opened his mouth to speak, closed it, and shook his head wearily.

He would feel no differently than Simon.

"You are my brother," Dominic said softly, "and I love you."

"As I love you, brother."

Then Simon smiled with all the pain of the time since his unbridled lust for a married woman had nearly cost Dominic's life.

"At least I won't have to serve much time in hell when I die," Simon said. "My hell has come to me on earth, and her name is Ariane."

23

For the rest of the day Ariane sat in her room and waited in dread for Simon to come and question her about her lack of virginity.

He did not.

Simon went about his duties as Dominic's seneschal without so much as looking Ariane's way. The chests were locked once more, the keys were given into Dominic's keeping, and no one spoke within Ariane's hearing about the missing dowry.

In fact, it was as though she did not exist.

As though Simon did not care why she came to the marriage without her maidenhead.

As though he did not care about his wife at all.

And why should he? Ariane thought bleakly. *I am his punishment. A mortification of his body for his sin of lust.*

I am his hell.

Ariane shuddered. The ripple of movement pulled discordant notes from the harp she held in her lap. Broodingly she looked down at the instrument, but it was her own dark thoughts she was seeing rather than the intricate, beautifully inlaid wood.

Aimlessly she walked around the room, strumming the harp, seeing nothing of the color and luxury and warmth of her quarters. Indeed, she felt more like a person in prison than a highborn lady.

But the prison was of her own making. Not by so much as a look or a word had the lord or lady of Blackthorne Keep indicated that Ariane was no longer a valued guest in their home.

Unhappily Ariane looked out one of the high slit windows that ran down the side of her room. If she leaned into the depth of the keep's walls and braced herself on the chill stone, she could see the sinuous ribbon of blue that was the River Blackthorne.

During the last of the ride to Blackthorne Keep, Ariane had enjoyed the silver rush and chatter of the river. It had reminded her of her own home, and the river that had been her companion on many a warm summer day. She had sat on the bank and played her harp, patterning her music after her own thoughts, the cries of the birds, the wind, and the distant calling of herders.

It seems like a dream, now. I was so innocent. So foolish. I trusted . . .

Too much.

A shout came from the bailey below, followed by the sound of the keep's stout wooden gate being opened. A horse's hooves drummed hollowly on the drawbridge, then clattered over the bailey's cobblestones.

Ariane went to another window just in time to see Simon exit the forebuilding and stride across the bailey toward the knight who had just ridden up. The pale flash of the knight's hair, and the supple grace of his dismount, told Ariane that Sven, the Glendruid Wolf's spy, had returned to Blackthorne Keep.

Simon's greeting was lost in the wind that gusted through the bailey. Together the two men strode toward the forebuilding's steps.

A cat the color of autumn bounded across the bailey and launched itself at Simon. Without breaking stride, Simon caught the beast, draped it around his neck, and petted it thoroughly while he listened to whatever Sven had discovered.

It seemed to Ariane that she could hear the cat's smug purring from four stories up.

She told herself that she didn't envy the cat being stroked by Simon's long, exquisitely knowing fingers. Yet in the next breath she admitted that she was lying.

Despite her brutal use by Geoffrey the Fair, Ariane had learned to treasure one man's touch, one man's caresses, one man's hands moving sweetly over her body.

Just one man.

The man whose punishment she had become.

My hell has come to me on earth, and her name is Ariane.

Ariane longed to explain to Simon how her maidenhead had been brutally taken. But she was afraid he wouldn't believe her.

No one else had.

I want him to believe me as no one has ever believed me!

I am not like Marie, a whore to lie down with every man and love none. I am a girl whose honor was dragged torn and bleeding from her body. I am a girl who screamed her betrayal to God.

And I was not believed.

Why should anyone believe me now? Even you, Simon, who has touched me as no one ever has.

Especially you.

The harsh cry of the harp jarred Ariane from her thoughts.

Footsteps sounded down the hall, coming from the staircase to Ariane's room. She looked around almost wildly, as though seeking an escape she didn't really want.

The steps paused at her door.

Simon? Have you finally come to me? Is this the hour when you finish what I could not on our wedding night?

The footsteps went on to another room, leaving Ariane undisturbed but for her wild thoughts.

Abruptly Ariane knew she must get out of the room or scream her anguish so that all the keep could hear. But she didn't want to pass Simon in the great hall and suffer yet one more of his cool, remote greetings. She didn't want to look into his eyes again and see the knowledge of his betrayal reflected there with such bleak clarity.

Ariane the Betrayed had become Ariane the Betrayer.

With a small cry, she began unlacing and stripping off the pale lavender dress that was one of the few she had brought from Normandy. She wanted nothing of her former land touching her. She wanted nothing touching her at all.

Except Simon.

Blindly Ariane reached for the Learned gift that she hadn't worn since discovering that the dress might be like Erik's animals — more clever by half than anything not human should be.

But right now Ariane didn't care what the dress was or was not. She wanted only to be warm when the winter winds blew. She wanted to feel cherished. She wanted to be free of her past and of the consequences of

Geoffrey's brutality. She wanted . . .

Simon.

The dress flowed over Ariane like a velvet benediction, caressing and soothing her flesh, her blood, her very soul. The cloth clung to her in the manner of a cat too long without petting. And like a cat, Ariane stroked it.

Silver laces glistened more brightly than sunlight on water, drawing together the edges of the dress from Ariane's knees to her collarbone. Silver stitches ran through the amethyst fabric, gathering like runic lightning inside the sleeves and making them flash with each motion of her arms.

As though in echo of the secret silver lightning, two human figures of the same profound, transparent black as Simon's eyes twisted and rippled sinuously through the cloth. No matter where or how Ariane looked at the dress, the figures were there, haunting her with the very thing she wanted and would never have.

Cloth seethed caressingly around Ariane's ankles, coaxing her to look at the silver and the black alike, demanding that she see the man and the woman locked in mutual abandon within the very threads of the weaving.

"Lie still, dress," Ariane hissed.

Serena's cloth will lie calmly around you. It responds only to dreams, and without hope there are no dreams.

The echo of Cassandra's words in Ariane's mind nearly shattered what small measure of self-control remained to her. With a curse that would have shocked anyone who overheard it, Ariane grabbed her mantle and flung it around her shoulders, blocking out the sight of the uncanny dress.

But not its caressing warmth. That Ariane needed as she needed to breathe fresh air.

Moving as though pursued by demons, Ariane stuffed her harp into its traveling case and slung it over her shoulder. On the way out of the room, she grabbed a basket that held her embroidery. Without regard for the delicate stitches and fragile silk floss, she dumped the contents of the basket onto a table.

Looking neither right nor left, Ariane walked swiftly down the stairs and through the keep to the forebuilding. There the guard looked at her in surprise, but said nothing as he opened the door for her.

The wind in the bailey was like a drink of cold, clear water. As heady as wine, as wild as Ariane's thoughts, the wind was a welcome companion. She let it rush her across the cobblestones and to the sally port in the heavy, wide gate that guarded the keep's security.

There the man known as Harry the Lame gave Ariane an odd look and a smile. His eyes saw both the white lines of tension around her lips and the tightness of the fingers clutching the handle of the basket.

" 'Tis a cold afternoon to be collecting herbs, Lady Ariane."

"I like the chill. And some herbs are best collected in late afternoon."

"Aye, madam. So Lady Margaret tells me."

"Is she in the herb garden now?"

"I believe so."

"Thank you."

Harry touched his fingers to his forehead in brief salute before he opened the sally port and allowed Ariane through.

She walked out with strides as crisp as the wind. When the path forked, she took the branch that led to the herb gardens. Not until she was out of sight of the sally port did she turn sharply aside, taking a narrow lane that led to the banks of the River Blackthorne. She had no desire to confront the Glendruid green eyes of Blackthorne Keep's lady.

Ariane wasn't the first person at the keep to be drawn to the river's edge. A path wound irresistibly through bracken turned gold by the wild, chill kiss of autumn gone to winter. The rocky point where the path ended was home to a handful of birch and rowan trees whose toughness was equaled only by their elegance of line.

In the most protected places, the trees still

clung to a few of their leaves, but the rest lay underfoot like coins flung carelessly to the ground. More leaves floated on the small river and caught among the cobbles that lined the banks.

Ariane walked through the golden landscape until she discovered a natural rocky bench that hadn't been visible from the upper lane. The faint polish of the stone's surface suggested that people had been coming to this place and staying to watch the water flow for as long as the River Blackthorne had run down to the sea.

With a ragged sigh, Ariane settled onto the time-smoothed stone. The empty basket dropped from her fingers. For a while there was only the sound of the river swirling gracefully over stones and the wind combing through branches naked of leaves.

Slowly Ariane removed her harp from its case and began to play. The sounds she made harmonized with wind and river and season, beautiful and yet bleak with the certainty of winter's killing embrace.

Gradually Ariane's thoughts turned to the nightmare that did not end with the coming of the day. The nightmare that had no end she could see. The nightmare that she still struggled to understand . . . what had happened and why and how she could weave that terrible thread into the pattern of the rest of her life.

Eyes closed, Ariane let the harp sing of unspeakable betrayal begetting more betrayal, of grief both savage and unrelenting short of the grave.

And perhaps, not even there.

"I thought it must be your fingers making the harp sing. But by Christ's blue eyes, you play dire notes. Have you been pining for me, my little cabbage?"

The music ended as though cut off by a sword.

Geoffrey. Dear God, it can't be!

Ariane' s eyes snapped open. Her nightmare was indeed standing in front of her, his mantle thrown back to reveal the armor beneath.

Geoffrey the Fair.

Tall, brawny, good-looking to the point of beauty, beloved by girls and noblemen alike, and a deadly fighter who loved to battle three to his one.

The sight of Geoffrey standing proud and powerful in his armor made Ariane's stomach turn over. Nausea climbed her throat as icy sweat broke on her skin.

"I thought myself rid of you," she said starkly.

Geoffrey smiled as though Ariane had called him her dearest heart. Eyes as blue and opaque as robins' eggs looked slowly at her, taking in the sleek black of her hair, the matchless beauty of her eyes, and the deep curve of her lips.

"By the saints, I long to bite that mouth again," Geoffrey said. "I have dreamed of hearing you moan and bleed while I lick it up like a starving hound."

Ariane fought nausea's tightening coils. She knew she must control her body enough to speak in her own defense, for no one else would.

No matter what happened, this time she would scream and curse and claw blood from Geoffrey's smiling face.

"What do you want," Ariane said.

There was no question in her tone, simply a demand that Geoffrey state his business.

"You."

"I do not want you."

Geoffrey laughed. "Still the coy maiden, I see."

"I am married."

"So?"

Geoffrey's shrug made the chain mail of his hauberk shift and gleam in the rich autumn sunlight.

"Unlike you," Ariane said, "I am honorable."

"Truly? Then why did you go to your husband deflowered?"

"Because you raped me!"

The smile Geoffrey gave her was the boyish one Ariane had once found charming. But no more. It revolted her that a man could look as innocent as one of God's angels and yet have the soul and the sensibilities of a pig.

"Rape? Nay," Geoffrey said, rubbing his gauntleted hands together. "Rather it was I who was ravished by your beauty. I lay slack-witted from wine and awakened to find your hands in my breeches."

"You are lying!"

"Nay, little cabbage. There is no need to pretend innocence. We are alone."

"Then why do you bother to lie?" Ariane asked scathingly.

"Lie? I but tell the truth. I am the one who awoke to find my rod in your mouth and then in your hungry wet —"

"Liar."

"Ah, I bring color to your little cheeks."

"You bring vomit to my throat."

Geoffrey laughed. "I shall stop it with my rod."

Abruptly Ariane realized that baiting her both amused and aroused Geoffrey.

Nausea coiled again, more urgently. Knowing that Geoffrey took pleasure in her feeble struggles had been one of the worst parts of

Ariane's nightmare.

"What? No more adorable protests?" Geoffrey asked. "Does that mean you long —"

"— to see the last of you, aye. Most fervently. Are you afoot? If so, I will give you a horse if you promise to ride it from my sight."

There was no emotion in Ariane's voice. Nor was there any in her face, save that which throttled rage streaked in red across her cheekbones.

"My horse is waiting in yonder woodland while I investigate the sound of harp music I had thought never to hear again."

"Then be gone. I promise I won't follow."

"I am wounded," Geoffrey said, holding his hand over his heart. "No sooner do I heal from that foul sickness and come to claim you than you spurn me."

"I am already claimed by Simon."

"That coward," Geoffrey said, dismissing Simon with a curl of his lip.

Ariane's breath came in with disbelief at the contempt in Geoffrey's voice and expression.

"Simon is the bravest knight I have ever known," she said, remembering her husband standing alone and outnumbered so that she could flee to safety.

"Is he? Then why doesn't he kill his faithless wife and throw her into the sea?"

"I am not faithless!"

"Truly? You came to him well-used by another man."

"*Ill* used."

"So well-used," Geoffrey continued, ignoring Ariane, "that you refuse to give your body to your husband because you long for the body of your first lover."

"I long to watch vultures feast on your bones!"

"Knowing that you are not a virgin, and that you refuse your husband, who will believe that you don't put your heels behind your ears for a knight such as Geoffrey the Fair?" he asked, smiling like an angel.

If Ariane had been pale before, Geoffrey's words leached the last hint of color from her. With unnatural calm she put away her harp, slung the carrying bag over her shoulder and stood up. At every heartbeat she regretted leaving her dagger behind.

'Tis a pity the weaver of Learned cloth didn't foresee the need to wear a weapon with this clever dress, Ariane thought bleakly. *I would trade my harp for my girdle and its dagger sheath.*

Ariane stepped toward the path. Geoffrey remained unmoving, blocking her way.

"You are standing across the path," she said evenly.

"Aye. Lift your skirts high, little girl. I have

394

come a long way to see your thighs open to me again."

"You will have to kill me first."

Geoffrey started to laugh. Then his laughter faded as he saw the certainty in Ariane's savage amethyst eyes.

"Have you told your husband?" Geoffrey asked harshly.

"That you raped me?"

"That I lay between your thighs until I was too weak to rise again."

"If my drugged memory serves, you sweated like a pig to rise even once. Your manhood was more like beached seaweed than the 'rod' you speak of so proudly."

A flush stained Geoffrey's unblemished skin. His smiling lips curled into something more like a snarl.

"But then, what would one expect of a craven who first drugs and then rapes a virgin?" Ariane continued softly. "No *man* would have to stoop so low."

Geoffrey lifted his mailed fist.

Ariane smiled like the witch she once had been.

"You try my patience," he said between his teeth.

"You try my stomach."

"Do you ache to feel my fists again?"

"I ache to see you in hell."

Spine straight, eyes unflinching, Ariane waited for Geoffrey to lose his temper as he always had when thwarted.

But somewhere between Normandy and the Disputed Lands, Geoffrey had learned caution. He considered Ariane curiously, as though he had expected to find something quite different.

And indeed he had. The weeping, ravaged girl of his memories had all but crawled beneath her saddle to avoid being noticed by Geoffrey during the trip from Normandy to England. She had spoken so rarely that the knights had taken to placing wagers on when she would say a word.

"What a pity that you have recovered your wits," Geoffrey said. "They were always the least appealing part of you."

"Thank you."

"Is your father here?" Geoffrey demanded. "Is that why you're so brave?"

Ariane blinked, puzzled by the direction of the conversation. Geoffrey had always been better informed about the baron's movements than Ariane had.

"Why do you ask me?" she said.

"Just answer me," Geoffrey said, "or I will go to Blackthorne Keep and tell your cowardly husband that you came to me today and begged me to give you the thorough plowing that he cannot!"

"Simon won't —"

"Believe me?" Geoffrey interrupted mockingly. "You tried that on your father, the man who knew you best. Did he believe you?"

Ariane closed her eyes and swayed as though she had been struck. Geoffrey's voice was resonant with sincerity and concern. It made others believe that he had those emotions.

But he used emotions rather than having them.

"Nay," Geoffrey continued smoothly. "Your father believed me, for I was but the poor victim of your wanton lechery. The bottle with the hellish love potion, the very witch brew you poured into my wine, was still tangled in your bloody sheets. It was all there for your father and the priest to see. And they did see it, didn't they?"

Then Geoffrey laughed with the malice he revealed only to whores and serfs.

Ariane wanted to put her hands over her ears, but would not give Geoffrey the satisfaction. Both of them knew all too well who had been believed and who had been betrayed.

Would you believe my innocence, Simon? You, who hate witches? You, who speak so savagely of being in thrall to any woman?

Especially a witch.

And even if you did believe me, what then?

Mortal combat with Geoffrey to determine who is truthful and who is not?

The thought made another cold sweat break over Ariane's body. Once she would have relished the chance to be vindicated by seeing Geoffrey die. But she no longer believed that truth was a useful shield against lies, particularly lies spoken by a knight such as Geoffrey the Fair. He had killed too many men, bandits and knights alike.

He enjoyed the sight of blood spilling over his sword. He yearned for it with an eagerness that was chilling.

No matter how quick Simon was, no matter how skilled, he was shorter and at least two stone lighter than Geoffrey. More telling than mere size, Simon lacked Geoffrey's blood-lust.

"Rumor says that Baron Deguerre is in England," Ariane said tonelessly.

"Then he comes to Blackthorne Keep."

"No word has come directly to me."

"Why should it? You are not beloved by your father."

Ariane made no argument with the truth. If her father had ever loved her, he no longer did. The last words he had spoken to her had made that very clear.

Whore. If I dared kill you, I would.

" 'Tis certain he hasn't come all this way

to see the wanton daughter who dishonored him," Geoffrey said as though following Ariane's thoughts.

"Perhaps he seeks an alliance with the English king instead of the king of the Scots."

"More likely your father scents weakness somewhere," Geoffrey said.

A slow smile crossed Geoffrey's lips. The smile was as cruel as Ariane's memories, but Geoffrey kept whatever he was thinking to himself.

Sensing that she was no longer the center of his attention, Ariane began edging beyond Geoffrey's reach.

"Of course," Geoffrey said, focusing on Ariane once more. "You."

"You think he finally believes me?" Ariane asked, startled.

"He believes the truth, which is that in the grip of an evil witch's potion, I plowed you as thoroughly as any oxen ever plowed a field."

Biting the inside of her mouth against the rage that threatened to overrun her control, Ariane eased farther from Geoffrey's reach.

"*You* are the weakness he scents," Geoffrey said. "You are the Norman fox set among the Saxon chickens."

"You are mad."

"No, simply more clever than other men,"

Geoffrey said casually. "The baron knows you came deflowered to your marriage, yet no hue and cry has gone up."

Geoffrey pulled his lower lip between his thumb and forefinger. Then he laughed as cruelly as he had smiled.

"The Glendruid Wolf and his loyal pup must be weaker than they seem," Geoffrey said in a low voice. "Trust that shrewd old carrion eater to know it and hurry in to pick clean the bones."

Ariane looked at the ground, afraid that Geoffrey would see the truth confirmed in her eyes. The Glendruid Wolf was indeed worried about his hold upon the Disputed Lands, or he would not have given his loyal brother over to a marriage that neither had sought.

You deserve a better wife than this cold Norman heiress.

But Simon's response to Dominic had been swift and painfully pragmatic.

Blackthorne deserves better than war. And so do you. Surely marriage can be no worse than the sultan's hell you endured to ransom me.

Too late Ariane caught the movement of Geoffrey's hand from the corner of her downcast eyes. Before she could jerk away, she was yanked so hard against Geoffrey's hauberk that the breath was driven from her body.

The smell of stale wine and something worse

washed over Ariane, making her swallow roughly. At close range, she could see that drink — and whatever passed for Geoffrey's soul — was slowly eroding the angelic purity of his face. The skin was becoming coarse. Burst blood vessels had left red traceries on his nose. His breath was as vile as his deeds.

"England hasn't been kind to you," Ariane said through her teeth. "Go back to Normandy, where people still believe your lies."

"I have my heart set on a noble widow."

"Then leave me and get to courting."

Geoffrey smiled. "The courting is done. 'Tis the widowing that remains. It won't take long. Then Carlysle will be mine, and you with it. It shall be as your father meant it to be."

"If you challenge Simon — and survive — the Glendruid Wolf will kill you."

"I shall survive, but it will be Simon who challenges me. No blood feud can come from that!"

"Go back to Normandy," Ariane said. "Simon won't challenge you. The Glendruid Wolf won't allow it."

"I think not, little cabbage. There will be no choice. You will see to it."

"I? *Never!*"

"Truly? Have I finally heard the last of your whining about rape?"

Smiling, Geoffrey shook off one gauntlet,

plunged his hand inside Ariane's mantle and jammed his fingers between her thighs. The smile on his lips instantly became a snarl of surprise and outrage. He yanked back his hand and released Ariane so swiftly that she staggered.

"Jesus and Mary!" Geoffrey rubbed his fingers harshly over the chain mail of his hauberk. "Since when have you taken to wearing hair shirt and nettles? You misbegotten slut, you have blistered my fingers with your tricks!"

Ariane's freedom registered sooner on her mind than Geoffrey's outraged complaints did. She caught her balance and was running toward the keep before he realized it.

"Come back here!" he shouted furiously.

Ariane picked up her skirts and ran faster, sending the harp banging against her back with each step.

Cursing and nursing his hand, Geoffrey ran toward the horse he had tethered out of sight in one of the keep's woodlots. He had no doubt that he could catch Ariane before she reached the keep.

Neither did Ariane.

She went no farther than a tangle of bracken, brambles, and rowan trees before she looked over her shoulder to see where Geoffrey was. He had his back to her and was running toward the nearby woodland where Blackthorne's foresters got much of the keep's lumber.

As Ariane had hoped, Geoffrey had chosen to run her down from the back of his horse rather than on foot, slowed by his hauberk, helmet and sword.

Unseen by Geoffrey, Ariane swerved aside from the trail and plunged deeper into the tangle. Branches raked over her mantle to the dress beneath, but found no hold there. The tough cloth resisted even the sharpest of the thorns.

When Ariane was certain she couldn't be seen from the cart road that led to the keep, she dropped to her knees and fought for breath. Hair fell into her eyes, for the thicket had raked her artfully coiled braids until they were half-undone. Impatiently she pushed the hair away and held her palm hard to her side where pain turned in her as a rogue knight's dagger once had.

Have I opened up that wound?

The thought froze the breath in Ariane's lungs. Frantically her fingers stripped laces open until she could see the wound just beneath her breast.

No blood greeted her eyes. In fact, the scar itself was barely a pale line drawn against the smoothness of her skin. With a broken gasp, Ariane sank to the ground, heedless of the leaf litter and earth that were soiling her mantle.

Soon Ariane was able to hear more than her own heartbeats and her own rasping breaths. She settled herself more comfortably, waiting to hear cries from Blackthorne's battlements when Geoffrey was spotted by the sentry.

The murmur of the river was overlaid by the calling of birds as they flocked together against the coming night. A cart whose axle needed grease groaned from the lane. Shouts from Blackthorne's battlements rose above the complaining of the axle.

Ariane cocked her head, listening intently. A fickle wind first chased away and then brought the sentry's words to her. Geoffrey's presence had been discovered, which meant he had no choice but to ride openly up to the gate.

She was safe. Geoffrey was too clever to maul her in public, and she would be quite careful not to get caught alone by him.

With a sigh of relief, Ariane stood up and pulled her mantle tightly around her. Bracken, fallen leaves, twigs, and bits of less identifiable matter clung to the bottom of the mantle. She flapped the edges impatiently, sending debris swirling. Holding the mantle more tightly about her body, she set off for the keep.

24

Sensing someone coming up behind him, Simon looked away from the strange knight who was riding up to the drawbridge. Sven's broad-boned face and pale, assessing eyes emerged from the shadows of the gatehouse.

"I heard of a strange knight," Sven said.

"Aye. The sentry spotted him riding out of the river woodlot."

Silently the two men stood and waited for a better view of the knight through the open sally port. As Simon waited, he absently rubbed the chin of Autumn, the huge tricolored cat who was draped, purring, around Simon's neck. The cat's sleek body was a mosaic of large patches of white, orange and black fur.

The knight approached the keep at a smart trot. He was riding a war-horse and was fully armed, though without attendants. A ragged pennant flew from his lance. His shield, too, was battered and darkened by hard use.

Autumn lifted his head and watched the knight approach with unblinking orange eyes.

Simon's own eyes narrowed as his instincts stirred, whispering of danger.

"Could this be one of Baron Deguerre's knights, come to tell us of his lord's visit?" Simon asked.

"I have heard of no knight this large, save the rogue who outwitted you and Duncan by riding into the Silverfells clan lands."

Simon grunted. "This one is big enough, but he wears colors of a sort on his shield and pennant."

The cross on the shield was blurred and crudely rendered, but still there for all to see.

"Aye," Sven said.

The knight turned onto the cart road that went directly to Blackthorne's moat. Though the bridge was lowered, the gate into the bailey was closed. Only the sally port was open, and it was too small for any but a man on foot.

" 'Tis Deguerre's sign," Simon said.

"Aye. A thin white cross on a black field."

Simon looked over his shoulder into the bailey. Autumn's fur stroked his cheek. Simon stroked the cat in return. The animal's muscular purring rumbled against Simon's throat.

Though an unusual number of the keep's people had found an excuse to be in the bailey so as to see the strange knight, Simon didn't find Ariane among those eagerly looking toward the bridge. Simon glanced up to the top of the keep. The shutters over Ariane's windows were barely ajar.

Sven followed Simon's glance.

"Your wife is collecting herbs," Sven said.

Simon's head swung back to the lithe descendant of Vikings who was Dominic's most trusted knight save Simon himself.

"Are you certain?" Simon asked.

"Aye. Harry mentioned it to me."

"Odd," Simon muttered. "Ariane has shown no particular interest in herbs before this time."

One of Simon's hands lifted and resumed stroking Autumn. Claws appeared and retracted with rhythmic ecstasy, though the cat's eyes never left off watching the approaching knight.

" 'Tis why Harry mentioned her leaving," Sven said. "He said she seemed quite strained."

Simon didn't respond.

"But not unduly so, considering what passed in the armory," Sven said under his breath.

Simon gave Sven a glittering glance. Dominic had demanded that only Sven be told the truth about Ariane's missing maidenhead and dowry, but Simon knew that few secrets were kept for very long in the intimacy of a keep.

Not that it would be Sven who gave away the game. Whatever secrets Sven held — and they were many — none showed on his face. But then, few things ever did. It was part of what made Sven so valuable to the Glendruid Wolf.

With the cat's low purring vibrating against his neck, Simon went back to observing the strange knight through the open sally port. He was close enough now to make out smaller details of armor and armament.

"I feel I have seen this one before," Simon said softly.

"Grey war stallions are as common as fleas on a hound."

"I wonder where his squires are?" Simon asked. "He looks a bit hard-used, but not poor. Surely he has attendants."

"Perhaps he has a squire in Deguerre's entourage."

"A squire's duty is to his knight."

"Perhaps this knight and the missing squire were part of Lady Ariane's escort," Sven said dryly. "Not many of them survived."

"And the ones who did lacked manners," Simon said. "They dumped Ariane and her handmaiden in Blackthorne's bailey and galloped off without staying for so much as a crust of bread."

"They must have felt unworthy to attend

the opening of the dowry chests," Sven said blandly.

Breath hissed between Simon's teeth in a Saracen curse that drew a sideways glance from Sven.

Autumn's long tail flicked in displeasure, pointing out to Simon that he was failing to please the lordly feline.

"Aye. Perhaps they did," Simon said. " 'Tis a pity. I would have enjoyed discussing their lack of manners with them."

"Here is your chance," Sven said, gesturing toward the man who had reined in at the moat. " 'Tis a great strapping knight astride yonder horse. You could question him with your sword until you tired of the exercise."

"A waste of time."

"Swordplay?" Sven asked, shocked.

"Nay. Questioning a lout that size. 'Tis my experience that brains and brawn rarely ride together, with the exception of my brother."

"Your mind is quicker than even the Glendruid Wolf's."

"But my body isn't as brawny."

"All knights should be as delicately made as you," Sven agreed sardonically.

Simon smiled. He was barely smaller than his brother, and he well knew it.

"Shall I greet this knight?" Sven asked.

"Nay. We will do it together."

Sven gave Simon a sideways look from eyes whose blue was so light it appeared almost colorless. Though Simon's fingers petted the cat with unerring rhythm, his clear black glance was focused entirely on the strange knight.

"Memorize him," Simon said so that only Sven could hear. "Be able to recognize him at fifty yards in the dark."

"Aye, sir."

"And Sven?"

"Aye?"

"If we allow this knight into the keep, be the shadow of his shadow. Always."

"What is it?" Sven asked in a low voice. "What do you see that I don't?"

"Nothing. Just a feeling."

Sven laughed softly. "A feeling, eh? I warned you, Simon."

"About what?"

"Living with witches. First you have uncanny cats like Autumn always with you. Next you have feelings. Soon you'll have the fey sight yourself."

"That is a pail of —"

Abruptly Simon cut off his words, for they were the very ones Ariane had used to describe love: *A pail of slops.*

A grim smile turned Simon's lips down at the corners. He doubted that Ariane had felt that way about the man to whom she had given her maidenhead.

Did he marry another, Ariane? Is that how you were betrayed? Did you spread your untouched thighs for the lie called love?

With an effort, Simon wrenched his thoughts back to the knight who was growing more impatient by the moment at his lack of hospitable greeting.

"Don't open the main gate until I signal," Simon called to Harry, who had been waiting thirty feet away. "And then, open only one gate. There is, after all, but one knight."

"In sight," Sven muttered.

"Aye, sir!" Harry answered.

"If we let him in," Sven said softly, "he will soon learn how few true knights we have."

"And if we don't let him in, we will insult my father-in-law."

Sven grunted.

"Come," Simon said. " 'Tis easier to watch the devil you have than to go hunting in hell for a different one."

Sven gave a crack of laughter and followed Simon through the sally port, but they walked side by side when they went across the bridge to meet the strange knight whose chain mail hauberk gleamed beneath his heavy mantle.

The cat on Simon's shoulders rode easily, its wise orange eyes opened wide. Despite the fact that Simon's hands were near his sword rather than petting Autumn, the feline made no protest. He simply watched the strange knight with unblinking, oddly predatory interest.

"How are you called, stranger?" Simon asked from the keep side of the bridge across the moat.

Simon's voice was civil and no more. He would have preferred that no strangers come to Blackthorne Keep until Dominic had more — and better-trained — knights.

"Geoffrey the Fair, vassal to Baron Deguerre," said the big knight. His smile was apparent across the width of the bridge. "Is this indeed the fabled Blackthorne Keep, home to the Glendruid Wolf?"

The admiration in Geoffrey's voice would have disarmed most men. Sven disregarded the implied compliment, for flattery was one of a spy's most useful tools.

Simon discounted it because he truly disliked Geoffrey. Nor could Simon have said why. He simply knew his distaste as surely as he knew that Autumn was no longer purring against his neck.

"Aye. This is Blackthorne Keep and I am Simon, brother to Dominic le Sabre. The man with me is Sven, a valued knight."

"I am honored to greet you," Geoffrey said.

"Is your lord far behind?" Simon asked.

"I'm not certain."

"How many are in his entourage? We will have to let the kitchen, falconer and gamekeeper know how many more we must feed."

"I don't know that, either, sir," Geoffrey said.

As he spoke, his hand rubbed across his face in a gesture of bone-deep weariness.

"Forgive my lack of information," Geoffrey said heavily. "I was one of Lady Ariane's escort from Normandy. The sickness . . ."

"We heard," Simon said.

"I have but lately come back to myself," Geoffrey admitted. "I have ridden hard to reach this keep, twice getting lost."

"Indeed?"

"Aye. I came upon a peddler four days' ride north, or perhaps it was five or six and not true north at all . . ."

Sven and Simon exchanged a look.

Geoffrey shook his head as though to clear it. "I am sorry, sirs. That foul illness laid me low. Even now I am weak. 'Tis relieved I am to find the shelter of Blackthorne Keep."

Sven and Simon exchanged another look.

"Is the Lady Ariane here?" Geoffrey asked when Simon remained silent. "She will vouch for my honor. We are old, old friends."

The fleeting smile on Geoffrey's mouth at

the word *friends* did nothing to increase Simon's charitable feelings toward the unwelcome knight.

On the other hand, it would be unwise to offend Baron Deguerre by refusing hospitality to one of his knights, and an ailing knight at that. Much as Simon wanted to turn his back on Deguerre's vassal, nobody knew Dominic's vulnerability better than Simon.

'Tis why I offered myself as a replacement for Duncan at the marriage altar.

Necessity, not desire.

But Simon knew he was telling only half of the truth to himself, and the lesser half at that. Even when Ariane was betrothed to Duncan, Simon had wanted her until he awoke sweating, fully aroused, teeth clenched against a groan of need.

He still did.

Abruptly, Simon signaled for the gate to be opened.

"Thank you, gracious knight," Geoffrey said, urging his stallion forward. "The baron will be pleased by your hospitality, for I am much loved by him."

As the stallion's metal shoes clopped hollowly onto wood, Sven flicked Simon briefly on the hand in a silent signal left over from the times when they had hunted Saracens through the night.

"Look," Sven said in a low voice. "Out beyond the millrace."

Simon looked, shaded his eyes against the dying sun, and picked out the form of a woman walking toward the keep on a seldom-used path. He needed no more than a glimpse of the graceful, flowing stride to recognize his wife.

"Ariane," Simon said beneath his breath.

"The herb gardens lie in another direction."

"Aye."

A groom rushed forward to take Geoffrey's stallion. Geoffrey ignored him, for he had just spotted the figure drawing closer to the drawbridge.

"Ariane!" Geoffrey said, anticipation in every syllable. "At last!"

He dismounted in an athletic rush, smiling like a child who has unexpectedly been given a cream cake to eat. Only when he saw Simon's bleak eyes did Geoffrey seem to remember that Ariane was now wed.

To Simon.

"Forgive me," Geoffrey said, wiping away his smile. "I must make a confession to you. In truth, Ariane is why I came to Blackthorne first rather than trying to find the baron. I have missed her the way I miss the sun in winter."

"Indeed," Simon said softly. "Why did you

not go to Stone Keep, then? 'Tis where Duncan of Maxwell resides."

Geoffrey looked blank for an instant.

"But . . . er . . ." Geoffrey fumbled for words, cleared his throat, and tried again. "The peddler said Ariane married another knight, for Duncan had been bewitched."

"Some said that," Simon acknowledged.

"You must know," Geoffrey challenged. "Why?"

"If you are the Glendruid Wolf's brother, then it is you who wed Ariane!"

" 'Tis a well-informed peddler you met," Simon said.

"You have my congratulations, sire," Geoffrey said.

"You may have them back."

"Few men are lucky enough to wed a maid who is beautiful, rich, and as passionate as a nymph," Geoffrey said, ignoring Simon's aloofness. "By the Cross, 'tis a wonder you can stand at all after a night spent between her . . ."

Again, Geoffrey appeared to realize too late where his words were going. He coughed, shrugged, and gave Simon a sheepish smile.

"I find no fault in my wife," Simon said evenly.

"Of course not. 'Tis the very thing I told the innkeeper at the Sign of the Fallen Tree when he talked of a cold marriage made in haste," Geoffrey said in a hearty voice. "A girl of Ariane's wanton nature would never be able to keep herself from her husband's bed."

Though Simon showed no outward response to Geoffrey's tactless words, Sven began measuring the knight for a shroud.

"Unless, of course," Geoffrey continued cheerfully, "Ariane were yearning for her first lover to the point that she couldn't force herself to permit another man entrance to her snug little, er . . . bed."

"I have known magpies that were less talkative than this creature," Sven said casually. "More fair of face, too."

" 'Tis a thing that can be cured," Simon said. "The speech, that is. The face is beyond mortal help."

"Have I offended you?" Geoffrey asked Simon. "By the Cross, you are a sensitive soul. But then, people with a sore spot do jump when it is touched, is that not so?"

Simon's smile was a simple baring of teeth.

"I meant no offense," Geoffrey said carelessly. "If my clumsy congratulations on your wife's sensual nature irritate you, I can only hope to be more precise with my praise in the future."

Sven shot a quick look at Simon, seeking

417

a sign as to how to handle the knight whose compliments were worse than any insults Sven had ever heard delivered to Simon's face.

A moment later Simon's fingers brushed casually against Sven's sword hand in an old signal for caution.

"Good evening, Ariane," Simon said, looking past Geoffrey. "Did you enjoy the herb gardens?"

"Ah, my little cabbage," Geoffrey said, turning quickly. "If you only knew how I have longed to be within your warmth again. You have bewitched my very soul. I wither out of your sight."

"Would that it were true," Ariane said. "I would lock myself in my room until you died."

With that, she went quickly to stand with Simon and Sven.

"I would be wounded, if I didn't know your heart of hearts," Geoffrey said, smiling at Ariane. "A married girl is a cautious girl, especially in the presence of her husband, yes?"

"I decided to play my harp along the river," Ariane said to Simon, ignoring Geoffrey.

"Ah, that explains it," Geoffrey said.

As he spoke, he gestured toward the bits of leaves and brambles clinging to Ariane's mantle.

"Careless of you," Geoffrey murmured. "A

jealous husband would think you had lain back upon your mantle and spread your legs for a lover."

Ariane went white and gave Simon a horrified glance. What she saw made ice condense in her blood.

She had never seen Simon so furious.

Nor so cold.

"Simon is a man of reason, not emotion," Ariane said thinly.

" 'Tis good that you know him so well," Geoffrey said in an earnest voice. "Some would think it cowardice rather than reason that guides your husband."

Sven said something in the harsh northern language of his mother.

"This fine knight," Simon said to Ariane, "believes himself well beloved by your father. Is it true?"

"Aye," Ariane said, making no attempt to conceal the bitterness in her voice.

"How well beloved?"

"As much as my father can love anything."

"Pity," Simon said. "I would rather feed this one to the pigs than feed pig to him at table tonight."

"Is that an insult?" Geoffrey demanded.

"Why would a man of reason insult a knight such as yourself?" Simon asked.

"Because you suspect that your wife is in

love with me. Because you —"

"Nay!" Ariane said harshly.

"— suspect that I am the man who took your wife's maidenhead in passionate battle. Because you suspect —"

Ariane made a sound that was both Geoffrey's name and a savage curse.

"— she is cold with you," Geoffrey continued, talking over all interruptions, "for she cannot endure another man after having known me!"

There was a stunned silence in the bailey.

All that prevented Ariane from clawing Geoffrey's smiling face was her husband's hand beneath her mantle, locked about both her wrists. Though she struggled subtly, she had no hope of winning free to do the damage she wished.

Nor could she undo the damage that had been done.

"If you were indeed my wife's first taste of love," Simon said evenly, " 'tis a miracle that she didn't swear off men entirely and take up the veil."

Before Geoffrey could speak, Simon turned to Sven.

"Show our guest to the stable," Simon said. "He can bed down with his stallion."

"Aye," Sven said. "This way."

When Geoffrey began to object about the

inhospitable quarters, Sven cut across his words.

"Be quick about it," Sven said curtly. "We have so many knights that the clean hay is soon taken."

Geoffrey hesitated, shrugged, and set off after Sven.

Ariane let out a long, ragged sigh. She looked up at Simon, wanting to explain how Geoffrey had twisted the truth to make it appear that she had compromised her honor today — and Simon's.

The words Ariane would have spoken fled as she confronted the clear black savagery of her husband's eyes.

"Listen to me," Simon said. "Listen to me very well. Whatever happened before you wed me cannot be changed. But if you have cuckolded me —"

"It wasn't as Geoffrey made it appear!"

"— leave now, before I find out. Run fast and run far or I shall catch you. Then we will spend eternity in hell together. Do you understand me, *wife?*"

Ariane wanted to speak, but the only word she could force past the constriction in her throat was Simon's name.

"I see that you understand," he said.

Abruptly Simon released his hold on Ariane's wrists. She drew in her breath swiftly, for beneath his cold fury she sensed that there was something more. Something worse. Something she, too, had known — the savage, consuming acid of betrayal.

"Simon," Ariane said, reaching out.

"Do up your laces," Simon interrupted curtly, stepping away from her touch, "lest you give the gossips of this keep even more to drool and snigger over than you already have."

Ariane looked down. Through the opening in her mantle peeked the trailing ends of silver laces. A flush consumed her pale skin when she realized that her dress was partly undone.

"It isn't what you think!" Ariane said passionately.

"What I think is that you are very fortunate the Glendruid Wolf values peace above war, *and that I value my brother above all else.*"

"My wound pained me," Ariane said. "I undid my dress to see if I had somehow hurt it anew!"

"Did your head pain you, too?" Simon asked silkily.

"My head?" Ariane asked, baffled.

"Aye," Simon said, turning, walking away with cool finality. "Your hair is even more undone than your dress."

25

Ariane got up from the supper table and went to her bedchamber with a few muttered words about being tired. The truth was that she hadn't been able to bear listening any longer to Geoffrey's insinuations strip away Simon's pride and her honor in front of the assembled knights of the keep.

Rather grimly Ariane wondered if Simon still thought that marriage was no worse than the sultan's hell Dominic had once endured.

The food grew cold on the supper tray Blanche had brought to Ariane's room, as Ariane simply sat and stared at nothing at all. Footsteps came and went in the hallway leading to the bath, but she took no notice.

Even the harp was no consolation. Ariane was finding that it was harder to abide Simon's pain and humiliation than it had been to endure her own. She hadn't caused her agony. But she was causing Simon's.

A knocking on the closed door dragged Ariane's attention from her own bleak thoughts.

"Yes?" she said.

" 'Tis Blanche."

"Enter," Ariane said without enthusiasm.

The door opened. A quick look around the room told Blanche that nothing had changed since she left.

"Are you not finished eating yet, m'lady?" Blanche asked a bit impatiently.

"I have no appetite."

"What of your bath, then?"

"My bath?"

"Aye, m'lady," Blanche said, irritated. "I have prepared a bath as you requested and laid out a warm chemise for sleeping and everyone else in the keep is already abed."

Blankly Ariane looked from her untouched supper to her handmaiden's face.

"Did I ask that you prepare a bath?" Ariane said, frowning.

"Aye, m'lady. Straight after you ate, you said. You said you couldn't bear something-or-other having touched your skin and you must wash no matter how late the hour."

"Oh."

Blanche waited, but Ariane said nothing more.

"M'lady?"

"Would you like to seek your own bed?" Ariane asked.

"Aye, most certainly. If you please."

"You are free."

"Thank you, lady!"

Cheeks flushed and eyes sparkling with anticipation, Blanche rushed out of the room, barely remembering to close the door after herself.

Ariane wondered if Blanche's new man — whoever he was — knew that his lover was already gone with another man's child. Perhaps he didn't care. Perhaps it was enough to share Blanche's breathless laughter in the darkness, to reach out and stroke warm flesh and be stroked in return, to hold another body close and hear ecstasy in each broken cry.

Abruptly Ariane stood, stripped off all her clothes, and pulled the pins out of her hair. As she shook her head, hair like fine black silk cascaded down her back to lie in heavy, smoothly shining waves to her hips. She gathered it up and began braiding it for the bath, but lost interest after a few twists. The moment she let go of the hair, it began unraveling.

She reached for her nightdress, only to find that her hands went to the silver laces of the Learned dress as though summoned. She was reluctant to leave the dress behind, even to bathe. She didn't know why, she simply knew that it was so.

As though expecting the answer to be found

in the fabric itself, Ariane looked at the dress.

And then she looked *into* it.

A woman of intense feeling, head thrown back, hair wild, lips open upon a cry of unbelievable pleasure.

The enchanted.

A warrior both disciplined and passionate, his whole being focused in the moment.

The enchanter.

Now he was bending down to her, drinking her cries even as he drew more sounds from her. His powerfel body was poised over hers, waiting, shivering with a sensual hunger that was as great as his restraint.

Simon!

Ariane saw him as clearly as she saw herself in the woman's wild amethyst eyes.

"Dear God," she whispered, dazed.

Ariane shook herself and looked around the room, half expecting to find Simon there. What she saw was a fire burned near to ash, a bed turned down for her use, and spare blankets piled across the foot of the mattress.

Blankets that would become Simon's bed when he came to the room.

If he came.

Ariane pulled the amethyst dress back on and laced it partway up as she paced the room. With each step the deep silence of the keep came back to her ears. Then the sentry called the time.

Simon should have come to the bedchamber by now. He had always come before now. Well before now, because Simon rose with the kitchen workers at the first crack of dawn to walk the battlements and check upon the well-being of the fields and people of the keep. Dominic walked with him, though he never required Simon's presence at such an early hour.

Marie.

Simon is with her.

The thought was like a dagger going into Ariane. Without stopping to think she lit a candle and left her room so quickly that the flame guttered. With an impatient exclamation, Ariane stopped long enough for the flame to recover.

Shielding the fragile flame with her hand, Ariane hurried to the opposite side of the keep, where Marie and Blanche shared quarters. There was no true door for the maidservants, simply a cloth screen that could be moved aside during the day.

" 'Tis Lady Ariane," she said.

"My lady," Marie said. "Please enter."

Ariane slid between screen and doorway before Marie was finished speaking. Amethyst eyes searched the room quickly, then more slowly.

"You're alone."

Ariane wasn't surprised to find Blanche gone. But she was surprised to find Marie alone. The dark-eyed woman had a lap full of sewing and a curious expression on her face.

"Aye. I am alone," Marie agreed. "Is there something you require, lady?"

"Simon."

"Then you will have to look elsewhere. Simon hasn't come to my bed since . . ."

Without finishing the sentence, Marie shrugged and began plying her needle once more with astonishing speed.

"Since when?" Ariane asked.

"Since my husband saw Simon sneaking from my tent, thought he was Dominic, and betrayed Dominic's band of knights into a sultan's ambush."

"God's blood," breathed Ariane.

"More like the knights' blood," Marie said.

Her small teeth flashed in the candlelight as she nipped off a thread that had knotted.

"Most of the knights were captured by the sultan's men," Marie continued, threading a new needle.

"Was Simon?"

"Aye. But none of the captured knights was the right one."

"I don't understand."

"The knight whom the sultan dearly wanted and whom Robert had betrayed wasn't among the captured knights," Marie explained.

"Dominic le Sabre?" Ariane guessed.

"Aye."

"Why did the sultan particularly want Dominic?"

"The sultan had a taste for torture. Dominic had the name of a very strong, very brave knight who bowed to no man. The sultan vowed to destroy him."

"What happened?"

"Dominic traded himself for the freedom of his knights. One of those knights was Simon."

"The knights were released?"

"Aye."

"And then Dominic was somehow freed?" Ariane asked.

"Aye. After a time."

"Then why . . . ?"

"Why does Simon hate me?" Marie asked. Ariane nodded.

"Simon was near my husband when Robert was mortally wounded during the ambush," Marie said calmly. "Before Robert died, he confessed to Simon what he had done to Dominic. And why."

"But Simon knew that Dominic was innocent of any sin."

"Aye," Marie said. "It was Simon rather than his brother who lay with me after my marriage to Robert. Since he heard Robert's dying confession, Simon hasn't touched me. He blames himself for what happened to Dominic."

"I thought you said Dominic was freed."

"He was. But only after he was tortured such as few men have been and survived."

Ariane tried to speak. At first nothing came out. She swallowed and tried again.

"In the armory," Ariane said. "Simon kissed you."

Silently Marie shook out her sewing, plucked a stray thread, and looked up at the woman who was close to her age in years, yet so far away in experience.

"Simon didn't kiss me," Marie said. "I kissed Simon. I suspected he was angry enough with you not to mind angering you in turn, so I kissed him. Simon hasn't willingly touched me since he heard Robert's confession."

"Never?"

"No."

"But the Holy Crusade was years ago!"

"Aye. Simon is a man of extraordinary passion. It will be many more years before he forgets. Or forgives me."

"He loved you," Ariane said painfully.

"Love?"

Marie laughed and smoothed the embroidered silk she was sewing. Her mouth was an amused curve as she knotted the thread, bit it through, and smoothed the knot until it was invisible. She picked up the needle and threaded it once more.

"Simon didn't love me," Marie said, sewing quickly. "I was simply the first woman he had bedded who did much more than lie on her back and think of God. My sexual skills all but enslaved him for a time."

Ariane couldn't hide her shock at Marie's bluntness, which only amused Marie more.

"You must have had a nun's childhood," Marie said.

"Far from it. My mother was forced by my father. It was the only way he could have her. She was a woman of unusual . . . gifts."

"A witch?"

"Some called her that. Here, I suspect she would have been called Learned."

"A witch," Marie said succinctly. "Did her gifts come to you?"

"Only for a time."

Marie gave Ariane a sharp look, then went back to her sewing, for a single look had told her that Ariane would speak no more on the subject of her own missing gifts.

"As a child I was stolen from my Norman parents and sold into a seraglio," Marie said as she sewed. "By the time Dominic's knights freed me, I was very experienced at pleasuring men."

"So you repaid the knights by becoming their . . ."

"Whore," Marie said without embarrassment. "Aye. 'Tis what I know best. 'Tis what I have been trained for since I was eight. That, and sewing."

Ariane blinked. "Trained to pleasure men? Why? I thought that sex was by nature a pleasure for men."

"There is the pleasure of coarse bread and water to feed hunger and slake thirst, and there is the pleasure of honeyed peacocks' tongues and dark, clear wine."

Marie shook out the bodice she was working on, tugged at a seam, and resumed sewing.

"For men who have the palate to savor peacocks' tongues," Marie said, "a skilled woman is a foretaste of heaven. Simon had known only coarse bread. For a time, I had great power over him. In the end, though, his love of his brother was stronger than his lust for me."

"That is what you regret losing?" Ariane asked against her will. "The power?"

"But of course. Why else would a woman trouble to learn what pleases a man?"

"Simply to bring him pleasure," Ariane said.

As she spoke, Ariane remembered how she had held and caressed Simon's hot, violently aroused flesh. And then she remembered something else. Her own feelings.

"And because it gladdens her to pleasure him," Ariane added, barely subduing a sensual shiver.

Smiling, shaking her head at Ariane's innocence, Marie stitched swiftly.

"You will never control your husband if you lose control of yourself," Marie said succinctly. "If you would have the whip hand, you must know how to kiss and when to bite, where to lick and how to suck, what to claw and when to soothe, how to put him in your mouth and when to put him in your body."

Appalled by Marie's matter-of-fact summation, Ariane could think of nothing to say.

"Ecstasy is power, lady," Marie said. " 'Tis the only power we women have over men. But for that, men own all of worth in this world and we own nothing, including our bodies."

Marie's cool assessment of the nature of what passed between men and women horrified Ariane, but even worse was her understanding that Marie had destroyed something in Simon as surely as Geoffrey had destroyed something in Ariane.

Simon can no more entrust his emotions to a

woman than I can entrust my body to a man.

Yet I must. I can no longer bear the sad savagery of the past. It must end.

It simply must.

Marie looked up, saw Ariane's expression, and sighed.

"Never mind, lady. You haven't the temperament for controlling Simon through harem tricks. You're far too sensual."

"I?" Ariane asked, startled.

" 'Tis in your music," Marie said. "It tempts me to seduce you myself. But you have eyes only for Simon and Simon is one of the few men I've ever met who is worthy of fearing, as that asinine Geoffrey may discover."

"Geoffrey." A malicious thought came to Ariane. "Why don't you seduce him?"

"I didn't think you liked Geoffrey enough to worry over his pleasure or lack of it."

"I despise Geoffrey."

"Ah." Marie smiled with faint cruelty. "I see."

She tugged at a final knot, shook out the bodice, and nodded with satisfaction.

"When Geoffrey tires of your handmaiden tonight —"

"Geoffrey is with Blanche?" Ariane asked, shocked.

"Aye. But only because I refused him, knowing Simon's dislike of him."

"Is it Geoffrey who got Blanche with child?"

"Probably. She is clever enough to know a well-placed knight's child is worth more than a peasant's spawn." Marie shrugged. "But she is no match for me. Nor is Geoffrey."

Ariane didn't doubt it.

"I will teach him to crawl naked across a swine pen just to lick the place where I have sat," Marie said. "I owe you at least that."

"Why?" Ariane asked, rather horrified.

"Your music. It says all that I haven't had words to say since I was eight."

Marie put aside her sewing basket and stood up.

"If you will excuse me, lady," she said, "I have certain implements to prepare for Geoffrey's . . . mortification."

Ariane opened her mouth. No words came out.

Marie smiled. "Nay, I never used such harem toys on Simon. I liked him too well."

"That wasn't what I was going to ask."

"It would have occurred to you sooner or later, and I value my life here. 'Tis as much kindness as I have known since I was stolen. God be with you in your dreams, Lady Ariane."

"Thank you," Ariane said faintly.

Marie smiled. "But if you wish for more substantial company than God, your husband is pacing the battlements."

Involuntarily, Ariane glanced overhead and held her breath, listening. She heard nothing but the ceaseless blowing of the wind. Then came a faint spattering of sleet against shutters.

"Another storm," Ariane said.

"Aye. 'Tis much colder at Blackthorne Keep than it was in the Holy Land."

" 'Tis too cold for Simon to be up there, that is certain," Ariane whispered. "He will take a chill."

"Go and tell him so."

"I shall," Ariane said, turning to leave.

"And while you do it, stand inside Simon's mantle, close enough to breathe his breath, so close that your nipples brush against his chest."

Ariane stopped.

"Then," Marie instructed softly, "set your hands most carefully on the bulge that is growing beneath his breeches."

Ariane's breath wedged in her throat.

"Measure him until he outgrows the reach of your fingers. Then undo his breeches and measure what you can with your mouth. Simon will be the warmer for it." Marie laughed. "And so will his sad nightingale."

26

The candle died in the fierce wind that howled around Ariane when she stepped onto the battlements. Her hair lifted and swirled as though alive. A flurry of ice-tipped rain stung her cheeks. She shivered but refused to retreat. The cleverly woven fabric of her dress kept much of the chill at bay. As for the rest . . .

Amethyst eyes sought the silhouette of Simon stalking along the battlements. At first Ariane saw nothing, for the wind had brought tears to her eyes. Then she heard fragments of conversation and turned toward the sounds.

Halfway across the battlements two men were standing near a brazier, warming their hands against the icy night. Sparks leaped up with each twist of wind, outlining the men in glittering swirls of light.

Without stopping to think how she was going to explain her presence on the battlements in the midst of night and storm, Ariane started for the men. Just before she reached the brazier, Simon spun around as though sensing her presence.

"Lady Ariane!" Simon said, shocked. "What are you doing here? Is Meg not well? Does Dominic —"

"I must speak with you," Ariane said distinctly, cutting across her husband's quick words.

Simon stepped away from the brazier. Taking Ariane's arm, he led her back just inside the stairwell, where the wind would be somewhat baffled. There a torch guttered and leaped fitfully, lighting the way for the next guard.

The whipping, unpredictable torchlight made Ariane's eyes appear wild. She wore no mantle, nothing but the fey dress whose textures haunted Simon's dreams. Shivers coursed visibly over her, yet she seemed unaware of her own cold. She was watching Simon with an intensity that in another woman he would have labeled passion.

But not in Ariane, the woman who withdrew from Simon's own passion.

"What is wrong?" Simon demanded.

"Nothing."

"Nothing? God's teeth, lady! You stand shivering in front of me in the middle of the night and say that nothing is wrong?"

Stand inside Simon's mantle, close enough to breathe his breath, so close that your nipples brush against his chest.

Ariane let the useless candle fall from her hand and stepped closer to Simon, then closer still.

"Cover me," she said in a shaking voice.

When he hesitated, Ariane bit back a cry. "Please, Simon. I am in need."

He opened his mantle and shifted the belt holding his sword so that the blade was at his back. Ariane stepped forward without waiting for him to finish.

When he closed the mantle again, Ariane was inside its heavy folds. Touching him.

Vivid heat flushed Ariane from her forehead to her heels as Simon's body pressed against her, changing her, seducing her into honeyed warmth. She felt as she had in her dreams; cherished, hot, sensuous to her very core. She wanted to pull Simon around her like a living blanket.

"Ahhhhhh," Ariane said raggedly, sigh and moan alike. "You always smell so good to me. And your heat . . . You are warmer than flame itself."

Simon's nostrils flared as he caught the scent that was Ariane's and Ariane's alone. He breathed deeply, drawing her into his body. Mixed with midnight and roses was a spicy trace of feminine arousal.

The scent of it sent a rush of searing awareness through Simon. Even his memories of

Ariane held in the thrall of healing balm and his caressing mouth weren't as vivid as the feel of Ariane's breasts pressed against his chest now, arousing him with each breath she took.

Simon's own breath came out with a sound that was halfway between a curse and a groan. To his surprise, Ariane tilted back her head as though savoring the warm rush of his exhalation and the urgency of his need. She inhaled deeply, infusing her body with his breath.

"Ariane?" Simon asked in a low, intense voice. "What is it? What drove you to me?"

She simply shook her head and pressed even closer to his body, fitting herself to him, giving herself to the dream that had haunted her since she had lain in healing thrall and learned that a man's hands could bring comfort instead of fear, pleasure instead of pain, ecstasy instead of nightmare.

Closing his eyes, Simon fought against the fierce rush of his desire. Of their own will, his arms contracted, overlapping the edges of the mantle as he drew Ariane even nearer to his body. Rather grimly he waited for her to realize what was pressing against her belly.

The feel of his wife's hands settling most carefully on the bulge growing beneath his breeches nearly brought Simon to his knees.

"I have dreamed of you, Simon. Have you dreamed of me?"

Surprise and desire hammered through him. He would have spoken, but Ariane was measuring him full well with her hands, taking away the possibility of thought, much less speech.

Breath hissed between Simon's clenched teeth as he felt his laces coming undone. He knew he should protest, should stop Ariane before she drove him over the edge of reason with passion only half-slaked, but he could not force himself to deny entry to her cool, searching hands.

She found him, freed him, stroked him from blunt satin tip to thick base and then beyond, cupping the aching flesh that was drawn up so tightly with hunger that it was all Simon could do to stand upright.

Simon ordered his arms to push Ariane away, but instead they contracted about her hips, bringing her even closer, cradling her thighs hotly between his own. The part of his mind that weighed and measured and reasoned expected Ariane to struggle against the blunt sexuality of the embrace.

Instead, Ariane pressed herself against Simon from breast to thigh, moving slowly, caressing him with her whole body. The erect flesh she held so lovingly leaped between her hands.

"This is madness," Simon hissed.

"Yes."

"Give me your mouth."

"Yes," she whispered.

Simon bent to receive Ariane's kiss, only to feel her pulling away from the embrace.

"No," he said huskily. "Don't draw back."

"I must!"

Clenching his teeth against words of disappointment, Simon released Ariane completely, keeping only the mantle around her.

Immediately she slid down his body like a warm, supple weight, vanishing entirely beneath the luxurious mantle.

"Ariane? Are you feeling fai—"

Simon's question ended in a gasp as her cheek smoothed over his erect flesh. Her skin was cool from the wind and her breath was warm from her body. It whispered over him in another kind of caress as she turned her head from side to side, stroking him. Then she caught him between her hands and brought him to her mouth.

"Dear God," Simon said thickly.

His whole body tightened like a bow. Had it not been for the stone wall against his back, he would have fallen. Ariane's mouth was hot, soft, wet, and her tongue was endlessly curious.

Simon took the wild loving as long as he

could. Then he sank the fingers of one hand into Ariane's hair and slowly, slowly, began to draw her head away from his body. She resisted at first. He thought the sweet pressure of her mouth tugging on him would be his undoing.

In the end, Simon's discipline and sheer male strength won out over Ariane's seductive caresses. But both he and she were trembling by the time Simon drew her up his body and buried his tongue hungrily in her mouth.

The kiss was as abandoned as Ariane's caresses had been, a hot mating of tongues that left both of them breathless, barely able to stand. Yet neither wanted to end the kiss. Each clung harder, closer, deeper, while the wind whipped Ariane's hair into a seething black cloud.

Beneath the mantle, Simon pulled off his gloves and loosened silver laces until his fingers could slide beneath cloth to touch Ariane's breasts. The chill of his fingertips against Ariane's warmth served to heighten the intensity of the caress, tightening her nipples in a dizzying rush. She moaned deep in her throat and swayed toward Simon, knowing only him.

It was a long time before Simon could force himself to release Ariane's mouth. He leaned heavily against the stone wall, caressing what he could reach of her breasts with hungry fingers, breathing as though he had been in battle.

"Simon?"

"The rest of your laces," he said huskily. "Undo them for me. If I let go of the mantle, the wind will have it."

"I would rather undo your laces."

"You already have."

"Not those on your shirt," Ariane said.

As she spoke, she ducked beneath the mantle and probed between the laces of Simon's shirt with her tongue. Then she began sliding back down his muscular torso, hungry for him in a way that she couldn't name.

Simon caught Ariane just before her mouth found him again. Muscles bunched as he lifted her upright once more. In the flickering light her eyes were wide, dark, shimmering with an unbridled hunger that made Simon's body clench. Her tongue darted out, touching the center of her upper lip as though catching up a drop of wine.

"You tasted as wild as the storm," Ariane said. "Let me taste you again."

"You will undo me," Simon said through his teeth.

"I enjoy undoing you."

"As sweet as your hands are, as hot as your mouth is, I would rather spill my seed inside your body."

Ariane trembled. After a moment she found Simon's aroused flesh with her hands. Breath hissed savagely over his teeth at her touch.

"But you don't want that, do you?" Simon said. "You don't want me sheathed within you. Why? You aren't a virgin to fear a man's hunger."

"No, I'm not a virgin . . ."

Ariane sighed and shivered. With one hand she slowly began drawing up the skirts of her dress. With the other, she held Simon tenderly captive. The fey cloth came as though summoned, riding up her thighs and swirling around her waist, leaving her naked but for the brushing of the mantle's white fur lining on her hips.

"Remember the friend I told you about?" Ariane asked.

Simon had difficulty concentrating on anything but his own heavy arousal and the feel of Ariane's dress sliding up his thighs.

"Friend?" he said thickly.

Following the instincts of her own need, Ariane brought Simon to the tight sheath that passion had transformed into a sultry, aching emptiness.

"Aye," she murmured. "My friend who was raped."

Ariane shifted, pressing herself against the rigid flesh passion had conjured from Simon's body. She rubbed over him, moistening him as surely as her mouth had. The next motion of her hips over him was easier, deeper, sweeter.

It made her want more. Much more. But she wasn't certain how to accomplish it. All she knew was that the feel of his blunt arousal caressing her made her want . . . *something.*

Simon groaned as he felt Ariane's sultry petals parting and gliding over him. Harshly he fought to control the need that had become a living thing tearing at his loins.

"Yes," Simon said raggedly. "I remember. Your friend."

Clinging to Simon, feeling the cold wind only as an exquisite contrast to the heat of their embrace, Ariane shivered with pure pleasure at the feel of him gently lodged between her thighs. Ecstasy swept through her in a hot, secret storm.

The breaking of Simon's breath and the sudden thrust of his body against her told Ariane that he had felt her sultry rain as surely as she had.

"I am she," Ariane said.

For a moment Simon didn't understand. Then he did.

He looked down at Ariane's face. She was fire and shadow, half-opened eyes smoldering, her mouth still flushed from his kisses.

"You?" Simon asked hoarsely.

"Aye. My first and only experience of a man left me torn, bloodied, beaten. Betrayed."

"Nightingale. My God . . ."

Simon trembled as he bent to kiss Ariane's eyes, her cheeks, her mouth. The caresses were both hungry and restrained. They made her feel bathed in tender warmth.

"I believed that this," Ariane's hips moved, measuring Simon even as she returned his kisses, "this instrument of silk and steel was meant to punish a woman."

Beneath Simon's short beard, his jaw muscles clenched against the sweet torment of being caressed by her softness and at the same instant knowing full well that there would be no release for him within her body.

Torn, bloodied, beaten.

Betrayed.

"I understand," Simon said huskily.

" 'Tis why I froze whenever you tried to touch between my thighs. I was frightened of being hurt again."

"Yes. I understand. Now."

Simon breathed kisses against Ariane's eyelids and sipped at the ends of her long lashes.

"But I'm not frightened of you anymore," Ariane whispered.

Simon said nothing, for he was afraid he hadn't heard her words correctly.

"Put your arm beneath my hips," Ariane said, remembering how Thomas had carried Marie from the armory.

Simon bent and did as Ariane asked, too surprised to ask why. The feel of Ariane's resilient, sleek bottom against his arm sent sensual lightning through both of them. Her knees gave way, making her cling all the harder to Simon.

"Help me," Ariane whispered.

The wind took most of her words, but Simon didn't hesitate. Her body was telling him everything he needed to know, more than he had ever believed he would have from his dark nightingale.

"Lift me," Ariane whispered.

Simon turned his back to the wind, letting it fold the mantle around both of them. As he took the weight of Ariane on his arm, her own arms went around his neck and clung. Her thighs parted and her legs wrapped around his body.

"Fill me, Simon," Ariane breathed against his lips.

With a throttled sound that was her name, Simon fit himself to Ariane as he had in his dreams, pressing gently and then harder, pushing slowly, deeper and then deeper still, feeling her sleek and wet and tight around him, welcoming him.

A long, unraveling sigh rippled from Ariane as she felt Simon parting her, penetrating her, stretching her . . . but not hurting her. The wonder of the sensuous joining trembled through her, ecstasy delicately raking her, calling a shimmering, passionate rain from her depths.

The sultry eagerness of Ariane's body drew forth a single hot pulse of response from Simon. He eased his way even more deeply into her, until he was locked within her, fully sheathed, more perfectly coupled with a woman than he had ever been in his life.

Ariane whimpered and clenched around Simon so tightly that he could barely breathe for the pleasure she gave him. The sensation of being held within a sleek, loving vise was extraordinary.

Suddenly Simon remembered what Ariane had said the first time she had held his naked, aroused flesh in her hands.

I am afraid of this. 'Tis made to tear a woman apart.

"Nightingale," Simon said hoarsely. "Am I hurting you?"

When Ariane opened her mouth to answer, all that came out was another of the odd, broken cries that had alarmed Simon.

Sweat bloomed beneath Simon's clothes as he fought against his deepest needs. Ariane was so hot around him, so tight, so sleek, she seemed to beg for an even deeper joining.

He knew he should spare her, yet he wanted only to delve more deeply, pushing himself in to the hilt.

Slowly he began to withdraw.

Unable to speak, Ariane clung to Simon, shivering with the violence of her response to being filled so perfectly by him, if only for a few moments.

"Ariane? Is even this too much?"

"Again," Ariane said finally, raggedly.

As she spoke, her nails scored against Simon's neck and she locked her legs more tightly about his body, trying to force him back inside her warmth.

Her strength was no match for his. He held her away, wanting to be certain that he wasn't forcing himself into her tight sheath.

Torn, bloodied.

Simon set his teeth. "Talk to me, nightingale. Tell me what you want."

"I — I must — have you."

"Like this?"

Ariane's breath caught as she felt herself stretched and stretched while Simon slowly penetrated her again. His name splintered on her lips.

"Am I hurting you?" Simon asked, withdrawing.

She shook her head. "Not — like that."

"You cried out."

"It was the beauty of —"

"This?"

Simon pressed into Ariane again, watching her eyes, and this time he didn't stop until they were so completely joined that the silken knot of her passion was drawn tautly against his body.

"Ariane?"

"Dear God, yes. *Simon.*"

The sound of his name breaking on Ariane's lips destroyed Simon's control. His arms closed even more tightly around her, locking her against him while he drove into her again and again, drinking the wild cries that came from her lips.

Ecstasy trembled inside Ariane, then burst, trembled and burst again and again, spilling through her to Simon. He gave it back to her pulse for pulse, caressing her soft depths even as he spent himself within them.

Then he held her, simply held her, until they could breathe without unraveling all over again.

Gradually the sound of the wind and stray lashes of icy rain reminded Simon that he was on the battlements and the sentry might come by at any time.

Reluctantly Simon began to lift Ariane off

his body. Her legs locked with surprising strength.

"We must go inside," Simon said.

Ariane's only answer was a sleek contraction of her body that made Simon's breath break.

And hers.

"Stay inside me," Ariane said against Simon's lips. "It feels . . . right."

" 'Tis the same for me."

Her mouth opened at the first touch of his tongue. For a long time they tasted one another in a hushed silence surrounded by the wind. Finally, unwillingly, Simon lifted his mouth.

"The sentry might come," he said against Ariane's lips.

"The sentry?"

"Aye."

Ariane turned to see if the sentry were close. The twisting motion of her body had a breathtaking effect on Simon.

"He is coming," Ariane whispered, turning back.

"We have a choice."

"Aye?"

"I can put you down and we can try to set our clothes aright before he notices."

"He is very close."

"Aye." Simon smiled rather fiercely. "Hold tightly to me, nightingale."

Before Ariane could ask what Simon meant, he was descending the stair. The sensations that came as he moved dragged a ragged, low moan from her. With a broken sound she clung to Simon, using every newly discovered muscle of her body.

When the spiraling staircase had turned enough to shield them from the sentry, Simon stopped.

"You can let go, now," he said.

Ariane shook her head and burrowed even closer to him.

Beneath the mantle, Simon's hand shifted until he could stroke the very petals that were stretched so tightly around him.

Ariane's eyes widened. She gasped at the sensations radiating through her from his probing fingertips. The gasp quickly became a moan. Ecstasy cascaded through her, sending a silky heat spilling over him.

"You are delicious," Simon said huskily, plucking at the sleek knot he had discovered rising from Ariane's softness. "I could take you again right now, right here, with all the people of the keep trooping by in a row. And you would let me, wouldn't you? God's teeth, you would beg me!"

"S-Simon," Ariane said brokenly, "what are you doing to me?"

"Does it hurt?"

"Nay, but — oh!"

Ariane's words were squeezed into silence as ecstasy's vise closed around her. Simon caressed her slowly, watching her, smiling as her heat blossomed once more between their bodies. While she convulsed gently around him, he lifted her until they were separate, then resettled her legs around his hips.

"Hold on to me," he said.

When Ariane obeyed, Simon had to bite back a groan. The feel of her lush softness pressed against his open breeches made his blood hot all over again.

He took the stairs swiftly and strode down the hall until he came to Ariane's bedchamber. The door was standing open. He kicked it closed behind them. The draft from their entrance made lamp flames stretch and sway. The fire in the brazier was little more than embers veiled in ash.

" 'Tis nearly as cold here as above," Simon said. "But it doesn't matter. The only fire I need is between your thighs. Unfasten my mantle, nightingale."

Ariane struggled with the big silver brooch that fastened Simon's mantle at his left shoulder. While she worked, Simon's mouth moved over her hands, nibbling, biting, licking, his tongue probing deeply between her fingers.

The sensual promise of the caresses speeded

Ariane's heartbeat, but not as much as the smoldering hunger in Simon's eyes when he saw that her hands trembled.

"Are you afraid?" he asked, knowing the answer but wanting to savor it from Ariane's lips.

"Nay. 'Tis just that you . . . unsettle me."

The breathless admission made Simon smile darkly.

" 'Tis done," Ariane said, finally freeing the mantle.

"Nay, my lady. 'Tis only begun."

Simon threw his mantle onto the bed. The white fur lining gleamed like silver in the shimmering lamplight. He lowered Ariane into the midst of it and swept her hair up over her head.

Her breasts were bared by the unlaced bodice and her skirts were well above her waist. Nothing of her femininity was concealed from Simon's eyes. He looked at her with a smoldering intensity that made Ariane's whole body flush with embarrassment.

And then Ariane didn't care about her nakedness, for Simon was equally revealed, standing proud and hard through the opening in his breeches. With a smile as old as Eve, Ariane reached out and delicately traced his erect flesh with her fingertips.

Simon's answering smile was hot and utterly

male. Impatiently he took off his broadsword and set it aside while Ariane's slender fingers teased him from tip to base and back again.

"You are magnificent, my lord," Ariane whispered.

Fire ignited at her words, drawing Simon even tighter, fuller, his life's blood coursing visibly beneath her fingertips. He shuddered at the certainty of his own potency like a torrent pouring through him.

"You have bewitched my body," Simon said huskily. "No woman has ever aroused me as completely as you do. I have just taken you and I must have you again."

"I am here."

Leaning forward, Ariane touched the tip of her tongue to him, stealing the sultry drop that she had summoned from the depths of Simon's need.

"You taste as the sun must taste," she whispered. "Burning."

"I taste like you. You are the fire burning me."

" 'Tis you, Simon." Ariane's tongue touched him again. "You are my sun. Before you there was only darkness."

Simon groaned and fought to subdue the urgency that was raking through him with sweet talons. When he could breathe again, he bent and slid one hand from Ariane's ankles

456

to the midnight triangle just above her thighs.

Her breath caught at the intensity in his look. "Simon?"

"Give me leave, my lady."

Slowly Ariane shifted her legs until there was no barrier to Simon's touch. He knelt between her legs. Gently his fingers parted her until he could trace the flushed, sensitive folds. Her breath broke and he knew again the sultry rain of her pleasure.

"You are more sensual than I hoped," Simon whispered, "hotter even than my dreams."

Two fingers probed, parted, then slid deeply into Ariane, stretching her. She gasped and felt pleasure surge sharply through her, spilling onto his hand.

"You're inside me," Ariane said, torn between surprise and desire. *"Touching me."*

Simon inhaled sharply. The heady spice of her response infused the very air he breathed, arousing him even more in turn.

"You hold back nothing," he said huskily, "hide nothing, give everything."

Simon felt his control unraveling, but he no longer cared. Ariane was trembling with forerunners of ecstasy, her every breath broken and as hot as the pulses his touch drew from her. The sultry, tangible proof that he wasn't caught alone in the sensual storm made it impossible for Simon to hold back any longer.

"Next time," he said as he slid his hands beneath Ariane's knees, "next time I will undress you and know you fully awake as I have known you in my dreams."

Simon caressed Ariane's legs, parting them even more.

"Next time," he said, "I will kiss you until you are silk and fire beneath my mouth and I can taste the delicious certainty of your ecstasy."

Ariane's eyes widened as Simon's hands shifted smoothly, powerfully, and she found herself suddenly with her legs draped over the crook of his arms, fully opened to him.

"But not this time," Simon said. "This time I must have you. *Now.*"

He drove into her, filling her completely.

Ariane gasped at the sunburst of fiery pleasure that blazed deep within her. The hard, complete joining was both overwhelming and exquisite. His name splintered on her lips, reflection of the ecstasy stitching through her body.

"Aye, my wild nightingale. No matter what happened in the past, this is the only truth that matters. You burn for me as no woman ever has."

Simon began moving fully within Ariane, watching their joined bodies, his whole being focused in the elemental union. Cries rippled from her lips, soft whimpers that spoke of sensuality unleashed, an incandescent truth that was beyond any shadow of lie.

Pleasure drenched her, infusing the very air with heat.

"Yes," Simon said huskily. "Bathe me in your desire. There is no need to talk of a past rape. No ravished maid could know the sensuous tricks you do."

Ariane barely heard the words, and even then they had no meaning to her. A muscular thrust of Simon's body had sent sweet lightning stabbing through her mind, cutting away all possibility of thought. Her being was racked with pleasure as her breath unraveled in a rippling cry.

"Aye, nightingale. Sing to me of fire. I don't care about the past. I care only about *this*."

Simon surged against Ariane, rubbing the sleek nub of her passion between their bodies. He smiled to feel her response, the shudder and the silken burst of heat. He vowed to feel it again and yet again, until he finally knew the depths of her sensuality.

And his own.

Ariane gave up trying to speak, for she no longer knew her own body. A sweet fire was sweeping through her, transforming her. She shivered in wild culmination and clung to the hard warrior who filled her so completely.

The smile Simon gave Ariane was as primitive as the caress of his teeth against her neck, her breasts, her ears. And with each careful bite he drove into her again, rocked against her, fitting himself deeply to her and then deeper still, drinking her cries as fire blazed through her again.

And still he thrust into her, taking her higher, going with her, sweat gleaming on their bodies like the fire that was consuming her, burning her beyond bearing.

Simon bent down, drinking Ariane's moans even as his powerful, driving body drew more sweet sounds from her.

With a cry Ariane arched up to Simon, her head thrown back, her hair an untamed cloud. He caught her there, held her arched and wild, his body motionless, poised over hers, waiting, shivering with a hunger that was as great as his restraint.

Then Simon felt unspeakable ecstasy ravish Ariane, heard it in her shattered cry. He thrust into her once more and let go all restraint, fusing himself to her with each savage, ecstatic pulse of his release, pouring himself into her until there was no past, no present, no lies, only the truth of a pleasure so great he thought he would die of it.

And it was just beginning.

He was as sure of that as he was of his own strength.

Slowly, tenderly, relentlessly, Simon began to arouse Ariane all over again.

A long time later, in the darkness when even the moon slept, Simon shuddered in the aftermath of an ecstasy so violent that it had left Ariane weeping in his arms, calling his name with each broken breath she took. He kissed her wet eyelashes, pulled her closer, and drew the mantle over both of them.

"Whatever came before this night does not matter," Simon said against Ariane's mouth. "But henceforth you will sing your sensual songs only for me, nightingale. Only for me."

The huskiness of Simon's voice didn't hide the steel will beneath it any more than his intense sensuality had concealed the sheer power and discipline of his body.

"I could never bear another man's touch," Ariane whispered. "I love you, Simon. 'Tis why I overcame my fear of a man's strength."

Simon closed his eyes. "Do not speak of the past again. It can only cause pain."

"But —"

He kissed Ariane's lips with great gentleness.

"You are everything I ever dreamed of having in my arms," Simon whispered against her mouth.

Simon tucked Ariane along his side and surrendered himself to sleep as completely as he had given himself to the shared body of their passion.

Ariane did not sleep as quickly. She lay awake for a long time, her breath catching, her passion spent, her heart aching with all that had been said.

And not said.

I seduced Simon all too well, Ariane thought despairingly. *He will accept his unmaidenly wife without complaint, for we burn too well together ever to burn separately again.*

But he does not believe me.

He believes Geoffrey.

No wonder Simon doesn't love me as I love him. He doesn't trust me.

Numbly Ariane wondered if she would ever escape from the nightmare of the past.

27

"Horsemen!" cried the sentry.

The urgent voice carried into the lord's solar, for the sentry was right overhead.

"Two leagues distant, at the entrance to the wildwood! I couldn't count them! They were gone too quickly!"

Simon and Dominic traded swift looks across the harvest tally books that were piled between them on a trestle table. The table had been used for breakfast and for working on the accounts as well, because there was no warmer room in the keep than the lord's solar.

"The wildwood?" Dominic muttered. " 'Tis not the commonly used approach."

"But 'tis the one that is hardest to see from the battlements," Simon said. " 'Tis also the quickest way from Stone Ring Keep. Were you expecting Duncan?"

"Not unless there were a dire emergency at his keep. There is snow on the peaks and ice in the highest fells. 'Tis no time to be traveling."

Dominic turned to one of the three squires

who was mending leather garments for use under chain mail tunics.

"Bobbie, tell Sir Thomas to sound the alarm."

"Aye, lord!"

The young squire set aside his leather work and ran from the solar.

"Edward," Simon said. "Attend me at the armory."

"Aye, sir!"

"John," Dominic said.

It was all he said. Though he had only recently selected John, Harry the Lame's son knew his duties as squire to the Glendruid Wolf. Harry had been one of Blackthorne Keep's most stalwart knights until he was lamed in a battle.

Simon and Dominic strode quickly to the armory, followed by the two lean youths who were barely old enough to grow a beard.

A bell pealed urgently over Blackthorne's fields, calling everyone to the safety of the bailey. Shouts echoed through the keep as knights, squires and men-at-arms ran toward the armory.

Though Simon and Dominic dressed with the speed of men long accustomed to the heavy, intricate trappings of war, the armory was crowded by the time the two brothers each accepted a broadsword from his squire.

Dominic's and Simon's movements as they fastened the swords in place were the same — quick, expert, calm. As always, Simon had the edge in speed. While Dominic was still settling his broadsword around his hips, Simon took his heavy winter mantle from Edward and fastened it around his shoulders.

The sight of the fur lining made Simon smile to himself. He would never again look at the silky white fur without seeing Ariane lying on it for the first time, her body all but naked, her skin flushed, her amethyst eyes blazing as she watched him sheathe himself deeply within her.

Nor had Ariane tired of the sensual sport in the nights that followed. She came to him as eagerly each night as he came to her. In truth, she came to him at dawn, as well. And once he had surprised her alone at her bath. It had been a sensuous revelation to both of them. He planned to find her there again.

Soon.

"What a smile," Dominic said, giving Simon an odd look. "Are you so eager for war?"

"Nay. I was just thinking of, er, something else."

"The coming night?" Dominic asked blandly.

Simon threw his brother a sharp glance.

Dominic grinned. "Did you think no one

had noticed that you and Ariane spend much time abed?"

"Abed? Nay," Simon said gravely. "We are simply doing as you and I did when we were children — hunting for feathered eels."

Dominic gave a shout of laughter that caused the other knights to look at him.

What they saw was their lord's scarred hands fastening the big Glendruid pin in place on his black mantle. The wolf's crystal eyes glittered balefully in the swirling torchlight, watching everything, promising grim retribution for any who caused the sleeping beast of war to awaken.

One by one the men looked away and went about their own work of preparing themselves to fight.

Simon and Dominic went quickly to the battlements, their metal chausses clicking as they walked. Their squires trotted after, carrying the helms that would be worn only if battle appeared imminent. The squires were both excited and a bit anxious about the outcome of a fight. Though the stonemasons had been working steadily, the wall around Blackthorne Keep still had a gap that was guarded only by wooden palisades.

The sentry saluted Dominic but had nothing new to add. The riders wouldn't be within sight again until they came to the open lane through the fields.

Under a lowering grey sky, Simon and Dominic stood in the center of the battlements, their uncovered hair combed by the cold wind, their long mantles whipping at their ankles, and their chain mail armor the color of a storm.

"Do you think it is Deguerre?" Simon asked.

Dominic shrugged. "Word of Deguerre has come to me every day since that braggart Geoffrey arrived ten days ago. Not once has the message varied."

"Which means that Deguerre has spent the past ten days progressing slowly north, recruiting knights, men-at-arms, and ruffians along the way."

"And whores," Dominic added.

"Like a man expecting to go to war."

"He claims to gather men for a new crusade to the Holy Land."

"No one believes him."

Dominic shrugged. "No one has called him false."

"Yet. But he will find that there is no cause for war in the Disputed Lands," Simon said.

Dominic said nothing.

"Despite the shrewd maneuvering of Deguerre's envoy, the king has accepted my marriage to Ariane," Simon said. "The Duke of

Normandy will also be appeased, as soon as the word of our marriage — and the gifts — arrive."

"The duke prefers to be called king," Dominic said dryly.

"King, duke or churl, he will be content with Ariane's marriage to me," Simon retorted. "I am already content. Therefore, there is no cause for argument with Baron Deguerre. He collects warriors in vain."

"Does he? Or does he merely bide his time until word arrives that Geoffrey the Fair has been challenged by Simon the Loyal and Geoffrey has been slain for his meddlesome mouth?"

"Deguerre will wait for that word until ice forms in hell," Simon said. "I can't be bothered swatting every dung fly that buzzes about the stable."

Dominic looked at the squires and curtly gestured for privacy. The boys withdrew to the relative shelter of the stairwell.

"Simon . . ." Dominic began, then sighed. "By the Cross, I had hoped it wouldn't come to this."

Tensely Simon waited, guessing what was troubling his brother.

"Let me send for Lady Amber," Dominic said finally. "She will cry the truth or falsehood of Geoffrey's accusations. Then there will be an end to his troublemaking."

"No."

Simon's flat denial was unexpected. It took a moment for Dominic to respond. When he did, he was as blunt as his brother had been.

"Why not?" Dominic demanded.

"I don't want to put Ariane — or Amber — through the agony of Learned scrying."

It was only half of the truth, but it was the only half Simon planned to discuss.

"God's teeth," Dominic snarled. "Amber would put an end to Geoffrey's lies."

"What lies?" Simon asked distinctly.

Dominic couldn't hide his shock. "Geoffrey says he is Ariane's paramour!"

"Nay. He merely insinuates it."

"But —"

"Have you or anyone else seen any sign whatsoever that Ariane has been less than faithful to me?"

Breath hissed out between Dominic's teeth in a vicious curse. His gauntleted hand smacked down on the stone parapet.

"Have you?" Simon demanded coolly.

"Jesus and Mary," muttered Dominic. "Of course not! Since Geoffrey arrived, I have no doubt of where and how that swine has spent every waking moment."

"With Sven as a constant, unseen shadow."

"Aye."

469

Simon shrugged. "Then there is no problem."

"Do not play the lackwit with me," Dominic said angrily. "I know full well that your mind is even quicker than your sword."

Simon didn't respond.

"Geoffrey is bragging from battlements to bailey that he has lain with Ariane," Dominic said.

"He has."

Dominic was too stunned to speak.

"My wife and I spoke of the past once, and only once," Simon said. "I have permitted no talk of the past since that night."

"Ariane told you Geoffrey was her lover?"

"She told me that Geoffrey had forced her in Normandy."

"Forced her?" Dominic asked. "Rape?"

"Aye."

"And Baron Deguerre still thinks of Geoffrey the Fair as his son?" Dominic asked in disbelief.

"Aye."

"Wasn't the baron told?"

"He was told," Simon said neutrally.

"And?"

"It happened the night Ariane was informed that Duncan of Maxwell rather than Geoffrey the Fair would be her husband," Simon said. "Geoffrey says that he was summoned to her sitting room, shared a final cup of wine with her, and found himself seduced."

Dominic's eyes narrowed. "He was believed?"

"Yes."

"Why?" Dominic demanded bluntly.

"There were traces of a love potion in Ariane's jeweled perfume bottle. The bottle was found in her bed, along with the blood of her lost virginity."

"Ariane told you this?"

"She told me that Geoffrey was responsible for her lost virginity. The details came from Geoffrey. He remembers the event with great . . . relish."

Dominic swore. He could well believe that Geoffrey enjoyed taunting Simon.

"What does Ariane say to his accusations?"

"We do not speak of the past. Ever."

"God's blood," said Dominic fiercely. "What a fine basket of eels this is!"

"Aye."

"What do you believe happened between Geoffrey and Ariane?"

Simon said not one word.

"By all that is holy," Dominic said in a low voice. *"You believe Geoffrey."*

For long, tense moments Dominic searched Simon's face with glittering grey eyes that closely matched those of the Glendruid pin.

Then Dominic swore wearily and looked away.

"Killing Geoffrey will not change the fact that I was not Ariane's first man," Simon said evenly. "Nor will I put the future of Blackthorne Keep at risk for a past that cannot be changed."

For a time there was only the wind and the random shouts of knights taking up defensive positions throughout the keep.

"You accept this?" Dominic asked finally.

Simon closed his eyes for the space of a breath. When they opened, they were as clear and unreadable as night.

"I will have no other wife but Ariane," Simon said.

Dominic's mouth flattened into a hard line. "Meg said as much."

Simon grimaced. "Glendruid eyes."

"Yes. She *saw* your acceptance of Ariane as she is today, rather than as the innocent maiden you had every right to require for your bride. 'Tis why I haven't sent for Amber and forced her truth down your stubborn throat."

"Thank you. I would not have Ariane shamed before the entire keep."

"And you? What of your pride?"

"It has taken worse blows."

"Has it?"

"Yes. When my lust for a married whore

472

nearly cost your life."

With a grimace, Dominic looked out over the keep's bare fields and mist-wreathed hills.

"What will you do when Geoffrey accuses Ariane of adultery?" Dominic asked. "And you know he will. He is determined to force you to challenge him."

"Sven will gainsay Geoffrey's lies."

"Sven has followed Geoffrey only since he came to the keep. I understand that it is possible Ariane and Geoffrey met just before then."

"Sven had best watch his words to you very carefully," Simon said with deadly clarity. "I can slay him without causing a war."

"He is your friend."

"Ariane is my *wife*."

Dominic looked at his brother's eyes and then looked away once more.

"If Blackthorne were strong enough to withstand war with Baron Deguerre," Dominic said, "where would Geoffrey be now?"

"Ten days dead," Simon said succinctly.

Eyes narrowed against the cold wind and an emotion that made his throat ache, Dominic waited until he could trust himself to speak.

"You stay your sword arm, and humble your pride, for the sake of loyalty to me," Dominic said.

"And for Meg. For your unborn child. For the children I now hope someday to have."

"In the Holy Land, you would not have done this."

"In the Holy Land I was a fool ruled by passion. Passion no longer rules me. I rule it."

Dominic's hand formed a fist on the parapet as he fought against the necessity of Simon's sacrifice. Simon was correct in his assessment of Blackthorne's vulnerability. They couldn't defeat a concerted, determined attack by forces such as Deguerre was assembling.

For a time Dominic closed his eyes and bowed his head as though in prayer. Finally he looked up at the brother he loved as he loved no one except his wife.

"I am in your debt," Dominic said, his eyes glittering with emotion. "I don't know if such a debt can ever be repaid."

"Nay," Simon said. " 'Tis I who am in your debt."

But Dominic had turned away and was striding toward the sentry. Only the wind heard Simon's protest.

"I can see them, lord!" called the sentry. "They are coming on like thunder!"

Dominic leaned into the wind as Simon hurried forward to stand alongside his brother once more.

The sentry was correct. The riders were coming swiftly.

"War-horses," Simon said.

"Aye."

"Look!" Simon cried. " 'Tis Lady Amber!"

"Are you certain?"

"Aye. The first time I saw her it was like that, her hair a golden fire all around her. By the saints, Erik is with her! See Stagkiller pacing at the stallion's side?"

"He is right," said Sven from behind them. "And that brown stallion is Duncan's. I know it well, having led it back to Blackthorne only this past summer."

"Thank God," Dominic breathed.

He turned and signaled to John, who came at a run.

"Signal the keep's people to return to their business," Dominic said. "And see that Lady Margaret is informed of the number of guests."

"Aye, lord," John said. He turned and sprinted for the stairway.

"We shall meet them at the gate," Dominic said. Then, to Sven, "Where is Deguerre's beloved knight?"

"I left off watching him when the bell summoned me."

"Was he abed?"

"Nay."

Dominic grunted. "Is Geoffrey recovered?"

"Aye, unfortunately."

"From what?" Simon asked.

Both Dominic and Sven gave him an odd look.

"Geoffrey was found in the swine pen yesterday morning," Dominic said neutrally.

"What?" Simon asked.

Again, Dominic and Sven exchanged a glance.

"Someone stripped Geoffrey naked and left him facedown in pig muck," Sven said blandly.

Simon looked at the two men, who watched him expectantly in return.

"Would that I had been the one to do so," Simon said dryly, "but I wasn't. Who dealt the fair knight his comeuppance?"

Without answering, Dominic turned and began taking the staircase with the smooth coordination of a highly trained warrior. Simon and Sven followed, matching Dominic step for step.

"If I had to guess who sent Geoffrey crawling naked through pig dung," Sven said as they emerged into the forebuilding, "it would be Marie."

"Weren't you there?" Simon asked.

"Nay. I am weary of watching him grunt and sweat over her at night and her over him.

When she is with him, I wait in the bailey until I see her leave."

"But why would she leave him naked in pig mire?" Simon asked, smiling at the thought. "She has been like a leech on him of late."

Sven shrugged. "Marie is a woman. Who knows what moves her?"

"You've spent too much time in the company of Erik," Simon said dryly. "You begin to sound like him."

"A man of rare wit and learning," Sven agreed, smiling.

"I believe Sven is right about Marie," Dominic said. "When I went to see Geoffrey for myself, I recognized some of the marks on his body from my stay in that sultan's cursed prison."

"Geoffrey had been tortured?" Simon asked.

Dominic smiled wolfishly. "You could say that. Or you could say that he had been used very thoroughly by a cruel harem girl."

"Marie," Simon said simply. "She never used those tricks on the three of us, but the rest of the knights learned at her hands just how close pleasure and pain could be."

"Aye," Dominic said.

"But why Geoffrey?" Simon said as they stepped into the forebuilding. "What had he done to attract Marie's vengeance?"

"Ask your wife," Sven said.

Simon's eyes widened. "What does Ariane have to do with Marie?"

"I don't know. I do know that your squire saw her go to Marie's room rather late ten nights ago."

"Ten nights . . . ?"

A curse hissed out from between Simon's teeth. He stopped dead in the center of the forebuilding.

"Aye," agreed Dominic, stopping as well. "The squire had heard about what happened in the armory, when Ariane drew her dagger."

"I will teach Thomas the Strong not to talk."

"It could have been Marie."

"She knows better."

Dominic smiled rather grimly. "Aye. Your Edward was afraid that Marie would do something rash to Ariane."

"Or vice versa," muttered Sven.

"When Edward couldn't find you, he went to Sven," Dominic said.

"I got there just in time to see Ariane run up the stairs to the battlements as though her skirts were on fire," Sven said, carefully not looking at Simon.

A flush that had little to do with the bracing temperature of the forebuilding tinted

478

Simon's cheekbones.

Sven laughed out loud, clapped his friend hard on the shoulder, and said nothing more about what had happened on the battlements between Ariane and Simon.

"Knowing that Ariane was safe, I went back to being the shadow of Geoffrey's shadow," Sven said. "Suddenly Marie appeared in the stable where he sleeps. She had his breeches undone before he knew what was happening. It was like that every night thereafter."

"No wonder you have looked short of rest," Simon said blandly.

"Marie has some interesting techniques. And tools. But in the end," Sven said, shrugging, "it is all much the same."

Simon waited, but Sven said no more.

"So how did Geoffrey end up in the muck?" Simon asked.

"I don't know. The past three nights, when Marie came to Geoffrey, I went to the gatehouse and dozed, knowing that Geoffrey wouldn't be getting into trouble until well after dawn."

Simon shook his head in silent sympathy for Sven's long, cold vigils.

"At dawn yesterday," Sven concluded, "the swineherd found Geoffrey in the muck. He told Harry the Lame, who came to me. I went to Dominic."

"What did you do?" Simon asked his brother.

"Geoffrey looked quite at home," Dominic said, smiling narrowly. "I left him there."

Simon laughed out loud. After a moment, he had a thought that wiped all laughter from him.

"What of Deguerre?" Simon said. "From what Ariane has said, Geoffrey is like a son to him."

"And you *are* a brother to me. If Deguerre objects to Geoffrey's quarters, he can teach Geoffrey to be less of a swine."

Simon grimaced. "Nay. 'Tis no fault of yours. You should have none of the burden of Deguerre's anger."

"Then permit Amber to use her gift. It can be done privately."

Simon closed his eyes. The passionate part of him, the part that had never willingly bowed to logic, wanted to believe that Ariane's maidenhead had been taken by rape rather than by seduction.

And yet . . .

For an instant Simon was standing on the battlements as he had ten nights ago, the wind icy about him and Ariane's mouth a soft fire between his legs.

She could not have been a raped virgin.

Nor do I care. It is enough that she wants

480

me as no other woman has.

And there is no doubt of that. I have bathed repeatedly in the sultry fountains of her desire.

A shudder of raw hunger went through Simon as he thought of Ariane's abandoned response to his caresses. He would spend a lifetime trying to get enough of her fire.

Thank God she isn't like Marie, getting pleasure only from controlling a man.

'Tis I who control Ariane's sensuality, not she who controls mine.

"Simon?" Dominic asked.

"Leave it be," Simon said roughly. "I find no fault with my wife as she is. Nothing Amber has to say about the past is of interest to me."

A black eyebrow rose. Silver eyes narrowed briefly.

Simon returned the look as directly and coolly as it was given to him.

"What of the present?" Dominic demanded.

"You are the master of tactics," Simon retorted. "Tell me, Glendruid Wolf, how is Blackthorne better served — by my accepting a bride whose sensuality and innocence once led her astray, or by my avenging a maiden who was raped by a dishonorable knight?"

Though neither man spoke aloud, both remembered what Amber had once said of Ariane's buried emotions: A scream never voiced. A betrayal so deep it all but killed her soul.

And this was what must not be avenged.

If Ariane had been raped.

Better, far better, for Blackthorne if Ariane's betrayal had been of the more normal kind, a maid seduced and then abandoned by a fickle knight.

No vengeance was required for that. Merely acceptance.

And Simon accepted Ariane.

Dominic let out a breath that was also a curse.

"I see you begin to understand," Simon said coolly. "Some truths are better not known."

Hissing Saracen phrases poured from Dominic as he swore over the trap from which even his tactical brilliance could find no escape.

"Aye," Simon agreed bitterly. "Aye and aye and aye! Listen to the wisdom of acceptance, Glendruid Wolf. *Let it be.*"

Grim-faced, silent, Dominic spun around and started for the gate. Simon and Sven followed closely behind.

The cobblestones were treacherous with ice in the shadows and glistening with dampness in the thin light of the day. Wind swirled, bringing with it the smell of snow. The thunder of horses' hooves over the wooden bridge and onto the bailey's cobblestones echoed throughout the keep.

Erik was the first to dismount. He looked from Dominic to Simon and then around the bailey.

"All appears normal," Erik said.

"It was until the sentry spotted your party coming from the wildwood," Dominic said dryly.

Erik swept off his helm and chain mail hood, revealing sun-bright hair and the golden eyes of a wolf. He threw back his head and whistled. The sound was high, haunting, like a pipe played by a god. It was answered by the equally haunting cry of a Learned peregrine.

Winter swooped down out of the low clouds and landed on her master's gauntleted forearm.

"Thank God all is calm," Erik said. " 'Tis too stormy for Winter to be of much use as a scout."

" 'Tis too stormy to be traveling at all," Sven said. "You should have waited for the storm to end."

"Cassandra feared that there wasn't enough time," Duncan said, dismounting.

"For what?" Dominic and Simon asked at once.

Erik and Duncan looked at Amber.

"To scry the truth before it is too late," Amber said.

"What truth?" Simon challenged.

The naked anger in his voice startled Amber, reminding her that Simon had once called her hell-witch. She took a deep breath and faced the man who was watching her with black eyes.

"Cassandra said you would know which truth we sought."

28

No sooner had Erik and Duncan arrived than sleet began to rattle across Blackthorne Keep's stone walls and pile in frozen heaps in the corners of the bailey. Erik's and Duncan's men were bedded down in every place where wind and ice couldn't reach. So were their horses.

The keep was fairly stuffed to the ramparts by suppertime. With trestle tables dragged up to form a huge U, knights from three keeps sat elbow to elbow for the length of the great hall, mopping up the last drops of meat juices with great hunks of fresh bread.

Only Geoffrey sat alone. He was at the far end of one of the trestle tables, as distant as possible from the lord's table. No squires attended Geoffrey. Nor did any knight from any keep choose to sit near him. The separation was enough that Geoffrey had to stand up and see to his own meal, for no one would pass food across the gap. Not even Sven, who sat just beyond reach.

It was the naked hostility of the Disputed Lands' knights toward Geoffrey that had made the Glendruid Wolf decree that no swords would be worn within the great hall. Dominic had considered banning daggers as well, but had decided against it. The squires had enough running about to do at mealtimes without having to carve meat for knights as though they were dainty highborn ladies.

Erik sat at the lord's table across the front of the hall, watching Geoffrey with eyes the color of fire. The silver dagger in Erik's hands gleamed as he turned the blade over and over with slow, almost lazy motions of his hands. The peregrine on a perch behind his chair was in a fine state of ire, her feathers ruffled and her feet so restless that her gold and silver jesses chimed ceaselessly.

The falcon's baleful golden eyes never left Geoffrey. Nor did Stagkiller's equally yellow glare. Torchlight gleamed on canine fangs as the wolfhound licked his chops and whined to be allowed to hunt.

"Erik," Amber said in a low voice. "Quiet your animals. You will make Geoffrey uneasy."

"A creature that sleeps in pig dung has no nerves worth our concern."

Laughter rose from the knights who were close enough to overhear. The story of the unpopular Geoffrey being found naked in the swine pen had passed through the keep as quickly as a storm wind.

Amber looked to Dominic for help in curbing her brother. She found Dominic watching Erik as carefully — if much more warmly — as Erik was watching Geoffrey.

"I told Cassandra she should come with us," Amber muttered. "Erik is thinking of cutting out Geoffrey's tongue."

Dominic made an approving sound.

"You are no help," Amber said unhappily. "Where is Meg? We could use one of her calming brews."

"She and Ariane are in the solar," Dominic said. "Meg wasn't feeling well enough to eat in this noisy hall."

Something in Dominic's tone made Erik, Simon, and Duncan turn to look at the Glendruid Wolf.

"Is Meggie's time at hand?" Duncan asked with the familiarity of an old friend.

"Nay, we have more weeks to wait, though we are both impatient to see our babe born."

As though in answer to Duncan's concern, Meg and Ariane walked into the hall from the lord's solar. Ariane came to stand by Simon. Ignoring the other people in the hall, she put her hand on Simon's shoulder in a silent bid for his attention. Nearby, Meg bent and murmured in Dominic's ear.

Simon missed the feral alertness that came

over Dominic, for Ariane had taken her husband's sword hand and was pressing his palm against her cheek.

"What is it, nightingale?" Simon asked.

"Nothing. I just wanted to touch you. Were we not in sight of the entire keep, I would kiss you most soundly."

"Hammer the keep. Kiss me."

Simon slid his hand beneath Ariane's headcloth and around her neck. The marvelous softness of her skin lured him. He tugged gently, pulling Ariane's mouth down to his own, shielding the caress behind the amethyst silk of her headcloth.

Meg went to Duncan, spoke so that no one could overhear, and then went to Amber. While Meg bent down to whisper to Amber and Erik, Duncan rose without any fuss and went to stand behind Simon. Simon didn't notice, for Ariane's dress had flowed forward over his legs, caressing his thighs beneath the table. Her lips parted and her tongue teased him very lightly.

Erik came to his feet in a lithe motion and walked down the length of the hall beside Amber. Together they stopped close to Geoffrey.

After one look at Erik's eyes, Sven put down his bread and moved away from the table. Within moments he had blended into the crowd of knights. Soon he was at Dominic's side, poised for any new orders that might come from his lord.

"All is ready," Meg said clearly.

"I love you, Simon," Ariane breathed against his mouth. "Soon you will be able to believe in me enough to love me in return."

The words shocked Simon. Ariane hadn't spoken of love since the first wild night when they had finally become true husband and wife. He hadn't known until this moment that he had longed to hear the words again.

Pleasure and pain streaked through Simon equally, for he knew Ariane wanted to be loved in return.

And he knew he could not. He would never again give a woman that much control over him. Even Ariane.

"Nightingale," Simon whispered.

Ariane stepped away so swiftly that she was gone by the time Simon reached for her. She turned and began walking rapidly down the long length of the trestle table where knights were no longer eating. They were staring at the amber witch who had taken off her head-cloth and shaken down her long golden hair.

Abruptly Simon remembered that it was the custom of Learned women to go with unbound hair when they sought knowledge — or vengeance.

"Ariane!" Simon cried.

She turned and gave Simon a look that was both gentle and fierce.

" 'Tis too late, Simon," Ariane said.

"Nay!"

Simon would have leaped to his feet, but Duncan had a heavy hand on each shoulder, forcing Simon to stay seated.

"God's blood!" said Simon, struggling against Duncan. "Let go! I must stop her!"

Duncan grunted and bore down with both hands, pinning Simon to the chair.

"Leave off," Duncan said through his teeth, "or I'll hold you with a blade between your thighs as you once held me!"

"Be still," Dominic said curtly to Simon. "Ariane has the right of it. 'Tis past time for the truth."

"Don't you see?" Simon snarled, twisting abruptly, trying to throw off Duncan's restraint. "If that bastard son of a whore and a swineherd raped Ariane, *I will kill him and to hell with the peace of Blackthorne Keep!*"

"I know," Dominic said, his face grim. "And I dearly wish I could let you carve Geoffrey into slices as thin as winter sunshine. But I cannot."

Duncan's powerful hands closed painfully on Simon, making it impossible for him to break free. Simon heaved up his body once,

490

twice . . . and then he went very still, saving his strength for a time when his captor was less attentive.

"I am sorry, brother," Dominic said, touching Simon's forearm with remarkable gentleness.

Then there was no more time for apology or regret. Meg was speaking in the clear tones of a Glendruid witch. The hall fell so silent that the gentle chiming of her golden jewelry could be heard throughout.

"Sir Geoffrey has insulted the honor of Lady Ariane. The lady has most forcefully requested that the issue not be solved by test of arms, for such would only jeopardize the peace that the Glendruid Wolf has worked so tirelessly to maintain."

A murmuring went through the assembled knights. Each knew what was at issue. Each had wondered why Simon had not challenged Geoffrey ten days ago, nor any day since.

Now they knew.

"Instead," Meg continued, "Ariane requested that Sir Geoffrey be put to the question in the Learned manner. Lady Amber has agreed."

"What is this nonsense?" Geoffrey asked, banging his empty ale cup onto the table. "All the world knows the truth of it. Lady Ariane is my —"

Geoffrey's words were cut off by the blade of a dagger pressed against his mouth. Thin lines of blood appeared at either corner.

"Lord Dominic prefers you alive," Erik said gently, "but I have no such desire and Dominic is not my lord."

Geoffrey tried to jerk back, but Erik's blade followed him, drawing more blood.

"You will behave in a seemly manner," Erik said in a soft voice, "or I will cut out your tongue. Do we understand one another?"

"Aye," Geoffrey said hoarsely.

But his eyes said he would kill Erik at the first chance. Erik's eyes blazed in return while his peregrine shrilled and lunged at the end of her jesses.

"Lord Erik," Dominic said clearly. "I would prefer you at my side."

Slowly, reluctantly, Erik lowered his knife and moved swiftly back to his place at the lord's table. Not only was he Dominic's guest, but Learned questioning did not permit force to be used unless the person being questioned attempted to struggle. Geoffrey was showing no further signs of resisting.

"Proceed when you are ready," Dominic said to Amber.

Meg gave Amber a compassionate look, knowing what the girl was about to undergo.

Amber didn't notice. She had eyes only for Ariane.

"Are you ready, lady?" Amber asked.

"Aye," Ariane said. "But are you certain you wouldn't rather question me?"

"Yes. 'Tis important that we know each one of Geoffrey's truths."

"Then we are lost," Ariane said curtly. "Geoffrey has no truth in him."

Geoffrey started to speak, but thought better of it when Erik stepped eagerly forward.

"Your turn will come to question Ariane," Meg said clearly, "if you require such a questioning."

Amber took a breath and let it out slowly, composing herself. Then she rested one fingertip on Geoffrey's cheek just above the place where blood had been drawn by Erik's knife.

As soon as Amber touched Geoffrey, she went pale. Sweat stood clearly on her skin. Her eyes were so dilated they were almost black. Only her clenched jaw kept her from crying out.

Whatever Amber sensed of Geoffrey when she touched him was intensely painful to her. Yet touching Geoffrey was the only way Amber could learn his truth.

Or his lies.

A visible shudder moved over Amber as she used her Learned training to control her response to touching Geoffrey the Fair.

At the lord's table, Simon felt Duncan's fingers clench in silent protest at what his wife was enduring.

"I did not ask for either Amber or Ariane to suffer this," Simon said through his teeth.

"I know," Duncan said, easing his grip. "Nor did Amber ask that God give her the ability to see truth. It simply is, and must be endured."

"Why did you permit it?" Simon demanded of Dominic.

"It was Ariane's right."

"To be shamed in front of the entire keep?" Simon asked savagely. "God's blood, she doesn't deserve it!"

"Yet she demanded it," Dominic said in a low voice. "I fear she was wronged, Simon."

"It's in the past!" Simon hissed. "Ravaged or seduced, it doesn't matter to me!"

"It does to Ariane."

I love you, Simon. Soon you will be able to believe in me enough to love me in return.

Simon went still as pain twisted through him. Too late, he understood Ariane's truth. She truly believed that he would love her if she proved herself to have been wronged rather than merely wanton.

"Begin," Amber said tonelessly to Ariane.

Ariane turned to Geoffrey, looking at him

494

for the first time since she had come into the room.

"The morning my father told me that I was betrothed to another," Ariane said clearly, "did you come to me privately and beg me to elope with you?"

"Nay, it was you who —"

"Lie," Amber said.

Her voice was like her face, without expression.

"Who are you to call me a liar?" Geoffrey snarled.

"Silence."

Though calm, Meg's voice was terrible to hear. It was the same for her eyes, a green that burned through to the soul.

"Amber's gift is known throughout the Disputed Lands," Meg said distinctly. "You may no more lie successfully to her than you could to an angel."

"Yet I say she has no right to judge me!" Geoffrey said.

"Truth," Amber said.

"Do you understand, now?" Meg said. "When Amber touches you, she discovers the truth or falseness of your responses. You believe she has no right to judge you, so Amber perceives your response as truthful."

"Witchcraft," said Geoffrey, crossing himself hastily.

Without a word Amber reached inside her tunic with her free hand and drew out a silver cross. Bloodred amber gleamed at five points of the cross that lay nestled in her cool hand. Her fingers closed around the cross for the space of four slow breaths, then opened again.

There was no mark anywhere on Amber's hand, no sign that the cross burned in protest at being held against her skin.

Geoffrey looked to the lord's table, where Blackthorne's chaplain sat.

"What say you, chaplain?" Geoffrey shouted.

"Have no fear of Satan within this keep," the chaplain said in a voice that carried easily the length of the great hall. "Lady Amber is like Lady Margaret, strangely blessed by God."

Stunned, off-balance, Geoffrey looked again at Amber's cross.

"Did you come to my sitting room that evening," Ariane said into the silence, "and did you give me wine to drink?"

"Aye," Geoffrey said carelessly, for he was still caught by the sight of Amber's cross lying coolly against her palm.

"Truth," said Amber.

"Did you put an evil witch's potion in my wine?" Ariane asked.

496

Geoffrey's head snapped around once more to face his accuser. The amethyst dress Ariane wore seethed quietly, making silver embroidery glitter and race like veiled lightning throughout the cloth. The jewels in her hair glittered as coldly violet as her eyes.

"Nay," Geoffrey said.

"Lie," Amber said.

A murmuring ran through the assembled knights. Ariane ignored it.

"Did that potion make my mind heavy and my body slack, unable to scream or fight?" Ariane asked.

"Nay!"

"Lie."

The murmur became a muttering of outrage. Warily Duncan looked at Simon.

Simon was absolutely calm, utterly in control of himself. With an inner sigh of relief, and a silent thanks to Simon for his restraint, Duncan eased his punishing grip.

Simon didn't move to take advantage of Duncan's looser grip. Soon the grip became more gentle still.

"Did you then carry me to my bed?" Ariane asked.

Silence, then, "Aye."

"Truth."

Ariane took a deep breath to still the hatred and contempt that made her tremble.

A scream voiced in silence.

"There, you raped me, and when morning finally came —"

"Nay!"

"Lie."

A betrayal so deep it all but killed her soul.

"— you brought my father up to see me lying naked in bloody sheets —"

"Never!"

"Lie."

"— and you told him that I had seduced you with a witch's potion."

"Nay! You —"

"Lie."

Ariane, the Betrayed.

The murmuring of her name and her betrayal went like a storm wind through the great hall, telling Geoffrey the Fair that Ariane had won.

"Then you —" Ariane began.

Geoffrey leaped out of his chair. Blunt fingers closed around Ariane's neck as though he would choke the truth to silence, and her with it.

With a savage cry Simon exploded free of Duncan's restraint and vaulted the lord's table, scattering costly goblets and plates in every direction. As one, Duncan, Dominic and Erik went over the table after Simon.

They weren't quick enough. Simon hit the

floor running. Knights took one look at the black hell of his eyes and scrambled to get out of his way.

Suddenly Geoffrey's high scream ripped through the hall. Ariane's long sleeves had whipped across his face. Livid streaks of red marked wherever the dress had touched his bare skin.

"Curse you to hell, witch!" Geoffrey raged. "I wish I had managed to kill you and your cursed husband when I attacked you in the Disputed Lands!"

Geoffrey whipped a dagger from beneath his mantle and raised the blade.

Simon's dagger flew in a blur of silver between the tables and buried itself to the hilt in Geoffrey's shoulder. Before anyone could draw a breath, Geoffrey was falling and Simon was upon him.

Simon snatched Geoffrey's dagger as it rolled from his numbed hand. Smoothly Simon returned the blade to Geoffrey, point first between his ribs, exactly where Ariane had been wounded by the renegade's dagger. When the blade could go no deeper, Simon twisted the haft sharply.

"May you spend eternity in hell," Simon said softly.

Geoffrey was dead before he hit the floor. Towering over his slain foe, Simon heard as though at a great distance the words of the knights within the great hall.

Geoffrey the Fair.

A renegade butcher.

Deguerre's beloved knight.

Dead.

Simon the Loyal has finally avenged Ariane the Betrayed.

A shudder tore through Simon when Dominic's hand gently gripped his shoulder. Rage receded, sanity returned, and Simon knew what he had done.

Hating himself for his unruly passions, Simon turned from Geoffrey's corpse to face the Glendruid Wolf.

"Again I have betrayed you," Simon said in a voice made harsh by restraint.

"You have defended your wife's honor and her life," Dominic said evenly. "There is no betrayal in that."

"I could have spared Geoffrey. I did not. Worse, if it were mine to do again, I know I would do the same . . . only more slowly, more painfully, until the swine squealed for me to end it."

Simon turned away, holding out his hand. "Lady Amber, I beg a favor of you."

Amber hesitated in the instant before she touched Simon. Her fingers jerked once, then were still. Her breath came out in a long sigh.

She watched Simon with haunted golden eyes, waiting for him to speak.

"Tell my wife," Simon said without looking at Ariane, "that I would have silenced the swine sooner, had Blackthorne been stronger."

"Truth."

"Tell my wife that I am certain of her fidelity to me."

"Truth."

"And finally," Simon said softly, *"tell my wife that I hold her in no greater regard for being certain of her innocence."*

"Truth."

Instantly Simon released Amber.

"I regret the pain I have caused you, lady," Simon said.

"There was none."

"You are as kind as you are beautiful."

Simon turned and looked at Ariane.

"Nightingale," he said softly, "are you at peace, now?"

Ariane couldn't speak. Tears wrenched her throat and spilled from her eyes, for she heard all that Simon did not say. Her reckless determination to prove her own innocence had caused Simon to betray the brother whom he cherished more than he cherished anything in life.

In defending Ariane, Simon had slain

Blackthorne's peace as surely as he had slain Geoffrey the Fair.

Marie's words about betrayal and the Holy Land echoed in Ariane's mind, telling her another truth that had been learned too late: *Simon is a man of extraordinary passion. It will be many more years before he forgets. Or forgives me.*

Ariane feared it would be the same for her.

29

"My lady?" asked Blanche.

"What is it?"

Ariane winced at the sound of her own voice. Geoffrey's death today had been enough to bring strain to anyone, but Baron Deguerre's messenger announcing the imminent arrival of his lord had been the final straw. Blackthorne Keep's nerves were strung to a high pitch as people waited to find out precisely when the baron would arrive, and more importantly, with how many warriors.

"I can't find your favorite comb," Blanche admitted unhappily.

Ariane barely heard. She was certain she had heard the sound of the sentry above the crying of the wind.

"M'lady?"

" 'Tis under the bed in the corner near the window," Ariane said curtly.

Blanche was halfway across the room to retrieve the comb when she stopped and spun back to Ariane.

"Your gift has come back to you!"

The words got through Ariane's preoccupation. She gave Blanche an impatient look.

"Nay," Ariane said. "I merely saw it there earlier."

"Oh."

Blanche went to the bed, got down on her hands and knees, and pawed through the draperies.

" 'Tis keen eyesight you have," Blanche muttered. "I can barely find the cursed thing with both hands."

"Did you say something?" Ariane asked.

"No," Blanche muttered.

As the handmaiden scrambled to her feet, she was grateful that the amber witch wasn't nearby to catch her out in a lie.

Ariane barely noticed Blanche as she combed and braided and piled her mistress's black hair high. Ariane was thinking of the coming night, when Simon finished walking the battlements.

She wondered if he were as angry with her as he once had been with Marie . . . or if Simon would come to his wife in the darkness, teaching her all over again that ecstasy was always new, always burning.

Nightingale, are you at peace, now?

Tears burned against Ariane's eyelids.

She was not at peace. She had risked more than she knew when she put Geoffrey to

Learned questioning, only to discover that the answer truly meant nothing to Simon.

But that same answer had forced him to again betray his brother.

Simon had not loved Ariane before.

He would not love her now.

"When do you think he will come?" Blanche asked.

"Simon?" Ariane asked huskily.

"Nay. Your father."

"Soon. Very soon."

"Tonight?" Blanche asked, startled. " 'Tis already quite late."

"It would be like the baron to arrive when everyone assumes he will wait."

"Oh. How many warriors will he have?"

"Too many."

A cry rang down from the icy battlements. Ariane listened, motionless, and heard the sentry announce the coming of Baron Deguerre through darkness and storm.

"My Learned dress," Ariane said. "Quickly."

Blanche brought the dress and stepped back after giving it to her lady, well pleased not to touch the fabric anymore.

Even as Ariane's fingers flew over silver laces, Dominic, Simon, Erik, and Duncan were sweeping through the keep, calling out orders to knights.

"A gentleman would have waited until tomorrow to come to the keep," Simon said under his breath, "when most of us wouldn't be abed."

"Deguerre is hoping to find our knights fully stupid with ale, and us along with them," Dominic said.

"Always the tactician," Simon said.

"Deguerre or Dominic?" Duncan asked dryly.

"Deguerre," said Dominic.

"Dominic," said Simon.

The Glendruid Wolf smiled sardonically.

The four men stepped into the bailey. Ice gleamed sullenly in the backlash of torchlight.

"Erik," Dominic said, "I ask you to conceal your cleverness. Let Deguerre think you are . . ."

"Stupid?" Erik suggested.

"That would be too much to hope," Dominic retorted. "Deguerre is diabolically shrewd. But if you are silent, there is at least a chance of surprising him with the clarity of your mind."

Erik smiled like a wolf. "I didn't think you had noticed."

Simon swallowed laughter as he picked his way across slick cobblestones. Erik's ability to see patterns where others saw only chaos had set the Glendruid Wolf and the Learned sorcerer at one another's throats more than once.

To Dominic, Erik was very much a double-edged sword. Yet Dominic could not help but respect the younger man's courage and uncanny mind.

When the four men were close to the gatehouse, Harry the Lame pushed open the door. Inside, a fire in the brazier burned like a great orange eye set amid an ebony chill.

"Do you think Deguerre will surrender his arms?" Duncan asked as he stepped into the gatehouse.

"Why shouldn't he?" Simon asked blandly. "You and your knights did. So did Erik and his knights. Neither of you owes fealty to Dominic. Particularly the sorcerer."

"Aye," Erik said under his breath. "The Glendruid Wolf has given me nothing but trouble."

"Thank you," murmured Dominic. "I didn't think you had noticed."

"What if Deguerre doesn't accept the ban?" Erik asked, ignoring Dominic.

"Then he sleeps in the fields with ice for his pillow and wind for his blanket," Simon said.

"You sound as though you relish the prospect," Dominic said.

"I would prefer the baron slept in hell with his beloved swine-knight than in the clean fields of Blackthorne Keep," Simon said.

Dominic gave his younger brother a wary look.

"Have no fear," Simon said tightly. "I am yours to command, so long as it doesn't add to what Ariane has already suffered."

Duncan and Erik exchanged a glance in the wavering torchlight. It was the first time either man had heard Simon put a boundary on his loyalty to the Glendruid Wolf.

"And if more suffering is required?" Dominic asked.

"Then, Glendruid Wolf, you had best restrain me more carefully than before. I find I am fed to the teeth with men who would torment a helpless nightingale."

"Not quite helpless," Dominic said dryly. "You saw the marks upon Geoffrey's face."

"Aye," Duncan muttered. "Lady Ariane must have fingernails like daggers."

"Not nails," Erik said. "A dress from the most accomplished weaver the Silverfells clan has ever produced."

"What do you mean?" Simon asked.

"Serena's weaving responds to Ariane as though she were an ancient Learned warrior commanding skills we have long since lost," Erik said.

"Explain," Dominic said bluntly.

"For Ariane, the dress is armor and weapon both. I wonder if Cassandra foresaw that."

"Just as you are wondering how you can use it to your advantage," Duncan said rather grimly.

As much as Duncan liked Amber's brother, Duncan hadn't forgotten who had set in motion the dangerous events that had ended with Duncan betrothed to one woman, married to another, and foresworn in the bargain.

"To *my* advantage?" Erik challenged softly. "Nay. To the advantage of the Disputed Lands. Like the Glendruid Wolf, I prefer peace to war."

The sound of many horses trotting toward the keep made the four men look at one another.

"A pity Deguerre isn't a peaceful lord," Erik said. "How many fighting men does he have with him?"

"I shall know when Sven returns," Dominic said.

"Ah, yes. The Ghost. I could use a man like him," Erik said. "There are places in the Disputed Lands that are . . . closed . . . to me."

"Should we manage to blunt Deguerre's sword, you may have Sven with my blessing. And his," Dominic added dryly. "Peace bores him."

"Lord," Harry said. "A knight comes."

"Alone?"

"Aye."

A chill moved through Simon.

" 'Tis more like a parley between enemies than a visit from a father-in-law," Duncan said under his breath.

"Simon," Dominic said. "Can you control your temper long enough to speak for me?"

"Aye."

"Then do so." Dominic turned to Erik. "Is your wolfhound a reliable, er, scout?"

"Aye."

"Can you send it to patrolling all the places more than one or two men might hide beyond the keep's walls?"

"Aye."

"Please do so. Quickly."

Erik whistled. The sound was as clear and carrying as that of a pipe.

Stagkiller materialized from the shadows just behind the gatehouse. Erik spoke to him in an ancient tongue. The wolfhound looked at Erik with unearthly golden eyes, then turned and trotted through the open sally port. A heartbeat later Stagkiller vanished into the darkness and wind.

Beyond the moat, a horse snorted and a knight spoke sharply. Harness and chain mail trappings jangled as the horse shied.

"Go," Dominic said quietly.

Simon walked out into the wind. His mantle lifted and whipped, showing flashes of the luxuriant white fur lining.

The knight's horse snorted again and stepped sideways. Though it lacked a war stallion's muscular power, the animal had a lean, long-legged look of speed about it. In the torchlight the horse's coat was as pale as the lining of Simon's mantle.

"Lord Charles, Baron of Deguerre," the knight said loudly, "comes not far behind me. Will Lord Dominic le Sabre, called the Glendruid Wolf, receive the baron?"

"Aye," Simon said, "if the baron will agree to leave all arms and armor at the gate. Lord Dominic permits no arms inside, unless they are locked in Blackthorne Keep's armory."

"By the Cross," the knight said, shocked. "Who are you to order the Baron of Deguerre?"

"Lord Dominic's brother and his seneschal," Simon said succinctly. "My words are his."

"You are Sir Simon, called the Loyal?"

"Aye."

"Husband to Lady Ariane?"

"Aye."

"I will take your brother's cold welcome to the baron."

The messenger turned his horse, spurred it, and galloped back into the night.

"What do you think he will do?" Dominic

asked Simon as he walked back into the gate-house.

"Leave enough armed men beyond the keep's wall to lay siege," Simon said.

"Erik?" Dominic asked.

"I agree," Erik said. "The baron will come inside with a handful of spies and assassins. When he has estimated the strength and temper of the keep, he will leave."

"Will he lay siege?" Dominic asked Erik.

Erik shrugged. "That depends on how much weakness he finds inside and what excuse he can cobble together to justify a battle, if that is what he seeks."

"Have you any other insights, Learned or otherwise?"

Erik narrowed his eyes until they were little more than gleaming yellow slits reflecting torchlight.

Dominic waited. However impatient he might become with the heart-stopping risks Erik was willing to take, he respected the Learned man's tactical abilities. It had taken a brilliant strategist to pull victory from the ruins of Amber and Duncan's forbidden love, and peace from the endless turmoil of the Disputed Lands.

"There are many possibilities," Erik said finally. "Too many. The baron could be bent on seeing his daughter well settled with an unexpected husband, or the baron could be bent on war, or he could be anywhere between."

"Aye," Dominic said softly.

"How is your Glendruid wife sleeping?" Erik asked.

"Badly."

"She dreams?"

"Yes."

"Even in the day?"

Dominic's breath caught. "At supper. Yes."

Erik's hands went to the sword that wasn't there. His fingers flexed and he sighed.

"Then there is more wrong than Geoffrey's death put aright," Erik said simply.

"What else is there?" Simon demanded.

"I don't know," Erik said.

"Nor do I," Dominic said. "But I know this — if there is a weakness, Baron Deguerre will find it."

The sound of horses cantering toward the keep came clearly in a pause between gusts of wind.

"He comes," Duncan said.

"Aye," said Dominic.

"Armed?" Simon asked.

Silence stretched like a harp string, then Dominic shook his head.

"Nay," Dominic said. "The baron is shrewd indeed. He will spy out the keep from the inside before he decides if he is insulted by my cold welcome."

Erik gave Dominic a quick, slanting glance, realizing that the Glendruid Wolf had hoped to anger the baron enough so that he would refuse to pass through the keep's gates.

"Subtly done, wolf," Erik said softly.

"But unsuccessfully," Dominic said. "Now we will have to find the baron's weakness before he finds ours."

"Are you so certain we have one?" Simon asked.

"Yes," Dominic said. "As certain as Deguerre is."

"In the name of God, what is it?" Duncan demanded.

"In the name of God, *I don't know.*"

30

Silently the four warriors watched Baron Deguerre ride up to the keep.

"Lower the bridge," Dominic ordered.

Within moments the bridge creaked down to lie across the moat. Deguerre rode over the planks without pausing. Five men came with him.

None of them wore chain mail or battle sword.

"The Baron of Deguerre greets you," said one of the knights.

Simon looked at the six men. Instantly he knew which one was the baron. Like Geoffrey, the baron was as handsome as a fallen angel. But unlike Geoffrey, there was nothing of dissipation in Deguerre's face. Intelligence and cruelty vied equally to shape his expression.

Simon found it hard to believe that his passionate nightingale had come from such a cold man's seed.

"Lord Dominic of Blackthorne Keep greets you," Simon said neutrally.

"Which is Lord Dominic?" demanded one knight.

"Which is Baron Deguerre?" Simon returned sardonically.

One of the knights rode forward until his horse threatened to trample Simon into the planks of the bridge. Simon stood in the middle of the bridge, legs braced against the wind, unmoving but for the whipping of his mantle.

"I am Baron Deguerre," said the man who looked like a fallen angel.

Simon sensed a stir behind him. Dominic came to stand at his side. In the cloud-ridden night, the crystal eyes of the Glendruid Wolf flashed eerily.

"I am Lord Dominic."

"What is this nonsense about not wearing swords within the keep?" the baron demanded.

"The Glendruid Wolf," Erik said from the shadows beyond the torchlight, "prefers to celebrate peace rather than war."

"Truly?" the baron asked in tones of wonder. "How odd. Most men relish the test of arms."

"My brother," Simon said, "leaves idle testing to others. It gives him more time to savor his many victories."

"But when someone foolishly forces Lord Dominic to take the field," Duncan added from the shadows of the gatehouse, "there is no more ruthless knight. Ask the Reevers — if you can find someone to talk to the dead."

Deguerre's hooded glance moved from the two brothers to the gatehouse, where Erik and Duncan waited.

"I regret that I can't offer better hospitality for your knights than the stable," Dominic said, "but there wasn't enough advance warning of your coming."

"Indeed?" the baron murmured. "My messenger must have gone astray."

Dominic smiled at the casual lie.

" 'Tis an easy thing to do in these lands," Dominic said. "As you will see, this is a place where success lies with one's alliances, rather than with one's own sword."

Dominic gestured to the men behind him. Erik and Duncan stepped into the uncertain light.

"These are two of my allies," Dominic said. "Lord Erik of Sea Home and Winterlance Keeps, and Lord Duncan of Stone Ring Keep. Their presence, and that of their knights, is why my hospitality must be limited."

With emotionless eyes that missed nothing, Deguerre assessed the men standing in front of him. Most particularly his glance lingered over the ancient wolf's head pin on Dominic's mantle.

"So," Deguerre said beneath his breath. "It has been found at last. I had heard rumors, but . . . ah, well, there are other ancient treasures not yet found."

Deguerre's glance cut to the man who both wore and was the Glendruid Wolf, noting the match between Dominic's ice-pale eyes and the uncanny crystal of the wolf's eyes.

"I accept your hospitality in the spirit in which it is offered," Deguerre said.

"Harry," Dominic said distinctly. "Open the gate."

Moments later, six men rode through the gate. Simon and Dominic flanked Deguerre the instant he dismounted.

"You will find the lord's solar more congenial than the bailey," Dominic said. "Your quarters are being prepared. If you don't object to sleeping in a half-built room that is destined to be a nursery . . . ?"

"Nursery," Deguerre said, glancing sideways at Dominic. "Then it is true. Your Glendruid witch is increasing."

"My *wife* and I have been blessed, aye."

Deguerre's smile was as cold as the cobblestones. "No offense intended, Lord Dominic. I, too, married a witch and had children by her."

The forebuilding's door opened, giving a hint of the heat and light to be found inside.

Servants hurried around, supplying a cold supper, a hot fire, and warm wine.

The men strode down the great hall to the solar's comfort. A woman stood silhouetted against the flames leaping in the solar's hearth. Her hair was unbound in the fashion of a Learned woman on a quest, but the hair was as black as betrayal rather than the rich gold of Amber or the fiery red of Meg.

"My lady," Simon said quickly. "I thought you were abed."

Ariane turned. She held her hand out, but it was Simon whose touch she sought, not her father's.

"Word of the baron's arrival came to me," Ariane said.

Her voice was like her face, without emotion, yet her Learned dress seethed restlessly about her ankles. The silver embroidery glittered as though alive, barely leashed.

Deguerre watched Simon's fingers interlace smoothly, deeply, with Ariane's. With eyes that were neither blue nor grey, but rather a shifting combination of both, the baron measured his daughter's heightened color at her husband's touch, and the subtle inclination of their bodies toward one another.

Had they been alone, they would have embraced as lovers embrace. Deguerre was certain of it.

"So," Deguerre said, "that, too, is true."

"What is?" Dominic asked softly.

"The marriage of Simon and Ariane was for love rather than for the convenience of kings or families."

"We are both well pleased with the union," Simon said succinctly.

The sensual approval in Simon's eyes as he looked at his wife said far more. The answering blaze in Ariane's eyes made them glow like gems.

Deguerre turned his intelligence toward assessing the lord's solar. Though the trappings were costly enough, they were nothing to what the baron had in his own home. For all his power and far-flung holdings, the Glendruid Wolf was not nearly as wealthy a man as rumor had suggested.

Which meant that Dominic could not afford nearly as many fighting men as Deguerre had feared.

The baron turned and looked at Dominic.

"I have heard," Deguerre said, "that your brother's loyalty to you knows no bounds."

"Simon's love for me is well-known, as is mine for him," Dominic said. "Be assured that your daughter could have no husband more highly regarded or closer to my heart than Simon."

With a grunt Deguerre flipped back the

cowl that had protected his head from the storm. Hair the color of hammered silver gleamed with reflected light. His eyebrows were utterly black, steeply arched, oddly elegant.

The chiming of tiny golden bells made the baron turn quickly. Despite his age, there was a fluidity to the movement that spoke of strength and coordination.

"Lady Margaret," Dominic said. "I thought you were asleep."

With a rustle of scented fabric and a sweet singing of bells, Meg walked to Dominic's side.

Deguerre's eyes narrowed at the obvious signs of Meg's pregnancy. The only thing more obvious was the bond between Glendruid Wolf and Glendruid witch. It was so strong it fairly shimmered.

"Baron Deguerre, Lady Margaret," Dominic said.

"Charmed, lady," Deguerre said, smiling, holding out his hand.

The smile changed the baron. He had been handsome before. Now he had an unearthly yet distinctly sexual beauty.

" 'Tis our pleasure to welcome you," Meg said.

If the baron's startling transformation from cool tactician to smoldering sensualist made any impression on her, it didn't show. She touched his hand as briefly as courtesy allowed.

"You have the beauty of fire, Lady Margaret," the baron said in a low voice. "And your eyes would shame emeralds."

Ariane's hand tightened suddenly within Simon's grasp. She well knew her father's ability to charm women. He had practiced it often enough on the wives and daughters of enemies.

Saying nothing, Simon brought Ariane's hand to his lips and kissed it soothingly.

"Her eyes would shame more than emeralds," Dominic said. "They would shame spring itself. There is no green more beautiful than Lady Margaret's Glendruid eyes."

If Meg had been indifferent to the baron's compliments, her husband's words made her flush with pleasure. For a long moment Dominic and Meg looked at one another, and for that moment nothing else in the room existed.

"Touching," Deguerre said coolly.

"Isn't it?" Simon said cheerfully. " 'Tis the talk of the land, the love of wolf and witch. Will you eat and drink?"

As Simon spoke, he gestured toward the lord's table. The servants had been hurrying back and forth, heaping dishes up until the table fairly buckled beneath the bounty.

Deguerre cataloged the food with a single glance.

"Much more has been sent out to your men," Simon said. "I hope it will be enough. No one seems to know how many retainers are with you."

"I would not have you cut into your winter stores," Deguerre said.

"There is no danger of that," Meg said, turning back to her guest. "This was the best harvest in memory."

"And all of it lies safely within the keep's walls," Simon added smoothly.

"How fortunate for you," the baron said. "Many keeps to the south of you suffered from untimely rains. For them, winter will be a season of trial and famine."

"Blackthorne has been singularly blessed," Dominic agreed.

Deguerre grunted.

Silently Dominic waited to parry the baron's next thrust as Deguerre probed for weaknesses within Blackthorne Keep.

"I expected a favored knight of mine to greet me here," Deguerre said, turning to confront Simon.

A stillness went through the lord's solar. Deguerre appeared not to notice.

"The knight is a very great favorite of my daughter's," the baron added, looking meaningfully at Ariane. "Is our well-loved Geoffrey here, daughter?"

"Aye," Simon said before Ariane could answer.

"Send for him," the baron said to Simon.

"I have sent your Geoffrey to his last place."

Deguerre's eyes changed, focusing on Simon with tangible intensity.

"Explain yourself," the baron said curtly.

Simon smiled and said nothing.

" 'Tis simple," Dominic said in a casual tone. "Geoffrey is dead."

"Dead! When? How? I have heard nothing of this!"

Dominic shrugged. " 'Tis true all the same."

"God's blood," Deguerre muttered. "I heard there was illness and men died, but not Geoffrey."

"Aye," Ariane said. "There was illness. Only a handful survived."

"Where are they?" Deguerre asked.

Simon smiled coldly. "I suspect I killed two of them in the Disputed Lands, and wounded the others. Perhaps they died, too. Geoffrey the Fair died today, at Blackthorne Keep, by my hand."

Deguerre's face became as expressionless as a blade.

"You are very free with the lives of my

knights," Deguerre said calmly.

"When I killed all but Geoffrey," Simon said, "they were outlaws wearing no lord's mark on their shields."

Deguerre's black eyebrows rose for a moment.

"And Geoffrey?" the baron asked scornfully. "Did you call him outlaw, too?"

"I could have. He admitted to it before he died. But before he approached Blackthorne Keep, he painted your device on his shield again."

For a time there was silence. Then Deguerre grimaced, hissed something beneath his breath, and accepted the loss of an ally within Blackthorne Keep.

"A pity," the baron said. "The lad had promise."

"Rest easy. His promise is being kept in hell," Simon assured him. "What of you, baron? Have you any promises you haven't kept?"

"None."

"Indeed?" Dominic asked sardonically. "What of Ariane's dowry?"

"What of it?" the baron asked.

"The chests were filled with rocks, dirt, and rotting flour."

Deguerre froze in the act of adjusting his mantle.

"What did you say?" the baron demanded.

Dominic and Simon looked at one another, then at Duncan. Grimly Duncan turned and left the solar, knowing that his wife would be needed once more.

Black eyes narrowed, Simon looked back at Deguerre.

" 'Tis quite simple," Simon said. "When the chests were opened, they contained nothing of worth."

"They left my estates filled with a ransom fit for a princess," Deguerre retorted.

"So you have said."

"Are you questioning my word?" Deguerre asked silkily.

"Nay. I am simply telling you what occurred when the chests were opened."

"What did Geoffrey say when he saw the empty chests?" Deguerre asked.

"He wasn't present," Simon said.

"Who of my men was?"

"No one," Simon said in sardonic tones. "Your fine knights dropped Ariane at Black-thorne Keep and bolted without so much as taking a cup of ale."

"More and more remarkable," the baron murmured. "What of my seals on the chests?"

"Intact," Dominic said succinctly.

"Extraordinary," Deguerre said, opening his grey-blue eyes wide. "I have only the word of Blackthorne Keep's knights that my spices, silks, gems, and gold were magically transformed to dirt between Normandy and England."

"Aye."

"Many men would assume trickery on the part of one lord or another."

" 'Tis likely," Dominic agreed.

Deguerre's smile was different this time. It was cold and triumphant with the assurance that he had found what he had hoped to find.

Greed was one of the oldest and most common of human weaknesses.

"Am I being accused of going back on my given word?" the baron asked kindly.

"No," Dominic said. "Nor are we requiring any payment from you. Yet."

Before Deguerre could speak, Amber came into the solar. She was wearing a scarlet robe, her hair was unbound, and the amber pendant around her neck gleamed like a pool of captive sunlight.

"Lord Dominic," Amber said, "you required me?"

"Nay, lady. I ask a favor."

Amber smiled slightly. "It is yours."

"The baron and I have a small mystery we would like resolved. Would you scry the truth for us?"

At Dominic's words, the baron turned and

examined Amber with keen interest.

"Amber is Learned," Dominic said to Deguerre. "She can —"

"I am aware of Learned gifts," the baron said succinctly. "It has been one of my life's studies. Does this lady have the gift of truth?"

"Aye," Dominic said.

Deguerre sighed with disappointment.

"Then you didn't steal the dowry for your own," the baron said, "or you would never bring a truthsayer within reach of you. Ah, well. Here, lady. Touch my hand and discover my truth."

Amber let out a long breath, calming herself. Then she touched Deguerre.

She cried out and would have gone to her knees if Duncan had not caught her. Despite the pain scoring her, Amber held to Deguerre's hand.

"Quickly," Duncan hissed.

"Did you cheat on your daughter's dowry?" Dominic asked the baron.

"Nay."

"Truth."

Instantly Amber withdrew her touch.

"Thank you, lady," Dominic said.

Deguerre watched Amber with rather predatory interest, noting what it had cost her to use her gift.

"A useful, if fragile, weapon," he said. "One

I had always hoped to own."

Duncan gave the baron a murderous look.

The baron smiled. "I believe the question is now mine."

Surprised, Amber looked at Dominic.

"If I may impose, lady?" Dominic asked reluctantly, holding out his hand.

Though Amber had never touched the Glendruid Wolf, she took his hand without hesitation. A tremor went through her, but it was quickly controlled.

"Was there anything of value in those chests when you opened them?" Deguerre asked Dominic.

"Nothing."

"Truth."

"Were the seals intact?"

"Aye."

"Truth."

"Remarkable indeed," Deguerre muttered.

Dominic lifted his hand from Amber's.

"My apologies," Dominic said. "I would not bring you pain."

"You did not, lord. There is great power in you, but no cruelty."

Deguerre smiled sardonically, for Amber had said no such thing about him.

"It appears," Dominic said, "as though one of your knights stole Ariane's dowry."

"One of mine? Why not one of yours?"

"The seals were intact. Your seals, baron. Not mine."

"Ah, yes." Deguerre shrugged. "Sir Geoffrey, I suppose. He was beloved by me and had free access to my records."

"And seals?" Simon asked.

"And seals."

"Now Geoffrey is dead and the dowry is lost," Simon said.

"Have you asked my daughter about it?"

"Why would we? She was more shocked than any of us," Dominic said. "If she knew where her dowry was, she would have told us instantly."

Deguerre looked at Ariane. "Well, daughter? Why haven't you found it for them?"

"I lost my gift the night Geoffrey raped me."

"Rape. Is that what you told your husband?" Deguerre asked with a cruel smile.

"Aye," Ariane said coolly. " 'Tis what Lady Amber told him, too."

Faint surprise showed on Deguerre's features.

"So you truly have lost your gift," Deguerre said thoughtfully. "The same thing happened to your mother when I had her on our wedding night. No witch wants to lose her powers, but a man knows just how to take them."

"You are mistaken," Meg said quietly.

Deguerre's head spun as he turned to stare at the small woman who had been so motionless that her golden jesses were silent.

"I beg your pardon?" Deguerre said.

"Union with a man can enhance rather than destroy a woman's power," Meg said. "It depends on the union. And the man. Since I have been the wife of the Glendruid Wolf, my powers are keener than ever."

"Fascinating."

Deguerre frowned. Then he shrugged and went back to the subject that interested him most.

Weakness, not strength.

"It would appear that Geoffrey was an untrustworthy craven who destroyed rather than enhanced Ariane's gift," Deguerre said indifferently. " 'Tis unfortunate that others must suffer for his acts, but that is the way of the world."

Simon went very still. The baron was radiating a kind of vicious pleasure that said more clearly than words that he believed he had at last found the weakness he sought at Blackthorne.

"When I agreed to give my precious daughter in marriage to one of your knights," Deguerre said to Dominic, "you promised that her husband would hold a keep in fief for you, a wealthy keep that suited Lady Ariane's high station in Normandy."

"Aye," Dominic said grimly.

"Tell me, Lord Dominic, *where is my daughter's keep?*"

"To the north."

"Ah. Where to the north?"

"Carlysle."

"Why is she not residing there as befits a lady with her own keep?"

"We are still recruiting knights for defense," Simon said in a clipped voice.

"There are fortifications to complete, as well," Dominic said.

"Expensive things, knights and fortifications."

Deguerre looked around the room with cruel satisfaction.

"You shall be hard put to support two keeps," the baron said, "no matter how bounteous Blackthorne's harvest was this year."

"I shall manage," Dominic said tightly.

Deguerre's smile was as cold as the night.

"And I shall stay hard by this keep," the baron said, "until what was promised to my daughter is given to her."

31

Long after Baron Deguerre had been settled in the lord's solar with his knights, Ariane waited alone within her bedchamber, her head bowed over her lap harp. Silently she prayed that Simon would come to her.

That he would forgive her.

I should have known Simon was too proud a man to hear of his wife's rape and not avenge it, no matter how carefully Meg and I planned to prevent just that.

I should have known!

But all I knew was my own need, my own pride, my own desire to be loved by Simon as I loved him.

Foolish.

Elegant fingers moved over the harp strings, calling forth a song that had no words, simply a cry as profound and compelling as Ariane's love for a man who could not love her in return.

By the blood of all the saints, how could I have been so selfish as to risk Blackthorne Keep for my own foolish desire? Simon will love no woman, just as I trusted no man.

Until Simon. He healed me.

But I cannot heal him.

Called by Ariane's fingers, rippling music haunted the room as surely as she was haunted by all that had been.

And all that would never be.

"Nightingale?"

Simon's voice was so unexpected — and so intensely desired — that for a moment Ariane was afraid to lift her head for fear of discovering that she only dreamed.

"Simon?" she whispered.

Gentle fingers stroked her cheek.

"Aye," Simon said huskily. "I expected to find you asleep."

"You weren't here."

Desire and something else, a hunger less easily named, turned within Simon at Ariane's words.

"Dominic needed me," Simon said.

"I know. He will have much need of you in the future."

Without looking up, Ariane set her harp aside.

"My father won't stir until he sees me in a well-furnished keep," she said tonelessly, "and Blackthorne impoverished. My reckless desire for the truth has destroyed your brother."

She expected Simon to agree, and then to turn away from her as he had from Marie.

Instead, Simon stroked Ariane's hair.

"We will find a way," he said.

"We?"

"Duncan, Erik, Dominic and I. We will rotate knights among the keeps if we must."

"Leaving all keeps weakened."

Simon said nothing.

"My father can be frighteningly patient," Ariane said, looking only at her clenched hands.

"Aye," Simon said.

"He has enough wealth to stay here until he has what he came for — a foothold in England."

Silence was Simon's only answer.

"You cannot beat Charles the Shrewd at his own game," Ariane said. "Unless the English king or Erik's father will lend you money to set up Carlysle Keep, my father will bring down Blackthorne Keep, and your brother with it."

"The king has many demands on his resources," Simon said. "In too much of England the harvest was poor."

"What of Erik's father?"

"Robert the Whisperer hates all Learned, even his own son."

Ariane shook her head in silent despair.

"Then we are lost," she said in a low voice.

The motion of Ariane's head sent locks of her hair over Simon's hand. Something that was almost pain pierced him at the cool, silken touch.

"Are you so angry with me that you can't even bear to look at my face?" Simon asked softly.

Ariane's head jerked upright. Simon was standing very close to her. His expression was grim. His clothing was half-undone, as though he were so weary he had begun pulling at laces while he climbed the stairs to his wife's room.

"I? Angry with you?" Ariane asked, surprise clear both in her voice and her extraordinary amethyst eyes.

"Angry that I betrayed your truth by not defending it sooner," Simon said bleakly. "Angry that the truth made no difference. Angry that I can't . . . love."

Ariane's heart turned over at the pain in Simon's eyes.

"Not even you," he said roughly, "my valiant nightingale. You, who have suffered so much at the hands of men. You, who saved my life. You, who taught me to fly as the phoenix flies, death and rebirth in ecstasy. You deserve . . . more than I can give you."

The pain in Simon's voice made Ariane ache. Tears shimmered against her black eyelashes.

"You have never betrayed me. *Never*," Ariane said. "You would have died to save my life when I was naught but a burden to you, a woman you married out of loyalty to your brother."

"You were never a burden to me. I wanted you the first time I saw you. I have never hungered for a woman like that, a fire hotter than any awaiting me in hell."

Ariane's smile was as sad as the tears she wept for Simon, and as beautiful.

Wanting. Burning. Desire.

Not love.

"I know now how much you wanted me," Ariane said, shivering with memories of Simon's intense, unbounded sensuality.

Simon saw Ariane's telltale response and felt his own blood ignite in answer, consuming the pain of a past that could not be changed, only accepted.

"You wanted me until you trembled with your wanting," Ariane whispered, "yet you never forced me. You have been gentle where other men have been cruel, passionate where other men have been calculating, generous where other men have been selfish. Angry with you? Nay, Simon. I am blessed in you."

"Ariane . . ."

Simon's throat closed. He could not have known Ariane's truth more clearly if he had lived inside her soul.

Slowly he lifted his hands and eased his fingers into the midnight beauty of Ariane's hair. As he tilted her face up, his lips whispered over her eyelashes, stealing the silver tears she had wept for him.

"When I think what was done to you by that swine . . ." Simon said hoarsely.

As he spoke, Simon's lips moved over Ariane's forehead, her cheekbones, her nose, her cheeks, her eyelids, her lips, worshiping her with kisses as soft as firelight. She trembled at the light touches and wept at the bleakness she saw in her husband's eyes.

"Don't think of it," Ariane said urgently. "I don't. Not anymore. Not even in my dreams."

"You were cruelly used, a betrayal so deep it all but killed your soul. Yet —"

"You healed me," she interrupted.

"— you came to me on the battlements and taught me what true passion is."

Ariane tried to speak, but the intensity in Simon's expression stole her voice.

"I took you," he said, "standing upright with my back to the freezing wind and your —"

A shudder of memory and desire and something more went through Simon, breaking his voice.

"— and your honeyed warmth sheathed me

completely," he said after a moment, his voice husky. "Yet you were all but a virgin when you came to me."

"I loved sheathing you."

The words were whispered against Simon's lips, feather touches that matched the delicacy of his own kisses.

"I know how well you loved it," he said huskily. "Your pleasure drenched me."

Simon felt the flush that stole up Ariane's body.

"I didn't mean to," Ariane said. "I couldn't . . . stop."

"I know," Simon breathed, biting her lips with exquisite tenderness. "I didn't want you to stop. I wanted to stand there forever with the icy storm around me and your sultry pleasure pulsing over me."

Simon's name became a whimper of pleasure as his tongue stole softly around the line of Ariane's mouth.

"You trembled and cried out just like that," Simon said, "and asked only that I thrust more deeply into you. Yet you were all but a virgin."

"I wanted you until I was wild."

"I wanted you the same way. And when it was done and neither of us could breathe for the ecstasy shaking us, you clung to me, holding me deeply inside you."

"I loved being joined with you."

"Yes," Simon said. "Your body told me. It wept your passion and I wanted to drink the scented tears. Never has a woman given herself more generously to a man, *yet you were all but a virgin.*"

A shudder tore through Simon, making the line of his mouth even more harsh.

"Simon?" Ariane whispered, not understanding.

"I should have been gentle," he said, his voice thick with regret. "I should have breathed kisses over your hair and your face and your hands."

While Simon spoke, he matched his actions to his words, breathing kisses over Ariane's hair and face and hands. She closed her eyes as desire stitched through her, making her tremble.

"I should have opened your clothing slowly," Simon said in a low voice.

Silver laces whispered free and amethyst cloth slid aside as his fingers moved over Ariane's dress. The cool air of the room only heightened the vivid heat of Simon's mouth as he bent down to Ariane.

"I should have praised your breasts," Simon said huskily against her neck. "They are perfectly made, silky, warm, and they beg so sweetly for my mouth."

Gently he kissed the crown of each breast.

The nipples drew taut and flushed, their pink a shade as deep as that of her mouth.

"Simon," Ariane began.

Then she fell silent as a slow, delicious shudder took her voice. Simon's tongue was caressing her lightly, drawing her nipples even tighter.

His hands traveled the length of the amethyst dress, undoing all the laces. He smiled to feel the cloth caressing him with tiny movements, heightening the sensitivity of his skin.

"I should have smoothed your dress from your body," he said. "I should have lingered over every newly revealed bit of flesh until you sighed and shivered and gave me what no man had ever asked for, only taken from you."

Closing his eyes, Simon very lightly drew his fingers down Ariane's legs. They parted for him with a rustle and sigh of fabric sliding away.

"Are you giving yourself to me?" he asked.

"Yes," she whispered. "Always."

Only then did Simon's eyes open.

"I saw you like this the first night," he said huskily. "And instead of telling you how beautiful you are, instead of gently coaxing passion from you, I spread you wide and drove into you as though we had been lovers for as long as we had drawn breath."

Ariane tried to speak, but Simon was bending down to her, caressing her with his hands, his words, his mouth. A low sound came from her throat as the tip of his tongue traced all the layers of her softness.

"They have an exotic fruit in the Holy Land," he said against her, caressing her. " 'Tis called pomegranate and its hidden flesh is more deeply pink than a ruby."

Pleasure radiated through Ariane, taking her breath even as it melted her body. Simon made a low sound and stole the sultry drops of her passion.

"You are like that pomegranate . . . tart even as you are sweet, flushed with color, meant to be slowly savored with teeth and tongue."

A luxuriant heat rippled through Ariane, arching her body in sensuous reflex. Simon had seen her move like that before, slowly, elegantly, held in the thrall of a healing dream whose reality still baffled him.

"I feel . . ." Ariane's voice unraveled as she looked into Simon's dark eyes. "I feel . . . I have dreamed this . . . before. Exactly this. Yet you have never kissed me thus."

"But I have kissed you thus," he countered softly.

Simon touched Ariane with the tip of his

tongue, circling the satin knot of her desire. She sighed and languidly arched again, moving as slowly as a dream.

"And you have answered thus," Simon said, "lifting to me, allowing me . . . everything."

"When?" she whispered, knowing it was true yet not understanding, echoes of a transcendent dream.

Heal me.

"In a dream," Ariane said. *"You healed me."*

"It was a Learned dream," Simon said, "infused with roses and midnight, moonlight and a wild promise of storm."

His teeth closed with exquisite delicacy. A slow, deep heat stole through Ariane, a burning that was all the more complete for its languid ease.

"I am on fire," she whispered.

"I can feel it, softer than my dreams. I didn't mean to take you that night, even in this way. But I mean to take you now, in every way."

A low sound was dragged from Ariane as her whole body succumbed to the seething, wondrous thrall of Simon loving her. He held her with hands both gentle and powerful. Whispered words praised her and lingering kisses savored her, heightening her fire until she burned silently, wildly, unable even to cry out.

Then Ariane looked at Simon and understood what it was to dream within a dream.

"I am yours," she said. "I gave myself to you before I even knew it. Now, knowing it, I give myself to you again."

Simon kissed Ariane slowly, completely, and tasted the certainty of her ecstasy.

"You are mine," Simon said. "And you taste of fire."

"Burn with me," she whispered. "I have been alone within this fire too long."

A shudder moved visibly through Simon. As he pushed away his clothes, he saw Ariane smile at the heavy arousal that stood revealed before her.

"Just seeing you turns my flesh to honey," she said, touching him. "Man of silk and steel. And pleasure. Dear God, the pleasure . . ."

Another wave of desire swept through Simon, shaking him.

"You make me as strong as a god," Simon said huskily.

Slowly he lowered himself, savoring her welcome as she made room for him between her legs, drawing them up around him, giving herself to him without reservation. Softly she parted for him, taking him even as she gave herself to him. He pressed deep into her, then more deeply still until finally they were complete within one another.

The taut, sultry perfection of the joining

nearly undid Simon.

"I am burning," he said, anguish and pleasure both.

It was the same for Ariane, an anguished pleasure consuming her like fire.

"We are . . ."

Burning.

And then neither one could breathe for the violent, silken ecstasy pulsing between them.

When it was finally spent, when there were no more ways to give and to take and to share, Simon gathered Ariane along his body and held her as though he expected her to be torn from his arms.

"There will be a way to defeat Deguerre," Simon said fiercely. "There must be. A lost dowry is not worth so many lives."

Ariane's arms tightened around Simon, holding him. Silently, passionately, she wished that her gift were intact.

If only the dowry could be found.

A vision burst over Ariane, holding her completely in thrall for a time that had no measure. She lay without moving, seeing only Stone Ring Keep's circle of stones standing tall and hard against the winter sky.

But this time there were two rings of stone.

Ariane blinked, shuddered, and found herself held within her sleeping husband's arms. Elation spread through her when she realized what had happened.

The Glendruid witch has the right of it. Union with the right man can enhance a woman's powers.

I am truly healed!

Eagerly Ariane turned to awaken Simon, but stopped before she spoke a single word.

My recklessness has cost Blackthorne too much already, Deguerre like a great silver vulture waiting for a bloody feast.

If I tell Simon, what will happen?

Elation drained from Ariane. Simon would insist on accompanying her to the Stone Ring. Dominic would insist that knights accompany the two of them, for should her father get wind of the dowry's recovery, he certainly would move to prevent it.

There were few enough knights as it was to defend Blackthorne. There were none to spare for even the swiftest trip to the Stone Ring. The fires from Deguerre's camps surrounded Blackthorne as though it were under siege.

Indeed, in a very real way, Blackthorne *was* under siege.

If I awaken Simon, he won't let me leave because he cannot leave with me. Simon the Loyal is needed here and now by his lord and brother.

But I am not.

I will steal away, find proof of my dowry,

and bring it back for Simon to fling in my father's face.

The thought made Ariane smile. It would give her pleasure to prove to her father that she was as much to be reckoned with as any cruel knight.

A sense of rightness stole through Ariane, a certainty of what must be done.

And how.

To leave secretly, I must find the keep's bolt-hole. Where has it been hidden?

After a few breaths a vision formed, torches burning in a long hallway where rooms opened on either side; buttery and barrels of salted eels, fowl with cool, faintly scaled feet hanging ready for the roasting spit, fruit both fresh and dried. Where the hall ended, the herbal began, rack upon rack of plants drying.

And beyond the last rack, dug deep into the hillside, hidden in darkness and stacks of twine, a small door was bolted shut.

Next, the horse. Surely someone has lost one in all this tumult. Perhaps one of my father's knights has a drunken squire or groom.

It took longer this time, for the loss was less precise. But slowly, slowly, a vision condensed from the darkness . . . a horse in Norman trappings standing with its broad rump to the wind and its nose in a Blackthorne haystack.

Carefully Ariane eased herself from Simon's arms. When he murmured as though in protest, she kissed him lightly and smoothed her hand over his cheek. He nuzzled against her hair, sighed and relaxed again.

"Sleep, my love," Ariane whispered. "All is well. I know where my dowry is.

"And I know how to save Blackthorne Keep."

32

"Vanished?" Simon demanded. "What do you mean she has vanished?"

Sven looked warily from Dominic to Simon. Sven had been on the Holy Crusade with both men. He would not relish fighting either of them, and Simon looked like a man on the edge of battle. Sven glanced in unwitting appeal to Meg, who was sitting on her lord's right in the solar's warmth.

"Softly," Meg said to Simon. "The baron is never far from us."

Simon's mouth flattened but he didn't disagree. Instead, he stood, pushed aside the remains of his midday meal, and stood close enough to Sven to touch him.

"Explain," Simon said.

Though soft, his voice was no less savage.

"Lady Ariane wasn't at morning chapel," Sven said quietly.

"Aye," Dominic said from behind Simon. "I thought she might have taken service with her father's chaplain."

"The one who called her a wanton and demanded penitence for a sin she never committed?" Simon asked in a low, scornful voice. "I don't think so. She would rather take service with swine."

"Ariane spoke to neither chaplain this morning," Sven said. "Nor is she bathing. Nor is she embroidering. Nor is she harping sad songs."

"What of the kitchen?" Meg asked. "She has been teaching them savory tricks with the stews."

"The guard Lord Dominic posted in the forebuilding said that no one but servants had gone out into the bailey," Sven said.

Dominic smiled and looked at Meg, who had once slipped past Sven while dressed as a servant. Sven saw the look and smiled ruefully.

"The guard was one of Blackthorne Keep's old knights," Sven said. "The servants are well-known to him."

" 'Tis no wonder Ariane stays away from the kitchens today," Meg said. "The devil's own storm is howling out there. Thank God the harvest is within the walls."

"But Lady Ariane is not," Sven said succinctly. "She is not at the wellhead. She is not in the barracks. She is not in the armory, the buttery, the privy, or any other cursed place I have searched."

"Deguerre," Simon said bitterly. "I will have his manhood for this!"

"Where would he hide her?" Sven asked in neutral tones. "He, too, is inside the keep."

Dominic looked at Meg again.

"Small falcon?" he asked softly. "How are your dreams?"

Meg closed her eyes. When they opened, they were haunted.

"I slept well enough before the storm," Meg said. "Better than in many weeks. As though something had been set aright."

"And now, while you are awake?" Dominic asked. "Do you dream?"

"When the storm broke during chapel, I felt as though I were out in it." She shivered. "It is very cold out there, my lord. Deathly cold."

"I know that all too well," Simon said. "I was out at the wooden palisade herding stonemasons as though they were stuborn oxen."

"Is the gap closed?" Sven asked.

"Soon," Simon said succinctly, "if I have to carry each icy stone myself. And I may. The storm shows no sign of dying."

"Aye," Meg said, frowning. "I didn't expect such a severe storm this soon in the season."

"Go to your herbal," Dominic said to his wife. "Your people will require balm to ease their chilblains."

Meg started to object, saw the determination in Dominic's eyes, and understood that he wanted her gone from the lord's solar.

"Of course," she said. "But —"

"If I need you," Dominic interrupted, "I will send for you very speedily."

"Aye," Meg said crisply, turning away. "See that you do."

As the sound of Meg's golden jesses faded from the solar, Dominic turned to Sven.

"Wait for a moment beyond the door," Dominic said. "I have a private matter to discuss with Simon."

Sven could well guess what the matter was. He turned and walked from the solar with a sense of frank relief. He did not want to be in the vicinity when brother quizzed brother on the subject of marital intimacy.

"Did you and Ariane quarrel over her rape?" Dominic asked bluntly.

"No."

"Over her father?"

"No."

"Over anything?"

"There was no anger between us when we fell asleep."

"Coldness?"

Simon closed his eyes as a wave of hot memories poured through him.

"Nay," Simon said huskily. "Far from it.

Ariane burns as no other woman on earth."

Dominic sighed and raked his fingers through his hair.

"It makes no sense!" snarled the Glendruid Wolf. "Why is she gone?"

"Perhaps she isn't."

"And perhaps eels grow feathers and fly to their spawning grounds," Dominic retorted. "The keep is not so large that a lady could be overlooked while wearing a Learned dress embroidered with silver lightning."

Simon had no argument, for what Dominic said was true.

"I will search for her myself," Simon said.

"Nay."

"Why?" demanded Simon harshly.

"If you go crying from the battlements to the herbal seeking your wife, Deguerre will seize the opportunity to run shouting to king and duke alike that we have murdered his precious daughter and hidden her dowry along with her corpse. Then all hell will be let out for breakfast!"

"I will be discreet," Simon said through his teeth.

"Joseph and Mary," Dominic muttered. "At the moment you look as discreet as a Norse berserker."

Simon barely managed to bite back a violent retort. A deep uneasiness was riding him. The uneasiness had begun as he helped the stone-masons and had increased with each stone laid.

Then the storm had come down from the north, making it all but impossible to lay stones.

Deathly cold.

"Put Leaper or Stagkiller onto Ariane's scent," Simon said curtly.

"Outside the keep? 'Tis futile. The storm will have washed away all trace."

"Begin inside, with the parts of the keep where Ariane rarely goes. If the scent is fresh . . ."

Simon didn't have to finish. Dominic was already calling for a squire to bring Erik to the solar with his wolfhound. Leaper was an easier matter. Dominic simply whistled and the grey hound emerged from beneath the table where she had been questing for scraps.

"Do you have something with Ariane's scent upon it, and only Ariane's?" Dominic asked.

"Her harp."

Dominic looked startled. "It isn't with her?"

"Nay. It is by the side of our bed."

For the first time, Dominic looked truly worried. Never had he seen Ariane when her harp wasn't within reach.

"Get the harp and go to the wellhead," Dominic said tightly. "We will begin there."

By the time Simon retrieved the harp and arrived at the level where the wellhead and garrison were, Stagkiller and Erik were already waiting.

"Stagkiller found no groups of men who had hidden without fires," Erik said to Dominic. " 'Tis simply too cold."

"Sven said the same thing. Nor are any of Deguerre's men heading for Stone Ring Keep or Sea Home."

"Better that they did," Erik said. "Cassandra will be planning unpleasant welcomes. We could use fewer of the enemy underfoot."

"Aye. By both your estimate and Sven's, Deguerre has at least two and probably three times the number of fighters we do."

"Were the Baron Deguerre outside the walls rather than lounging at table in the great hall, I would say we were under siege," Erik muttered.

"As it is," Dominic said dryly as Simon walked up, "we are merely under the *threat* of siege."

"Who courses first, Leaper or Stagkiller?" Simon asked baldly.

"Leaper," Dominic said. "She has free run of the keep. No one will remark her comings and goings."

Dominic bent to the slender hound, gave her a low command, and indicated the harp in Simon's hand. Though most of her kind were good only for running game that had been driven into the open by beaters, Leaper had a fine nose and a keen desire to use it. Most often it was Leaper who discovered game, rather than the slow-footed peasants wielding sticks.

Leaper sniffed the harp, sniffed again, sniffed a third time, and then looked at Dominic. A movement of his hand sent the hound to work.

Palm on Stagkiller's head, Erik watched the slender grey bitch quarter the wellhead room, searching for fresh scent. When she reached the stone stairway that spiraled through the corner of the keep, she whined softly.

Instantly Dominic was at her side.

"Up or down?" he asked.

"Down," Simon said. " 'Tis less used by Ariane."

Another signal sent Leaper down the stairs. The men followed in a rush of booted feet on stone. Before they reached the herbal, Meg was standing in the doorway looking alarmed. Her hand was wrapped around Leaper's leather collar.

"What is Leap—" Meg began, only to be interrupted.

"Release her," Simon said urgently.

Meg let go of the collar without a word.

Leaper slipped by Meg's long green skirts and vanished into the herbal with Meg and the men hard on her heels. Simon grabbed the lamp Meg had been using and waited to see what the hound would do next.

The varied and pungent smells of the herbal confused Leaper, but only for a short time. Another sniff of the harp and the bitch was casting about once more. Soon she had the scent and was off again, threading deeper and deeper into the herbal's dark recesses.

At the same moment Meg and Dominic realized where Leaper must be going. Dominic looked quickly at Erik, shrugged, and decided that the Learned sorcerer had kept more important secrets than the location of Blackthorne Keep's bolt-hole.

Leaper's long muzzle held to a line on the floor as though she were on a tight leash. She trotted up to the stacks of twine and sacks waiting to be used, scrambled over them, and whined at the bolt-hole's door.

"Open it," Dominic said tersely.

Simon did so and held the lamp aloft. Nothing but a dark, cramped tunnel looked back at him.

The air that rolled into the room from the tunnel's small mouth was frigid. A dim, distant circle of light and the moaning of the wind were the only signs that the tunnel ended.

Leaper shivered with cold and whined with eagerness to follow the scent trail. Dominic shook out a leash, secured it to Leaper's collar, and started toward the tunnel.

"Stay here," Simon said, grabbing Dominic's arm. "You are needed at the keep, not I."

After a moment of hesitation, Dominic turned the leather over to Simon and stepped back from the tunnel. Simon handed the harp to Dominic, bent, and followed Leaper into the opening. The darkness of Simon's mantle merged instantly with that of the tunnel.

Hound and man emerged in a leaf-stripped willow thicket. Though it was still afternoon, there was a twilight pall to the day. Beyond the thicket, snow skidded along parallel to the ground, blown by a merciless wind.

Following Ariane's scent would be extremely difficult. Nor did Simon see any sign of tracks. He stepped into the storm anyway, for Ariane was somewhere out there in the icy wind.

Leaper lost the scent no more than a few yards from the thicket. She whined and quartered and whined some more, until Simon dragged the lean, shivering hound back into the tunnel.

"She lost the scent just beyond the thicket," Simon said curtly as he emerged into the herbal's aromatic calm. "No tracks."

His eyes said much more, blacker and more wild than the storm. Like Leaper, he was shivering from the icy talons of the wind.

"Stagkiller," Simon said, turning to Erik. "I doubt that he can scent what Leaper cannot, but 'tis our best hope."

No one said it was their only hope until the storm ended and the Learned peregrine could be flown.

Stagkiller sniffed deeply of the harp and bounded into the tunnel. So large was the hound that his head brushed the ceiling.

Tensely Meg and the men waited.

Soon, too soon, Stagkiller's unhappy howl lifted above the wind.

"Lost the scent," Erik said succinctly.

"Was there another scent in the tunnel?" Dominic asked.

Erik whistled a command that was both shrill and oddly musical. Stagkiller's howling ceased. Very shortly the thick-furred hound emerged from the tunnel. Erik took Stagkiller's huge, savage head between his hands and spoke to him in an alien tongue.

The hound went back into the tunnel again. It was several minutes before he returned and glided up to his master.

"No other recent scents but hers and Simon's," Erik said.

"Ariane was alone when she left?" Simon asked, dazed. "Why would she leave the keep's warmth in the middle of a savage storm?"

"Perhaps it wasn't storming when she left," Dominic said.

"Perhaps it wouldn't matter if it had been," Meg said. "A woman who would charge a war-horse with a palfrey doesn't lack courage."

"Perhaps she didn't leave willingly," Erik said.

"She was alone," Dominic said. "Your own Learned hound can attest to that."

"Aye. But her father is a warlock. Who knows what mischief he could brew?"

Simon became very still. "What are you saying?"

Erik shrugged. "The man has some Learning. I can sense it in him. But his is the kind of Learning that once divided Druid from Druid, clan from clan, and man from his soul."

"If Deguerre has harmed Ariane, he is a dead man," Simon said distinctly.

"First you must find his daughter and prove that he has done evil," Dominic said.

"Why else would Ariane leave if not forced?" Simon asked fiercely. *"There is no reason."*

560

The sound of footsteps in the hallway silenced the men.

" 'Tis only Amber," Meg said quickly. "I asked her to help me."

With a low muttering of relief, they recognized the golden glow of Amber's hair in the doorway to the herbal. She had a smile on her face and a comb set with bloodred amber in her hair.

"What are you doing here?" she asked as she spotted the men. "Surely you have more urgent duties than chilblain balm."

"Have you seen Ariane?" Simon asked starkly.

"Not since early this morning. I passed her in the hall and she told me my missing comb was caught behind the torn lining of my travel chest."

Meg made a startled sound.

"I went to the chest, and there it was!" Amber said. "Isn't it wonderful that Ariane's gift has come back to her?"

Simon was too stunned to speak.

Erik wasn't. As soon as Amber mentioned her recovered comb, a single pattern had condensed from a chaos of possibilities.

"Ariane has gone after her dowry," Erik said flatly.

"Are you mad?" Simon asked. "She is afoot in a winter storm! The cursed dowry could be anywhere between here and Normandy!"

Erik's tawny eyes narrowed as he reassessed the possibilities that had tantalized him ever since he realized that the dowry had been stolen.

Simon started to speak, only to be stopped by a curt gesture from Dominic.

"I believe," Erik said slowly, "that the dowry went with Geoffrey to the Disputed Lands. If so, the dowry lies somewhere between Stone Ring and the Silverfells."

"She would have told me," Simon said.

"You wouldn't have let her go without you," Meg said.

No one said what all knew: Ariane had gone alone rather than ask Simon the Loyal to leave his lord and brother in his time of need.

"Have two horses readied," Dominic said to Simon. "You should quickly overtake her. Lord Erik, will you and your Learned animals accompany Simon?"

"With pleasure."

"What will you tell Deguerre?" Simon asked Dominic.

"Nothing. Ariane has avoided him at every opportunity. With luck, he won't even know she has gone."

"And if you aren't lucky?"

"Ride hard, Simon. I would like my wife to begin sleeping well again."

33

Simon and Erik rode as though pursued by demons, but they didn't overtake Ariane. They went as far north as Carlysle Manor, but she wasn't there. Afraid they had passed by her in the night and storm, the men spent a miserable time trying to sleep while Stag-killer coursed the countryside, searching for any sign of Ariane's camp.

The hound got nothing for his trouble but clots of ice between his toes.

Simon was up well before dawn, much to the wonder of the manor's small staff. He had little interest in breakfast, for he kept thinking of Ariane out in the storm.

"She must be lost," Simon said tersely.

Erik sliced cold meat with his dagger, speared a piece of cheese and a slab of bread, and dumped the lot in front of Simon.

"She is a finder," Erik said curtly. "She can no more be lost than the sky can lose the ground."

"Then why haven't we overtaken her?" Simon demanded.

Erik had no answer that would soothe Simon's pain. All he had was the truth and a pattern that became more bleak with each hour the storm raged.

"Stagkiller found no sign that we had passed Ariane in the storm," Erik said. "She must have gotten a horse somehow. She is somewhere ahead of us."

"It is so cold," Simon whispered.

"She wears Learned cloth."

"Is that enough to keep her warm?"

"Eat," Erik said, ignoring the question. "We will ride until the storm eases. Then I will send my peregrine aloft."

But the storm didn't lose its strength until the men were at the edge of the sacred Stone Ring itself. The standing stones were not visible, for an icy mist clung to the ground. Erik and Simon reined in their weary horses while Stagkiller flopped on the ground and panted great puffs of silver that were quickly swallowed in mist.

The peregrine stepped from her saddle perch onto Erik's gauntlet, fluffed her feathers and opened her beak as though already tasting the freedom of the wind. Erik whistled with piercing clarity. The falcon answered with a rill of music too sweet by far to have come from a predator's throat.

With a swift movement of his arm, Erik

launched Winter into skies that matched her name. The falcon's narrow, elegant wings flared and beat rapidly as she climbed into the icy mist.

Simon watched the bird with fear and hope combined. Long after the brilliance of the mist-veiled sunlight made his eyes water, he stared into the distance, his whole body tense.

But it was nothing to the tension Simon felt when Winter quickly arrowed back down out of the sky with a long, keening cry. The Learned man whistled back and forth with his peregrine until Simon wanted to shout at them.

Then Erik turned and looked at Simon with grief in his tawny eyes.

"*Nay,*" Simon snarled fiercely. "I won't hear it! *Ariane is alive.*"

Erik closed his eyes for a moment before he told Simon what neither man wanted to know.

"Ariane . . ." Erik's voice faded into an aching thread of sound. "Ariane is beyond your reach."

"*She is alive.*"

"Ariane lies motionless within the second ring of stones," Erik said carefully. "That is all Winter was permitted to see."

"Permitted? What in the name of —"

"The second ring," Erik interrupted curtly,

"can't be weighed or measured or touched. It simply *is*. You have never acknowledged that. Therefore, alive or dead, Ariane lies beyond your reach. We shall see if she also lies beyond mine."

Erik urged his horse forward. Tensely Simon watched. Once he had tried to track Meg into a sacred ring. He had failed. Then he had tried to help Duncan track Amber, only to be brought up short by another sacred circle of stones. Again he had been baffled by the ancient secret of the stones.

If there is any secret, Simon told himself savagely. *If!*

Yet even as he doubted, fear blossomed in a soundless black rush.

What if she is there and I cannot reach her?

No answer came to Simon save the growing certainty that the ancient places would test him as they had tested Dominic and Duncan in turn.

But unlike the other men, Simon feared he would fail. He had neither Dominic's shrewdness nor Duncan's berserker will.

How can I find something I can't see or hear or touch? How in God's name did Dominic and Duncan manage?

Erik's horse stopped as though it had been turned to stone.

"It is closed to me," the Learned man

566

shouted angrily. "By all that is holy, it is closed!"

Fear and anger combined in Simon, making him savage. He spurred his horse toward the ancient monoliths whose faces were veiled in mist. His horse galloped up the hill and then stopped as though brought up against a keep's wall.

Simon had been expecting as much. He kicked free of the stirrups and landed with catlike grace on the uncertain ground.

"There is no place I won't go to find Ariane," Simon shouted at the stones, "and to hell with what *is* and what is *not*."

Like a warrior going into battle, Simon strode toward the monoliths looming out of the mist ahead of him.

"Ariane! Do you hear me?" he called.

Nothing came back to him but a falcon's clear, keening cry rising from the throat of a Learned man.

Simon set his teeth and kept walking. Tall stones rose on either side. He stalked between them without looking to right or left.

"Ariane!"

This time even the falcon didn't answer.

Simon kept walking. He walked to the mound in the ring's center, circled its base, and saw no sign that anyone had crossed the snowy ground since before the storm. He scrambled to the top and looked around with a wildness he barely could contain.

He saw nothing but wind stirring mist into ghostly shapes that faded as soon as he looked at them.

"Ariane! Are you here?"

Not one sound came back from the mist.

"Ariane! Where are you?"

"Inside the second ring of stones," Erik called from beyond the mist.

"Where is the second ring?"

"The mound is its center."

"I am there. *Where is Ariane?*"

"Inside the second ring."

"Show her to me!" Simon yelled savagely.

"Even if Stone Ring permitted me inside, I could no more show you Ariane than I could show a rainbow to a man with no eyes!"

Simon's answer was a raw sound of rage.

"You are what you have chosen to be," Erik shouted, "a man bounded by logic. You have held on to your blindness too long. Now you are paying the cost of seeing truth too late. Ariane is beyond your reach!"

Simon gave an anguished cry that was also Ariane's name. The echo came back in ghostly whispers.

You are what you have chosen to be.

Ariane is beyond your reach.

But Simon could not accept losing Ariane.

"I will see her!" Simon shouted to Stone Ring itself. "Do you hear me? I will see her!"

Spectral whispers became the sound of wind stirring through nearby branches, branches that were laden with blossoms.

But no tree grew on top of the mound.

No flowers bloomed in winter.

And the wind did not move.

Yet the sound came again, a murmuring, rustling, mourning sigh; wind that could not be blowing through a tree that didn't exist; wind ruffling impossible blossoms until they spoke with a thousand soft tongues.

Hurry, warrior. She is dying. Then you will be one with me, ever living, always dying, forever grieving for a truth learned too late.

Chills coursed over Simon. The part of him that weighed and measured and touched fought back fiercely, denying that he had heard anything more meaningful than wind over rock and ice.

And a part of Simon was driven to his knees by a whispering, measureless torrent of grief that was not his. Not quite.

Not yet.

Hurry, warrior.

See.

He looked around with black, wild eyes. He saw nothing that he hadn't seen before.

"How can I see?" Simon cried. "Help me!"

Nothing came back to Simon except the certainty that Ariane was nearby, and her life was slipping away, taking her forever beyond the reach of any living man.

Love? What a pail of slops that is!

A ragged sound was torn from Simon's throat as he heard Ariane's sardonic words spoken by a thousand petal-soft tongues. But the whispering did not cease at his cry. It continued, telling him more than he thought he could bear, recalling a conversation only he and Ariane had shared . . . her courage and his cold response.

As soon as I am well once more, I will endure the marriage embrace. For you, my loyal knight. Only for you.

I want more than clenched teeth and duty.

I will give you all that I have.

And she had.

"Ariane!" Simon cried.

No answer came, not even the thousand whispers that could not exist.

Simon closed his eyes and fought the emotions that threatened to squeeze breath from his throat. His hands formed fists on his knees and he shook with the power of his longing.

"Nightingale," he said in an anguished whisper, "I would give the heart from my body to see you again."

Wind threaded through the branches of a nearby tree, set petals to stirring until they sighed.

Open your eyes, Simon.

See.

Yet even before Simon opened his eyes, he knew that Ariane was within reach, knew it in a way that couldn't be weighed or measured or touched.

She was at his feet, lying huddled on her side, wrapped in her mantle. Where the wind had blown her mantle aside, an oddly muted amethyst cloth was revealed. The silver laces and embroidered lightning were only darkly gleaming, almost tarnished. Her skin was pale and cold as snow.

If Ariane breathed, Simon could neither see nor hear it. Nor did she awaken when he lifted her, called to her, tried to shake her from the grasp of cold.

Her body was slack, unresisting, as cold as he had once accused her of being.

"Nightingale . . ."

Loss turned like a dagger in Simon's heart. As he lifted her gently into his arms, packets of spices and gemstones tumbled from her mantle.

Union with the right man can enhance a woman's powers.

"Curse the dowry," Simon said through

clenched teeth. "It wasn't worth your life. Nothing is!"

He kicked aside the spices and priceless gems. Then he held Ariane hard against his body, willing her to awaken, to look at him, to smile.

To live.

All that awakened were a thousand soft tongues whispering the words Simon had once spoken.

I am not Dominic or Duncan. I will never give that much of my soul to a woman. I will never see the rowan bloom.

Yet Ariane had come to Simon with her ravaged innocence and shocking bravery. She had burned wildly for him, giving him more than she had believed she had to give; her trust, her body, her very soul.

I love you, Simon.

Simon's gift to Ariane had been his body.

And now she was cold beyond his warming.

Petals stirred, whispered, shaping words from stillness, murmuring to Simon, repeating his own words, wounding him until he bled the very tears he had fought against crying. More than he knew had died with Ariane. More than he had believed existed.

With great gentleness, Simon wrapped Ariane in his own mantle, saw her hair once more black against the soft white fur. Slowly he lowered Ariane to the ground, removed his sword, and set it between her hands.

"No warrior ever had more courage than you," Simon said as he kissed her cool cheek. "Your bravery humbles me. Wherever you are, may the rowan bloom for you."

Then Simon bent his head and wept as he hadn't since he was a child. As he wept, fragrance drifted down over him, softness brushing his cheeks like kisses.

Open your eyes.

Slowly Simon opened his eyes and saw an ancient rowan blooming in the midst of winter. He saw, and knew that the truth he had seen too late was his own.

Blossoms drifted into his hands, petals from a tree that could not exist, blooming in a place that could not be.

Yet he saw the rowan bloom. He held its blossoms. He touched their transcendent beauty. He breathed their impossible fragrance as though it were life itself.

It is.

You saw too late. Now you are as she is, between two worlds, warmth bleeding into cold.

You may hold my tears and live as you did before, trusting your soul to no one. Or you may release my tears and accept what comes.

With a shudder, Simon opened his hands

and let the rowan's tears drift over Ariane, giving everything to her, more than he had ever believed he could give.

And he feared only that it would not be enough.

When the first flower touched Ariane's cheek, she seemed to stir. When the second blossom caressed her, she shivered and drew a sharp breath, as though she had been too long without air. The third and fourth and fifth flowers rained down, and then there were too many to count, a swirl of warmth and fragrance permeating everything.

Simon sensed life rushing through Ariane's body as certainly as it pulsed through his own. She stirred as though awakening from sleep. Then her eyes opened, and they were amethyst gems reflecting the beauty of a sacred tree blooming in the midst of winter.

"Simon?" she whispered.

He gathered Ariane's living warmth into his arms, felt the strength of her arms circling his neck.

"I give to you the gift of the rowan," Simon whispered against Ariane's lips.

And the gift was love.

Epilogue

Baron Deguerre stood at Blackthorne's moat bridge and saw the rowan's triumph riding toward him, borne on the backs of horses that followed Ariane with neither lead rope nor groom to harry them into obedience. Each horse carried a burden of sacks filled with spices and silks, with gold and silver, with precious stones, with all that had been taken from Ariane by treachery and betrayal.

But it was not the dowry that convinced Deguerre of his defeat. It was the pommel of Simon's sword, a crystal as black and clear as Simon's eyes. Held impossibly within the crystalline midnight was a single luminous blossom.

Baron Deguerre looked at the rowan flower within the sword, called for his horse and led his knights away from Blackthorne Keep, for he knew no weakness remained there for him to exploit. Nor would there be any in the future. Even Charles the Shrewd had never discovered a way to undo love.

Carlysle Manor became part of Rowan

Keep, home of Ariane the Beloved, a woman whose hands drew joy from her harp and whose gift assured that no child wandered lost and alone away from the keep's safety.

Simon's sword came to be called the Rowan, after the uncanny blossom encased within its black crystal pommel. In time, Simon himself was called the Lord of the Rowan.

For it was Simon who had discovered what even the Learned did not know . . .

The sacred rowan is a woman born long, long ago, a woman whose refusal to see love cost first her lover's life, then the lives of her family, her clan, her people.

But not her own life. Not quite.

In pity and punishment she was turned into an undying tree, a rowan that weeps only in the presence of transcendent love; and the tears of the rowan are blossoms that confer extraordinary grace upon those who can see them.

When enough tears are wept, the rowan will be free. She waits inside a sacred stone ring that can be neither weighed nor measured nor touched. She waits for love that is worth her tears.

The rowan is waiting still.

Author's Note

One of the questions I am most often asked by readers is "Your Western and contemporary romances were so successful, what made you decide to write medieval romances?"

The answer involves a true story that really is stranger than fiction. I wouldn't have dared to make it up, because no one would believe it! Here is how it goes . . .

For twenty-six years I have been well and truly married to the only man I ever loved. In addition to being husband, lover, friend, and father of my children, Evan is my writing partner. (We write as A.E. Maxwell and as Ann Maxwell.) Evan is also a hardheaded contrarian who loves to argue so much he'll take either side of any issue.

In the course of doing research for *The Diamond Tiger*, Evan and I went to Britain. As Maxwell is a Scots name, we decided to drive to Scotland. My maiden name, Charters, is also Scots, a corruption of the name Charteris.

Evan and I weren't chasing family ties, we

just wanted an excuse to see a new piece of the world. We jumped in our rented car and set off north, sitting on the wrong side of the car, shifting with the wrong arm, and driving on the wrong side of the road.

By the time we crossed the border into Scotland, we were bored with super highways. We turned off into the first country lane we found and began winding along the edge of a windswept, shallow bay. When I spotted some distant ruins rising out of the land, I was ecstatic; I had been wanting to photograph ruins, but everything I had seen so far in Britain had been depressingly well kept.

We chased the ruins over roads that got more and more narrow until we came to a Scottish National Trust site. The site was closed for the season. But the ruins were there for all to see — and photograph.

While Evan set off to read the historical plaques, I started taking pictures. After a few minutes, Evan called to me in an odd voice and waved me over to where he was. When I got there, he simply pointed to the plaque. The magnificent red ruins were of a castle called Caerlaverock [Meadowlark's Nest], which had been built in the twelfth century.

The castle had been the Maxwell Clan stronghold.

Evan and I were stunned by the coincidence of time and place and us. We hadn't been seeking family landscapes in Scotland; we hadn't even known they existed. Yet here we were in Caerlaverock . . .

When we finally left the castle, we were full of questions. We collared one of the locals in a pub. He told us there was a place called Maxwellton [Maxwell Town], near Dumfries. There was a museum there devoted to Maxwell Clan history.

We went to the museum. While Evan admired the assortment of weapons and armor, I wandered off to look around. There was a map of all the clans. The Charteris Clan was there, too, a tiny little fingernail clinging to the edge of the Maxwells' vast lands.

Beneath the portrait of a fierce-looking Maxwell was a short history of the clan. Soon after I started reading, I was laughing out loud. Evan came over, wondering what was wrong with me.

When he started reading, he discovered what I already had: the Maxwells were a Norman warrior clan that had fought on the wrong side of every major battle after 1066 . . . including the Spanish Armada. Three times an English king took Caerlaverock after a very long siege, pulled down the castle, and stripped the Maxwells of titles and lands.

Three times an English king was forced to give back the lands, the titles, and the castle to the Maxwells, so that the clan could guard the western approach to Britain.

The fourth time Caerlaverock was pulled down, it stayed in ruins. The lands and titles were given back to the Maxwells, but not the right to "crenellate" (build a castle).

The Maxwells were contrarians to a man.

And nothing much has changed in nine centuries.

Evan led me away from lost battles to the museum's archives. There he pointed to several huge, leather-bound volumes. The books were Maxwell family genealogies compiled in the nineteenth century. Intrigued, I began leafing through them.

The longer I looked, the more silent I became. Each page I turned took me farther back in time; and on those yellowed pages I saw again and again a name from my own American childhood: Charters.

From the first moment I had seen Evan in California in 1963, I felt that I knew him in some impossible way. He had felt the same. Now we understood why.

Maxwells and Charters have been marrying one another for nine hundred years.

When I looked up from the ancient genealogies into the green eyes of my very modern warrior, I knew that I would write medieval romances.

And I have.

— Ann Maxwell (a.k.a. Elizabeth Lowell)

The employees of THORNDIKE PRESS hope you have enjoyed this Large Print book. All our Large Print books are designed for easy reading — and they're made to last.

Other Thorndike Large Print books are available at your library, through selected bookstores, or directly from us. Suggestions for books you would like to see in Large Print are always welcome.

For more information about current and upcoming titles, please call or mail your name and address to:

THORNDIKE PRESS
PO Box 159
Thorndike, Maine 04986
800/223-6121
207/948-2962